A Joyful Christmas

A Joyful Christmas

6 HISTORICAL STORIES

CYNTHIA HICKEY, LIZ JOHNSON
VICKIE McDONOUGH, LIZ TOLSMA
CARRIE TURANSKY, ERICA VETSCH

BARBOUR BOOKS
An Imprint of Barbour Publishing, Inc.

A Christmas Castle ©2013 by Cynthia Hickey
A Star in the Night ©2011 by Liz Johnson
An Irish Bride for Christmas ©2008 by Vickie McDonough
Under His Wings ©2011 by Liz Tolsma
Shelter in the Storm ©2009 by Carrie Turansky
Christmas Service ©2011 by Erica Vetsch

Print ISBN 978-1-64352-634-8

eBook Editions:
Adobe Digital Edition (.epub) 978-1-64352-636-2
Kindle and MobiPocket Edition (.prc) 978-1-64352-635-5

All scripture quotations are taken from the King James Version of the Bible.

This book is a work of fiction. Names, characters, places, and incidents are either products of the author's imagination or used fictitiously. Any similarity to actual people, organizations, and/or events is purely coincidental.

Cover Photograph © Sandra Cunningham / Trevillion Images

Published by Barbour Books, an imprint of Barbour Publishing, Inc., 1810 Barbour Drive, Uhrichsville, OH 44683, www.barbourbooks.com

Our mission is to inspire the world with the life-changing message of the Bible.

Member of the
Evangelical Christian
Publishers Association

Printed in United States of America.

Contents

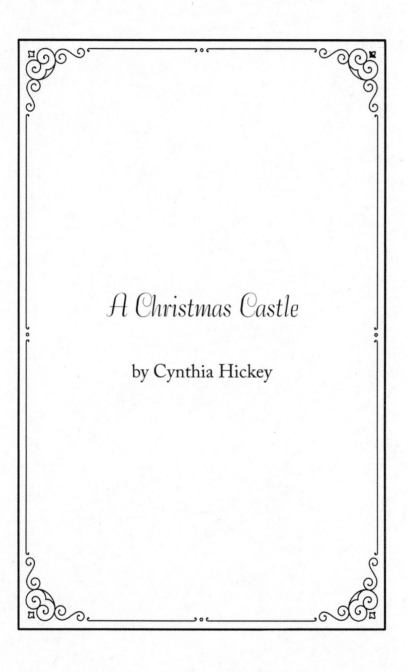

A Christmas Castle

by Cynthia Hickey

Chapter 1

December 1867
Prescott, Arizona

Annie Morgan looped her horse's reins over the hitching post, slung her rifle over her shoulder, and marched into one of the many saloons in Prescott, Arizona. Every head turned in her direction. Every conversation ceased. Every glance increased her heart rate.

"I'm looking for Bill Morgan." She lifted her chin, causing her floppy hat to slide to one side. She righted it and glared at the bearded faces turned toward her. "Well, is he here or not?" Her insides quaked. *Please, somebody answer before my last nerve flies out the window.* Her new husband should have been at the livery to meet her. Instead, the grizzled old man who worked there had sent her here.

"He ain't here." The bartender swiped the inside of a glass with a towel. "Maybe you ought to check his land. Heard tell he ain't left it in a couple of days." He grinned at a group of men playing cards. "If you're his new bride, I'm betting he's got a surprise for you."

Well, Annie had one for him too. The man didn't make a good impression by not meeting her. So far, he wasn't anything like his letters. "Can you direct me to his land?"

The man snickered. "Head straight west about half-a-day's ride. There's a big pile of junk with a sign that says, 'Morgan's Ranch.' If you veer to the northeast a bit, you'll find your nearest neighbor, a man named Carter. He has another surprise for you." He winked at the card players.

This town seemed full of surprises, and Annie had a feeling they weren't pleasant ones. "Thank you kindly." She straightened her hat and shoved through the swinging doors. Something strange was going on, and she aimed to find out what.

Sure enough, four hours later she stopped in front of a sagging fence with a weathered sign stating MORGAN'S RANCH. In the distance, brown cattle grazed, walking over and around a mound of dirt covered on one side by more weathered boards. A few mustangs stood, heads down, in a nearby corral. Chickens squawked, running free.

Annie dismounted and led her horse through a gate ready to fall off its hinges. Already her head spun with a list of things that needed improvement. She'd mention them to Bill at the first opportunity.

She lifted her face to the sun. Although a chill filled the air, the day's moderate weather amazed her. Back home, snow covered the ground and cold bit at your cheeks. She'd heard tell, though, that the area could have snow after the first of the year, if not sooner. It'd be nice not to have to worry about freezing when a body rolled out of bed in the mornings.

Had her new husband lost cattle because of a shoddy fence? Could he possibly be out looking for them? What had she gotten herself into? The letters she'd received from Bill proclaimed him an ambitious man. Annie's first impression showed otherwise.

Certain that God had led her to wed Bill Morgan, sight unseen, she'd had no qualms about leaving Missouri and traveling to Arizona. Now she hovered beside her gelding, filled with indecision. Where was the man?

Seeing no house, Annie let her horse graze on dried grass and wandered the strange land. A small stand of trees—oak, pine, and another she thought might be the Arizona ash she'd heard about— bordered what she hoped was a creek. Bill had written her about one. She headed in that direction, letting her hat hang down her back by its drawstring.

Sure enough, a clear stream ran over rocks. Annie dropped to her knees and splashed her face with the frigid water before cupping her hand for a drink.

Crashing sounds in the nearby brush had her spinning and grabbing for her gun. A wiry-haired mongrel appeared, tail wagging. She grinned. "Well, hello there, boy. Do you live here?" She scratched behind his ears. "Could you possibly be Scout?"

The dog answered with a slobbery kiss.

"Where's your master, boy?" Annie straightened and glanced around. The land showed promise. Not as fertile as Missouri, perhaps, but promising all the same.

The sun sat low in the sky, and the temperature dropped. Forgetting her irritation at Bill's nonappearance, now she was worried. She snapped her fingers for the dog to follow and headed for the mound of junk.

Wait. A board cross next to the creek caught her attention. She rushed over and read the crude letters burned into the wood. BILL MORGAN. REST IN PEACE.

She fell to her knees. This must be the surprise the townsmen thought so humorous.

A widow before ever meeting her husband. Tears pricked her eyes. What would she do now? There was nothing left for her in Missouri. No parents, no family. Why would God bring her this far only to leave her alone again?

Planting her hands on her thighs, she pushed to her feet. First order of business: she needed to find the house, then the neighbor who supposedly had another surprise for her.

Slapping her hat back over her braids, she headed for the pile of wood around the mound, leaving Scout to continue investigating whatever he felt the desire to stick his nose in.

If she had to sleep outside, it wouldn't be the first time, but she needed to start a fire. Once the sun slipped below the horizon, the temperature would drop fast.

She stopped by the mound. Her heart sank. Why was there a door propped against the dirt?

"Hold it right there, mister." Drake held his shotgun on the trespasser and tried to ignore the tight hold of the child sitting on the horse behind him. He prayed there wouldn't be gunfire, not with the little one so close. *She's already seen enough violence in her life.*

The stranger put his hands up and turned to face Drake. When he tilted his head, his hat fell, releasing mahogany braids that reached to his—no—her waist.

"You're a woman." Sparks flew from hazel eyes. He couldn't recall ever seeing a prettier woman, leather pants or not. She must be Bill's bride. He'd told him she was scheduled to arrive that day.

"Last time I looked in the mirror, I was."

"But you're wearing britches." Drake shook his head and lowered his gun. "Who are you?"

"Annie Templeton. No, it's Morgan now, and you're on my land."

She sure wasn't what Drake expected. Bill had filled him with tales of a lady. A woman excited about helping him run his ranch. Drake needed to get to town more, or at least make the rounds of neighbors. "When did you get in?"

"I arrived a little bit ago, expecting to meet my new husband, but instead. . ." She waved a hand toward the creek bed. "We were married by proxy not more than a week ago. Who are you?"

"Drake Carter. I'm your closest neighbor. My place is an hour's ride from here, right across the boundary line." He reached behind him and lowered May to the ground then tossed her pack next to her. "Since you're Bill's widow, seems like this is your new daughter, May."

Annie's eyes widened, and her skin paled, making her freckles look like drops of watered-down coffee. "Daughter? Bill didn't say anything about a child."

"Well, he had one." Drake dismounted. "Guess you found the grave."

"Did you bury him?"

"Yep, two days ago." He nudged May forward. "Found the little one and the dog sitting all alone in the house." The child shrank back against him and stuck her thumb in her mouth.

"I'm obliged." Annie took her lower lip between her teeth. "How'd he die?"

"Scoundrels after his land." Drake shrugged. "I was checking the boundary fence and heard gunfire. By the time I got here, it was too late." Seemed like most folks died that way out here, or by disease. He studied the pretty woman in front of him. How would she manage several hundred acres of land and cattle all on her own? What if Hayward returned with his hired hands? The poor thing wouldn't stand a chance.

"Where's the house?"

"You're looking at it."

She frowned. "Where?"

"That door leads to a dugout. A good-sized one too. I reckon Bill dug out a good ten-by-fifteen foot of space."

"A hole in the ground?"

Drake didn't think it possible, but she paled further. He took a step forward in case she fainted. Instead, she whipped her rifle around and had it pointed at him before he took the second step. "Whoa." He held up his hands. "I mean you no harm. I thought you might faint."

"I've never fainted in my life." She narrowed her eyes. "Child, come over here behind me."

May shook her head and ducked behind Drake.

"Go on, sweetheart. This is your new mama." He lifted her and set her down by Annie. "She ain't never had a mom. Hers died in childbirth. It's always been her and Bill."

"How old is she?"

"Four." Drake didn't feel right leaving the two alone, but there wasn't much help for it. The sun was setting fast, and he needed to get home. "I'll show you around the place, then I've get to git." He pulled on the flimsy dugout door. "Come see your place. Bill installed a new cookstove a short while ago, most likely in preparation for your coming. He hadn't gotten around to putting in a stovepipe yet. I'll light a lantern, but take care on the steps leading down. A couple of them need repairing." He rushed down the stairs and lit a lamp on the table before watching Annie, who now clutched May's hand like a lifeline, enter.

"It isn't much, but it'll do until you get a proper cabin built. There's two bunks, a dry sink, a table, two chairs, and that's pretty much it." He'd lived in a dugout while building his own cabin and hadn't thought much of what a woman would think until now. The place sure looked sparse. And dirty. "That crack over there is big enough to point a rifle barrel through if the need arises. It's also all you've got in the way of a window."

"Oh my." She released May's hand and turned slowly in a circle. "It's. . .different." She speared him with a glance. "Without a husband, how can I be expected to build a cabin?"

Right. Looks like Drake had another job added to his list. "Bill already cut the lumber."

She pressed her lips together. "I'll make do. Thank you for taking care of. . .May." She plopped on one of the bunks, releasing a cloud of dust.

"I reckon you could sell out and head back to where you came from." Drake crossed his arms. He refused to allow himself to feel guilty. Annie should've made sure things were more to her liking before hitching herself to a man like Bill.

"You'd like that, wouldn't you?" She tossed her hat on the rickety table. "After all, didn't you say Bill died because of his land? Are you offering to buy, or should I wait for the next no-good scalawag to make an offer?"

"Now, wait one minute." Did she just compare him to the men who killed Bill? He ought to leave her to her own devices. He turned for the door. "I'm an hour's ride due east. You can't miss the house. After I buried Bill, I've been coming every day to tend to the stock. Now that you're here, I've plenty work of my own."

"Wait. My apologies. It's. . . I've got a lot to take in right now. I'd offer you a cup of coffee, but. . ." She waved a hand.

"The shelves are fairly well stocked. There's what's left of Bill's cash in May's bag, and he's got a running credit at the Grayson's. You let me know if I can help you in any other way." He took the steps two at a time until he darted back into sunshine. Closed in spaces always made him feel as if he were in a cage. The six months he'd lived in a dugout were the longest of his life.

He called to his horse and then mounted in one motion. From this higher vantage point, he could see all the improvements that needed to be made. He shook his head. If he offered, it'd take up most of his day, and he still had a ride home. But the good Lord wouldn't look kindly on a man who didn't offer. He'd be back tomorrow with May's clothes and a hammer and nails.

With a click of his tongue, he steered toward home, his mind listing the things he could accomplish in a day and the things that would take longer. Between his place and Annie's, he'd be busier than a three-legged dog after a jackrabbit.

He laughed, envisioning the first time Annie would try to give May a bath. He still had the teeth imprints in his hand from his one attempt.

Oh to be a fly on the wall in that dugout tonight.

Chapter 2

Annie rolled off the cot, keeping the quilt wrapped around her shoulders. Seemed yesterday's mild weather had given in to winter's cold. She padded to the cookstove and added more kindling to the low embers.

What had she gotten into? She cast a glance to where May still slept. She hadn't liked letting the child go to bed filthy, but exhaustion won out. Today a bath would definitely be in order.

With the fire building in the stove, she perused the contents of the shelves and decided on flapjacks for breakfast. Later she'd make their hole in the ground habitable. She had a trunk arriving on tomorrow's stagecoach with a few of her mother's things. She hoped they'd help make the place a home.

She faced the table. May sat staring up at her with big eyes the color of blue bonnets.

"You can go play while I fix breakfast." Annie picked up a cast-iron skillet. "Do you have any toys?"

May shook her head and stuck her dirty thumb in her mouth.

No toys? "Not even a doll?"

Another shake of the head.

Well, Christmas was on the horizon. Annie was a fair seamstress. She'd sew May a doll, and the little girl a dress to match. Just because Annie found wearing pants more convenient didn't mean that the child shouldn't have the option to choose for herself.

What if May didn't like her, even after Annie took care of her? Annie had no younger siblings and had rarely had neighbor children to play with. She glanced at May. She'd treat the girl like a small adult; she didn't know any other way to respond to a person. Hopefully it would be sufficient. With her own melancholy and mentally absent mother, Annie definitely knew what not to do in regard to raising a child.

She dropped a blob of lard onto the hot skillet and listened to the pleasing sizzle. She had a bit of red flannel in her trunk. Maybe May would enjoy making ribbons to decorate greenery around the dugout. As a child, Annie had loved decorating for Christmas. Since it appeared she now had a young'un of her own, she'd introduce the little girl to some of the things she'd loved and give them some time to get to know each other.

After mixing the batter, she poured some into the hot skillet. Soon the smell of frying flapjacks filled the room. "Okay, May, I'm going to tell you everything I need to do today. You help me remember." What did one talk about to a little girl with eyes as big as saucers?

"First thing is to get as much of the dust out of here as possible. That most likely means washing the linens. Then we need to find the hole in the chicken coop and round up them feathered rascals." She glanced out of the corner of her eye. May's gaze never left her. Annie smiled. "Then, I think we'll give you a bath."

"I hate baths!" May dashed up the stairs and out the door.

Annie removed the pan from the fire and raced after her. Outside, she barreled into the little girl and wrapped her arms around her to prevent taking them both to the ground. May pointed toward the gate. Scout dashed from the woods and barked, running to May's side.

Squinting, Annie made out the form of four men on horseback. She whirled and dragged May into the dugout. "Stay here." She grabbed her rifle and headed back outside.

Annie aimed her gun at the biggest target: a man dressed in black sitting tall on his horse. "State your business." She narrowed her eyes.

"My name's Ben Hayward." He removed his hat. "I'm here only to welcome you to Prescott, Mrs. Morgan. It isn't every day that a comely widow moves to these parts. I've come to offer my services."

She snapped at the still barking dog. "Hush, Scout." The noise set her nerves on edge.

"In what capacity? If you've come to make an offer on my land, you can turn around and leave. I have no intention of selling."

"Mrs. Morgan." Hayward swung a leg over the horse to begin his dismount.

"Don't bother getting down." Annie's arm was starting to shake from holding the gun steady for several minutes. "You can talk just as well from the saddle."

Hayward sighed. "I haven't come to make an offer on your land but rather to offer you my hand in marriage."

"Whatever for?"

"Women are scarce out here, and one as beautiful as yourself shouldn't be left to tend to a ranch alone. I'm willing to care for you and the child while joining our acreage together. It's a winning situation for both of us."

"Are you the skunk who murdered my husband?"

"Now, Mrs. Morgan, that was an unfortunate accident. I made the man a fair offer, and he pulled a gun on me and my men." Hayward held up his hands. "We mean you no harm."

"Turn around and leave, Mr. Hayward, before I put a bullet through your scheming heart."

Drake slowed his horse at the sight of Annie struggling to lift her gate into place. Why didn't the stubborn woman wait for him? He grunted. Had he even mentioned he'd be back today? He stopped and dismounted. "Let me do that. It's too heavy for you."

She rubbed the back of her gloved hand across her already dirty face.

Instead of making her unattractive, the fruits of her hard labor appealed to Drake, and he pulled away to focus on the task at hand. It wouldn't do to pay too much attention to Annie. He was here to do a job, nothing more.

"Thank you. The sorry thing was already falling, but then one of Hayward's men knocked it completely down when I refused to marry him. The whole fence looks like it would fall with a brisk wind."

"Marry who? The hired hand?" This couldn't be good. In town less than twenty-four hours and already Annie had a target on her back. There had to be more to Hayward's attention than water rights.

"No. Mr. Hayward."

Drake lifted the gate into place. "I take it he didn't care for your answer."

"Nope." Annie leaned against the fence and helped hold the gate while Drake hammered. "I don't understand the man's intentions." She stared toward town.

"I'm wondering whether the man's thirsting for more here than water." Drake motioned her to step back while he swung the gate back and forth. "That ought to hold. What else would you like me to do?"

She tilted her head. "Don't you have work of your own?"

"Yep, but I can't rest easy knowing what a mess Bill left you." Nor, could he, in good conscience, leave her be while a snake like Hayward hung around.

"I need to give May a bath. Could you round up the chickens and fix the coop? Oh, and there are a couple of pigs rooting in the woods. Can you build an enclosure for them?"

"Sure." Easy enough jobs.

"And tomorrow, I've a trunk coming in on the stage. I don't feel comfortable going into town with Hayward sniffing around. Could you fetch it for me?"

Drake sighed. He knew offering his help would result in a lot of nonsense. Why didn't the woman hire someone to deliver the dratted thing? No help for it now. He guessed if it all came down to most desirable job, he'd rather muck out a pigpen, fix a chicken coop, and waste a day riding to town than try giving May a bath.

Annie marched to the dugout and disappeared inside its dark depths. Within a few minutes, she returned with a plate of flapjacks.

"Eat," she said. "I'll call when lunch is ready."

Drake watched her retreat back into her hole. A beautiful but strange woman. He wondered what caused her to let go of the familiar and travel west to marry a man she'd never met. He shrugged.

He needed to get things fixed as soon as possible and avoid Annie

Templeton Morgan as much as possible. He had no desire, or time, to get tangled up with a woman no matter how pretty, and it was none of his concern as to why she married Bill. It was his Christian duty to make sure she didn't harm herself or the child, and that was best done by making repairs around her property.

The flapjacks melted in his mouth. Maybe he could work out a way of having Annie cook for him in return for repairs. He hated his own cooking. When he'd finished, he set the plate on a stump and got back to work.

A shriek rose over the sound of Drake's hammer. He whirled, hand on the butt of his gun. He relaxed and chuckled.

Annie had a kicking May slung over her shoulder as she marched toward the creek. This, Drake had to see. He propped his tools against the fence and jogged after them.

"The water's cold!" May squirmed until Annie dropped her into the creek.

"If you hadn't knocked over the tub, you would have a warm bath."

"You're mean." May threw a handful of mud at Annie. It hit with a splat and slid down the front of her faded yellow shirt.

Drake crossed his arms and leaned against a pine tree. The scene before him beat working for sure.

Annie pulled a bar of soap from her pocket, toed off her boots, and waded into the creek after May. She wrapped an arm around the flailing child and started scrubbing.

"Your lips are turning blue." Drake didn't know what he'd expected, but it sure wasn't for Annie to join the child in the cold water.

"No doubt." Annie grunted and took both her and May under the water. They came up sputtering, and Annie struggled to drag May back to the bank.

Drake stepped forward and offered her a hand. He froze at the sight of her wet blouse clinging to curves better left disguised. He averted his gaze and pulled.

"Thank you." Annie slung May back over her shoulder and headed home. "Next time I tell you to take a bath, I'm guessing you'll listen, and don't think you're going to get out of helping me mop up the mud in the house."

Maybe Annie would be all right out here after all. Drake shook his head and followed. He'd never met a more strong-willed person, male or female. Poor little May didn't stand a chance.

By the time he entered the dugout after fetching his tools, Annie and May huddled together by the stove. May sat on Annie's lap, her head tucked under the woman's chin. Well, what do you know? Maybe Drake had been too easy on the little tyke. Her father too. All the child needed was a firm hand and then a consoling shoulder when it was all over.

"I'll get you something to eat in a bit," Annie said over her shoulder. "Gotta take the chill off first."

"No hurry." Drake backed out of the small space. "I'll work on the coop." He'd have to take his meal outside. Just stepping into the dugout caused his heart to race. There didn't seem to be enough air to breathe, not to mention the lack of space for a man well over six feet tall.

The coop sat behind the dugout, out of sight of the road. Drake found the hole. Looked chewed through by an animal. He nailed a couple of boards over the hole. Once he found the chickens, Annie would have fresh eggs every morning.

He didn't know how many fowl Bill had, but he found a rooster and three hens among the forest's foliage. He tossed them into the repaired coop and then stretched the kinks from his back.

"Now it all makes sense." Hayward stepped from the trees, a cigar dangling from his lips. "The lovely widow doesn't want me because she already has you. Well played, Carter. A beautiful woman, desirable acreage—why, you've got it all."

"What is it you want, Hayward?" Drake's fingers itched for his gun.

"Don't play stupid." Hayward blew a smoke ring in the air. "I want the mineral rights to this land. Bill flashed gold all over town. The fool even tossed several nuggets on the bar. It's simple really, what I'm after. His having a beautiful widow only sweetened the pot."

"You can't have her if she's already married to me."

Chapter 3

Drake wanted to bite his tongue. What would Annie do if Hayward confronted her with the fact she was marrying him? He struggled to keep his composure. What a blasted fool. How was he going to tell Annie they were getting married?

"We have ourselves a predicament, Mr. Carter." Hayward tossed his cigar butt at Drake's feet. "I want this land we stand on and the creek that runs through it. Somewhere on this land is gold, unless Morgan lied, which I doubt."

"Did he actually say he found the gold here?" Drake kept his fingers close to his gun and crushed the burning ember of the cigar under his boot. Drake knew Bill had found gold, but it wasn't on this land. Most likely it was found somewhere else and brought to Arizona in a saddlebag. Either way, that type of rumor could only spell danger to Annie—and to him.

"Not in so many words." Hayward frowned. "But his meaning was clear. When a man buys horses with gold, people take notice. I want this land, and I intend to have it."

"Over my dead body."

"I don't kill, Mr. Carter." Hayward melted back into the shadows. "Until next time."

No, he just let his hired hands kill for him. Drake's blood ran cold. The man was as heartless as a rabid wolf and every bit as dangerous. Drake couldn't waste any time in coming up with a plan to protect Annie and May. He hadn't thought to marry, but he would if it kept them safe.

After a few minutes without seeing any more signs of Hayward or his men, Drake gathered his tools and meandered back to the dugout. He'd decline the offer of lunch and head back to his place. His mind whirled like a dust devil, and he wasn't any closer to coming up with an answer to his loco remark to shut up Hayward. He needed to find a different solution than getting hitched.

As he rode home, he expected to feel a bullet rip between his shoulder blades. Tension knotted his shoulders.

He, a grown man, had raced away from a woman like she was a porcupine ready to stab him with her quills. He shook his head. If being around a good-looking woman left him this addled, he definitely needed to get to town more.

Tomorrow. He sighed. He'd promised her he'd fetch her trunk tomorrow.

Smoke rose on the horizon. Drake's mouth dried up. He spurred his horse to a gallop and raced for home.

Annie pulled a small drawstring bag out of May's things and peeked inside. Gold? Was there gold on her land? Was that why Hayward was determined to claim it?

She glanced around the dugout. Where could she hide it? Why hadn't Mr. Carter mentioned it, or had he not even bothered to go through May's few items of clothing? From the looks of the child yesterday, Annie would guess not.

The spittoon. She'd clean it out and stuff the bag in there. With no one around who chewed tobacco, the gold should be safe and left undetected from marauders.

She didn't deserve the money. Having never met Bill, much less loved him as a wife should, she didn't feel she was due the inheritance. But she knew from his letters that he had no one else, and she had nowhere else to go. Her gaze fell on May. She'd take care of the land and the money for the sake of Bill's daughter.

Leaving the child wrapped in blankets, Annie donned her clothes and slipped out into the morning cold to take care of the stock and gather eggs. The peace of the morning surrounded her with a gentle embrace. She might feel guilty at enjoying land she felt she had no claim to, but for the first time in her life, she had something that actually belonged to her.

Scout bounded to her side and sent the chickens into a panic. Annie laughed and glanced at the repairs Mr. Carter had managed to make the day before. The next thing on the list would be to fix the fence. She could do that herself. None of the chores were too difficult if she set her mind to doing them.

She studied the dugout. Surely there was a way to make the place look less like a junk heap. She pulled her coat tight. But the dugout served its purpose of keeping out the cold. Most likely, it would stay cool in the summer as well. Maybe she could live with its ugliness for a while.

Would Mr. Carter bring the trunk today? If so, he wouldn't show up until at least the noon hour. She finished collecting eggs and headed back to the dugout to fix breakfast.

A cloud of dust rose on the horizon. She set the basket on a stump and grabbed her rifle. Surely Hayward wouldn't bother her so early in the morning.

Cattle and horses thundered toward her. Annie whistled for Scout and dashed inside the dugout. Underground was the safest place she could think of to be in a stampede. She gathered May in her arms and waited for the pounding of hooves overhead. None came. Instead, a whistle pierced the day. She slowly emerged into the sunlight.

Drake marched toward her, his face set in grim lines. Soot marked his skin and clothing. Strange cattle mingled with hers.

"What's happening?" Annie peered into his face.

"You're coming with me to collect your trunk." He slapped his hat against his thigh, sending puffs of dust and ashes into the air.

"Are these your cattle?"

"Yes."

"I don't understand." Whatever it was, she didn't want to hear it.

"My place is gone. Burned to the ground. House, barn, everything."

"Hayward?"

"That's my guess." Drake slapped his hat back on his head. "So we're going into town and getting hitched."

Annie froze. "Excuse me?"

"We're getting married. I told Hayward we were."

Fire burned through her limbs. If she didn't know better, she'd think smoke came out her ears. "And why, pray tell, would you do something so stupid?" She stuck her hands in her pockets to prevent herself from punching him.

"It's the only way to keep you and May safe. If you're married,

Hayward can't pester you to marry him. Any deals he wants to try to make would go through your husband." Drake waved an arm at the mingling cattle. "I've combined our stock, removed the boundary fence, and come to stay until I have time to build another house. I can't do that unless we're married. It wouldn't be proper."

"Neither is doing all that without consulting me!" Annie stepped close enough that her nose practically touched his chin. "I haven't been married a month yet, nor widowed for much less time than that. Perhaps I don't wish to wed again."

"Do you have a better idea?" Drake planted his hands on his hips and stared into her eyes.

My, a woman could forget herself. His eyes were so blue. No, there were other things to contend with. "We were doing just fine as we were."

"I can't ride back and forth every day. I can't watch both places at the same time."

"Then I'll care for myself." Annie whirled, grabbed her basket of eggs with enough force to send several crashing to the ground, and stomped down the stairs of the dugout.

The man was plumb loco. She slammed the door and cringed as dirt rained on her head. She set the basket on the table and plopped on the edge of her cot. May watched her, silent as usual unless the subject of a bath came up.

Was there reason in Mr. Carter's proposition? True, having a man around full-time would be convenient and safer, but Annie had always dreamed of a proper proposal. Her first marriage occurred on paper. Why did she expect another one to be better? She took a deep breath and filled a kettle with water.

If today was going to be her wedding day, she might as well wash up. She ran her hands down her buckskin pants. Since she'd

grown old enough to know her own mind, her insistence on wearing britches had been a point of consternation with her ma.
Now the idea of wearing a dress seemed foreign. What would
Mr. Carter think if she started dressing like a woman? What should
she care? Pants were more practical.

Would God ever send her a man to love, or would her marriages
always be ones of convenience? And what about Christmas? The dugout had no room for a tree. Annie doubted May had ever experienced
Christmas, and it had been years since she had. What a silly woman,
worried over something as trivial as holiday decorations.

She stood and cracked eggs into the skillet. "Go tell Mr. Carter
that breakfast is almost ready."

May dashed outside. She returned by the time Annie set plates
of scrambled eggs and bacon on the table. "He says he'll eat outside."

"I don't think so." She exited the dugout and approached Mr.
Carter by the well. "If I'm to marry you without a proper proposal,
then the least you can do is eat with your soon-to-be family." She
crossed her arms.

"I don't like closed-in spaces."

"Then how in tarnation do you expect to have a place to sleep?"
Annie glanced around her land. "I don't even have a barn."

"Reckon I didn't think that far ahead."

She narrowed her eyes. "There's no time like the present to get
over your fears. Come on." She marched away, knowing without looking that he would follow. She grinned. No man liked to be outwitted
by a woman.

Ignoring the fact that Mr. Carter paused at the dugout's entrance,
Annie took her seat at the table, raised the wick on the lantern to cast
more light around the room, and waited. Drake joined her with all
the enthusiasm of a man going to his own hanging.

"So, you'll marry me?" He sat across from her.

"I reckon, although I've heard of better proposals." She flushed at the sight of her cot behind him. "May will sleep with me, and you can have the other cot."

"Fair enough." Mr. Carter spooned a healthy serving of eggs onto his plate. "We'll head into town after breakfast and hunt down the preacher."

"And fetch my things." Annie set her hand over his and gave it a squeeze.

He raised a startled glance.

She glared at him. "Here's a warning for you. If you try to take my gold, I'll shoot you, husband or not."

Chapter 4

Annie followed her husband-to-be into town with May perched on the horse behind her. At least this wedding would have a physical groom in attendance.

By the time they reached town, snow flurries drifted from a gray sky. Annie shivered and pulled her wool coat closer around her. She could feel May's shudders and wondered how much credit Bill had at the mercantile. Clearly, they both needed warmer coats.

She peered in the window of Grayson's as they rode past. A scarlet dress adorned a headless dress form. What would it feel like to dress like a girl for once? A woman? She shrugged. A dress around a rundown ranch. Britches were more practical. She ran a hand over her thigh. Besides, she was the one who killed the doe whose skin she'd used.

Mr. Carter stopped in front of a clapboard building with a small steeple. He dismounted and helped May down from the back of Annie's horse. With her heart in her throat, Annie followed him inside. Marriage was forever, "till death do you part." And she knew less about this man than she'd known about Bill. At least with Bill, she'd corresponded over the course of several months.

"Are you okay?" Mr. Carter removed his hat. "It's not too late to back out, although I still think marriage is the safest recourse."

"No, I'm not changing my mind. There's strength in numbers, and we can't fight together unless we're wed." She wiped sweaty palms down the legs of her pants and wondered again about purchasing a dress. How would Mr. Carter look at her if she looked like a woman?

Would she see admiration in his eyes or the same weary resignation he exhibited now?

He crooked his arm and gave her a small smile. She slid her hand in the crook of his elbow and allowed him to lead her to the pastor's residence. Before she knew it, Annie Templeton Morgan added Carter to her name.

"Your trunk is most likely at the livery. Is there somewhere else you'd like to go while we're in town?" Mr. Carter escorted her outside.

"The mercantile, please." Annie had a list in her mind and knew that a full day back and forth would make trips to town few and far between.

He nodded. "Why don't you do that while I rent a buckboard for your trunk? You should probably buy necessities for the winter too. Mine burned with the house."

Annie took May's hand and rushed across the street. Pa rarely wanted to wait while Ma shopped. Perhaps her latest husband was the same.

A bell tinkled over the door when she pushed it open, and a round woman behind the counter greeted them with a smile. Annie sent May to sit by the woodstove radiating heat in the center of the store while she browsed.

"I'm Mrs. Grayson," the shopkeeper told her. "Is there something I can help you with?"

"I'm Mrs. Morgan—no, now Mrs. Carter." Would she ever be able to keep her names straight? Annie leaned closer to the woman. "I'm looking for a doll."

"For the little one?" Mrs. Grayson grinned. "Oh, hello, little May. I remember you from when you visited with your pa in the spring." She lowered her voice. "I have just the thing. A pretty, curly haired doll with a blue dress." She pulled a box from under the counter. "I've yet to set them on the shelf."

"Do you have a child's dress to match?" Annie peered under the lid. Her breath caught at the doll's beauty. She'd always wanted one.

"We do." Mrs. Grayson came around the counter and led Annie to a rack of readymade clothing. "This looks about the child's size." She removed a dress the same shade as May's eyes. The garment had white ruffles around the neck and hem. It was perfect. "What about for yourself?"

Could she? Annie looked down at her calico blouse and stained britches. "The dress in the window." She exhaled. She was buying a dress. Had she lost her mind? Pa would say she was growing silly in her adult years. She didn't care. A red dress for Christmas!

"Lovely. Do you need flour, sugar. . .?"

"Yes, and heavy coats. I'll be back in the spring to settle my account." On a whim, she grabbed a forest-green man's shirt from the rack and added it to the pile, along with wool and cotton to sew clothing. If Mr. Carter's food had burned, then so had his clothes, and he needed something under the tree on Christmas morning too.

For as long as Annie could remember, she'd wanted something of her own. Now she had land, a child, and a husband. One more thing than her poor ma and pa had had. Poor sharecroppers, they'd rarely had anything to call their own, much less land. She'd work hard to keep all three, whether her marriage had love or not. Over time, God willing, they could at least have mutual respect.

"Which account should I put these on? Mr. Morgan's or Mr. Carter's?" Mrs. Grayson opened a thick leather-bound book. "Or should I combine the two?"

"Yes, please." She supposed she'd have to let her husband know.

May tugged on Annie's sleeve. "That man is staring." She pointed.

Annie turned to the window. Mr. Hayward stood on the sidewalk. He tipped his hat and continued on his way. "Add some ammunition to that pile of supplies, would you, Mrs. Grayson?"

So much for flights of fancy. Life would be spent keeping May safe and holding on to her land. There wasn't time for foolishness or daydreaming or wondering *what ifs* about love.

Drake hitched the horses to the buckboard and glared at Hayward as the man paced the sidewalk in front of the mercantile. He was sure it was all around town that the Widow Morgan and he were hitched. Word spread fast in those parts. Why couldn't the man leave well enough alone?

If there was gold on Bill's land, he would have said something. Even a fool who bothered to ask questions would know Bill recently came from California. That's how he'd had the funds to purchase his land in the first place. He'd earned the gold working in a gaming hall.

Drake had told his neighbor plenty of times not to flash the nuggets around, but he'd wanted to buy the supplies to build a cabin for his new bride. Drake shook his head. All for nothing. Now he was dead over a squabble. Drake hooked the tugs to the evener. And now he was married with a child.

Life could take a huge turn in a short amount of time. It was all a man could do to keep up.

Horses hitched, he led them across the street in order to load the supplies. Hayward nodded and moved toward the saloon. Good riddance.

Annie came out of the mercantile. "Why doesn't he shoot us and get it over with?" She boosted May into the wagon. "If that's his intention."

"I don't think he intends to kill anyone." Drake watched the man push through the saloon's swinging doors. "Bill was an accident, Hayward said. He said Bill fired first."

"You believe him?"

"I do. If Hayward was a murdering a man, we'd be dead for sure. No, he intends to run us off or force us to sell, and he'll burn us out if he has to."

"Like he did you." Annie marched back into the mercantile and returned with her arms loaded.

"I'll get those. You watch May." He took the bundles from her.

"I can carry things." Her eyes flashed.

Drake didn't think she could get any prettier than when riled. "Let me do the heavy work. A woman has enough to do. Hasn't a man ever taken care of you?"

She tilted her chin. "No. I don't want a man to take care of me. I want a man to let me work alongside him as God intended."

"How so?" Drake leaned against the wagon. This ought to be interesting.

"Do you believe in the Bible, Mr. Carter?"

"Drake."

"Excuse me?"

"It's Drake. We're married, and yes, I believe in the truth of God's Word."

"Then you know Eve was created as a helpmate for Adam." She crossed her arms and fixed her eyes on his.

"Point taken. Suit yourself. We'll load the wagon together." He marched inside and slung a bag of flour over his shoulder, chuckling as Annie struggled to do the same. He wanted to tell her to take the smaller things just to get her riled again but thought better of it. The ride home was long, and could be even longer with an angry woman.

By the time they got the wagon loaded, snow fell heavier. It'd most likely turn to rain by morning. Drake looked at the pile of supplies and shook his head, knowing he'd have to go back to the livery to get a canvas covering. Seemed like women required a lot of things. He would start on a shed first thing in the morning in which to store it all, and then he'd start a cabin, weather permitting.

He hoisted himself on the wagon seat and flicked the reins. Annie's thigh brushed against his, sending a wave of heat through the layers of both their pants. Separate cots or not, he doubted he'd get much sleep that night. Not with her breathing a few feet away and him having to sleep inside such a closed-in space like the dugout.

"Here." Annie draped a thick wool coat over him. "I bought us all new coats."

"Really?" Knowing she'd thought of him warmed him more than any coat. He took another look at her and May. Sure enough, they both wore new coats. Good thing, because with the way the snow was coming down, the horses would be knee deep in the stuff by the time they got home.

"I'm much obliged." He didn't begrudge her the pile in the back of the wagon. As sweet as she was proving to be, he'd be hard pressed not to shower her with gifts himself. Maybe he should have gotten hitched a long time ago.

Late afternoon looked like nightfall when they reached home. Drake sent the females inside while he unhitched the animals and sent them to their corral and lean-to. He stomped his feet to warm them. The supplies could stay where they were. Covered with the tarp, they'd be all right until he found a place to put them. Bill would have piled them in a corner of the dugout, but Drake wanted to make the place less crowded. Maybe he could find a lock that hadn't burned in the fire at his place.

He gazed at the door. It'd be dim in there. Airless. He shuddered, whether from cold or nerves, he didn't know.

Annie opened the door. "You coming?"

"Yeah."

She stepped out, wrapping a blanket around her shoulders. "You're afraid. Why?"

The time had to come sooner or later. "When I was twelve, I went camping with my older cousins and followed them into a cave and got lost. I had no lantern and headed farther away from the opening. It took until the next day until I found my way out. Can't stomach small places to this day."

She tilted her head and peered up under the brim of his hat. "I can't make the dugout larger, but I can light a second lantern, and you can have the cot by the window so you can see the sky."

He wanted to kiss her. Grab her close and claim her lips. No one had ever been so thoughtful of him. Yet now he was married to a woman who didn't love him but wanted to make sure he was comfortable. He had nothing to give her in return but protection. He prayed it would be enough.

Chapter 5

Annie woke to darkness. Sometime during the night, Drake must have extinguished the lanterns. She smiled at his bravery. She wouldn't say a word. If he could sleep without a lit lantern, they'd save on fuel.

Glancing at his cot, she noted it was empty. The lack of laziness on Drake's part, even before their marriage, warmed her despite the chill in the room. It wasn't as freezing as the cabin back home, but even in a home underground, winter made itself felt.

She glanced out the slit of a window. The sun was just beginning its peek over the mountains, painting the sky with coral and pumpkin. A light dusting of snow covered the ground. Oh she hoped they'd have a white Christmas.

After lighting a lantern, she set to starting a fire in the stove. Breakfast would be ready by the time Drake returned from morning chores. She glanced at May and decided to let the little one sleep. Annie had lost sleep during the night because of the child's thrashing. May likely needed more rest.

Half an hour later, Drake returned with a pail of milk and a few eggs.

"We have a milk cow?" Pleasure rippled through Annie. There was so much she needed to discover about her new home.

"Two, now that I've combined our stock." He grinned. "Breakfast smells good."

"Flapjacks and bacon." His presence made the dugout that much smaller. How would they make it through the winter with three people in such a tight space? "Sit. It's about ready."

Maybe she could make cheese to sell at the mercantile. No, the long trek into town wouldn't make that practical. She smiled. For once, she'd have more food than three people could eat. The West truly was a land of milk and honey.

"I'll wake May." Drake gently shook her shoulder. "Time to rise and shine, sweetheart. After breakfast, I'll work on a shed for the supplies," he said, turning to Annie. "I'll have to use some of the wood intended for the cabin, but with Bill's gold, we can replace the wood easily enough."

Annie's hand stilled, spatula suspended over the flapjacks. Had Drake married her for the gold? Her heart sank. Too late to back out now. He'd known Bill better than she had anyway. He had as much of a right to it as she did, if you didn't factor in that she had been Bill's wife. She'd never laid eyes on the man. She sure would like to be loved for herself though. Someday, God willing.

She sighed and slid the flapjack onto a plate. "That's fine. I'm going to unpack my trunk and work on making this hole in the ground look more like a home." Annie smiled at May. "And we'll go looking for greenery to decorate with."

"Why?" Drake set his fork on his plate and glanced around the room. "Isn't it small enough in here without adding unnecessary things?"

"I've been looking forward to a real Christmas for years." What if Drake thought celebrating was a waste of time? She slumped in her seat. Pa hadn't liked holidays, but Bill's letters said he had. Annie should have known better than to get her hopes up.

"Are you wanting a tree too?"

"Yes, even if only a small one." She tipped her head toward May. "I doubt she's ever had a Christmas. Look how excited she is." The little girl's eyes were as large as owl eyes, and she transferred her attention from Annie to Drake and back so fast that Annie thought her head might fall off.

"You can't be excited about something you've never had."

"Just a small tree in the center of the table." Annie wasn't going to budge on decorating. No matter how small the space, there was always something that could be done. She forked a bite of flapjack and lifted it to her mouth, her gaze not leaving Drake's face.

He ate like a man who hadn't eaten in weeks, shoveling the food into his mouth as fast as possible, glancing out the window every few seconds.

Despite the rumbling of his stomach, Drake dreaded mealtimes in the dugout. Now that he was hitched, he wouldn't ask to eat outside anymore, for risk of hurting Annie's feelings. But now the crazy woman wanted to take up more valuable space with frilly decorations. His leg jerked up and down, bumping the table.

"What is that noise?" Annie bent to peer over the table.

Drake put his hand on his leg to still it. "I didn't hear anything."

"Are you feeling closed in right now? The sun is streaming through the window."

A slit of a window barely big enough for a rifle barrel. "I'm fine. Tell me why decorating for the holidays is so important to you." Anything to take his mind off the walls closing in.

"When I was real little, we celebrated, but then life got tough. Pa took to drinking, and anything happy or frivolous flew out the window." Annie reached over and refilled Drake's coffee with a white speckled pot. "During my correspondence with Bill, he said he liked the holidays. I got my hopes up is all. We don't have to."

A tremor in her words belied the bravado. There was no way Drake could let the holidays go uncelebrated now. Not if it meant he'd hurt her feelings. He reached across the table and placed his hand over hers. "Do what you want."

Tears filled her eyes. Drake stood and fled outside. Nothing scared him more than a woman's tears.

Having a woman around to cook and serve him with a smile was nice, but Drake missed his own homestead. It hadn't escaped him that with his land and Annie's, they were quite wealthy. Not to mention Bill's pouch of gold. Yep, they were sitting pretty.

He selected the lumber he would need for the shed and located Bill's saw between the pig shelter and the fence. Sometimes the man stuck things in the oddest places or left them where he'd used them last. It might take Drake months to get the place operating correctly. Maybe he should consider hiring an extra hand, if they had a place for the man to sleep. Someone to help him make improvements, care for the stock, and build a cabin.

He grinned. The place was turning into a regular ranch. Between the two of them, they had approximately fifty head of cattle, three pigs, five chickens, a dog, and a family. Something Drake didn't think he'd have for a while yet, if ever.

After measuring the space for a shed a bit smaller than the dugout they called home, he hammered a simple frame together and then cut a hole for a door. If the shed was as warm as the dugout usually was in the winter, he'd suggest they move into it and get above ground. Dugouts felt too much like a grave. But, the wind would tear at the shed.

Scout sniffed around him as he worked. Then the dog stiffened and barked.

Drake studied the horizon. A lone figure of a horseman stood silhouetted against the sun. Drake still didn't know for sure why Hayward didn't shoot to kill. After all, with him and Annie gone, the land and stock would go up for sale. Most likely, a man could get them for next to nothing. He switched his attention as Annie and May came out of the dugout.

More than likely, she would make good on her promise to find some greenery. With Christmas only two weeks away, he figured she'd want to get it done before too much snow fell.

His heart stopped. Winter meant long days indoors. A lot of time spent in the dugout. He was doubly grateful for his new coat, knowing he'd use every available moment to step outside to work, no matter what the temperature.

By the time he started nailing boards to form the shed's doors, Annie and May had returned from the woods with their arms full of evergreen boughs. Drake glanced back at the horizon. Another silhouette joined the first.

Annie glanced that way then at him, before ushering May back into the dugout. She returned within minutes with her rifle cradled in her arms, instead of the evergreens, and marched in the direction of the unwanted visitors.

"What are you doing?" Drake stood.

"I'm going to send them on their way."

"No you're not." He took the gun from her. "They're likely to shoot you."

"Not if I shoot them first." She crossed her arms. "We shouldn't have to worry about folks watching every move we make."

Sweet one minute and like a caged boar the next. Drake had no idea living with a woman could be so interesting. "You can't go getting yourself killed. You have May to think of."

"I do." She nodded. "If something should happen to me, like it did to Bill, I want you to take her." She reached for the rifle.

Drake held it over his head. "Stop it. You're acting loco."

"I could just take it from you." Her eyes flashed. She was prettier than a snow-filled winter night.

His mouth crooked. "How do you reckon?"

She opened her mouth to say something, snapped it shut instead, and kicked his shin. The toe of her boots sent a shard of pain rippling through him. He loosened his grip. She jumped, grabbed the rifle, and continued her march toward the men.

The little wildcat. Drake rubbed his shin and then followed, grabbing his gun from where he had leaned it against the pigpen. "Have you always been this stubborn?" he asked, catching up with her.

"Most likely." She strode right up to the men and took aim. "What are you doing on my land?"

"We're outside the boundary fence," one of them replied.

"You're too close. What do you want?" Annie cocked the hammer. "Answer carefully if you don't want to meet your maker today."

She was going to get them killed. Drake stepped next to her, holding his gun loose at his side. "I'd do what she says, men. She isn't one to listen to reason."

"Hush," Annie hissed out the corner of her mouth. "You're not helping."

"And you're plumb crazy. My leg hurts."

"You shouldn't have taken my gun." She glared at him, lowering her guard.

He whipped the rifle from her hands. "Go on, men. Git. Tell Hayward we're not selling."

"There are ways to make you."

Drake shrugged, not taking his eyes off Annie's red face. "Yep, I'm sure there are."

Annie planted her fists on her hips. "You tell Hayward that if he shows his face around here, I'll shoot him." She lowered her voice and stepped closer to Drake. "But I won't really. I just want to scare him." She whirled and stormed back to the dugout.

Drake burst out laughing as the men rode away. A little bitty thing like her, scare a man like Hayward? He doubted it, but he'd like to see her in a face-off with the man. If guns weren't involved, that is. He had a feeling he'd miss the feisty Annie if something happened to her.

Of course, with her spirit, and if he were a betting man, Drake might just have to put his money on Annie winning.

Chapter 6

Drake stopped at the door to the dugout and peered inside. The place had been transformed. Green swags covered every surface they could lie on. Pinecones and red ribbons were scattered among the greenery.

The room didn't look as crowded as he'd feared. Instead, Annie had managed to bring the great outdoors inside.

Colorful quilts lay across both bunks. A crocheted runner ran down the center of the table. A two-foot pine tree took center stage, stuck in an empty coffee can. The place looked like Christmas. Like a home. Drake didn't have a clue how to react. He turned and dashed back outside.

His growling stomach could wait. He dropped to a stump and placed his head in his hands. What was the matter with him? First, he'd blamed his caginess on the dugout, but that wasn't the truth. Annie made him nervous, plain and simple. The way she looked up at him with those sparkling hazel eyes, the curve to her lips, the dusting of freckles—it was enough to make a man crazy. Not to mention the little snuffling sounds she made in her sleep.

Annie's heart sank. Drake hated the decorations. If not for the smile on May's face, she'd take everything down this minute. She sliced the fresh loaf of bread for sandwiches. Eventually he'd come back for lunch. After all, he did the work of two men and needed sustenance.

Sighing, she placed slabs of ham between the bread and handed it to May. "I'm going to take your new pa's lunch out to him. You stay here and eat. I'll be right back."

"Yes, Mama." May dutifully took a bite.

Annie's heart swelled. *Mama.* What a wonderful word. Maybe someday she'd hear the word wife fall from Drake's lips.

She found him slumped on a log. "Here's your lunch."

"Thank you." He exhaled loudly, sending her heart to the ground, and accepted the plate with two sandwiches.

"I apologize if I overdid the holidays. Would you like me to remove some decorations?" She twisted her hands together. "May is thrilled, but if it bothers you. . ."

He held up a hand. "It isn't the decorations."

"Then it's me." She forced the words past her frozen lips. Her husband disliked her, couldn't stand to be around her. "I'll let you be as much as possible. I know you felt you had to marry me, but. . ." She turned to leave.

He reached out a hand and grasped her elbow. "It isn't you. Please, sit and have one of the sandwiches."

She faced him, studying the grave intensity in his blue eyes. His brown hair curled over his collar. What would it feel like to run her fingers through those silky strands? Would he push her away or close his eyes and lean closer?

"Are you sure?"

"Positive." He handed her one of the sandwiches. "I see you unpacked your trunk. The dugout looks wonderful. A woman's touch makes all the difference. Please don't change anything on my account."

Confusion filled her mind. She took a bite of her food and stared at the almost finished shed. The wood gleamed new against the weathered boards of the chicken coop and pigpen. "Where will you build the cabin?"

"At first, I thought about building on the boundary line, but I like the idea of being closer to the creek. How about moving the corral fencing and putting the house where the horses are now?" He fixed his gaze on her.

Did he really want to know her opinion? No one had ever cared before. She looked at her land with new eyes. "I love that stand of birch. In the springtime, the green leaves will be so pretty against the white trunks. Can we build it there? That isn't far from where you'd planned."

Drake looked in the direction she mentioned. "I think that's a wonderful idea. We could call our ranch Birchwood. I'll make a branding iron to fit the name."

"Birchwood." She liked it. She cast a shy glance at Drake. "It sounds fancy."

He set his plate on the ground then leaned back on his arms. "This will be one of the finest ranches in northern Arizona in a few years. Why shouldn't it have a fancy name? I'll build us the finest two-story cabin you've ever laid eyes on. May will be the spoiled princess of our kingdom. When she grows up, no man will be good enough for her, and I'll meet them all at the door with my shotgun." He chuckled then stood. "Enough daydreaming, I've lots of work before the day is done, and I want to check the fence line."

She watched him go, his back strong and straight. Sure, May would be spoiled, and already the little girl owned a piece of Annie's heart, but Annie had always thought God would bless her with many children.

Was it wanton to crave Drake's arms around her? To wonder about the true physical side of marriage? She sighed and picked up the empty plate. She ought to be grateful she'd married a kind man, even if she did have suspicions regarding his interest in the gold. Things could have been worse. She could have been stuck with a fat man who hit her. But it sure would be nice if Drake didn't try to avoid her so often.

She'd liked their conversation about the ranch and wanted more enjoyable times together. Maybe she could draw him out at supper. Ask him more about his plans for their future. And maybe, if she had a moment of bravery, she'd tell him about hers.

What a fool he was! Annie sat there next to him, willing to share his lunch, and he'd babbled on about a romantic name for the ranch. What was wrong with him? Ranches didn't need romantic names. This was the wilds of Arizona.

He needed to get away and do some thinking. He headed to the corral, saddled his horse, and decided to ride the split-rail fence, checking for spots that needed fixing. A cold wind picked up, and he pulled his coat tight, thankful for Annie's thoughtfulness.

Until he'd gotten himself hitched, he hadn't realized how lonely he'd been. Seeing Bill occasionally and the rare visits to town didn't satisfy like the company of a woman. God sure knew what He was doing when He'd made women.

At one section of fence, Drake dismounted and studied the broken rail. To his trained eye, it was clear it had been sawed through. Had it been springtime and the cattle grazing a larger area of the ranch, most of Annie's stock would have disappeared in a very short time. He tried to remember whether Bill had ever told him how many head of cattle he'd owned. The last time he'd checked, Drake had counted only fifty.

Was that how Hayward planned on running them out? By rustling the cattle? Drake almost expected to see Hayward and his men gallop over the nearest hill. Instead, the horizon contained nothing but trees and heavy gray clouds.

Looked like rain. Drake shivered and tugged up the collar of his coat. He'd best head home before the sky unleashed its burden.

He straightened. A blow to the back of his head drove him back to his knees. Darkness overtook him.

With the thickest of the two quilts wrapped around her, Annie stood in the doorway of the dugout and watched for Drake. A slow rain fell, chilling the air and increasing her worry.

Night had fallen an hour ago. Suppertime had come and gone.

Drake had said the decorations didn't bother him. Had he lied? Had he left to do a chore and decided to keep riding? No, that wasn't possible. Not for an honorable man like Drake. But really, how well did Annie know him?

He'd combined the ranches without consulting her—not that it was a bad thing—made plans to wed her without a proper proposal, and mentioned the gold at regular intervals. She shook her head. Drake Carter was not out to harm her and take what belonged to her. Something else was wrong.

She hurried back into the dugout and grabbed her coat. "May, we've got to go look for your pa. Put your coat and mittens on, please." Annie grabbed her rifle and filled her pockets with ammunition before rushing May out of the house.

Please, God, let him be safe. Once she'd saddled her horse, she hefted May into the saddle and climbed on behind her. She'd follow the fence line, like Drake had said he would earlier.

The rain fell harder, soaking through her coat. Annie hunched over May, trying to keep the little girl as dry as possible. Why hadn't they found him yet? They'd long since passed the halfway mark on the property line, and night had erased day, leaving them riding through inky darkness. How would they ever find him?

Despair threatened to choke her, and Annie pressed against May, taking comfort from her presence. Surely God hadn't made her a widow twice in less than a month.

Wait. Drake's horse stood, head hanging, under a tree. On the ground next to the fence was a bump on the ground that was quickly covering with snow.

Annie guided her horse to his and slid to the ground. The bump wasn't a mar in the landscape but Drake, who didn't move when she approached him. "Drake?"

How would she get him home? She knelt in the mud by his side and checked for signs of life. A faint breath from his lips brushed her face. He was alive! Praise God. Her throat clogged with unshed tears.

She shook him. "Drake, please get up."

He groaned and rolled from his stomach to his back.

"If you can get on the horse, I can get you home." Annie tugged on his arm until he sat up. "What happened?"

"Someone surprised me and hit me on the back of the head." Drake put a hand to the back of his head. "I'm bleeding. You look blurry."

"I'll care for you when we get home." She scooted closer until he leaned on her shoulders. "Climb up, and I'll ride behind you." She prayed May was able to sit on the other horse alone.

With much effort, Annie helped Drake onto the horse then mounted behind him. Seemly or not, she pressed closer, giving him as much of her body heat as she could. With the reins of May's horse clutched in her hand, she set off.

Her arms ached from keeping Drake from tumbling to the ground, taking her with him. By the time they reached home, the dugout had never looked better. Annie helped May down and sent her into the house to change into dry clothes before she turned her attention to Drake.

"I'm fine." He slid down, and his knees buckled. He leaned heavily on her for a moment then straightened. "I'll put the horses away."

"You'll go to bed." Annie propped her shoulder under his arm. "The horses will have to wait."

"You're a bossy little thing."

"Yes I am." She struggled to stay upright under his weight and steered him inside and toward the cot. He sprawled on it with a moan. Her face heated as she stared down at him. She was the only one available to strip him of his wet clothes. Well, they were married, after all. "May, hide under the covers. Don't peek out until I say so."

Removing the soggy coat was no big deal, but by the time Annie's fingers worked on the buttons of Drake's shirt, she was shaking. The fact that he stared at her, eyes stormy, not moving, his chest rising and falling under her hands. . .made her want to turn tail and run.

If doing so wouldn't put him at the risk of catching pneumonia and dying, she would have without a second thought.

When she moved to the buttons of his long underwear, Drake's eyes darkened. "Get the fire going and tend to May. I can finish this." He cleared his throat, his hand resting for a moment longer than necessary on hers.

She slid free. Her breath hitched as she turned away. What had she been thinking undressing him? What must he think of her? She busied herself tending to May. Anything to stay busy and not dwell on how she'd felt tending to him.

Annie Templeton Morgan Carter had fallen in love with her husband and had no idea what to do.

Chapter 7

Yesterday Drake had still had a fever and drifted in and out of consciousness. Today he seemed much cooler but still slept later than usual. Annie sponged his forehead and prayed. Lying on the wet ground for hours had left him struggling to breathe, and other than fighting his fever, she had no idea what to do. She'd tried tea but could only get Drake to take a few sips. What if his fever came back while she wasn't paying attention?

The dugout was easy to keep warm, but snow fell steadily outside, lazy flakes covering the ground with a light powder. She didn't know much about caring for stock. The pigs and chickens were easy—she'd had them back home—but cattle were another story. At least she knew how to milk a cow. "Please, get up quickly," she whispered. "We need you."

Would God hear her prayers in an underground home? Silly

woman, of course He would. Her ma always said He was with her no matter where she abided, but right now, Annie felt alone and helpless.

"Mama?" May leaned against her.

Annie pulled the little girl into her lap. "Are you hungry? I can fix you some oatmeal if you'll keep putting cold water on your pa."

May nodded and took the rag from the bowl of water. "I'll make him better. He won't die like my other pa."

Annie prayed not. Each day, May's affection for her new ma and pa grew. Now one of them lay at death's door. What would that do to a small child? Annie was almost grown when her parents died of influenza, not a young'un still in need of raising.

One of the cows set up a bellow, reminding Annie she hadn't done the milking yet or gathered the eggs. "I need to do the chores. Keep wiping his face with cool water until I get back. Then I'll fix breakfast. Come get me immediately if he gets worse." She grabbed her coat and hurried outside. She'd need to hurry. What if Drake got worse and May didn't recognize the signs? What if she came looking for Annie and got lost in the snow?

She glanced over her shoulder, barely able to recognize the dugout in the snowy dawn. Surely once the sun fully rose anyone could find their way around, even a child. Annie worried too much.

Or maybe she didn't worry enough. Her steps faltered. Her hand shook as she reached for the milk bucket next to the cows' lean-to. Would Drake be out of harm's way if she'd gone looking for him sooner? How did he get a bump on both the front and back of his head? It seemed to her as if someone had hit him, and he fell forward, striking his head against a rock.

She slumped on the milk stool, her fingers already growing numb from the cold. With Drake gone, she'd have no choice but to sell out. She couldn't run the ranch on her own, not with the repairs it needed and a cabin and barn to build. She'd put on a brave face when Hayward approached her, but it was all an act. Fear took root in her stomach and grew, spreading its branches through her heart and mind.

For the first time in her life, someone wanted what she had and would do anything to get it. She shook the bad thoughts from her mind and let the splat of milk hitting the tin pail soothe her. Scout whined and sat next to her.

"Where do you stay out of the weather, boy?" Annie feared for him out in the winter cold. If not for Drake already feeling overcrowded, she'd invite the dog inside.

When she finished milking, she forked hay into the manger and moved to the chicken coop. By the time she finished hunting eggs and feeding the stock, the sun sat a few inches over the nearest eastern rise. She didn't know why, but she expected to see Hayward or one of his men up there, on horseback, watching everything that went on at Birchwood. She smiled. Even if Drake changed the name, the ranch would stay Birchwood to her.

With a basket of eggs in one hand and a bucket of milk in the other, Annie headed back to the dugout. In her hurry, milk sloshed over the rim of the bucket, soaking the hem of her pants.

She shoved open the dugout door and stepped sideways down the steps. After setting the eggs and milk on the table, she turned to the bed. Drake sat up, blanket pulled to his chin, gaze on her.

"You're up." Her heart fluttered. He was awake and looking very fine.

"Thanks for your ministrations." The blanket covering his bare chest slipped.

Annie's cheeks darkened, and she turned away. He wanted to tell her not to worry, that they were married and her looking upon him wasn't unseemly, but embarrassment over his vulnerability had him yanking the blanket up to his chin. He glanced at the sheet Annie had hung the first night in order to allow him to strip to the waist in privacy.

She nodded and pulled it partway closed. "Do you feel like some oatmeal?"

"That would be wonderful." His stomach rumbled. "And coffee, please." He moved his legs over the side of the cot and tried to stand. He wobbled like a newborn calf. Maybe he wasn't ready to get up.

"You'd better not be trying to stand," Annie called from the other side of his privacy curtain.

He grinned. She sure was a bossy little thing. "No ma'am."

She screamed.

Shoving the curtain aside, he lunged for the table. His hand came inches from a scorpion ready to strike. He jerked upright and fell back, tangling himself in the quilt curtain and falling to the bed.

"What is that?" Annie's shriek rang against his ears.

Drake fought against his fabric prison. "Don't touch it."

"It's a scorpion." May glanced up from her bowl of oatmeal.

"A what?" Annie's eyes were huge in her pale face. "Is that a type of insect?"

Managing to free himself, Drake stood. "Yep. Very poisonous too. Most dangerous part is a person doesn't know how badly they'll react until they git stung. Guess he's been hiding in here because of the cold."

May grabbed her boot and squashed it. "Gone now. My other pa got bit once. Said it felt like his hand was on fire."

"Are there more of them?" Annie glanced around the floor, her words trembling.

"Most likely. We do live in a dugout. It's full of bugs." Drake leaned against the table, struggling to breathe through lungs full of sludge.

"I haven't seen any before." Annie slowly climbed onto the chair.

So, she was afraid of something. Drake had wondered. "Bill built the dugout sound with a good roof. Otherwise, bugs would be dropping on you while you sleep." He grinned.

"You're enjoying this!" She crossed her arms. "I want a proper cabin built immediately."

She sure was pretty when riled. Sometimes he felt tempted to start a fire between them just to see her eyes spark and her cheeks brighten.

He figured he'd work on a bigger bed before building a cabin and concentrate his efforts on making Annie his wife in every sense of the word. But first, he'd court her. With Christmas looming, he needed to come up with a gift. He'd go back to his burned cabin and see whether he could find his ma's ring. Maybe, with some polishing, he could make it lovely again. The sapphire stone would suit Annie just fine. He'd kept it in a metal lockbox. Surely, the fire spared that.

Clearing her throat, Annie nodded at him.

"What?" He turned in a circle. "Is there a bug on me? Oh." His long johns had slipped low on his hips, leaving more bared than not. He grabbed the fallen quilt and wrapped it around him. Face burning, he met her gaze.

Laughter bubbled from deep inside him. Clearly, his new wife wasn't overly shy. He'd never had time for false, coquettish women. His lips twitched. Within seconds, they both laughed like a couple of loons.

"Isn't anyone going to clean the smashed scorpion off the table?" May asked, looking from one of them to the other.

This made Drake and Annie laugh harder. Annie finally climbed down from the chair and handed Drake his clothes. "Not that I don't admire the scenery, but it isn't proper."

Her glittering eyes made Drake hotter than his fever had. He hurriedly donned his clothes and scooped up the scorpion with a piece of bark before tossing the thing into the stove. The simple act of dressing left him exhausted. A fine sheen of perspiration covered his forehead.

"You've overdone things." Annie set his breakfast in front of him. "It takes time to recover from a chill." She placed a cool hand against his forehead. "No fever. That's good."

"I'm just weak. It'll pass." It had to. He didn't cotton to Annie having to do the chores that belonged to him as the man of the house.

He took her hand in his. "Sit with me."

"Okay." She did, her gaze not leaving his face. "Is there something on your mind?"

A whole lot of things he wasn't quite ready to voice. "I don't like to eat alone."

"All right." She folded her hands on the table and continued to watch him.

He squirmed under her stare and struggled to find something to talk about. Something more serious than romantic notions about a ranch. "How long have you been afraid of bugs?"

"How long have you been afraid of the dark and small spaces?" She smiled.

"Point taken." He spooned oatmeal and honey into his mouth. Why did he feel tongue-tied all of a sudden? It couldn't be because she had caught him stumbling around the dugout in his under drawers. No, it had to be the fact that there was no one on earth in whose company he'd rather spend his time. The feeling was foreign.

Strength seemed to return with food. "I'm going to ride to my burned cabin and see if I can salvage anything."

"Should you? I mean. . . ." She took a deep breath. "It isn't my place to stop you, but you've been ill."

"I'll be fine. I'll keep my wits about me. No one is going to catch me unaware this time." He scooted back his bowl.

"If you aren't home by the noon hour, I'll come looking."

He patted her hand. "I'll be home."

Something bumped under the table. He looked under to see May crawling on the dirt floor. "What are you doing, sweetie?"

"Looking for bugs so Ma isn't scared."

"You're doing a fine job." He looked into Annie's teary eyes and clasped her hand. "We've a fine little family, don't we?" Nice, the way it was, but he wanted more. Much more. A big cabin, a passel of young'uns, and Annie by his side until the day he died. Now if he could work up the courage to say so. . .

She nodded. "The best." She fussed with her hair and stood. "I'd best clean up from breakfast. Be careful, Drake. I don't relish being a widow again so soon."

He chuckled. "I'll do my best to see that doesn't happen." He yanked on his boots and grabbed his coat and hat. With a final glance at Annie's lovely face, he headed out the door, praying he wouldn't collapse from exhaustion, and cursing his stubborn male pride.

Something about having a family made him want to be a hero in their eyes. A man had no time to be sick.

Chapter 8

Annie watched Drake ride away then closed the dugout door on the cold winter day. How could she have said the thing she'd said? Heavens, she was as wanton as a saloon girl. If she wasn't careful, she'd drive her husband away.

Sighing, she stacked the breakfast dishes on the drain board then reached for her yarn. She wanted to knit Drake a muffler for Christmas, along with a scarf and mittens for May. If she didn't work fast, the holiday would be upon them and she wouldn't be ready. She checked her seat for bugs then sat down.

It hadn't occurred to her that a house underground would contain pesky insects. Not that she hadn't seen plenty of bugs in Missouri, but most didn't run across the kitchen table with intent to harm. She'd be sure to check her bed covers before sliding in each night. She shuddered. Drake must think her a silly woman.

While May continued to search for bugs, Annie knitted, the click-clacking of the needles soothing her. With each stitch of the blue yarn, she envisioned how it would look with Drake's eyes. Heavenly, that's how. It should be a sin to look as fine as her husband. Surely the angels in heaven had nothing on his looks.

Scout barked outside. Annie set aside her work and peered out the window. Hayward sat on his horse, just feet from the house. Why hadn't the dog barked an earlier warning? What would the man do if Annie pretended not to be home?

"I see the smoke from the stovepipe, Mrs. Carter. I know you're home."

Bother. Annie shrugged into her coat and grabbed her rifle. "Stay in the house, May."

"Yes, Mama. I'm finding all kinds of bugs to toss in the stove."

Annie shuddered and went out to meet a two-legged pest. "You aren't welcome here, Mr. Hayward."

"Now, ma'am, is that anyway to greet a neighbor?" He dismounted and approached her, hands held loosely at his sides. "I've come to make another offer on your land."

"My husband and I have no intentions of selling." Maybe a bullet in his backside would convince the man. Words didn't seem to have any effect. "There is no gold on my property, if that's the illusion you're under. We've told you time and again."

"It's still prime land. With what I'm offering, you could afford to build a grand house, worthy of a fine lady such as yourself." His gaze ran over her pants and scuffed boots. "Maybe purchase yourself a wardrobe of fine fashions."

"I have no need of such things."

"That dugout must be mighty crowded now that you've hitched

yourself to Mr. Carter." He grinned. "Had you taken me up on my first offer, you would be dining on china this evening."

"Fine food with swine is still slop."

The man's eyes narrowed. "You're a stubborn, foolish woman."

She shrugged and lifted her gun. "I've been called worse." *Please, don't let him see my knees shaking*. She struggled to hold her aim steady. "Get back on your horse and ride, Mr. Hayward."

"What of the child? Doesn't she deserve better than. . .this?" He waved his arm.

"She's the princess of her castle and is happy."

"I found another scorpion, Mama." At the doorway, May held out a jar with another of the evil creatures inside.

Mr. Hayward laughed. "Some princess." He turned and marched back to his horse. "There are other ways of convincing folks to sell out. I'll be back to show you one." He mounted and galloped away, leaving the gate open behind him.

Annie sagged and eyed the jar with disgust. "Throw that away. Jar and all." She leaned against the corral fence and closed her eyes. Why did the man insist on visiting when Drake was gone? Did he sit away somewhere and watch to see him leave? She had half a mind to ride to Drake's property and fetch him home right away. She lifted her gun to fire a warning shot but set it down before doing so.

No, he had his reasons for checking his land. She'd leave him to them. Casting her eyes on the sky, she sent up a prayer for her husband's safety.

Contentment spread through her as she looked around at all God had blessed her with. A field of cattle and other stock. A warm home for the winter. A husband willing to work hard in order to better their lives. Yes, she was indeed blessed and didn't need some high-handed cattle baron telling her otherwise.

She looked down at her pants. She had a half-finished dress in her trunk, nestled under the new scarlet gown. Maybe she should finish it. If she did, maybe folks would look at her differently. Even go so far as to give her more respect. She shook her head. If Drake came home to the sight of her in a dress for the first time for no apparent reason, he might think she'd lost her mind. Besides, a dress wouldn't make people like Mr. Hayward any kinder. She rubbed her face, her mind a muddle.

Wearing a dress was a new concept, one she'd toyed with for the last year since receiving letters from Bill. She straightened her shoulders. She'd do it. All she needed was to attach the bodice to the skirt, and she'd be decked out in a sunshine yellow calico when her husband came home. Then she'd save her britches for chores.

Drake hefted a heavy beam out of the way and stopped to catch his breath after a fit of coughing. He prayed he'd caught nothing but a cold. It wouldn't be good to have pneumonia. There wasn't a doctor closer than town. The fact that his fever seemed to stay away gave him hope, but his head pounded something fierce.

Under the last scorched piece of wood, he found the lockbox, intact. Inside was his ma's ring, and his deed to his land. He tucked the box into his saddlebag and continued searching through the rubble for anything spared by the fire.

There wasn't much. A few tin dishes and some tools. No matter. The lockbox was the important thing. He glanced to where the barn had once stood and laughed at the sight of his laundry frozen stiff on the line. He'd forgotten he'd washed a couple of shirts and a pair of pants. Thank the good Lord, he had a change of clothes now. The ones he wore would most likely stand on their own if he let them. He grinned, remembering the sight of Annie's own stained buckskins.

If she were that pretty in men's clothes, what would she look like dressed in women's? He doubted his heart would be able to take the sight without exploding.

Having salvaged all that he could, and with saddlebags bulging, he turned his horse toward home. Never in his wildest dreams would he have thought he would ever call a dugout home. Went to show it wasn't the walls a man built but the people who lived within those walls that made the place special—that and the God who put them together.

Once home, he brushed down his horse, gave it some feed, then turned to the house. There were other chores that needing doing, but a nap would have to come first. Exhaustion dragged at him. He hefted his shoulder bags and headed to the dugout, stopping when he noticed unfamiliar hoof tracks in the snow. He sprinted for the house.

"Annie!" He barged inside and stopped.

She turned, wearing a bright dress, her hair piled high on her head, and a shy smile on her face. "You're back."

"You look like spring." He swallowed past the lump in his throat, all thoughts of a nap having flown out the slit of a window.

She brushed her hands down her skirt. "Do you like it? I just finished it today. Made May a skirt too."

Sure enough, May wore a yellow skirt with her nut brown blouse, her hair tied into neat braids adorned with leather strips.

Drake set his bag on the table. "I think you two must be the prettiest gals in Arizona."

He thought his grin might split his face in half. For Annie to don a dress meant she might harbor feelings for him. At least he hoped. It had to be a sign of good times ahead. "What's the occasion?"

"I started sewing it when Bill proposed. I thought it was time to wear it."

Oh. She'd made the dress for Bill. Stupid of Drake to think it was for him. Why would she go to extra trouble for a man she barely knew? He noted the curtain rehung and headed for his cot. "I'm in need of a nap. Call me when lunch is ready." He ignored the hurt look on her face and ducked out of sight.

He dropped his boots to the floor with a thud and fell back on his thin pillow. Idiot, harboring dreams that Annie could grow to care for him. Him! Drake Carter, a full-grown man afraid of the dark. Most likely she laughed herself to sleep at night long after she blew out the light.

He heard her shush May and rolled to his side, his gaze landing on the tiny window. Barely any light managed to squeeze inside, but it was enough when he laid eyes on Annie's face. Now the winter sun barely broke through the gloom in his heart. Hitched to a woman in love with another man. What had he expected? She hadn't had time to grieve before he'd practically forced her to marry him.

What did she say to make him angry? Annie glanced down at her dress. He didn't like it. What was she going to do with the red one now? She'd feel foolish wearing it. Didn't Drake understand she wanted to look pretty for him?

She plopped into the nearest chair. Marriage was confusing. Crossing her arms, she rested her head on them and stared at the fire in the stove. Tears burned her cheeks, leaving paths as hot as the fire's flames.

"Why are you crying, Mama?" May burrowed her way into Annie's lap.

"No reason. Sometimes women cry." She wrapped her arms around her daughter, breathing in her clean scent. She'd managed to give her a sponge bath before Drake returned. The sweet thing hadn't fussed much at all, other than completely soaking Annie by the time they were finished.

"You're crying?" Drake stepped from around the curtain. "Do you miss Bill that much?"

Annie shook her head. "I didn't know Bill, so how could I miss him?" She swiped her hands across her eyes, wanting him to disappear back to his cot. She must look a fright with her eyes red and watery.

Instead, he knelt beside her. She turned her face away, only to have him turn it back to face him. "What did I do?"

"I put on this dress for you! Oh, you're such a. . .a. . . Oh." She pulled away and stormed outside.

The wind cut through the thin fabric of her dress. Why couldn't she have left things the way they were? She didn't know any other way of letting him know she loved him other than cooking, cleaning, and donning a silly dress.

"Annie?" Drake followed in his stocking feet.

She hid a grin. They'd both freeze to death from their foolishness. "Go back inside before you take ill again."

"You wore a dress for me?" He stood so close behind her, she could feel his body heat.

She nodded. "I'm sorry if you don't like it."

His arms wrapped around her waist, turning her in toward him. "Of course I like it. I thought you did it for Bill."

"You silly fool." She cupped his cheek. "Can't you see that I—"

A shot rang out.

Chapter 9

Drake shoved Annie behind him and down the dugout steps. He followed, making a beeline for his cot. More shots rang outside. He shoved his feet into his boots. If he should die that day, it wouldn't be in his stocking feet.

"Of all the days I choose to wear a dress." Annie shoved aside the curtain and pushed his rifle into his hands. "I'm hampered by yards of fabric, and we've a gunfight to tend to."

She made it sound as simple as gardening. "By the way, I should've mentioned that Hayward came by while you were gone. He threatened this very thing when I ran him off at gunpoint."

"Why didn't you tell me?"

"I didn't have the opportunity." She planted her fists on her hips. "I'm telling you now."

"Of all the. . ." He shook his head and upended the cot to get it out of the way so he could have better access to the window. The last thing he wanted right now was an argument. As soon as Hayward was dealt with, Drake had every intention of getting back to his previous conversation with his wife.

Hayward and six men circled the dugout on horseback, hooting and hollering, firing shots in the air like a bunch of drunken Indians. Drunk was probably true. Why else would the man leap from threats to lawlessness?

"May, get under the table." Drake pointed and watched as she scampered to do his bidding. "Annie, you too."

"I will not." She grabbed her gun. "I intend to fight with you. There's power in numbers."

True enough, and they were definitely outnumbered. If something were to happen to her, though, he'd never be able to live with himself. "Then stay away from the window."

"Right." She gave a nod. "I'll shoot from the door."

"No." He yanked her back. "Fine, shoot with me from the window. But don't fire unless they actually aim for the house. I think they're only trying to scare us."

"Then I'm going out to show them we aren't afraid." She whirled and headed for the door. "They won't shoot a woman. This way, I'll distract them, and you can protect me from in here."

"Absolutely not." The thought made his stomach churn.

"Trust me." She cast him a smile and sailed out the door.

Rifle aimed, Annie marched toward the galloping men. The winter wind whipped at her skirt and sent shivers through her. Her boots crunched on the thin layer of ice over the snow. Scout's barking promised to annoy everyone within earshot.

It wasn't that she meant to act foolhardy. Far from it. But sitting back and waiting for Hayward to make a move didn't sit well with her. He needed to know they wouldn't bow to his demands. "Stop this instant."

The men reined to a halt in front of her, eyes wide, most likely because of her stupid bravery. Hiding shaking legs was one thing a skirt was good for, and hers were as shaky as leaves on a windy fall day.

"So your husband sends you to fight his battles." Hayward leaned forward, arm resting on his saddle horn.

"His rifle is aimed at your heart, Mr. Hayward, while mine is aimed at your head. I guarantee we won't both miss."

"Should I shoot her?" One of his men glared at her. "She looks like she can handle a gun and might be a threat."

"Of course she can handle a gun, you fool." Hayward shook his head. "We don't want to shoot anyone, Mrs. Carter. Hand over your weapon and the deed to your land."

"Hard to do when I don't know where it is." She grinned. "I'm guessing it's safe in a bank deposit box in Prescott." If it needed a key, she'd be in trouble. The only proof she had that she had been married to Bill was a slip of paper in the bottom of her trunk, right under the newer sheet with Drake's name.

"Bank is open. We could take a ride." Hayward motioned for two of his men to skirt around her.

"Not a wise move, Hayward!" Drake's gun barrel showed through the open window. "You put one finger on my wife, and I'll put a bullet through your gut."

Annie knew the situation could spiral out of control faster than a twister across the prairie. Somehow she needed to calm the rising tempers. "Gentlemen, there's no need. . . ." She took a step forward.

One of the men's horses jerked, yanking hard on its bridle. A shot rang out. Something tugged at Annie's skirt.

She glanced down to see a rip through the fabric. "You shot my new dress." She leveled her gun at Hayward. "You've come on my land, given orders to me and my husband, threatened the welfare of my child, and ruined a perfectly good dress. I'm starting to get riled."

Hayward climbed from his saddle and strolled, hands up, to within a couple of feet of her. By the time the rancher reached Annie, Drake had rushed to her side.

"Not one more step." Drake's shoulder brushed Annie's. Immediately she felt as safe as if she were wrapped in his arms. "The land isn't for sale. Last time we were in town, I informed the sheriff of your actions and filed a complaint. He's sure to be suspicious if we don't show up alive within a couple of weeks." He narrowed his eyes. "Who do you think they'll look for first?"

Annie didn't know anything about a complaint. Maybe Drake was bluffing. If so, he had a great poker face. She could believe what he said with very little convincing.

By the way Hayward glared, she wasn't sure how much he believed. "Sheriff Olson is a friend of mine. I don't see him taking anyone's side but mine."

"Does that mean he can shoot us?" Annie leaned into Drake, her voice barely louder than the horse's breathing.

"Nobody is shooting anybody."

One of Hayward's men fired a shot in the air. "I got a whiskey waiting at the saloon. Either we get this gunfight started or I'm leaving."

As one, Drake and Annie transferred the aim of their guns to the whiskey-loving man. Annie shivered again. If she'd known it would take so long to run Hayward and his men off, she would've grabbed her coat. Her fingers tingled, threatening to grow numb. If it did come down to shooting, she wasn't sure she could hit the side of a barn.

"Go in the house, Annie, before you freeze." Drake stepped in front of her and took steps back, forcing her to move behind him.

"Only if you go." She felt his sigh rather than heard it. She hated to disobey him. After all, she'd vowed to honor her husband, but she wouldn't be able to live with herself if she hid in safety and left him to the devices of a man such as Hayward.

They shouldn't be doing this. Meeting violence with violence would not be the way God would have them handle the situation. Sure, Annie tried to reason with Hayward, but on the other end of a gun. She lowered her rifle and put a hand on Drake's shoulder. "Put the gun down, Drake."

"What?"

"We aren't handling this right. This isn't the way God would want us to act." She was sure of it, even more so as peace flooded her.

Drake nodded and propped his rifle on his shoulder. "Hayward, we aren't going to fight you over this. If you want our land, take it. By force, by law, however you want, but we will not start a gun battle with you."

"You're going to let God fight for you?" Hayward laughed, his steps halting two feet from Drake.

"Yes, I reckon that's exactly what I'm doing." Drake shrugged. "If you take Annie's land, we still have mine. We'll be fine, unless you plan on killing us outright." He backed closer to the dugout, raising the barrel of his gun a bit to discourage any eager trigger fingers. Not that he didn't trust God but rather that he didn't trust man. If

Annie didn't want a gunfight—and Drake agreed it was the least desirable option—then they'd wait Hayward out in the safety of their home. That Drake didn't already have a bullet between his eyes attested to the fact that Hayward possibly didn't want gunfire any more than he did.

"I didn't come out here to flap my jaws." One of Hayward's men aimed his pistol at Drake. "Somebody's taking a bullet."

"No." Annie pushed forward.

Drake tried to shove her out of the way at the same time Hayward stepped up. The bullet took the man in the back, toppling him into Annie. They both fell. Drake whipped his rifle into position and shot the other man off his horse. The five men who had remained silent observers turned their horses and galloped away, leaving Drake and the others in a state of shock.

"Help me." Annie rolled Hayward off her and pressed her hands to the hole in his shoulder.

"Are you hurt?" Drake pulled her to her feet and ran his hands down her arms, eyeing the blood across her stomach.

"No, but he is." She kept the pressure on Hayward's wound, this time using the hem of her skirt. "How's the other man?"

So much for no violence. Drake knelt beside the man he'd shot and felt for a heartbeat. Nothing. His shot had taken the man in the heart. He leaned back on his haunches, sick at knowing he'd killed a man but comforted in the fact the other man drew first. Drake was only defending the woman he loved. "This man is dead. Let's get Hayward inside."

Together they dragged Hayward inside and laid him on the table. "Annie, get the fire stoked. We've got to warm ourselves as well as Mr. Hayward. May, can you find me some clean rags?"

The little girl scampered off to do his bidding. Using his Bowie knife, Drake cut the man's shirt from his body and rolled him over so he could assess the damage. The bullet seemed to have gone through his shoulder and out the upper flesh of his arm. Good. He would survive, and it didn't look as if there was the need to dig a bullet out of his flesh.

After building the fire, Annie lit another lantern and placed both beside Drake, making it easier for him to see. The way she seemed to know his needs without his expressing them amazed him. It was as if the two truly were one.

"I think if we clean this good and keep him warm, he'll be fine and on his way home by Christmas." Another body added to an already crowded dugout. Drake shuddered as the walls closed in.

Annie's once sunny dress was stained with blood, her carefully upswept hairstyle falling around her face in disarray, yet the warm look in her eyes closed out the winter and bloodshed, leaving summer with them instead. With her here, Drake could survive the close quarters.

He could survive anything.

"I'm going to change, if you can care for Mr. Hayward." Annie plucked at the bodice of her dress.

"I can handle this." What he wasn't sure about was the idea of her changing behind a simple blanket while he was wide awake and standing only a couple of feet from her.

Hayward groaned, drawing Drake's attention back to him. "Don't move. I've got to get a bandage on you."

May handed Drake a handful of clean bandages. "Is he going to die?" Her eyes were wide and caught the flicker of the fire's flames.

"No, sweetheart. He won't die." Not if Drake could help it. "Why don't you sit on your bed and say a prayer?"

May nodded and scampered off.

Drake grinned, thinking on how the soft words of his wife had kept him from shooting Hayward himself and possibly having Annie killed in the process. One less thing on his conscience when God called him home.

When he'd heard the shot and seen her fall, he thought his world would stop spinning. Thank the Lord, they were both unharmed. Now he'd do his best to save the life of the man who started it all.

"I'm sorry." Hayward opened his eyes. "I'm a fool."

"You saved my wife's life, Mr. Hayward. There isn't enough gold in the world for that." Drake wrapped the fresh linen around his shoulder and tied it tight. "We've a few nuggets if you want it. I count it a small price to pay."

"Keep your money. I'm thinking on heading to Montana. Heard the cows almost raise themselves up there."

The man was a dreamer. Not a bad thing unless it consumed you. Drake glanced at the curtain. He had all he'd dreamed and more.

Chapter 10

Christmas morning! Annie leaped from bed, eager for breakfast—flapjacks with the last of their honey. Drake had shot some quail the day before, and she would prepare them for their Christmas dinner.

Hayward had left for his own place the day before, and Drake no longer slept curled on the floor beside his cot. Annie glanced at the kitchen table where she'd stuck wrapped packages around the tiny tree. She'd stayed up late many nights working on the scarves and mittens.

Oh! A small square she didn't recognize sat among the others. Her heart leaped. Had Drake gotten her a gift? Would today finally be the day when she found the opportunity to tell him how much she loved him? With the cramped space and their unwanted guest, the opportunity hadn't presented itself again after Hayward showed up with his men.

Annie grabbed a mixing bowl from the shelf and measured out the ingredients for breakfast. May would be so excited to find hair ribbons in her stockings when she went to pull them on, not to mention the wooden horse Drake had carved for her. The little girl was in for a day she wouldn't forget, probably her first real Christmas. And definitely the most enjoyable one for Annie in a good long while.

She hummed a new carol she'd heard right before moving to Arizona—"What Child Is This?"—and thought about Drake's response when she put on the red gown. If the way his eyes lit up when she donned the yellow one was any indication, he'd be speechless.

She couldn't count the number of blessings God had bestowed on her in the last few months. A husband, a home, and a child, food on the table, and money in the bank in the form of cattle. She knew other blessings would come to mind later, but these were the most important ones. She was a blessed woman indeed.

Hot water boiled for coffee, and flapjacks sizzled. She moved to wake May while glancing to where Drake slept. Why hadn't he awoken yet? Most mornings he rose and slid aside the curtain before she got out of bed, completing morning chores then coming in to breakfast.

"Merry Christmas, honey." Annie pulled the quilt off May. "Breakfast then presents. How does that sound?"

"Wonderful, Mama." May bounded to the table. She reached for the presents then withdrew her hands and sat on them.

Annie grinned. That was as good a way of not grabbing things as anything she could think of. She skirted the table and stood in front of Drake's quilt. "Drake?"

When he didn't answer, she moved aside the curtain. His cot was empty, the blankets pulled up. He must have forgotten to slide the quilt aside in his hurry to get outside. Well, she'd finish making breakfast and have things ready when he returned.

She rubbed her hands together, as excited as a child. She'd never given anyone gifts before and only received them when the church back home took pity on her and her parents. She couldn't wait to see May and Drake in their new clothes or see May hug her doll. Breakfast ready, she locked the door and hurried to dress in her Christmas finery.

Drake pounded the last nail in the bed frame. It might not be as big a piece of furniture as he hoped to have some day, but it would do for now. Tonight, God willing, Annie would become his wife in every way. Once he got a proper cabin built, then May could have this bed and he'd make a much larger one for himself and Annie. For now, the mattress would have to be filled with straw, but soon he'd start collecting feathers and give Annie something as soft as a cloud to sleep on.

The bed would also have to serve as seating. He grinned. It would take up a lot of space, but with the table shoved against it, the bed would make a fine bench.

Snowflakes danced like angels as he straightened from under the tarp and grabbed one end of the bed. If he hefted and dragged slowly, he ought to make it to the dugout with the frame in one piece.

Perspiration dotted his forehead. The cold air cut into his lungs. He leaned against the dugout door to catch his breath, slipped, and then rolled down the steps, landing in a heap at the feet of a queen in red.

"I'm sorry." Tears welled in Annie's eyes. "I opened the door to call you to breakfast. I had no idea you were leaning against it." She held out a hand to help him up.

He lay like a stranded fish, mouth opening and closing in an attempt to breathe. Finally, he pulled forth words. "You are the most beautiful thing I've ever seen."

Her cheeks pinked. "You hit your head when you fell." She turned. "Come eat. May is waiting for her presents."

Once they'd eaten and the dishes were cleared, Drake folded his hands. "There's something I've always wanted to do once I got a family, and that's read from the book of Luke at Christmastime. But my Bible burned in the fire, so I'll have to recite it the best I can."

"I've my ma's Bible." Annie jumped up and dragged her trunk from under the bed. "I think that's a wonderful tradition to start."

His face flushed. Whatever made Annie happy, he'd do to the best of his ability. He especially loved it when she was pleased with one of his ideas. Nothing built up a man more or made him feel stronger than the encouragement of a good woman.

She handed him a Bible with a worn leather cover and opened it to the Christmas story. "Ma didn't read out loud from it much, but I found this story once when I was hoping for presents. No gifts came that year, but the story filled an empty spot in my heart."

Drake would make sure she had gifts every year of their lives. Never again would sweet Annie want for anything, not if it was in his power to give it. He started to read, " 'And it came to pass in those days, that a decree went out from Caesar Augustus that all the world should be taxed. . . . And she brought forth her firstborn son, and wrapped him in swaddling clothes, and laid him in a manger; because there was no room for them in the inn.' "

Like their dugout, Bethlehem had been bursting at the seams, and the same as in that town of long ago, God provided the room needed for the celebration of Christ's birth. Drake finished reading of the angel's visit and closed the Bible.

"Now, presents?" May asked.

"Yes, now the presents." Drake ruffled her hair, noting the shiny blue ribbon. "You got new ribbons?"

"They were in my stocking." She wrinkled her brow. "Isn't that a strange place for them?"

"Very." He laughed then sobered as Annie handed him his gifts. He opened them, more than pleased with the shirt and muffler. "You are a fine seamstress, Annie." He stood. "I've something to show you that will test your skills if you don't mind a little snow."

"I love snow."

What could he possibly have for her that he couldn't bring in? Annie headed for the stairs, anticipation adding a skip to her steps.

"Wait. There's something else I want to give you first." Drake reached for the box on the table.

With trembling fingers, Annie peeled off the thin slices of bark he'd tied on in place of paper. Inside was a small wood box with a gold clasp. The type of box that one might keep small treasures in. Holding her breath, she opened the box. Tears sprang to her eyes at the sight of the ring. "It's beautiful."

"No more so than the woman on whose finger I hope to place it." Drake took the box from her. "Will you wear it?"

She put her hand over her mouth and nodded, tears falling in steady rivulets down her cheeks.

"No longer are you the woman I married to save our land, but the woman of my heart. The other half of me." He slid the ring on her left ring finger.

Sobs shook her shoulders. He loved her as a husband loved his wife. She could hardly see through her tears. "I don't know what to say."

His eyes glistened. "Your response to the next gift will tell me all I need to know." Taking her hand, he led her up the steps and outside.

Waiting for them was a pine bed, big enough for two. When the implications of the bed occurred to her, Annie didn't need a coat to warm her. Her face burned. "How will we fit it in the house?"

"I've thought of that." Still holding her hand, Drake turned her to face him. "Will you share this gift with me?" His Adam's apple bobbed, showing his nervousness.

Knowing his emotions mirrored hers made Annie's decision that much easier to make. "Yes, I'd be most pleased to share my gift with you."

"I wish I had a finer place to share this day with you." He took her other hand in his and pulled her close.

"Anywhere that you are is a castle to me, my husband." She peered into his face. "I love you. I tried to tell you the other—"

He put a finger over her lips. "Merry Christmas. I love you." He bent and claimed her lips.

Annie felt like the most important woman in the world. She didn't care that she stood with snow covering her head and catching on her lashes or that the wind bit through the fabric of her dress. Drake's kiss warmed her to her toes and made her feel like the richest woman in Arizona.

Cynthia Hickey grew up in a family of storytellers and moved around the country a lot as an army brat. Her desire is to write real but flawed characters in a wholesome way that her seven children and five grandchildren can all be proud of. She and her husband live in Arizona, where Cynthia works as a monitor in an elementary school.

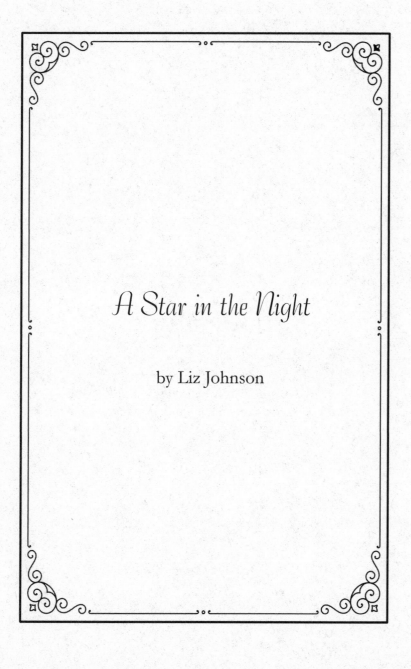

A Star in the Night

by Liz Johnson

Dedication

For Judy and Ann, first readers and faithful friends.
Thank you for your encouragement, kindness, and example of joy.

Chapter 1

December 3, 1864
Franklin, Tennessee

Although it had not yet snowed that morning, Cora Sinclair sniffed the air for any sign of a coming storm. Despite the frigid breeze, oh, how she wished it would snow now. How she wished the pure white flakes would cover the ground stained with the blood of thousands. At least until Christmas.

Pulling her cloak tighter around her shoulders, she ventured a swift glance at the white columns and brick walls of Carnton. Unable to control her emotions, tears filled her eyes, and she shuddered as memories of the last two days in the grand house flooded through her.

"Has it really only been two days?" She spoke to herself, as no servants could be spared to walk the half mile with her to her home.

While the sun rose, illuminating the barren trees and scarred earth, Cora could not help but envision the soldiers who had marched over this very land. Her gaze darted around the grassy fields, looking for signs of any soldiers still there.

The silence turned eerie, and more shivers ran down her arms.

There! What was that shadow in the tall grass?

Fear rooted her feet in place as the shadow moved.

Surely it wasn't a Union soldier who'd lost his regiment, interested in taking a woman as a prisoner. Was it?

Why had she been so swift to assure Mrs. McGavock that she could safely find her way back to the cabin she shared with her grandfather? Why hadn't she waited until someone could be spared to join her?

Cora tried to swallow but found the lump in her throat was actually her wildly beating heart. A strangled sob tore from her as the shadow moved again. And again.

She tripped over her feet as she backed away, falling hard on her hip. Closing her eyes, clutching the lapels of her cloak, and pulling her shoulders up to her ears, she waited as the rustling grass drew near. When the movement stopped, she squinted at the bright red fur and round eyes of a little fox several yards away.

Jumping to her feet, she threw decorum aside, picked up her skirts, and ran toward the small cluster of trees that hid a wooden cabin just off the Harpeth River.

Her breath came in ragged gasps as she reached the outer ring of sycamore trees, and she leaned heavily on a sturdy trunk until her breathing returned to normal. Dark auburn waves had escaped the knot at the nape of her neck, and she pushed them behind her ears, her hands growing damp from the streams of tears down her cheeks.

Suddenly the swelling sunlight shimmered off a piece of gold.

Her mind had to be playing tricks on her again. She blinked

several times, but the soldier didn't vanish. In his Union-blue frock, and covered with branches up to his waist, he sat perfectly still against the base of a tree. His right arm hung at an odd angle, the fabric there more purple than the deep blue of the rest of his coat.

She took a tentative step toward him. "Are you—are you. . . ?" She didn't know what she was going to ask, but he let out a low, pain-filled groan, effectively halting her words and the hand she reached out.

Cora jumped back, snatching her hand to her chest. As she concentrated on his shoulders, they rose and fell in a shallow rhythm.

"Papa!" she yelled. But she was much too far away for her words to carry to her grandfather.

Racing over the uneven earth between giant trees, she finally reached the clearing dominated by the one-story log cabin. She nearly crashed into the front door when the handle did not unlatch on her first attempt. After yanking on the rope again, the lever on the inside of the door rose, and it swung open.

"Pa–papa." She swallowed, trying to catch her breath as the old man with silver hair slowly pushed himself from the rocking chair in front of the fireplace. He still held the family Bible open. "Please. There's a soldier in the grove. We have to help him."

Cora didn't realize how much the fire in the stone hearth warmed the cabin until she stepped back into the freezing cold, her teeth chattering. Stepping next to her grandfather, she leaned into him as a coughing fit seized his body. That same cough had kept him from accompanying her to Carnton when the fighting finally finished and Mattie ran to their home asking for help with the wounded.

Papa waved off her look of concern and trudged against the wind as she led him toward the fallen man.

When they reached the soldier, he hadn't moved, but his shoulders continued to rise and fall. Papa quickly laid one of the blankets he'd brought with him on the ground. "Help me roll him onto this."

Together they pulled the brush off of him and then gently laid him on his side. Rolling him onto the blanket seemed the only option, as he was much too big to lift. He never stirred as they situated him in the middle of the makeshift travois, or as Papa slipped one of the blankets under his arms and covered him with the third.

"Take that corner," he said, and Cora bent to pick up the edge of the blankets at her feet.

It took them several tugs to get the blanket moving, but once it began sliding over the roots and foliage, they continued at a steady pace all the way back to the cabin.

They dropped the blankets next to the fire, and the soldier moaned but made no other movement until Papa rolled him onto his side. Just as the discoloration of his overcoat suggested, the telltale round hole from a minié ball marred his right shoulder.

"Boil water, and get some clean cloths," Papa directed. "We need to take it out."

Cora carried her teapot to the corner of the room near the door and filled it from the large tub of creek water there. Then she slid the pot onto the cast-iron stove, which Papa had added to the cabin just a couple of years before the war began. While she waited for the water to begin bubbling, she hastened to the bedroom, rummaging through the single trunk at the foot of the bed. Her hand finally landed on soft, white cotton, and she removed a pair of much-used petticoats. She had outgrown them more than a year before, and had been saving them in case she needed to mend her only other pair.

Heat rose in her cheeks as she realized that her underthings would soon be tied around a man to whom she had never even been introduced. Staring into his face, she tried to perceive the kind of man he might be and how he had come to be in their woods. Was he a deserter? Or had he simply lost his way and been separated from his regiment?

Mud-caked curls clung to his temples, and dark lashes convulsed, but his eyes never opened. Unruly whiskers covered his cheeks and chin, but he was not altogether unattractive. The slope of his broad shoulders and quirk of his colorless lips made her heart beat unusually fast, and her stomach filled with a sensation she could not name. Certainly it was only concern for his well-being. Someone cared about this man and waited for his return.

Was he married? Was his wife waiting at home for him, terrified of reading his name listed among the missing or dead?

Just the thought forced her to put her mind on the task at hand. She ripped the cloth in her hands into even strips, as Papa struggled to remove the man's coat.

"Let me help you."

Papa looked up and smiled as they rolled him to his stomach. "Will you pull on that cuff?"

Soon they had stripped away his outer clothes and piled them on top of the satchel he had carried, leaving only his undershirt and the red stain that covered nearly the whole of his back. Papa sliced the saturated fabric with his knife, until they could clearly see the man's injury.

Cora bit down on her lower lip to keep from crying out at the sight, and she blinked several times in order to rein in her emotions.

Papa's hand shook as he held the knife over the wound, and she reached out. "I'll do it, if you like." Her eyes pleaded with him to refuse her offer, but he did not. He simply handed her the blade.

"Good. I'll hold him down. You cut out the minié ball." Papa leaned down on the man's shoulders, pressing him into the floor.

She pinched her eyes closed as she poured steaming water over the weapon and into a basin.

"God, give me a steady hand," she whispered as she touched the point to the jagged opening. Blood immediately bubbled from the hole, and she gulped another breath as she pressed in deeper until metal met metal. The tip of the blade scratched and prodded at the foreign object, and the soldier cried out.

Cora jumped at his agony but didn't stop digging until the projectile poked out of its aperture. She snatched the minié ball away then pressed on the seeping wound with one of the strips from her petticoat.

Papa's knee cracked as he stood and walked toward the cabinet near the kitchen table. He pulled out a glass decanter and swiftly returned to her side. "We have to make sure it's clean, or he'll develop a fever."

She agreed, nodded, and pulled back the cloth as Papa poured the amber liquid into the injury. The muscles in the man's back bunched and quivered, and he let out several groans, but still he did not open his eyes.

By the time they had bandaged the wound and cleaned up after the surgery, the sun had set, and the only light in the room came from the flickering fire.

When another coughing fit took hold of Papa, Cora put her hand under his elbow and helped him toward the bedroom. "Why don't you go to sleep? I'll stay up and make sure that he doesn't take a turn for the worse." She looked over her shoulder at the sleeping man, a pang of fear eating at her stomach.

How could she possibly lose another man to the wounds of this battle? Already the faces of the men haunted her dreams.

"Thank you," Papa mumbled as he pressed a kiss to the top of her head. Despite his stooped shoulders, he still stood nearly a head taller than her. "Call me if there's any change."

"I will."

Papa left the door to the bedroom mostly open as Cora walked past their patient to the jumbled pile of clothes on the floor. Folding them piece by piece, she cringed when she held up the long jacket, covered in blood and grime from the floor of the surrounding forest. As she folded it, a piece of paper fell from an interior pocket. She bent to pick it up, surprised that there was no envelope or address on what was clearly a letter.

Many men carried them into battle. Letters to send to their loved ones if they didn't make it home, but this one was simply folded in half.

Glancing into the handsome features of the man before her, she opened the page filled with long, even pen strokes. What secrets hid beneath his long, brown lashes? Was he dreaming of the woman to whom this letter belonged?

Her stomach clenched at the idea of reading another woman's post, but she pressed on. How would she know where to address it if he did not survive?

My dearest Bess,

If you're reading this, then you know that I won't be coming home. I cannot express to you how sorry I am to leave you and our son on your own. But I trust that God will hold you close during these difficult days. I have loved you with my whole heart and will eagerly await the moment when we can meet again in glory.

The closing words swam before Cora's eyes, and she had to stuff the letter back into the jacket pocket before it made her cry any harder.

Every letter just like it—and the reason for them—had made her sick to her stomach as she'd passed water and tea to the soldiers crowding the house and yard at Carnton. If only she could share that pain and grief with someone.

But who could understand? Papa needed her to be strong. And the McGavock family would be consumed with caring for the wounded for months.

The faces of those wounded men and the women who waited for them to return were memories she had to carry on her own.

Straightening her shoulders, she brushed her fingertips over her eyelids and cleared her throat. As she set the captain's folded uniform at the foot of his pallet, she shot him one more glance.

But this time, something had changed.

His stunning brown eyes stared back at her, sending her stomach to her toes.

Chapter 2

Jedediah Harrington's shoulder burned like it rested in the fireplace. The pain that had almost certainly woken him also indicated that something else was amiss. As he opened his eyes, he remained still, taking in his surroundings and trying to place the room.

It wasn't an overly large room, but it felt as though families had grown and loved each other in this place. It looked like a home ought to, with a gentle blaze below the stone mantel at his back and a kitchen table and benches on the far side of the room. Even at the distance and with only the light from the fire, he could see that the corners of the furniture had been rounded by years of use. The only other place to sit was an equally worn wooden rocking chair.

Twisting slightly against wooden floorboards, he looked around until he spotted the skirts of a young woman near the foot of his bed.

When his eyes made it to her face—all smooth lines, soft freckles and pink lips—she glanced up at the same moment and immediately darted to the other side of the rocking chair, holding it carefully between them.

"My papa is in the other room." She stretched her finger over his head, but Jed didn't have the strength to follow her movement again. Did he look like he was a danger to her? Certainly she thought so.

He managed a small nod, immediately regretting the way it made his head swim. Resting his ear against the thick blanket spread below him, he opened his mouth but found that he had no voice.

The woman took a tentative step around the chair, keeping one hand on it, probably to use as a weapon if he made a wrong move. "Do you need some water?"

Again he tried to speak. Again he met with the same outcome, so he offered an almost imperceptible nod, trying to limit the pounding behind his eyes. All but her lower half disappeared to the far side of the room, and water rang against the bottom of a tin cup.

He tried to swallow, his tongue like a desert, so he waited until she returned.

"Drink this," she whispered as she knelt by his head. The tin cup she pressed to his lips tasted of metal, but the water tasted like rain in a drought. He tried to guzzle the entire contents of the cup, but she pulled it back every few swallows. "Not so fast. You'll spill all over."

Finally it was empty, and she stood and took several small steps away, as though their nearness had been too intimate for two people who had never been introduced. He immediately missed the sweet scent of lavender and gentle touch of her hand.

He cleared his throat and closed his eyes for a long moment. "My na—" His voice cracked, and he had to try again. "My name is Jedediah Harrington. Nearly everyone calls me Jed."

She squinted as though uncertain if she would believe him. After a long pause, she whispered, "Cora Sinclair."

The fractured grin he offered must have broken through at least one of her reserves, as she brought a hand to the high neckline at her throat but responded with a faint smile of her own.

"How did I end up here? Where are we?"

"I found you in the woods not far from here, so my grandfather and I brought you to our home. I removed a bullet from your shoulder and patched it up the best that I could."

Suddenly the memories crashed through his mind. "I was shot by Confederate scouts. We're about a mile from Franklin. There was a skirmish." She confirmed his memory only with a quick motion of her head. "I was headed to Ft. Granger when I stumbled on the troops. I was just trying to get around them, and someone shot me off my horse. They took my weapons." But had they taken the War Department missives he had been carrying to General Schofield?

His gaze darted around the room looking for his gear, for he knew that the leather satchel that had been hanging over his shoulder and across his chest no longer rested there.

"Where are my things?"

Cora glanced over her shoulder to a pile of neatly folded clothes on the floor near the door to the bedroom she had indicated earlier. "It's all there. Your coat and vest and shirt." She blinked long, fair eyelashes before continuing. "And your bag also."

The missives could be of little use to General Schofield or anyone else at Fort Granger in the aftermath of the unexpected skirmish, but he could not afford for them to fall into enemy hands either.

Could he trust her to keep him safe until he could return to Washington? What if she had already called rebel troops to come and get him?

But if her intent was to turn him over, why hadn't she left him to freeze?

Oh, and it had been bitter there beneath that tree. He had been there for at least three nights, blacking out for long stretches of time. But he'd never forget the cold. Somehow he'd pulled branches and leaves over himself, in an attempt to retain any heat still in his body, and it must have worked.

"Why did you bring me here?"

Lines appeared on her forehead, and she tilted her head to the side, escaped strands of her rippling hair falling over her shoulder. "I couldn't leave you outside to die, could I?"

"I'm an officer in the Federal army. You're from Tennessee." He looked toward the ceiling, letting his gaze settle on the rough-hewn rafters. "Most would have."

When he looked back, her face turned gentle, her blue eyes compassionate, and she sank into the rocking chair. "This is not my war. I have no stake in it."

"No brothers? What about your father? A beau?" A sad smile tugged at the corners of her mouth, and remorse pinched his stomach when he realized he was the cause of her sorrowed expression.

"My father died when I was very young, and my mother also. I was their only child, and I was raised by my grandfather and grandmother—she died last year. He's all I have now." Her gaze jumped to the bedroom door then returned to meet Jed's. "I haven't lost anyone I love, and the men here aren't fighting to preserve my way of life."

Her hand fluttered to the corners of the room, and he understood. She had never owned slaves, never owned a plantation or probably even concerned herself with politics. This war wasn't her choice.

But could she really be as harmless as she seemed? Nashville had been under Northern control for several years, but nearly twenty miles south, this battle in Franklin only served as a reminder that many pledged their allegiance to their homeland, not to those in power.

She leaned closer. "You have nothing to fear from my grandfather or me," she said, as though reading his mind. "You will be safe as long as you're here."

An unexpected chill swept his body, and Jed cringed as the muscles in his shoulder contracted, piercing the wound with fire again. He closed his eyes against the throbbing pain, Cora's pretty face appearing on the back of his eyelids. He wouldn't soon forget her tenderness or compassion.

Suddenly Cora's cool hand rested on his cheek, her eyes studying his face.

"You should rest," she whispered.

Doubts about her honesty seeped into his mind, and he wanted nothing more than to walk out of the cabin and return to his home, to Bess. If only he could push himself off the floor, put his coat back on, pick up his bag, and leave. But wishing did not give him the strength to do so, and he shivered again.

"Let me check your wound again." She leaned over his back and rolled back the blanket covering his shoulders. She inhaled sharply as she jumped to her feet, quickly returning with fresh bandages in hand.

He could not refrain from flinching when an icy, wet cloth touched his bare skin.

"I'm sorry. I should have warned you." The cloth swiped like hot coals over his back. "You're bleeding again."

"Of course." He bit down on his bottom lip to keep from letting on how much pain even her gentle touch caused. It seemed like hours before she firmly pressed another bandage in place and secured it with a piece of cloth already wrapped around his chest.

As she pulled the cover back over his shoulders, he asked, "May I have another blanket?"

"Are you cold?"

"Yes."

She spread another blanket over the layer already in place and then knelt beside his head, putting her palms on his cheeks and forehead. "You're very warm. You shouldn't feel cold."

"I do." A yawn caught him unaware, making him stutter. "So very cold." He closed his eyes, and the pressure building at his temples begged him to succumb to a long night of sleep in front of a fire and free of the outdoor temperatures he'd suffered.

"Let me get you more water before you go to sleep."

She scurried across the room, but he could not even ward off slumber until her return as he sank into the darkness of oblivion.

Chapter 3

How is he?"

Cora glanced up from where she knelt by the captain as her grandfather carried in an armful of logs for the fire. "The same." She pressed her palm to the cheek of the man on the floor. But his eyes didn't move, and his face remained unchanged. "I made him drink more water, but he won't eat."

Papa unloaded the logs onto the pile next to the hearth, tossing a few of the smaller ones onto the already radiating fire. "How does the wound look?"

Jed's muscles twitched as Cora peeled back the sodden bandage. Even though she'd washed it and changed the bandage several times, the ragged flesh and pungent odor made her cringe every time.

"Do you think it's getting any better?" She couldn't keep the hopeful lilt out of her voice.

His hands on his hips and leaning clear forward, Papa shook his head. "It's hard to tell. Truth be told, I'm more concerned about that fever."

"I gave him some ginger tea." She held up a half-empty teacup. "Well, as much as he would take. But it doesn't seem to be helping."

Still deep in sleep, Jed's legs jerked. Cora shot her grandfather a helpless look and sighed.

"Keep pouring the tea down, but make sure it's not too warm." Papa sat on one of the benches along the table, his eyebrows drawn tight and usual smile a distant memory. "I don't know that there's anything else we can do for him."

Cora's stomach lurched, and she knew it to be true. The captain had suffered a fitful sleep for nearly two days, never fully waking up. She had done everything she knew to do. He needed a doctor. And she knew exactly where one could be found.

Certainly there were still surgeons tending to the wounded at Carnton. If the thick, black smoke rising over the tree line was any indication, all of the fires there burned day and night, for boiling water and cleaning surgical instruments. For the men. Those wounded soldiers.

They were in so much pain, and the chloroform administered by the doctors only numbed the injured. But the fires hadn't blocked out the metallic smell of artillery fire still lingering in the air mixed with the sharp odor of unwashed bodies.

Her stomach jumped again, bile rising in the back of her throat as the memories of the injured men leaped to mind.

She didn't want to go back there. Ever.

She didn't want to see those men still recovering. Or have to again cross the field where so many soldiers had marched toward the

Union line in Franklin.

"It's getting late." Papa dragged her from her thoughts. "Will you sleep in your bed tonight? You need to get some rest. I can stay by him."

Cora's gaze shifted to the single doorway on the far side of the room then back to her patient. "No. I'll stay up with him. If there's a change, I want to be here." She dipped a clean rag in a basin of cool water, using it to bathe Captain Harrington's face. Above his dark eyebrows, past his ear, and under his broad chin. *My, but he is handsome.* "Just in case."

"All right. Good night then." Papa walked past her and bent down to kiss the top of her head before disappearing into the dark bedroom. She heard him unsnap his suspenders and the rustle of cotton as he hung up his shirt. With the door all the way open, his rhythmic snoring soon echoed through the cabin as it did every night.

After cleaning and rebandaging the wound on the captain's back one last time, Cora crawled to her rocking chair. Fighting sleep and the haunting dreams that waited just behind closed eyes, she picked up her mending, one ear always listening for a sound from the mat at her feet. Her eyelids drooped as she pushed the floor with her toe, the crackling of the fire and squeaking of the chair her only companions as her mending dropped to her lap.

The clock on the mantel chimed twice, jerking Cora from unwelcome images dancing through her dream. Wrapping her arms around her stomach, she curled as tightly as she could, trying to erase the faces of the men at Carnton who would never return to their loved loves. Uninvited tears leaked down her cheeks, and she swiped her knuckles across them, her heart broken for the families who'd lost their husbands and fathers, brothers and sons.

She shivered despite the heat from the smoldering embers.

Tossing another log on the fire before kneeling next to the captain, she brushed his hair from his forehead. Heat radiated off him stronger than ever before, while barely discernible chills made his teeth click together.

She pressed her hands to Jed's cheeks. She barely knew him, yet she was responsible for him. Even though she'd never met the other woman, Cora owed it to Bess to make sure Jed returned home.

He needed a doctor and medication, but taking him to Carnton could mean a fate worse than the one he faced on her floor. The Confederate troops at the main house wouldn't look kindly on a Yankee. Even if he was an injured officer. If taken captive, the captain could spend the rest of the war—possibly the rest of his life—behind bars.

"I wouldn't wish that on anyone," she whispered to the shadowed face. "What if you were sent to a prison, and I had no way of finding Bess to tell her what happened? Oh, Captain. You have to wake up." A single tear slipped down Cora's cheek, as she sent up a silent prayer for his healing.

The air smelled of frying ham, the meat sizzling not far from where Jed lay, still on the floor. For the first time in days his stomach rumbled, a not-altogether-unpleasant sensation for a man who had thought his life was coming to a slow and painful end.

When he twitched his shoulders, pain eased through his back, rolling through the muscles like gentle waves on the beach. Heaving a sigh of relief that it no longer burned like an unquenchable fire, he ventured to open an eye and lifted his hand to wipe the beads of sweat from his forehead.

Suddenly a pan crashed to the floor, and a familiar voice hollered, "You're awake!"

In a flurry of skirts, Cora knelt beside him, her cool fingers paradise on his cheek. "I supp—ose I am." His voice cracked with disuse, but she ignored him as her soprano filled the room.

"I was so worried. Your fever just kept getting worse and worse last night. I tried to give you ginger tea, but you wouldn't drink much of it. This morning I thought you might be getting better, but I couldn't be certain." As they locked eyes, her hands ran over his face and down his neck before she jerked back, her cheeks tinged pink and gaze dropping to the floor. "How do you feel?"

Jed barely suppressed a grin at her familiar actions. He couldn't blame her. She'd clearly been watching over him for days, and he had no objections to a pretty gal touching him like that. "Better." He wheezed, and she rose to her feet like a doe in the morning light. When she returned with a cup of water in hand, she lowered herself just as gracefully.

"Drink."

He did as ordered, gulping greedily as she held tin to his lips. When the water was gone, he rested his head back on the mat, taking several deep breaths. A sharp aroma mixed with the woodsy scent of the fire and spicy lye soap that had certainly been used to clean the blankets on which he slept.

"Is something burning?"

Cora's eyes grew round as she scrambled to her feet, all sense of grace abandoned. She muttered to herself as a skillet sizzled and clanked against the small cast-iron stove in the corner next to table.

"I've ruined dinner." She sighed to no one in particular just as the hinge on the front door lifted and her grandfather stepped inside.

"Well, well. It's good to see that you're awake finally," the old man said. He squatted near Jed's feet, eyeing him with equal parts suspicion and interest. "How do you feel?"

Jed twisted to get a better view of the wrinkled features, not sure if there was more to the question than what the other man had said. "Better, sir. I appreciate your hospitality. You and Miss Sinclair have been more than kind."

Nodding thoughtfully, the man slapped his own thigh as he stood. "Well, if you're going to stay here awhile, you might as well call me Horace."

"Very well. Will you call me Jed, then?"

Horace nodded, putting his fists on his hips. "Do you feel well enough to sit up, Jed?"

"I'm not sure. Shall we give it a try?"

Maneuvering Jed into a seated position turned into quite the ordeal even with Cora and her grandfather at each of his elbows. By the time he leaned against the log wall, cool gusts of wind seeping through cracks in the chinking between old logs, he needed to lie down again. But he fought the drowsiness as Cora handed him a bowl filled with a thin broth. As he tried to lift the spoon to his mouth, it clattered back into the bowl.

Immediately by his side, Cora offered him a gentle smile. "May I help you?" She didn't hold out her hand for the bowl or even move to take it back, but her posture indicated immediate help should he ask for it.

"I can do it." Making a fist with his right hand several times, he stretched and practiced the movements. Forearms crying for mercy after days of disuse, on the third try he managed to get a half spoonful of brown liquid to his mouth. It tasted better than any feast at his mother's table in Maryland ever had.

After finishing more than half of his evening meal, he set the bowl aside and leaned his head back as the old man opened the big Bible and read aloud the story of Ruth and Boaz.

Cora's eyes remained firmly on the red fabric in her hands, her needle never slowing. Maybe it was the fresh log on the fire or just Jed's imagination, but Cora's cheeks seemed to glow with extra color when Mr. Sinclair reached the end of the story.

Had Cora slept at the foot of his bed like Ruth had with Boaz?

What a foolish thought to have about a woman he'd barely met. He hadn't thought to be married since the war began, but if he had a wife as kind and pretty as Cora, perhaps he might think on it more. But there was no use. He would be moving along shortly. Mrs. Puckett wouldn't hold his room at the boardinghouse for long. And first there would be a stop at the farm in rural Maryland, tucked between rolling green hills.

Bess would be there, and she deserved an explanation, even if he had none to give.

When the Bible was safely stored on the kitchen armoire, Mr. Sinclair excused himself to look in on their only remaining livestock. "When the Army of Tennessee came through and took our horse and chickens back in sixty-two, we couldn't pay them to take that hog off our hands." He laughed.

His exit seemed Cora's cue to put away her sewing. As she walked past him toward the bedroom, she stopped but did not turn to face him. "Papa will help you lie down to sleep tonight." She took another step then thought better of it. "You should put an address on your letter to Bess in case you ever need to mail it."

His eyebrows pulled tightly together. "Did you read that letter? You had no right." He hadn't even read it.

"It fell out of the pocket of your jacket as I was folding it." Her head dipped low. "And a wife has a right to know if her husband isn't coming home."

Jed nodded slowly. "I agree. That's why I'm taking it to her."

Her gaze sought his, blue eyes reflecting the flickering flames. "I don't understand."

"Bess is my sister. Her husband and I were on an assignment together." The lump in his throat refused to be cleared, so his words sounded like a bullfrog. "And he won't be returning to her."

If only they hadn't been separated. If only Grant hadn't run into those scouts. If only.

Cora blinked several times, biting on her lips so hard that they disappeared. "I am sorry for your sister. And for you, as well."

"Thank you." Jed sighed quietly. "If you're sad for anyone, it should be my nephew, Matthew. He'll never know his father, who was a good man. Grant took good care of my sister, and he was shaping up to be a good father to that little one."

"Do you have a letter like that for your wife?"

"My wife?" She nodded, as though encouraging his memory. "I'm not married."

"There must be someone waiting for you."

He shook his head. "Just Bess and my parents."

Her hand shot to her cheek, covering something that looked like relief. "They deserve letters too, I think." With that she bolted from the room, disappearing into the bedroom and closing the door softly.

If she'd given him a chance, he'd have told her. He had letters for them. Letters in envelopes, addressed to his childhood home. But he wouldn't need to have them sent yet.

Chapter 4

The cold December days passed quickly, but still Jed didn't move from the floor. He tried to stand on several occasions, always refusing Cora's help. And each attempt left him weak and defeated. While his color improved, his scowl grew deeper with every passing day. And it was that attitude that concerned Cora most.

Three days after his fever broke, she approached his pallet carrying a plate of stew. "Will you let me help you to the table?"

"I can take care of it myself." As if to prove his point, he pressed his palms against the floor. He didn't budge. But his face twisted in pain.

"You're too weak." She set the plate down, crossed her arms, and shook her head. "You were seriously ill for four days and faced the elements unprotected for at least two. And you lost a lot of blood. It's going to take you some time to regain your strength. Please, won't you let someone help you, Captain?"

He cocked his head to the side, closing one eye almost all the way. The corner of his glower crept upward, his face slowly transforming. "Captain?"

The skin at her throat burned instantly, and she covered her cheeks before the red stain became obvious to him. He trapped her in his gaze like the rabbits Papa snared near the riverbanks. She could not escape without telling him the truth. "Yes—well—it is your rank. . .and I just thought that. . .it seemed too. . . I wasn't certain that it was proper. . ." Breaking eye contact, she stared at her brown boots. "I hardly knew you, but I had to call you something."

His laugh surprised her, rich with mirth, the opposite of the scowl that had taken up residence.

"Don't your men call you Captain?"

"Of course. I've just never had anyone as pretty as you call me that before."

Her cheeks burned stronger, and she wrinkled her nose against the telltale sign of her discomfort. "Well, should I have called you Mr. Harrington?"

She peeked up to see one of his shoulders rise and fall. "Call me whatever you like. But Jed is fine."

"Miz Sinclair! You home, Miz Sinclair?"

Cora's head snapped to the narrow gap where the wooden planks of the front door missed meeting the frame. "I'll—I'll be right there." She spun back to Jed, her eyes like saucers. "Quick. You must hide," she whispered. "No one can know you're here. Since Papa is out checking his traps, you must let me help you."

He nodded quickly as she wrapped an arm around his waist, careful to avoid the bandages still tied in place. Her shoulders tingled where his arm rested across them. She'd cleaned his wound, washed his face, and combed his hair, yet none of that had made her stomach churn as this informal pose did.

"Where to?"

His question pulled her back to the urgent present. "The bedroom?"

On shaking legs and leaning heavily on Cora, Jed shuffled across the room. His eyes closed tightly, but his feet never stopped moving. Just as she stepped away from his side, her visitor knocked loudly. "Miz Sinclair?"

She practically pushed Jed to sit on the bed, and then she raced back into the main room, closing the bedroom door on him. Nearly missing his folded uniform and leather bag, she caught a glimpse of it just before answering the knock. Scooping them into her grandmother's trunk, she could hardly breathe for rushing when she swung the door open on a familiar face from Carnton.

"Mattie! What brings you all the way down here?" The cold December wind had her quickly motioning the petite woman inside and helping her off with her damp shawl.

"Missus Carrie sent me to check on you. To make sure you made it home fine." Mattie rubbed her dark hands together. "And she wanted me to check on your papa. Is he feelin' better?"

Of all the things to ask! With a house full of wounded soldiers, Carrie McGavock, the mistress of Carnton, wanted to check on her and Papa. Mrs. McGavock's kindness had always made her a favorite of Cora's. And Mattie was an extension of that same gentle spirit.

"Oh, yes. He's doing much better. Please thank Mrs. McGavock for her kindness."

Mattie turned her back toward the fire, thawing from the freezing rain. "I thought I saw 'im checking 'is traps when I was walking up."

Cora smiled. "Yes. He wanted to make sure they didn't freeze before he cleaned them." Mattie's eyes drifted to the pallet on the floor at her feet, but she seemed to stop herself before asking a personal question. Quicky Cora piped up, "Would you like a cup of tea before you go back?"

Mattie shook her head. "Missus Carrie needs me back right away. But she said I should ask if you have any blankets or cloth for bandages."

"Then there are still wounded men there?"

"Oh yes. They're packed into every room in the house, 'cept the sitting room."

"From both sides?"

"Not many Yanks left." Mattie pulled her shawl from her shoulders, holding it in front of the fire. "They left without their wounded, so them that could be moved were taken prisoner."

Cora's stare shot to the bedroom door before she could stop it, and a chill that had nothing to do with the howling wind shook her shoulders. If anyone knew there was a wounded Union officer in her home, Jed would be headed to the same prison as those other poor souls.

Of course, Mattie and even Mrs. McGavock wouldn't tell Jed's secret, their compassion stronger than most. But what if one of them had an accidental slip of the tongue? Cora couldn't live with herself if she endangered his life.

"Those poor men." Cora sighed.

Mattie offered a half smile. "Maybe the war will end soon."

Cora had nothing to offer in return. They'd all hoped the war would end soon. They'd been hoping that for years. Even as isolated as she and Papa were, nearly a mile from Carnton and that much farther from the rest of the town, they'd hoped and prayed for an end to the bloodshed. The men dying on these fields weren't her brothers, but they were someone's kin, and they haunted her as if they were her own.

"I should be getting back." Mattie's view dropped again to the pallet at her feet. "Can you spare some blankets and such?"

Cora's knees rattled. She couldn't give Mattie the quilts spread out on the floor. Some of them held bloodstains from the captain's wound. If anyone looked closely at them, they'd know she was hiding something.

"Let me just check the bedroom." Her legs could barely hold her as she stumbled toward the closed door and slipped into the room. But it was empty. She spun around, expecting to spy Jed in every corner. He was nowhere to be seen.

She'd have to find him later. After Mattie left.

Grabbing the only extra bedcover from her mattress and the last pieces of her old petticoats, she hurried back into the main room. Mattie had tied her wrap tightly about her shoulders and hugged the items that Cora handed to her.

"Thank you, Miz Sinclair."

"You're quite welcome, Mattie. Be safe."

Mattie smiled and disappeared out the door in a flourish, leaving Cora to find her missing soldier.

Jed wasn't sure he'd ever be able to move again. His head spun, and all of his limbs shook with the effort it had taken to crawl beneath the bed. He couldn't risk being seen by anyone, even a house slave from the next home over. He just needed to get back to Washington and his assignment there as a special courier for the quartermaster general.

He'd just have to make his legs move long enough to get back there.

When Cora said farewell to the other woman, Jed forced himself to roll from his side to his stomach. Using one hand, he pushed against the wooden bed frame until he was all but free of the quilt, which hung to the floor.

"Jed!" Cora's footsteps stopped the moment she entered the room. "What are you doing on the floor? Where did you go?"

Pushing himself to his knees, Jed rested an arm on top of the mattress as he drew several quick breaths. Cora stooped next to him, her hands reaching out but not touching him. Her dark blue eyes unblinking, she simply stared at him.

"I've put you and Horace in danger just being here." He looked away, through a clean glass window toward the grove of trees where he'd been injured. "I have to go back to Washington."

She stood to her full height. "You're in no shape to travel." Placing her hands on her hips, she imitated a stance his mother had often taken when he was a boy. "Besides, we have no means of transportation. Our horse was taken two years ago. How could you possibly make it hundreds of miles on foot?"

"If the rebels knew that you were hiding me, you could be imprisoned. . .or worse." His eyes swept back to hers, and he very slowly pushed himself to his feet. "You've been so kind to me, but I can't put you at risk. I have a job to do back in Washington. The War Department will want to know where I am."

Cora crossed her arms over her chest. "You can't leave. It's not safe for you"—she motioned to the great beyond—"out there. And you don't have the strength."

Could she see the way his legs trembled beneath Horace's ill-fitting trousers?

It didn't matter. He didn't have a choice. They'd already been far kinder than they should have been to a Union soldier. He wouldn't jeopardize them any longer. Neither would he argue the point with Cora, whose eyes flashed with something akin to fire.

So he stayed through the afternoon, eating more at noon than his stomach wanted, but he would need the energy from rabbit stew. As he sat on the table bench next to Horace and scraped at a piece of wood with his knife, the sun began to set.

Supper was a quiet affair. Cora mentioned Mattie's visit and looked as though she might say something about his intent to leave but bit her tongue instead.

The wind howled past the cabin later that night as the fire dimmed to embers. Horace had been snoring for at least thirty minutes. Jed could only assume that Cora had also succumbed to sleep after a long day.

Pushing himself off his mat, he sat up and rolled to his knees. Groaning as he stood, he walked over to his uniform and slipped the stained and ripped fabric back into place. He reached into his leather bag and pulled a letter from the other papers. The sound as the paper tore in his hands seemed to echo even above the wind, and he whipped around to make sure Cora hadn't heard and come to investigate. The room remained still as he scribbled a short note and left it on the table next to Horace's spare set of clothes.

As he settled the strap of his bag across his chest, Jed glanced over his shoulder once more as he opened the door, the wind wailing as though it were crying. A quick glance around the room did not calm the sensation that he left something behind, his stomach a knot as his gaze landed on the bedroom door. He could not stay with Cora, so he stepped into the frigid winds of the night.

Chapter 5

Cora awoke with a start, at once feeling something was amiss. Papa continued to snore in the bed on the opposite side of the room, so she donned her shawl over her white cotton nightgown and tip-toed into the main room. Jed's pallet lay empty, his uniform gone.

Her stomach churned, and the hair on her arms stood on end. She didn't even have to read the note on the table to know where he'd gone. But she read his messily written words nonetheless.

Dear Horace and Cora,

Thank you for your kindness. I will be forever beholden to you. I must return to my duties in this war now, but I pray that God will protect you both. I hope our paths will cross again.

Sincerely,
Jed Harrington

Cora smiled at the scrap of paper in her hand. He hadn't mentioned his rank or regiment, or even which side of the war he fought for. Still protecting them, even if they didn't need it. No one else would ever see this note. She rolled the paper in her hand and clasped it under her chin.

Not even Papa.

As she stood at the window and wondered how far Jed had gotten during the night, her stomach plummeted. The night was full of dangers: wild animals and rebel forces, not to mention a river that ran much higher and faster than she'd ever seen it before. Jed had still been so weak when he left. Would he ever make it back to Washington?

"You fool," she whispered to the window just as gentle white flakes peppered the floor of the clearing.

"I hope you're not talking to me."

Cora jumped at her grandfather's voice, nearly dropping Jed's note. Clutching it in both hands at her waist, she offered Papa a weak smile. "Of course not." She nodded toward the trousers and shirt folded neatly on the table. "The captain is gone."

"Gone? But he could barely walk yesterday."

She nodded and looked through the snow and trees, hoping to see his form making its way back to them. "After Mattie's visit, he told me he wanted to leave. He was afraid he put us in danger. Afraid there might be a visit from one of the Southern soldiers, who wouldn't take kindly to us caring for an officer from Washington."

Papa grumbled something under his breath as he turned back to their room.

Cora couldn't seem to move her feet. Eyes alert, she held her breath for long intervals as she waited for Jed to return.

But he didn't.

Not while she made biscuits for breakfast. Or while she heated water on the stove to wash their clothes that afternoon. Not even as they ate their evening meal.

Cora couldn't taste the potatoes she'd grown that summer in her own garden as she put them in her mouth. Every time the wind rustled the leaves outside their door, her head spun to see if it might mean the captain's return.

It never did.

As Papa opened the family Bible later that night, Cora picked up her knitting, something she could do and still keep watch. When the fire was so low that he could no longer read by its light, Papa stood.

"I need to find more firewood tomorrow."

"Why?" Cora's attention jumped at her grandfather's unexpected announcement. "We had plenty stored up. It should have gotten us through the winter."

He nodded grimly. "When the river rose, it flooded our woodpile. Only the logs on the very top are dry enough for us to use."

Her heart sank, and tears jumped to her eyes. "But we worked so hard to gather enough to last the whole winter."

Cupping her cheek with his weathered hand, he tilted her face up to look into his eyes. "Don't worry. God will provide for us. Didn't you hear what I read tonight?"

Oh, she hadn't been paying any attention for worry over Jed's safety.

"I'll be leaving early," he said. "I'll have to look farther away from the river. Those trees close by will be as wet as our pile."

"Be careful," she pleaded. "There might still be soldiers out there." Her mind didn't conjure an image of soldiers seeking help but the bodies of those at Carnton who they could not help.

Cora had to look away, the back of her eyes burning as she blinked quickly. She didn't want to remember the faces she'd seen.

But it didn't seem to matter. She saw them every night in her dreams.

"What's wrong, Cora-girl?" Papa placed his large hand on her shoulder, but still she could not look him in the eye. "Why are you so sad?"

She wiggled her head back and forth, biting her lips against the longing to tell him the whole truth. How she wanted to tell him of the memories and faces that caused her anxiety to bubble like water in her teapot. But he had enough concerns with replenishing the firewood and helping them survive the winter and the war.

She could not give her burdens to him, so she patted his hand and whispered, "Please don't concern yourself with me."

Papa rubbed her shoulder again. "If you're certain."

"I am."

He took to bed, but Cora could not drag herself out of her rocking chair to follow him. She tried to focus on the steady rhythm of his breathing after he fell asleep and the clacking of her needles. Tried to wipe the terrible images from her mind. But as her chin fell to her chest and her eyes closed of their own accord, the faces she mourned played across her mind.

"Jed!" Cora screamed, waking herself from the nightmare where the captain's face joined the others. Tears trickled down her cheeks, and she swiped at them, rubbing her eyes with her fingertips, trying to press that terrible image from her mind.

It was good that he had left. She might have fallen in love with him, ending up one of those women left to wonder if her love would return.

The sun had just broken the plain of the horizon line as she set aside her yarn and pushed herself from the chair, refusing to give her body opportunity to fall back asleep. Wrapping her arm around her waist as she walked toward the window, she shivered against the chill seeping through the wall, where beams of light broke through breaks in the chinking.

Then as if she were still asleep, Jed's form materialized between two trees in the distance. She smiled to herself, as though this were her mind's way of apologizing for that awful dream. But the figure continued walking and then stumbled, barely catching himself on the trunk of a tree. He pushed himself up again, favoring his left arm. The side on which Jed had been shot.

Cora was in the yard, racing toward the figure, before she fully recognized that he was more than her imagination.

"Jed! Jed. . ." She fell to the ground where he had tripped, resting her hands on either side of his ice-cold face. "You're freezing. Let me help you inside."

For once he didn't object, silently allowing her to wrap her arm around his waist as she pulled his arm around her shoulders. They stumbled at the threshold, slipping through the doorway, which she'd left wide open. She led him inside, and he collapsed to the floor in front of the fire.

Immediately she knelt at his side, helping him take off his sodden coat and soaking boots. "What were you thinking? You could have died out there." She shook her head and glared at him as she hurried to pour him a cup of chicory root that Papa had left on the stove before leaving that morning.

He pulled a blanket from the pile on her grandmother's trunk and hugged it around himself, leaning toward the fire. "I–I'm sor–ry." His teeth chattered, and his entire body shook. "I shouldn't have left."

Handing him the steaming tea cup, she muttered, "That's the smartest thing you've ever said to me."

Sipping the hot drink, he sighed. "You were right. I didn't have the strength to make it very far, and I ran into rebel scouts near Franklin. The town is still a terrible mess, but I was able to hide in a barn until nightfall, and then I came right back here." He looked away from her, clearly ashamed, but she couldn't be certain if it was caused by his leaving or having to return. "Should I not have returned?"

She glanced down and realized that her arms were crossed, one hip stuck out in a pose not unlike one her grandmother had often struck. Lowering her hands to her sides, she shrugged. "I never asked you to leave."

"I'm sorry."

"Very well. You may stay. As long as you promise not to leave until at least Christmas."

His face turned thoughtful. "Another two weeks here?" She nodded, and he took a long sip of the bitter coffee substitute. "Agreed."

Chapter 6

In the days that followed, Jed's health improved rapidly, his strength returning in waves every day. Each evening he fell soundly asleep after working steadily alongside Cora and Horace to take care of their home. As the snow melted and daytime temperatures rose, they all spent much of their days collecting firewood to replace what had been ruined by the flood.

When all the trees were picked bare as high as they could reach, the two men felled one of the sycamores farthest from the cabin, dragging it in parts to the yard.

The ring of the ax splitting new firewood didn't seem out of the ordinary to Cora as she cut thick slices of bread to complement their lunch.

"The way that boy's going, we'll have enough heat to last two winters." Papa chuckled to himself as he plunged the dipper into the barrel of drinking water, sipping right from the ladle.

Cora spun around, knife still in hand, and glared through the window. Jed stood next to the stump in the yard, resting his forearm on the long ax handle as he gently rotated his shoulders and stretched his back. Marching to the door, she flung it open and pointed her knife at him. "What in heaven's name are you doing?"

Jed had stripped off the red-checked shirt he'd borrowed from her grandfather and even rolled up the sleeves of his white undershirt. He swiped an arm across his forehead and quirked one eyebrow. "Whatever it is that I'm doing, I'm sure there's no need for violence."

"What does that mean?"

He nodded toward her hand, the corner of his mouth lifting in an ever-so-slight grin. "I don't know. You're the one holding a knife."

Cora looked at the blade then back at Jed before realizing he was teasing her. "All right then." Lowering her hand to her side, she put her other fist on her hip. "You know you shouldn't be out here chopping wood."

"I know. There are several cracks in the chinking that need to be fixed. Horace said we could start that tomorrow."

She glanced over her shoulder at Papa. "Did you ask him to daub the cracks?" Jed began to speak, but she cut him off. "Oh, it doesn't matter. You're working far too hard for someone who could barely walk five days ago."

"I feel good." As if to prove his point, he picked up a piece of the tree, centered it on the stump, and split it evenly with one slice of the tool, barely favoring his left arm. "This is good for me. Well, this and all your good cooking."

His attempt at flattery would get him nowhere, but she wasn't going to argue with the fool either. If he wanted to injure himself again, that was his choice. No matter the nagging concern that forced her to look back at him once more before returning to the meal preparations. Or was it the way his handsome features glistened under the midday sun?

Certainly she felt only concern for him, as someone who had been under her care. The way her heart fluttered at the sight of him hard at work was nothing more than a natural apprehension. Wasn't it?

The long hours of labor and so many late nights caring for Jed finally caught up with Cora that afternoon as she washed the dishes. She yawned loudly and often, battling the heaviness of her eyelids. Finally conceding to rest her eyes for a moment, she dropped into her rocking chair and had just dozed off when Jed stomped his boots clean just on the other side of the door.

Through one eye, she glared at him as he stepped into the home. When he looked over and caught her gaze, his smile fell. "Were you resting?"

She shook her head, fighting the desire to succumb to sleep once again. "Not quite."

He fastened a button below his chin. He'd put the red cotton shirt back on over his undershirt, although his cheeks still glowed from the exertion. "Don't let me keep you from whatever you were doing. I just needed. . ." His voice cut off as he lowered himself to a seat at the table. A wry grin spread across his face. "Well, I guess you were right. I don't have as much stamina as I thought."

She opened her mouth to say she'd told him so but bit her tongue instead. Pulling her knitting from her basket, she asked, "Where's Papa?"

"He was just going to finish stacking the wood that I cut and then go down into the cellar to bring up more smoked ham."

They'd been alone many times, but Jed was nearly fully healed, and her stomach fluttered uncomfortably. She pressed her hand to it while consciously averting her gaze. She knew his features by now. Knew the way his hair fell across his forehead and his hands curled into fists. Knew that gleam so often in his eye that meant he was teasing her.

But sitting alone with him as he pulled out the fair scrap of syc-amore he'd been carving for days felt strange and new, and not even a distant relative of the concern she'd felt for his wellbeing. And not altogether unwelcome.

Slamming her eyes closed against the curious feelings brewing within, she was soon lulled by the consistent rasping of knife against wood and gentle motion of her chair.

Jed flinched as the knife in his hand scraped his thumb, nearly draw-ing blood. He had to focus on the little figure emerging from the lumber, despite the way the sun shone through the window, turning Cora's hair to the color of honey. He admired the graceful lines of her cheek as her face was turned away from him, yet he couldn't make out the words she mumbled.

"Hmm?" He leaned toward her, still unable to see her face.

She took a deep breath, nearly a sob. "Just hold on. Hold on. The doctor will see you soon."

Jed jumped to his feet, moving silently across the room. When he reached her side, she swung her face toward him, her eyes closed and silver trails slipping down her cheeks. And then she wailed so loudly that he leaped back, nearly tripping on his own boots.

He'd heard that terrible sound before. The night that he'd tried to leave for Washington—he'd thought it was the wind.

Her breath hitched, and more tears streamed down her face, but still she didn't wake.

What if she woke up and was angry that he'd been there? He shot a glance toward the door. But what if she awoke and was frightened to be alone?

Considering all the nights that she'd stayed by his side as his fever raged in front of this same stone hearth, he owed her at least the same. So he pulled over the bench and sat right next to her as her gentle features twisted in pain and something akin to fear.

Utterly helpless, he did the only thing he could think to do. He slipped his hand into hers and squeezed gently. Her fingers were long and soft, the opposite of his callused, chapped hands. But she clung to him, clenching his hand with each stuttering breath.

The longer she clutched his hand, the easier her breathing became. Her tears dried, and the pinched features of fear relaxed until she slept, finally at peace with the world inside her own mind.

Jed lost track of time as he whispered prayers of serenity over her, hunched so close that his lips brushed her hair. When Horace opened the door, Jed jumped enough to jolt Cora from her rest as well. Her eyes darted between Jed's face and her two hands, still clinging to his. Hopping to her feet, she dropped his hand and pressed her palms to her face. Her eyes open wide, she just stared at him before shaking her head slowly.

"I'm so embarrassed," she whispered. Without warning, she bolted, disappearing behind the bedroom door, refusing to emerge even to join them for supper.

Jed sat across the table from Horace that evening, his eyes staring only at his plate, focused on the memory of the way Cora's cheeks had burned with embarrassment. He'd wanted to scoop her into his arms and hold her until she confided what made her cry in her sleep. But he hadn't done it. For propriety's sake and her composure, he'd stayed rooted to the floor.

His stomach fell, and he set down his fork. If her pride got in the way, she might never let him close enough again to learn what was really going on in her head.

"Was she crying in her sleep?"

Jed jerked his head up to look the other man in the eyes. Nodding slowly, he said, "Yes, sir."

Horace rested his chin against his chest, his shoulders sloping to his elbows, the furrows above his eyes growing deep. "I don't know what to do. It's every night since she came back from Carnton—since she came back from tending to those men."

"Those men?"

White hair bobbing, Horace mumbled, "She went to Carnton after the battle. The house had been turned into a hospital, and Carrie McGavock sent word that Cora should go help if she could." The old man's hands shook as he folded them on the table next to his plate. "Her grandmother would have known what to do now, but all I can do is stay awake at night listening to her sobbing and pray that God will give her rest."

"I understand." Jed's eyebrows pulled together. "Have you tried touching her arm or holding her hand?"

"She won't let me near." The sadness in Horace's eyes was a punch to the gut for Jed. "It's like she can feel that I'm close by, and she thrashes out like a trapped raccoon."

Jed swallowed the fear that he might hurt the old man's feelings and pushed forward in the hopes of helping Cora. "She let me hold her hand today."

"I know."

"I'll hold it again tonight." He glanced over his shoulder at the bedroom, longing to give her some semblance of peace in her sleeping hours.

Objections crossed Horace's face as clearly as if he'd spoken them aloud. It was improper. Her reputation could be ruined. What if she awoke while Jed was there and was even more embarrassed? "I don't think that's a good idea."

"Sir, I realize there are a lot of reasons why I shouldn't, but if it could help your granddaughter rest peacefully. . .even for one night . . .would it be worth it?"

Horace heaved a loud sigh, the love for his only grandchild filling his eyes with compassion. "I suppose so."

That night, after the chores were done and the cabin was closed up tightly, Jed waited on his pallet until a new cry joined the wind whistling between the logs. He knocked softly on the door of the bedroom and waited until Horace let him in, and then he sat on the floor between the two beds and reached for Cora's hand.

She wrapped her fingers around his, her breaths slowing to a steady rhythm until she finally rested.

Chapter 7

Y ou attended West Point, but did you graduate?"

Jed laughed at her. "Of course I graduated. It was my dream to be a soldier, and I wasn't going to squander it."

"Why a soldier?" Cora picked up another handful of kindling, filling in larger cracks between the cabin logs.

As Jed stirred his bucket of mud and straw, which he would use to fill the smaller spaces and seal the openings, his eyes shifted down, his eyebrows drawn tightly together. "My father wanted me to run the farm—"

"In Maryland?"

"Yes, but my great-grandfather fought with George Washington, and I grew up hearing stories of those battles. Those men at Valley Forge were my childhood heroes, so when I entered the academy my only regret was that I wouldn't have a noble war to fight as they had."

Cora pressed another piece of wood into place, keeping her gaze on Jed's face. "And now that you have a war?"

Jed shook his head, his hand never stopping, lest the mud harden beyond use. "It's not romantic, but it is noble to fight for what you believe in."

"What about the farm? What will your father do?"

"Grant and Bess were going to farm it." A painful expression seared through his eyes. "Now, I suppose he'll give it to my nephew. I'm a lifelong soldier." Suddenly a yawn cracked Jed's jaw. Leaning against the rough timber of the outside of the cabin, his eyelids drooped.

"Are you not sleeping well?" Cora asked as she pressed the last pieces into place. "You look terrible."

Jed grinned at her. "*I* look terrible? If you're not careful, you'll look worse." He stirred the sloppy mess, moving as though he would pitch it at her.

She ducked and screamed. "Don't you dare!"

Taking a menacing step toward her, he waved the stick of muck in her direction. "Oh, wouldn't I? I'll show you what terrible looks like!"

She shrieked and ran from him, picking her skirts nearly up to her knees as she bolted around the side of the house. His breathing loud and close behind her, she knew she couldn't outrun him. He had returned to almost full health and strength, so she hid around the corner of the cabin. When he rounded the building, still growling and waving the muddy stick, she jumped out and screamed.

He plunged to his backside in an instant, his bucket flying and covering him in the sticky daubing. Cora fell to her knees beside him, laughing harder than she could ever remember.

With his forearm Jed swiped at the black streaks that covered his forehead. "This is awful." His face remained stoic, but the lilt in his voice gave away his good humor.

"Just don't waste any of it," Cora managed between fits of laughter. "You still have to fill in the cracks between the kindling."

"Thanks for the reminder," he grumbled, his hand shooting out to wipe a black stripe down her cheek, his smile suddenly matching her own. "Now we look alike."

She grimaced as she poked the mark on her face and then inspected her finger, her eyes squinting and nose wrinkling at the dark coating. "I suppose I deserved that." He nodded mutely before they both broke out in laughter again.

When her stomach hurt too much to continue, Cora pushed herself up, taking in the sticky mess before her. "Do you think you can salvage any of that and finish fixing the wall?"

"I think so."

"Good. Then clean up. It's almost Christmas, and we still don't have a tree." She looked off to the eastern sun, her lips pulling into a straight line. "My mother always had a tree. She came over from England and said the Royal family had a tree every year. When I was young, she read an article about them putting decorations on their trees, so we've been doing that almost my whole life."

"What else did you do to celebrate Christmas with your parents?"

Her gaze turned wistful, still not turning back to him. "My mother had a beautiful voice, so she often sang Christmas songs as we baked sweet breads."

"What did you sing?"

"Oh, anything that came to mind. But 'Joy to the World!' was her favorite, and we would sing it over and over." Cora bit her lip, her smile growing. "Mama and I would spend weeks baking on her brand-new step top stove. No matter how cold the outdoors, we were warm as fresh pie in front of that fire. And oh, the pies we made!" Turning back to Jed, she didn't try to hide her pleasure at the memories flowing forth. "When the pies were done my father always tried to steal a bite of the peach, but it wasn't for him. Mama bundled me up in a cloak that covered me to my toes and wrapped scarves around my head. And then we carried baskets full of sweets to our neighbors, stopping at each house on our street to wish them a happy Christmas." She swallowed hard. "I do miss them sometimes."

Jed's deep, brown gaze turned soft, his eyes never wavering from hers. "What happened to your parents?"

Cora shook her head. She didn't want to talk about it right now. She only wanted to think on the happy memories, the times of laughter and joy.

Jed's hand reached for hers, familiar like she'd dreamed of it fitting so perfectly into his own. When he squeezed gently, she sighed. "They died of yellow fever when I was twelve, so my grandparents took me in." Jed pressed her hand again and opened his mouth to speak, but she cut him off before he could respond. "It's not as painful now as it was once. I just wish I wasn't such a burden on Papa."

"A burden? But you take care of this whole house."

She waved off the flattery. "He worries about me." She pursed her lips and looked over Jed's shoulder. "He doesn't say that, but I know it's true. He worries about what will happen when he's gone. Who will take care of me?"

Jed squared his shoulders and spoke with a boldness unusual even for him. "Did you never have a beau? There must have been men who wanted to marry you."

Heat threatened to burn her cheeks again, but she forced herself to respond to his question. "I was barely sixteen when the young men at church in town began leaving to fight." She could offer him only half of a smile. It wasn't as though she had never wanted to marry. It simply wasn't an option now. The man that she could love and respect would be fighting until the war ended. Just like Jed, who would soon be returning to Washington.

And if she loved him, she'd become one of those women with a broken heart. One of the ones left behind. One who might never know the fate of her beloved. That was a worry she could never manage, one she could not carry on her own.

Pain filled her stomach, but she forced a happy expression and spun away. "Get yourself cleaned up. We have a tree to find."

By the time Jed washed his hair with the thick soap Horace had loaned him, changed his clothes, and caught up with Cora, who was stuffing a burlap bag into the bottom of her sewing basket, all trace of her sadness had vanished. She'd tried to cover it at the time, but he knew he'd upset her by asking about a beau. He'd just been unable to stop the question from rolling out, even if he didn't want to admit why it mattered.

"Are you ready?" she asked. He nodded, his stomach rolling at the bright smile she offered. "Good. Get the ax. We have quite a trip to make before it gets dark."

"Why do we have to go so far?"

She laughed at him over her shoulder as she trotted away from the river headed west. "There aren't many fir trees in this area, so Papa planted a small grove of them, but he didn't want them to be too close to the river. He said it was bad for them to be in ground that is too wet."

They trudged through the groves of sycamore and towering oak trees, both shivering with each step, despite the sun high in the sky.

"Are we almost there?"

Cora didn't bother answering his question. She simply led the way between two trees that had blocked the view of a cluster of twelve or fifteen small firs, their tops about even with his shoulder. Jed squinted at them, not sure if his eyes played tricks as to their color. "Are they. . .that is, they look blue."

She nodded enthusiastically, as she ran up to one on the right side. "They are. They're called concolors and appear to be both blue and green. And just wait until you cut it down."

Jed did as he was told, swinging the ax at the base of the young tree until it split and toppled to its side. As he leaned over it, he caught the scent to which he knew Cora had been referring. "It smells like oranges."

"I know." She laughed. "Isn't it wonderful?"

He agreed and joined in her Christmastime merriment as he hooked his arm around a branch to drag it back home. As Cora prattled away about the corn they could pop and string around their beautiful tree, Jed's mind continued drifting to what would take place later that night. Long after the popcorn was wound around the tree, he would sit on the floor next to her and hold her hand until morning came.

But he couldn't be there for her forever. After all, Christmas was a week away, and then he would leave. He had to go back to his post in Washington, but he didn't want to leave her alone with her nightmares.

Just as he started to speak, his heart heavy with her internal agony, large flakes of snow began to drop before their eyes. Cora held out her mittened hand as though she could catch the white flecks before they melted. "Don't you just love snow? It feels like it washes away everything wrong with this world. Like it could cover every ugly thing."

Jed stepped toward her, putting his hand on her shoulder, but she didn't turn toward him. "What is it that you want to be covered?"

She shook her head, hunching her shoulders away from his touch. "I saw a lot of things that I can't seem to forget."

"Is that what you dream about at night?"

She whirled toward him, her face a mask of vulnerability and pain. "How did you know?"

"I hear you sometimes." He swallowed the lump in the back of his throat telling him not to tell her the whole truth, took a breath, and pushed forward. "And I hold your hand while you're sleeping."

Her knitted mitten covered her mouth as tears welled up in her eyes. She blinked twice but couldn't seem to stop the quivering of her chin. "I'm mortified," she cried as she turned and ran.

Thankful he had the strength to catch her, Jed dropped the tree and chased her several steps, finally wrapping his hand around her wrist just firmly enough to stop her. "Please, don't be ashamed. Tell me what it is you dream that makes you cry so hard."

She shook her head, her gaze on his hand, still clinging to hers. "I can't tell you."

"Why not?" He tucked a snow-flecked strand of her hair behind her ear, leaving his hand on her cheek and wishing that he could protect her from all the awful things of the world. "Have you forgotten that I've been in this war for four years? I've seen terrible things too."

Her chin rose until she looked into his face, if not quite into his eyes, tear tracks still marring her apple cheeks. "There were so many men. The uninjured soldiers kept bringing the wounded into the house until they filled every room. I brought them water and blankets and passed out supplies. And I was fine. The blood didn't bother me until they brought in Danny Pa—car." Her voice hiccupped on the last word, and Jed did the only thing he could. He pulled her into his embrace, tucking her head under his chin. She nuzzled into the shoulder of his wooly coat.

"What happened to Danny?"

She hiccupped again, her shoulders shaking under his hands. "His arm was gone."

Jed smoothed her hair with one hand while rubbing circles on her back with the other, his cheek resting on top of her head. "Was he the only one with a missing limb?"

"No. . .but he was the youngest. He couldn't have been more than fourteen." The damp spot on his coat swelled as she sniffed softly. "When I was wiping the dirt off his face, it felt like a brick in my stomach. He was someone's son. They all were. Even the ones being buried behind the house were someone's family."

"Oh, honey," he murmured into her ear. "I am sorry."

Her arms slipped around his waist until she held him as tight as he hugged her. "After that, every drop of blood was another mom or wife or daughter who would never see the man she loved again. I couldn't stop thinking about those faces until it made me physically ill."

"And now? Is that what you see when you dream?"

She nodded into his shoulder, rubbing her cheek against his arm.

"I am sorry that you've seen such terrible things." Resting his ear atop her head, he inhaled the lavender and rosemary scent of her hair. "Do you know that in the Good Book it says to cast all your care upon Him; for He careth for you?"

"Ye—es."

"Do you think you could try to do that? Could you give these memories and nightmares to God?"

Her breath caught loudly. "I'm not sure."

He didn't have easy answers, so he whispered a prayer over her. "Heavenly Father, please give Cora peace. Help her to cast these terrible memories upon You. Take them far from her mind. And please give comfort to the families of those men who won't be returning home. We pray in Your name. Amen."

Long after his prayer ended, they stood among the trees holding each other as snow covered the ground all around them. Finally, when her grip on him loosened, she leaned back just far enough to look into his face. "Thank you, Captain."

He meant to say that he was happy to help. He meant to offer another gentle word of comfort. He meant to give her a soft hug and then let go.

He did none of those things.

Instead he took one look into her sapphire eyes and leaned down until there was just a breath between their lips. He waited for a moment, giving her ample opportunity to pull away.

She didn't.

When their lips finally met, Jed's heart pounded so hard that he was certain she could feel it. She tasted like the sweet peach preserves they'd eaten together at lunch—a meal he wanted to share with her for the rest of his life.

The unexpected thought crashed through him, turning his stomach to stone. He'd fallen in love with the woman in his arms, but he could not take her home with him.

Chapter 8

Cora's hands moved automatically, drawing the needle and thread through the thick blue wool. Each stitch blended with the rest of the frock, but she didn't pay attention. Her ears stayed attuned to the sound of Jed's ax breaking apart the last of their renewed firewood supply. When the consistent rhythm stopped, she quickly bundled her project into a sack and tucked it into her sewing box.

A voice in her head asked why she even bothered. She was in no danger of Jed returning to the house as long as Papa was still in the cellar. After all, Jed had made certain that they hadn't spent any time alone since their kiss.

Her stomach danced at just the memory of the strength in his arms and the compassion in his voice as he'd spoken that prayer over her. Being in his arms had been everything she dreamed of, sharing her first kiss with the man she loved. But her love wasn't enough to make him stay, and a band around her heart constricted with that certainty.

She'd fallen in love with a man and become her own worst nightmare, the woman left behind to wonder.

When the front door opened, she wiped a wayward tear from her cheek, hunching over her knitting.

"Where's Jed?" Papa asked as he set down the items he'd brought up from storage.

"I suppose where he usually is lately." Her tone sharper than she meant, she quickly offered a softer follow up. "I'm sure he's whittling somewhere by himself. He's been doing that a lot."

Papa walked over to the fireplace, clapping and rubbing his hands in front of the flames. "Is everything all right between you two? I haven't seen you spending much time together lately."

"I'm sure everything is fine." That same voice in her head gnawed on those words.

If that's really the truth, then why is your heart breaking?

Papa shoved his hands into the pockets of his trousers so hard that his suspenders pulled taut over his white shirt, a sure-tell sign that he was about to broach a subject with which he was uncomfortable. "Your dreams seem to be getting better."

Cora glanced into his dear, weatherworn face. "They are."

"Did something happen to help?"

Her eyes drifted to the corner of the room, filled almost entirely by the tree now adorned with strings of popcorn and bright-red bows made of ribbon, gifts from her mother. "I suppose talking with Jed helped."

One of Papa's furry eyebrows lifted in an arch. "When did you talk with him?"

"A few days ago."

Papa nodded in a way that indicated he understood a lot more than he let on. "What did he say?"

Eyes still on her sewing, she said, "I'd rather not speak of it right now."

Papa knelt by her chair, resting both of his hands on her arm. "Why won't you let me in? Why won't you tell me what burden it is that you carry?"

Tears blurred her vision. "I can't."

Christmas morning dawned bright, the sun sparkling off the thin layer of fresh snow blanketing the front yard. Cora stood by the window, enjoying the simple beauty for nearly thirty minutes, her mind recounting the promise she'd forced Jed to make. He'd said he would stay until Christmas, and she knew he would not stay even a moment more. This would be their last day together.

Even if he had been distant since their kiss, she would miss his presence in their little home. His voice sometimes filled the whole room, and his laugh forced her to join in.

"Merry Christmas, sweetheart."

She turned into Papa's embrace, holding him close. "You too."

Boots thudded against the outside door frame, and Jed stepped into the room, his cheeks rosy from the cool morning. "The chores are done," he announced.

"Merry Christmas, Jed." Papa shook the other man's hand with a firm grip. "Thank you."

"My pleasure. What's for breakfast?"

Both men turned to Cora, whose face must've turned as pink as Jed's. "Oh my! I haven't even started it." She motioned to the rocking chair. "Sit down. It'll be ready shortly."

She broke several eggs into the cast-iron skillet and cooked them until they stopped wiggling. Then she added thick pieces of ham, which sizzled when they hit the pan. While warming several biscuits from the day before, she set the table with the last of her orange marmalade.

Cora barely tasted the food as she ate, but Jed and Papa enjoyed it immensely if their mumbles of appreciation between bites were any indication. "Just like your grandmother used to make," Papa sighed at one point.

The morning meal finished quickly, and as Cora washed the plates, Jed pulled the bench near her chair. Papa handed him the Bible. "Start in Luke, chapter two."

Jed did as he was told, beginning just as Cora settled into her seat. " 'And it came to pass in those days, that there went out a decree from Caesar Augustus that all the world should be taxed.' " In a clear timbre Jed read the story of Mary and Joseph's journey to Bethlehem and the birth of the Messiah, and the angels and shepherds who were there that first Christmas night.

When he had finished, Jed set the heavy book on the bench beside him, and Papa prayed over them. He prayed for an end to the war and a peace to come again. He prayed for their safety inside the little cabin, but when he asked God to protect Jed when he returned to Washington, Cora bit on her lip to keep from letting a sob escape.

Papa was the first to give his gifts, a beautiful knitted shawl for Cora and an old knife he said he'd intended to give to his only son. But now it seemed fitting that Jed take it with him.

Next Jed handed them each a small parcel wrapped in paper and twine. "Open them at the same time," he urged.

"You didn't have to do this." As Cora's fingers opened the paper, a perfectly carved wooden angel fell into her hands, the feathers of its wide wings and cherubic features etched with precise detail. "Oh my." Her thumbs ran across the smooth edges, her mouth hanging open in awe.

"This is remarkable craftsmanship." At Papa's words Cora glanced over to see a manger resting in his palm. Even at a distance, she could see the lines of straw Jed had so meticulously fashioned into the soft wood.

Jed's smile carried all the joy of a gift appreciated, and Cora warmed into it. "Thank you. These are beautiful."

"Well, I meant to make a star too." He ran his fingers through his hair. "I just ran out of time. Lots of wood to cut." He chuckled, the first time in days.

"Well, now it's my turn." She handed a small paper-wrapped parcel to her grandfather, who thanked her profusely when he opened it to reveal a blue shirt. "For Sunday services when they resume, I thought."

"It's very nice. Thank you."

"And for the captain." Cora stretched to pass him a substantially larger burlap bag.

A line formed between his eyebrows as he reached into the carrier, recognition lighting his eyes only when he pulled the folded pile of cloth into the light. "My uniform." He flipped the frock over, his smile growing at the clean material. His finger traced the small stitches around the mended hole. "You fixed it."

"Good as new, I think. Do you like it?"

He caught her eye, his smile nearly making her forget that the uniform meant that he would be leaving. Tonight.

That night Jed stood with Cora so close to the door of the cabin that firelight illuminated them through the window, flashing on the polished brass buttons of his blue frock. He held both of her hands gently in his, looking anywhere but into her eyes. He hadn't made any secret about having to return to Washington, and he'd kept his promise to stay through Christmas. They'd both known this was coming, yet somehow he felt as though he was letting her down and betraying the affection growing in his own heart.

"I have to go tonight. It's safer for me to travel in the darkness."

She nodded. "I know."

He squeezed her hands, offering a subtle smile. "Thank you again for mending my uniform."

"You're welcome, Captain." Her head turned so that she could look in the direction of the grove of fir trees, near where they'd shared their kiss. "Thank you for all you've done. For the firewood and—and. . .well, for helping me put my worries into God's hands." Her voice cracked on the last word as tears spilled down her cheeks.

"Please don't cry." He brushed away one of the tears with his thumb. Forcing out a strained sigh, he closed his eyes to the pain flickering across her face.

"I'm sorry," she whispered, lips drawn tight.

As her tears made their trek near the corner of her mouth, he physically fought the urge to kiss them away. Wrestling the impulse to pull her tight and relive that moment in the forest that he'd taken such caution not to repeat for fear that this night would be harder than it had to be, he latched back onto her hands and took a small step back.

"I care for you, Cora. I truly do." He shook his head, as he butchered his attempt to explain his mounting love for her without breaking her heart further. "The truth is that I care about you far too much to leave you to wonder whether I'm ever coming back. I won't let you be one of those women in your nightmares." He hung his head, even though she still refused to look at him. "I don't know how much longer this war will last, and I can't promise you that I'll be able to return."

Suddenly her head whipped back toward him, her eyes locking with his. "Then don't go!"

"I would stay if I could. You know that, right?"

Her eyes filled with another batch of tears, and she nodded.

"You're going to meet someone. . ." Jed had to stop to clear his throat, unable to get out the words he needed to say. "You're going to meet an amazing man and have a wonderful family. Any man would be lucky to love you."

I certainly was.

Her eyes turned dark, brooding like the sea, the firelight transforming her features into shifting shadows. She'd probably never been to Maryland, but as he let go of her hands and stepped into the woods, he knew he could never be home without her.

Chapter 9

Cora inhaled the sweet scent of fresh snow as she traipsed across the wide field in front of Carnton, holding out her mittens to catch the flakes before they melted. Her breath curled into a cloud floating above the frozen earth. The ground before her had long since been washed clean by the summer rains and leveled by Mr. McGavock's plow. Someone just passing through might never know that this land had once been marred by the shells of the Union army.

Not all of Franklin had returned to normal more than a year after the battle, but almost a mile from the hub of the fighting Cora's little world had resumed as it once had before the war. Before the nightmares.

Before the captain.

As she entered the stand of trees, her eye instantly caught the small stones laid out in the shape of a cross at the base of the tree where she'd first seen him. She knelt by them and wiped each rock clean of the light dusting of snow.

As she'd done every day for a year, she whispered a prayer for Jedediah Harrington, wherever he might be, giving all of her concern for him to the only One who could take away her anxiety.

"This year could have been miserable," she whispered so quietly that the morning birds continued to sing. "But I will continue to cast my cares upon You, for You careth for me. And for Jed too."

As she stood and resumed a steady gait back toward the cabin, a slow smile curved her lips. The war had ended in April according to the newspapers, and still there was no word from Jed, but she would wait until there was. He'd made no promise to ever return, but deep in her heart, Cora knew that if he was able, he would come back to her.

So she hoped. And she continued to pray.

As she entered the clearing, the snow began falling in earnest, and she could barely make out the figure of her grandfather walking along the side of the cabin.

"Papa!"

He turned and waved. "I'm going to get some water. Did Carrie like her new dress?"

"Very much! I'm going to start dinner. Hurry back." He waved again, resuming the path toward the small inlet from the river.

It wasn't until Cora reached the front door that she spotted six wooden stars on the windowsill. Running the last few steps to them, she snatched one, turning it over and over in her hands as though it would reveal what she hoped to be true. Her stomach in knots, she spun on the spot.

"Jed?" Her voice barely a whisper, she tried again. "Jed!"

And then he was there, stepping out from behind a tree, marching across the yard. Unable to wait for him to reach her, she sprinted toward him, throwing her arms about his neck when they met. His embrace nearly stole her breath, or was it the way her heart doubled its speed?

"I have missed you," he whispered into her ear. His smile wavered as he put his hands on her waist and pushed her a half step away, his gaze running from her head to her toes as though confirming she was truly in front of him.

She blushed but didn't dare look away from the face she'd longed to see all these months.

"I'm not too late, am I?" The tone of his voice turned serious.

"No. I haven't even started dinner yet."

His laughter, so rich and familiar, covered her like a second cloak. "Not for dinner. For you."

"For me?"

His face pinched in serious concentration. "When I left, I told you to find a good man. Have you found someone else? Are you married? Am I too late?"

Her mirth as deep as the conviction in his voice, she laughed heartily. "No! Of course not. How could I marry someone else when I have been in love with you for more than a year?"

The relief that crossed his face brought a boyish grin with it as he swooped down and kissed her soundly, his arms wrapping about her shoulders as he made her forget everything but them. Her toes curled, and she tried to smile as joy bubbled deep in her stomach. He had been more than worth the wait.

When he finally pulled back, his smile only radiated brighter. "I wanted to ask you to wait. Do you know how much I wanted you to wait for me? But I just couldn't put you through that."

"I know." She brushed the snow from his whiskers before cupping his cheek with her hand.

"And then I couldn't stop thinking about you. About your sweet smile and beautiful eyes. About getting home to you."

"But your home is in Maryland."

Pressing both of his hands to her cheeks, he laughed. "My home is wherever you are, so I returned as soon as I could."

"Did you see Bess?"

His smile dimmed. "Yes. I delivered her letter on my way to Washington and stopped again on my way back here. That letter broke her heart, but I believe she's beginning to find hope again. Matthew is walking now, and she chases after him. A neighbor that we grew up with asked if he could court her, so there may be a wedding on the farm soon."

"What else did you think about while you were away?"

He grinned like a cat who had stolen a bowl of milk. "About how I owed you a star to add to your set. So I just kept carving them for you."

She tossed a glance over her shoulder at the row of stars leaning against the window. "They're beautiful. Thank you."

"I have about a dozen more in my saddlebags."

"A dozen?"

"I told you. I couldn't think of anything but you." The intensity in his gaze deepened.

"I'm so glad you're here in time for Christmas! But I don't have a gift for you."

"You've already given me the best gift I could ask for." He leaned in to briefly press his lips against hers.

She dove back into his arms, wrapping hers around his back. But as soon as she tucked her face into his shoulder, she realized something was different. "Where's your uniform?"

"I resigned from the War Department."

"But your job? It was your dream."

The corner of his mouth tilted up. "You're my new dream."

Tilting back to look into his face, she bit her bottom lip to keep from smiling. "How long can you stay this time?"

He pressed his lips to hers quickly and passionately, the kiss fueled by the same fervor she'd carried in her heart for a year.

"Forever."

Liz Johnson is the author of more than a dozen novels, a few best-selling novellas, and a handful of short stories. She works in marketing and makes her home in Phoenix, Arizona.

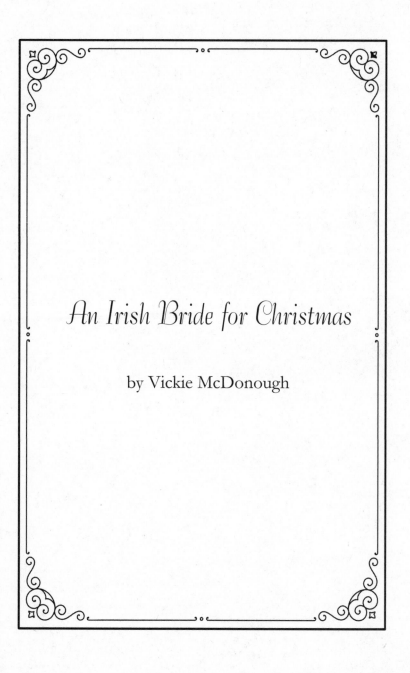

An Irish Bride for Christmas

by Vickie McDonough

Chapter 1

1880
Prairie Flats, Illinois

W here's Mama and Poppy?" Rosie hugged her rag doll to her chest and stared up at Jackson with worried brown eyes.

Unshed tears blurred the view of his niece as Jackson knelt in front of her. He blinked them away for fear of scaring her. He could handle his own grief, but seeing his niece crying for her parents nearly gutted him. How could he make the four-year-old understand that they'd just buried her mom and dad—that they weren't coming back?

Help me explain it to her so she'll understand, Lord.

He picked up Rosie and hugged her tight, needing solace himself. "Remember when Bandit got bit by a snake and died?"

Rosie looked up at him and nodded. Her eyes shimmered with unshed tears.

Maybe she understood more than he gave her credit for.

"We had to bury him, and then you and your mama put flowers on his grave and your poppy made a cross for it. Remember that?"

Rosie's lower lip trembled, and she nodded. "He's in doggy heaven. Poppy said so."

"Well, that's what happened today. Your mama and poppy died in a stagecoach accident"—he didn't want her to know they were shot by robbers—"and now they're in heaven with Jesus."

"But *I* want them." Tears dripped down her cheeks.

Jackson hugged her tight. "So do I, sweet pea; so do I. But Jesus needed them in heaven with Him. I'm going to take care of you now."

Jackson swayed back and forth as Rosie clung to his neck, crying. Why couldn't it have been him who died instead of Ben. Instead of Amanda.

God, I have to say I don't understand this. I know You see all and know all, but why this? How am I supposed to run Lancaster Stage alone and raise a little girl? Rosie needs a mother and a father, not an uncle who knows next to nothing about caring for a child.

He raked his hand through his hair. He'd agreed to keep Rosie while Ben and Amanda went to a nearby town to celebrate their fifth anniversary, but he didn't know they wouldn't return. Now Rosie was the only family he had left in the world. He needed her as much as she did him.

Jackson looked around the small room where he lived behind the stage office. It smelled of leather and saddle soap from his evenings spent polishing harnesses and bridles. He hadn't had time to sweep the floor all week. The windows were so dingy he hadn't needed a shade to cover them, and there was only one bed. He hated all the reminders of his big brother and his sister-in-law in their house—a house left to him and Ben when their mother had died—but that was where Rosie should be.

He flipped the quilt back and laid Rosie on the bed, pushing back his emotions. He didn't understand why God hadn't protected Ben and Amanda during the stage robbery. It seemed a simple thing for the God who created the universe to deflect a few bullets.

But Jackson knew his brother wouldn't sit by and watch another of their stages being robbed. Most likely, Ben had tried to stop it— and now he and Amanda were dead.

Rosie was an orphan, and he had a two-man business to run alone.

He drew the carpetbag out from under his bed and blew the dust off. He'd pack his things while Rosie slept and then take them back to the neat two-bedroom home next door.

A few minutes later, he took a crate from off the back porch and packed up his coffee, sugar bowl, and cup and plate. He rarely ate there, preferring Amanda's fabulous cooking and open invitation to dine with them. What would he and Rosie eat now? He wasn't much of a cook.

Setting the crate by the door, he put the carpetbag on top of it. Rosie would miss her mama's homemade sugar cookies. Maybe one of the church ladies would let him chop wood in exchange for some.

Entering the door to the stage office, he stared at the map with pins in it marking the four places where their stagecoaches had been robbed in the past three months. Why had they been targeted? They were just a small-time operation, transporting people and freight that arrived in Prairie Flats, Illinois, by train to the small area towns where the train didn't go. They rarely carried anything of great value, although someone seemed to know whenever they had a payroll ship-ment on board. With a shaking hand, he picked up a pin and stuck it in the spot where Ben and Amanda had died.

He dropped into a chair. Lowering his head to his arm, he let the tears he'd held back for the past few days flow.

Jackson awoke to someone knocking on the stage office door. He glanced around, wondering why he'd fallen asleep at the desk. Suddenly everything rushed back to him.

The rapping increased.

Rosie! He dashed into his room, and his heart slowed when he saw his niece curled up on his bed, hugging her dolly.

Someone pounded again, and Rosie stirred. Jackson hurried through the office, wiped his damp eyes, and opened the door. Judge Smith, the mayor, and the mayor's wife stood on the boardwalk. They seemed an odd trio to offer condolences, but he hoped they would do it quickly.

The judge cleared his throat. "May we come in, Mr. Lancaster? It's warm for late November, but that wind is stiff."

"Of course." Jackson stepped back, allowing the three to enter. Rosie appeared at the door between the two rooms, hair tousled from sleep, and leaned against the jamb.

"How can I help you, Judge?"

He glanced around the office, and Jackson noted when the man's gaze landed on Rosie. "Perhaps it would be best if Mrs. O'Keefe took the child in the other room while we talk."

Rosie's eyes widened, and she raced toward him. Jackson scooped her up, concern mounting. What could these men have to say to him that they didn't want Rosie to hear? Had someone discovered the identity of the robbers?

Mrs. O'Keefe ambled to the back of the room and peeked through the door to his private quarters. Jackson narrowed his eyes at her rudeness.

"*Tsk tsk*. Would you look at this, Judge? You'll see for yourself what I've been talking about. This is no place for a child to live."

To Jackson's surprise, the judge and mayor joined Mrs. O'Keefe at the door of his room. With the news of the two deaths, a funeral to plan, and a precocious young one to care for, he hadn't gotten his normal chores accomplished. Sure, his place was a bit disorderly at the moment, but what did that matter to them?

"I don't see nothing all that much out of the ordinary here. He's a single man, Maura."

"But he can't raise a child in a place like this. That's my point." She eyed Jackson over the top of her glasses, pressed her lips together, and shook her head.

Jackson shifted Rosie to his other arm. "Just what is this all about?"

The judge sighed and turned to face him. "Mrs. O'Keefe has petitioned the courts to get custody of your niece."

"What?" Jackson backed up against the door, clinging to his niece. She wrinkled her brow and looked from him to the judge and back. "Now you listen here. Rosie is *my* niece. My flesh and blood. We belong together."

"You sure you want to be talking about this in front of the child?" The judge lifted his brows.

No, he didn't, but he wasn't about to let Mrs. O'Keefe get her paws on Rosie. "Not really, but there's no point discussing it. I'm all the family she has, Judge." Rosie must have sensed his distress, because she laid her head down on his shoulder and hugged his neck, nearly choking him.

"You're a single man, living in a—a hovel, for lack of a more decent word. A little girl has no business living here and being raised by an unmarried man. Isn't that right, Harvey?"

Harvey O'Keefe gave Jackson an almost apologetic glance before nodding at his wife. The man had yet to utter a single word. Maybe

Jackson had one ally in the bunch.

"I've made my decision, Mr. Lancaster. Rosie is a young and impressionable child. You're a single man and shouldn't be tending a little girl. It isn't proper. I'm giving temporary custody to Mrs. O'Keefe."

Jackson's already-crumbling heart shattered in two. "You can't do that. We're family, and family stays together."

The judge laid a hand on Jackson's shoulder. "I know this is a difficult thing, son, especially after losing your—" He looked at Rosie. "Um. . .well, you know. You can see your niece regularly, but you've no business tending to her physical needs. If you know what I mean."

Jackson shook his head. This couldn't be happening. He wanted to run out the door with Rosie and leave town, but his business was here. He had people and clients who relied on his service. And if he left, he'd have no way to support Rosie and no home.

"This isn't right."

"Let me have the child." Mrs. O'Keefe held out her hands, a smug smile on her plump face.

Rosie whimpered. Jackson cast the judge a pleading glance. "There must be something I can do. She needs me. I'm the only familiar person left in her world."

"I'll give you the chance to get her back. If you marry in the next month—say, by Christmas—I'll grant you permanent custody of your niece. Otherwise, she'll stay with the O'Keefes." The judge put his hat on and buttoned his coat.

"Can't this wait—at least until tomorrow? We just buried Rosie's parents this morning." Jackson searched his mind. There had to be some way to fix this nightmare.

"Prolonging the matter won't make it easier. You have until

Christmas." The judge reached for the door, and Jackson stepped aside. He turned the handle then stopped. "Hand over the child, Mr. Lancaster."

"No," Rosie cried.

The tightening in Jackson's throat had nothing to do with Rosie choking his neck. He'd never broken the law before, although he was highly tempted now. But if he ran with Rosie, what kind of life could he give her? As much as it pained him, he had to follow the judge's orders.

He untangled his niece's arm. "It will be okay, sweet pea. You go home with this nice man and lady; then I'll come see you every day until you can come back home."

"I have cookies and milk waiting for you." Maura O'Keefe smiled congenially for the first time and held out her arms.

"I like cookies. Can Uncle Jack have one?"

"Maybe when he visits tomorrow." Mrs. O'Keefe patted Rosie's head.

"Can Sally come?"

Mrs. O'Keefe wrinkled her brow. "Who is Sally? Not a dog, I hope."

Rosie shook her head. "No, she's my dolly."

Jackson's legs trembled and his head ached. Rosie had never known a stranger, and that alone could make this horrible situation bearable. He couldn't stand the thought of her crying for him and him unable to console her.

"I can come to your house and eat cookies." She wriggled, and Jackson reluctantly set her down. She took Mrs. O'Keefe's hand and waved at him.

"You'll bring her clothes to the house later?" Mrs. O'Keefe lifted her brows at him.

He nodded, too stunned to move. Silently Mr. O'Keefe followed his wife outside. Shutting the door, Jackson slid to the floor, unable to digest all that had happened.

He'd lost everything he held dear in one day. A frigid numbness made his limbs feel heavy, weighted.

Why is this happening, God? How will Rosie get along without me?

"And how in the world am I supposed to find a bride by Christmas?"

Chapter 2

Larkin Doyle stared with her mouth open as Maura O'Keefe strode into the house with a little girl in tow. What in the world had the woman done now?

"This is Rosie Lancaster, and she's going to live with us. Rosie is in need of cookies and milk." Maura eyed Larkin with her brows lifted, and Larkin understood the silent message.

The lass tugged at Larkin's skirt. "I like cookies." The brown-eyed urchin stared up at her.

Reaching out a hand, Larkin smiled. "Then, wee one, we must go find some."

Rosie took Larkin's hand without hesitation. "You talk funny."

"Aye, 'tis true. I come from Ireland, which is why I talk as I do." The charming child won Larkin's heart immediately.

Larkin put a shallow crate upside down on a chair and set the child at the table. She gave her two gingersnaps and a glass half filled with milk. As Rosie nibbled the snack, Larkin studied her. The girl's brown eyes were so dark Larkin could barely see her pupils, and her wavy hair was only a few shades lighter. What a lovely lass she was. "Is that good?"

Rosie nodded. "Mama makes sugar cookies."

How sad. Did the lass not understand that her mum was gone? Larkin brushed a strand of hair from Rosie's face and tucked it behind her ear.

Wilma, the O'Keefes' cook, entered with a bucket over her arm. She glanced at Rosie. "Well, what have we here?"

"This is Rosie. She'll be stayin' here awhile."

Wilma pursed her lips and set the bucket down. She leaned toward Larkin. "Not another attempt to replace the baby Maura lost?"

Larkin shrugged, hurt by Wilma's callous words. "Rosie, I must go talk to Mrs. O'Keefe for a moment. You stay with Wilma."

Rosie scowled but nodded. She dipped the corner of her remaining cookie in her milk then stuck it in her mouth.

Larkin gave her a third cookie then patted the lass's head. "I shall be back in a minute."

Rosie picked up another cookie and waved at her.

Larkin hurried through the dining room, past the elaborate table, and into the parlor. Mayor O'Keefe sat in his favorite chair, hiding behind his newspaper as he often did. She located Mrs. O'Keefe in the spare bedroom, tapping her index finger against her thick lips.

"I was going to give this room to the girl, but I simply can't have her destroying the décor. This furniture was far too costly to allow a child to live here. Too, if we have guests, I'll no longer have a place to put them."

Larkin didn't ask but knew that meant Rosie would be sharing her room. She didn't mind but would have liked to have been asked rather than having Mrs. O'Keefe instruct her as to how things would be. But wasn't that always the case?

You're a servant here, not a daughter—and you'd best remember that, Larkin Doyle.

As much as she'd hoped for a loving family to live with after her parents had died, that hadn't happened. The O'Keefes had taken her in and given her a nice place to live and decent clothes to wear, but she was not an adopted daughter. Perhaps Rosie would fill that coveted position.

"May I ask why the lass is here?"

"You may." Mrs. O'Keefe sidled a glance her way as she closed the curtains on the lone window. "Rosie's parents were buried today. A single man the likes of Jackson Lancaster isn't fit to raise a child—a girl, at that. Besides, he didn't want the responsibility, so I very graciously offered to take in the orphan."

"'Tis a sad day when family refuses to care for family." Larkin's ire rose at the uncle who coldly turned his back on such a darling child. What a horrible ordeal Rosie must have been through.

"Give the girl a bath after she eats her cookies, and find something to put her in. Her uncle was supposed to deliver her clothes here, but with the lateness of the hour, he may not come until tomorrow."

"Aye, mum." Larkin hurried back to the kitchen. Wilma nodded toward the table. Larkin's heart stopped when she saw Rosie's head leaning against the table. Poor lass. Larkin lifted her up.

"I want Uncle Jack!" Rosie suddenly went rigid and struggled to get free. Larkin set her down for fear of dropping her. The lass slumped to the ground, tears pooling in her eyes. "I wanna go home."

Larkin clutched her chest as the memories of her parents' deaths came rushing back. She knew what it felt like to lose those she loved and to become an orphan.

Cuddling the girl, she patted her back. "There, there, 'twill be all right."

Uncle Jack. The poor child must be crying for the very man who'd refused to care for her. What a horrible beast he must be. Even though she was a Christian woman, if she ever got the chance, Larkin intended to give him a piece of her mind.

The sun peeked over the horizon, sending its warming rays across Jackson's back. He knocked on the O'Keefes' door then rubbed his hand across his bristly jaw. He should have taken the time to shave this morning, but after another nearly sleepless night, he'd been anxious to see how Rosie had fared and to get her clothes to her so she'd have something fresh to wear. Shoving his hands in his coat pockets, he waited. Maybe he was too early.

A noise on the other side of the door indicated someone was coming. His gut tingled with excitement while at the same time he worried about Rosie's well-being. Had she cried last night? Had she asked for her mama? For him?

A pretty young woman with thick auburn hair opened the door. Her green eyes widened at the sight of him and then narrowed. "Might I help you?"

He brushed the dust from his jacket and smiled. "I'm Rosie's uncle. I've brought her clothes and have come to see her."

The woman's cinnamon-colored brows dipped. "She's not yet awake. The wee lass had trouble getting to sleep last night, so I thought it best not to awaken her this morning. I'll take her clothes."

Disappointed, Jackson handed the small satchel to her. "Could I come back and see her later?"

She scowled and stared at him as if he were a weevil in a flour sack. He glanced down at his clothes. Did he look that bad? Or had something else twisted her pretty mouth like a pretzel?

"You'd best come back after the family has had breakfast. Mrs. O'Keefe can talk with you then."

She started to shut the door, but he stuck out his foot, holding it open. "Wait. I don't need to talk to the mayor's wife. I just want to see my niece and make sure she's all right."

"The lass is fine, other than having a difficult time sleeping in a strange bed. I tended her meself. Really now, I've other duties to attend to. Come back later."

Jackson stared at the closed door, feeling empty and alone. He looked up to a window on the second story, wondering if Rosie might be there. Would she look out and see him?

Backing away, he stared at the big structure, one of the few brick houses in Prairie Flats. White columns holding up the porch roof gave it a Southern flair. The house was much nicer and probably warmer than Ben and Amanda's clapboard cottage. But strangers couldn't love Rosie like he did.

Please, Lord, show me how to get her back. Comfort Rosie, and help her not to fret.

Shoving his hands in pockets, he crossed the street to Pearl's Café. He'd get breakfast, check on today's stage, and then go back to see his niece.

At the café, he pulled out a chair and stared out the window. He could just make out one corner of the O'Keefes' home from here. He thought of the gal who'd opened the door. She was a pretty young woman, even with that pert nose scrunched up at him and her eyes flashing daggers. What had he done to upset her so?

Maybe she hadn't had her morning coffee yet. He remembered seeing her walking down the boardwalk and shopping at the mercantile on occasion but had never met her before. Her singsong accent was unexpected on the Illinois prairie, but it was lovely and intriguing.

Two hours later, Jackson knocked at the O'Keefes' fancy front door again. The wood-carver had done an excellent job on the twisted columns. Jackson tapped the dainty gold door knocker several times then pounded on the wood with his knuckles.

Finally, the Irish gal opened the door, her eyes widening again at the sight of him. He was glad he'd taken the time to shave and change clothes.

"Wait here and I shall get Mrs. O'Keefe." She closed the door in his face, not even allowing him to step into the parlor. Was she always so rude?

Jackson slumped against the jamb, anxious to see Rosie. The longer he waited, the more his anxiety grew. Were they purposefully avoiding him? He glanced at his pocket watch.

The door creaked and suddenly opened. The mayor's wife pulled a shawl around her shoulders and stepped outside, her lips pursed.

"What is it you need, Mr. Lancaster? Surely you must know that as the mayor's wife I'm a very busy woman. I can't have you disturbing me constantly."

Jackson lifted his brow. Two visits constituted constantly bothering her? "I'm here to see Rosie."

Mrs. O'Keefe let out a *tsk*. "It's not good to trouble the child. She's been through enough."

"Seeing me won't upset her. She loves me, as I do her."

"Yes, well, the judge gave me custody, and if she sees you, she'll just want to be with you—and not being able to do so will frustrate her. So, you see, it's better if she doesn't see you at all."

Jackson ground his back teeth together as his irritation rose. "The judge said I could see her every day. I want to see Rosie now."

Mrs. O'Keefe backed up a half step but glared over the top of her wire-rimmed glasses at him. "I simply can't have you interrupting things here at your leisure. We will go talk to the judge and get this matter settled now."

She disappeared back into the house. Jackson wanted to ram his fist through her glass window but knew that wouldn't accomplish anything other than proving that he wasn't fit to care for Rosie. He gazed up at the cloudy sky. "God, I need help here. I can't lose Rosie."

Moments later, he followed Mrs. O'Keefe as she marched toward Judge Smith's office. Jackson prayed the man wouldn't be in court so the matter could be settled quickly. He had his own work to do.

The mayor's wife stormed into the judge's offices, past the surprised clerk, and knocked on his private door.

"Now see here, madam, you can't—" At Mrs. O'Keefe's glare, the thin clerk slumped back into his chair. Mumbling under his breath, he yanked off his round wire glasses and polished them.

Mrs. O'Keefe knocked harder. Jackson had never been in the judge's offices and glanced around the opulent room. It smelled of beeswax and leather furniture. Two chairs sat on either side of a small round table, and a fine Turkish rug decorated the shiny wooden floor. The clerk's cherrywood desk was nicer than anything Jackson had seen in a long while.

"Come in, Andrew." The judge's deep voice resounded through the closed door.

Mrs. O'Keefe opened it and plowed right in. "It's not Andrew, Roy. It's Maura."

Jackson sighed and followed her. *That's just great. She's on a first-name basis with the judge.*

"Roy, Mr. Lancaster here was at my door this morning at a most inappropriate hour, demanding to see his niece. I simply can't have that man coming and going anytime he chooses. As the mayor's wife, I'm a very busy woman."

The judge lowered his spectacles and glanced at Jackson. "That true, Lancaster?"

Jackson shrugged and resisted the urge to fidget. "Yes, sir, but I thought Rosie would need a fresh change of clothes when she arose. That's why I went so early."

The judge turned his gaze on Maura. "Sounds reasonable. The child needs her clothes."

"Yes, but then he returned in a few hours."

"That's because I didn't get to see Rosie, and that helper of yours told me to come back. I was worried how she fared last night." Jackson crossed his arms, irritated that he had to explain why he wanted to see his own niece.

"You see, Roy, we have guests constantly, and I can't have this man coming in and upsetting the girl when I have a dinner party to prepare for."

Judge Smith sighed. "I can see your point, but you can't keep the child from her uncle."

Jackson's hopes rose for the first time.

"Lancaster, I'm guessing Sundays are slow for you. Am I right?"

He nodded, unsure what that had to do with anything.

"How about Wednesdays?" the judge asked.

"Sometimes busier than other days, sometimes not. Just depends." Jackson swallowed, not liking where his thoughts were taking him.

"All right. Maura, you let the man see his niece twice a week—on Sundays and Wednesdays."

"But—," Maura squeaked.

"That's not—" Jackson stepped forward.

Judge Smith raised his hand. "I've made my decision. Lancaster can see his niece for two hours every Sunday afternoon and Wednesday evening." He smacked his gavel down as if he'd made a court decision.

Jackson's heart plummeted as the sound echoed in his mind. He combed his fingers through his hair, holding them against his crown. He promised Rosie that he'd take care of her. She would think he'd lied to her—that he'd deserted her.

A ruckus sounded in the clerk's office. "Someone said Jackson Lancaster is in seeing the judge. That true?"

Jackson recognized the voice of Sheriff Kevin Steele and stepped into the other room. The sheriff's steady gaze turned his way. "Sorry to have to tell you, Lancaster, but your stage has been robbed again. The driver's been shot."

Chapter 3

Larkin squirmed in her chair as Frank Barrett leered at her over his cup of cider. She broke his gaze and pushed her carrots around on her plate, uncomfortable with his attention. Even though some might find the man of average height with sleek dark hair and pale gray eyes handsome, something about him gave her the shivers. She couldn't help comparing him to Jackson Lancaster's rugged, often disheveled appearance that made him look like a boy in need of a mother's care.

"It was very benevolent of you to take in the Lancaster orphan. Must have been quite a shock for her to lose both parents at once." Frank turned his attention to Maura. "How is she adapting to life here?"

"As well as can be expected. Although I do believe Judge Smith made a grievous error allowing that scoundrel uncle of hers to visit. He had the nerve to return her a half hour late, and then the child pitched a royal fit when it was time for him to leave. I simply don't understand what she sees in him. He didn't want to keep her, after all."

"I can see how his visits would be disruptive and not in the best interest of the girl."

Maura picked up her glass and lifted it as if in a toast. "Exactly how I feel. The child has enough worries without pining for the very uncle who gave her away and refused to care for her. His visits will only prolong her healing process."

Larkin narrowed her eyes but focused on her plate. Maura allowed her to attend the O'Keefes' dinner parties but made it clear that she was to remain silent unless directly asked a question. To Maura, Larkin represented a trophy of the woman's hospitality and generosity. Taking in an orphan somehow set her above her peers—at least in Maura's mind. And now she had two.

Larkin took a bite of mashed potatoes covered in Wilma's thick beef gravy, but its flavor was wasted on her. Why did Maura always refer to Rosie as "the child" or "the girl" but never by her name?

Had she done that when Larkin first arrived? Searching her mind, Larkin couldn't remember. She'd been a distraught twelve-year-old, having lost her parents to illness only a few years after they had arrived in New York. The deplorable conditions on the boat from Ireland had caused her mother to take sick, and she never recovered. Then her da caught the same sickness and died.

She didn't dislike living with the O'Keefes and was grateful to them for taking her in, but at nineteen, she longed for a home of her own—a family of her own.

Maura wanted Rosie so badly that she was willing to offer her a home when nobody else would, but one spilled glass of milk and

Rosie had been relegated to eating in the kitchen. Thankfully, dinner tonight was later than normal to accommodate Frank Barrett's busy schedule, so she'd been able to sit with Rosie while she ate and had put her to bed before dinner.

"Don't you agree, Miss Doyle?"

Larkin's gaze darted up at Mr. Barrett's question. One she hadn't heard. "Um. . .'tis sorry I am, but I did not hear the question." She swallowed hard, irritated that her accent thickened whenever she was flustered.

"I said that the Lancaster girl is far better off here than with her uneducated uncle. Don't you agree?"

Maura stared at her as if awaiting her agreeable response. Larkin knew it was better to deflect her answer than step in that miry pit. "Why do you refer to Mr. Lancaster as uneducated? He speaks clearly and runs a successful business. I wouldn't think an uneducated man could do that."

Mr. Barrett's brows lifted at her defense of Jackson Lancaster. She wasn't even sure why she defended him, since she despised the way he had abandoned Rosie.

"You'd be surprised what a man can do when he sets his mind to it." Frank narrowed his eyes at her.

His interest in her was undeniable, but she did not return the attraction. A sinister air encircled the man, and even though he was a friend of the O'Keefes, Larkin intended to keep her distance.

"I'd best look in on Rosie and make sure she's sleeping soundly." Larkin pushed back from the table, and Mr. O'Keefe and Mr. Barrett both rose.

"There's no need for you to check on the child, Larkin. I'll have Wilma do it."

"Beggin' your pardon, mum, but you asked me to tend Rosie. I wouldn't want Wilma to be off helping in the bedrooms when you might have need of her here." She rushed out of the room before Maura forced her to stay, grateful to be away from Mr. Barrett's leering.

In her room, she found Rosie still asleep, with both hands under her cheek. Larkin brushed a lock of hair out of the girl's face. She was such a pretty child. And resilient, even after all that had happened. Larkin's heart warmed. Maybe someday she'd have a sweet daughter like Rosie.

Rosie bounced on her toes and ran to the door. "Is he coming?"

Why was the lass so eager to see the uncle who didn't want her? Perhaps she was unaware that he had abandoned her. Larkin shook her head, finding it difficult to understand why the man wanted to spend time with Rosie now. Did it ease his guilt? She looked through the tall, narrow window at the front entrance. "Here he comes now."

She tied Rosie's cloak under her neck and opened the door. The lass raced outside. "Uncle Jack!"

He picked her up and tossed her into the air. Childish giggles echoed in the quiet of the late afternoon, warming Larkin's heart. She was so glad to see Rosie smiling.

"I sure missed you, sweet pea."

"I'm not a pea." Rosie locked her arms around his neck and hugged him tight.

"Ready to go?"

Larkin's heart skittered as he turned to walk away. "Mrs. O'Keefe needs a word with you, Mr. Lancaster."

His dark brows dipped down. A muscle ticked in his jaw. "Why?"

Larkin shrugged. "She didn't tell me. Only that I must inform her when you were here."

He sighed, and his broad shoulders drooped a bit. He shifted Rosie to his right arm. "All right. Let's get the inquisition over so Rosie and I can have our time together."

"We going home?" Rosie patted her uncle's clean-shaven cheek.

"We'll see, sweet pea."

Larkin ushered him into the parlor. "Please have a seat and excuse me while I find Mrs. O'Keefe."

Darting out the door, she swiped at the band of sweat on her brow. Odd that she would be perspiring in early December. She located Mrs. O'Keefe upstairs in the spare room where the woman was sorting her Christmas decorations.

"I'll have to order some new ornaments this year. Some of the old ones weren't packaged properly and got broken."

The look she cast in Larkin's direction told her that Maura blamed her for the damage. "Mr. Lancaster is here. He's anxious to be off with Rosie."

"Hmm. . .we'll just see about that."

Downstairs in the parlor, Rosie's uncle stood as they entered. "Good day, Mrs. O'Keefe."

"Humph. It's been a busy day." She glanced at the mantel clock. "Since Rosie was half an hour late returning last Wednesday, you may only keep her an hour and a half today."

Mr. Lancaster's eyes shot blue fire. Rosie cast worried glances from one person to the next and clung to his neck.

"Now see here, I was only late because one of my coaches cracked a wheel. I had to see about getting it repaired since it was due to go back out the next morning."

Maura waved her hand in the air. "No matter. I want the girl back by six o'clock so she can get her dinner."

"She can eat with me." He stood rigid, like a soldier, holding Rosie in one arm.

"That wasn't part of the judge's deal. Also, I want Miss Doyle to accompany the child on her excursions with you."

Jackson Lancaster looked as if he could have strangled Maura.

Larkin stared at her, stunned by her declaration. "But, mum—"

Maura zipped an angered glance her way. Larkin swallowed, remembering the times as a child that she'd been punished for her disobedience. "Aye, mum. As you wish."

"No! Rosie is my family, not yours." Mr. Lancaster headed for the door. "The judge made no conditions and said nothing about my visits being supervised."

"You can accept Miss Doyle's chaperoning or not see your niece at all."

"We're leaving." He slung open the door and stormed out.

"Go with the man. Make sure he returns the child on time tonight."

Hurrying to do Mrs. O'Keefe's bidding, Larkin donned her cloak and followed the pair outside, feeling like an unwanted stepchild. He didn't want her company, but she didn't dare refuse Mrs. O'Keefe's orders or she'd be out on the streets. Hurrying to keep up with his long-legged gait, Larkin took two steps to his one. Rosie peered over his shoulder and waved. Larkin smiled at her.

Mr. Lancaster stopped suddenly, and Larkin plowed into his solid back. He turned quickly, grabbing her arm and steadying her. "Sorry. Look, Miss Doyle, I don't need anyone watching over my shoulder during my time with Rosie."

Larkin studied the ground rather than his fierce blue eyes. "I don't doubt that a'tall, but you wouldna want me to get into trouble for not complying with Mrs. O'Keefe's wishes, would you, now?"

Indecision darkened his gaze. Finally, he heaved a sigh. "I guess not. Follow me, then."

She hurried to keep up, running a bit to draw even with him. He loosened Rosie's arms from his neck and tossed her in the air again, gaining a wide grin from his niece.

"Do it again, Uncle Jack."

"One more time." He tossed her high, this time catching her and cradling her in both arms as one would hold an infant. Leaning down, he pressed his lips against Rosie's cheek and blew, making a sputtering noise.

Melancholy washed over Larkin. His actions reminded her how her da had played with her as a child.

"That tickles." Rosie giggled and rubbed her cheek.

Jackson Lancaster chuckled for the first time, and it took her breath away. A dimple in his tanned cheek winked at her before it disappeared as his expression sobered. She found his ruggedness appealing, much to her dismay. She didn't want to like the man after what he'd done.

Something didn't add up. Was Maura wrong in her opinion of him? Who told her he didn't want his niece? From what Larkin had seen, the man was willing to fight to spend time with Rosie.

They approached a small clapboard house painted a cheery buttery shade. Rosie peered over her uncle's shoulder. "That's *my* house."

Larkin nearly stumbled. This was Rosie's home? There was nothing unsavory on the outside of the cute cottage, other than it being much smaller than the O'Keefes' overly large house. Mr. Lancaster opened the door, then stepped aside and allowed her to enter first.

The house had a slight musty smell, but it *had* probably been closed up since Rosie's parents' deaths. A stairway led up to the bedrooms, most likely. A simple kitchen was to her left, and on the right, the parlor was decorated with a pretty floral wallpaper and a colorful rag rug. A small settee looked abandoned under the front window. Two rockers sat turned toward the fireplace. Everything was neat and tidy. All it needed was a family.

Surprised at the emotion that swept over her, Larkin crossed to the parlor window and looked past the lacy curtains that were held back with a matching tie to the cozy front yard. This was just the kind of place she'd dreamed about whenever she thought of having a home of her own—something simple but cozy. She felt a tug on her hand and looked down.

"Come see my room." Rosie's wide gaze beseeched her to follow.

Larkin looked at Mr. Lancaster, and he shrugged. "Make yourself at home. I thought Rosie might like to get a few of her toys to, uh. . .take back with her."

Larkin didn't miss the huskiness in his voice when he thought of having to return his niece. Like the morning sun bursting over the horizon in all its glory, she realized the truth. This man dearly loved Rosie and was pained by their separation. So why didn't he keep her?

"C'mon, Larkin." Rosie leaned sideways and pulled her along. He followed them.

Upstairs, Rosie went into her room, but Larkin stood out on the stairway landing, looking in. The furniture in Rosie's small room consisted of a little bed and a chair. Three crates turned on their sides held her few toys and another pair of shoes that looked to be her Sunday best. A book of children's stories leaned sideways in one crate, and a ring-toss game sat across from it. Another crate was filled with more than two dozen blocks of various sizes. Three empty pegs were attached to the wall at a height that the girl could manage.

"Would you like to take a book, game, and blocks back to the O'Keefes'?" Mr. Lancaster asked.

Rosie shook her head, her braids swinging back and forth. "No. They need to be here for when I come home."

Larkin couldn't help glancing at Mr. Lancaster. The longing look in his blue eyes took her breath away.

If she comes home, Jackson couldn't help thinking. Miss Doyle looked uncomfortable in the doorway. He'd made it clear that he didn't want or appreciate her presence, but he hadn't thought what it meant for her. Mrs. O'Keefe sounded like an ogre, and he didn't doubt that she'd be quick to punish Miss Doyle if she refused to accompany him. Obviously she hadn't wanted to come with him any more than he'd wanted her to join them.

Ignoring her, he dropped to the floor and picked up one of Rosie's books. "Come here, sweet pea, and I'll read to you."

Rosie complied and sat on his lap. He couldn't help glancing at Miss Doyle. She stared at him with a surprised look. What? Did she think he couldn't read?

He tried to forget she was there as he read the story "The Three Bears" from *Aunt Mavor's Nursery Tales.*

Miss Doyle's soft floral scent drifted through the room when she untied her cloak and laid it over her arm. She leaned against the doorframe, watching him. Feeling guilty for being so rude to her, he looked up. "You can sit on Rosie's bed, if you like, or in the parlor."

Relief softened her pretty features, but she didn't enter the room. "If you're sure 'tis all right, I *would* like to sit in the parlor. . . and give you and Rosie some time alone."

Appreciating her consideration, he nodded and watched her leave.

Rosie nudged him in the belly with her elbow. "Read more, Uncle Jack."

After he read three stories from the children's book, she wanted to play with her blocks. He built several towers, and she knocked them down, laughing with delight.

Being with Rosie made him realize he'd missed her more than he thought. Staying busy with work had helped keep his mind off the situation, which angered him whenever he thought about it, but working sure hadn't helped him to find a bride. He simply had no time to court, not that there were many unmarried women *to* court.

"I'm gonna build a house." Rosie collected her blocks in a pile and started stacking them.

It bothered Jackson that she didn't seem to miss him nearly as much as he missed her. In fact, she seemed to be getting along quite well without him. He stared at a knothole on the wall. Children were adaptable. Not so with adults.

He stood, and Rosie looked up at him. "Go ahead and make a house. I need to talk to Miss Doyle for a few minutes."

"Her name is Larkin."

He smiled. "That's a pretty name."

With the tip of her tongue in the corner of her mouth, Rosie carefully set another block on her growing stack.

Jackson entered the parlor and found Miss Doyle in Amanda's rocker. He wanted to be irritated, but instead, he thought she looked as if she belonged there. He walked closer and noticed her eyes were shut. For the first time, he wondered how hard Mrs. O'Keefe worked the girl—and surely having an active four-year-old had only added to her burden. How had Larkin Doyle come to live with the O'Keefes?

Jackson stepped on a board that squeaked, and Miss Doyle jerked and opened her eyes. "Ach, sure now, you frightened me. I fear I must have dozed off." She sat up and ran her hand over her hair.

Jackson dropped into Ben's rocker. A shaft of longing and sadness speared him. He missed his brother so much. Not just because of the business, but because Ben was his best friend.

"Are you all right, Mr. Lancaster?" Miss Doyle leaned forward in her chair.

Jackson nodded, irritated that she'd witnessed his grief. He turned his face away from her, trying to force back the tears stinging his eyes. He lurched to his feet and went to stand by the window.

"I want you to know, I'm sorry for your loss."

He couldn't respond with his throat clogged as if someone had shoved a rag down it.

The rocker creaked as she stood. He could sense her standing behind him. "I lost both me folks in a short while, leaving me an orphan, like Rosie."

Jackson didn't want her comfort—didn't want her in Ben's home. She was a member of the enemy's camp. He whirled around so fast that Miss Doyle took a step backward, her eyes wide. "Rosie is not an orphan. She has me."

Miss Doyle blinked her big green eyes. "Then why did you give her to Mrs. O'Keefe?"

Jackson clutched his fists together. All the anguish and pain of the past week came rushing to the surface. He leaned into Miss Doyle's face. "I never gave Rosie up. She was stolen right out of my arms."

Confusion, and maybe even a little fear, swirled in her eyes and wrinkled her brow.

Guilt washed over him for taking his frustrations out on her. He glanced out the window again and noticed the sun had already set. Shadows darkened the room, and he turned at a shuffling in the doorway. "It's time to go, sweet pea."

Rosie's lip trembled in the waning light. "No. I want to stay here with you."

Jackson crossed the room and knelt in front of her. "That's what I want too, but we can't. Not yet."

"Why?" Tears dripped down Rosie's cheeks.

"Because the judge said you have to stay at the O'Keefes' until. . ." He cast a glance at Miss Doyle. How much did she know?

"I don't wanna go." Rosie dashed back to her room.

Jackson sighed and stood. It was so hard to take her back when he wanted to keep her so badly. He found her on her bed and picked her up.

"No. . .I don't want to go." Rosie kicked at him and pushed against his chest. "Put me down."

Holding her tight with his jaw set, he carried her outside, not even checking to see if Miss Doyle followed. Another chunk of his heart broke off and lodged in his throat.

Chapter 4

The window in the stage office door rattled as the door opened. Mrs. Winningham entered, followed by three of her six boys, reminding him of a mother duck with her ducklings.

Jackson laid his pencil down and rubbed his forehead. Ben or Amanda always handled the bookwork. Trying to make all those numbers line up wasn't something he enjoyed, but it had to be done.

He stood and forced a smile in spite of the headache clawing his forehead.

The young widow Mabel Winningham had made her interest in him well known, at least to him. She wasn't especially pretty, with her hair all pinched tight in a bun and those too-big-for-her-face amber eyes and buck teeth, but she was friendly enough. "Good day, Mr.

Lancaster." She smiled, batting her eyes, reminding him of an owl.

The first of her boys, a three-foot-tall blond, stopped beside her. The last two, identical twins with snow-white hair, plowed into the back of their brother.

"Hey! Stop it." The older boy spun around and shoved one of his brothers, knocking him backward into the other boy. Both landed on the floor, staring wide-eyed at their attacker. They turned in unison to look at each other, and as if they passed some silent code, both wailed at the same time.

Mrs. Winningham grabbed the shoulder of the oldest boy. "Bruce, you stop treating your brothers that way."

"They started it," he whined, sticking out his lip in a pout that would have swayed a weaker woman to his side. "They conked me in the back."

"Sit down over there." She pointed to the extra chair near the window. "Bobby, Billy, stop that caterwauling. I can't hear myself think."

Jackson pinched the bridge of his nose, thankful that the other three Winningham boys were at school and not here. How did their mother find the energy to deal with them all day after day? He couldn't help feeling sympathy for her.

"Sorry about that, Mr. Lancaster." Her lips turned up in an embarrassed smile. "But boys will be boys."

He was certain she knew all about boys. Bruce knelt in the chair, blowing steam rings on the window Jackson had just cleaned the day before. "What can I help you with, ma'am?"

She patted her head, not that a hair was out of place, what with it all being stuck down. Did women use hair oil?

"I wanted to make sure that you know my sister will be riding your stage from River Valley to here the week before Christmas. I'm concerned for her safety, what with all the robberies and, well. . .you know."

He sighed inwardly. She wasn't the first person to challenge him on a passenger's safety, and he of all people knew the danger. "I'm working on hiring an extra man to ride shotgun. Before the robberies started, we had no need for a guard."

"Well, you certainly need one now." She hiked her chin and looked at him with piercing tawny eyes.

Evidently she wasn't interested in winning his heart today. Thank goodness. He needed a wife, but he wasn't ready to take on a whole tribe. One little girl was enough for now.

Suddenly she softened her expression, and he swallowed hard.

"Ethel's not married. I was hoping you might come to dinner once she's here."

Uh-oh. Jackson glanced at the calendar on the wall. Just two weeks to find a bride. Was he that desperate? At least the sister most likely didn't have a half dozen boys.

Surely some other woman—one without six hooligan kids—would like to marry a man who owned his own business and a nice house.

"Uh. . .thanks for the invitation, but I'm pretty busy right now, running things here by myself."

Her gaze hardened. "Well, maybe after Christmas. Let's go, boys." She spun around and yanked the two toddlers up from where they were wrestling. Bruce marked a *B* inside one of the many fog circles he'd blown on the window. He pointed his finger like a gun and pretended to shoot Jackson and then jumped out of the chair.

Jackson closed the door the boy had left open and watched through the window as the Winningham tornado blew down the street. He wondered how the slight woman managed to feed and clothe all those boys, much less keep them in line. He made a mental note to go hunting and take her some meat. But maybe it would be better if he delivered it after dark, so she wouldn't know who'd brought it. He didn't want her getting the wrong idea.

Jackson sat at his desk and opened the center drawer. Mabel Winningham's name had been at the bottom of his list of prospective brides—a very short list. He licked the end of his pencil and drew a line through her name.

Elmer Limley, the town drunk, had a daughter who was a few years older than Jackson. The spinster had never married and hid herself away in her home, doing mending for a few of the town's wealthier people. He'd often felt sorry for Thelma Limley. She was as homely as a stray mutt, but she was kind. She'd be nice to Rosie, but he didn't want his niece exposed to the likes of Elmer Limley. For the time being, he left Thelma's name on the list.

He'd even penciled in Larkin Doyle's name, not that the quiet woman had ever shown any interest in him. But if he married her, he'd never be free of Mrs. O'Keefe's meddling.

He stared out the window, watching a wagon slowly move by. He'd never thought too much about getting married before but always figured he'd marry for love like Ben had. Amanda had come to town to visit a family that used to live in Prairie Flats. The first time Ben saw her, he'd acted like a schoolboy with his first crush. Jackson smiled, remembering.

Ben and Amanda had lived only five short years together, but they'd been years of love and laughter. That's what Jackson wanted. A home he looked forward all day to returning to. Not one where he'd have to hide out in the barn because he'd married a woman he had no feelings for.

But couldn't love grow out of such a situation?

For Rosie's sake, he had to do something. He had to find a bride in just two weeks.

Tapping his pencil on the desk, he thought of all the smaller towns that his stage visited. Was there a woman in one of those places willing to marry quickly—a woman who'd be good to Rosie? His needs didn't matter so much, just as long as Rosie was back with him.

Looking up at the ceiling, he sighed. "I need some help, Lord. How do I find a wife so fast? Guide me. Show me where to look."

"Please help, Father. I can't lose Rosie."

Jackson tied his two horses to the ornamental iron hitching post in front of the O'Keefes' large home. Arriving to pick up Rosie definitely felt better than returning her. Even after two weeks, she still cried and fussed when he had to leave. In fact, her fits seemed to be getting worse rather than better. He ran his hand down his duster, making sure he looked presentable, and knocked on the door.

"He's here. Uncle Jack's here." Rosie's muffled squeals on the other side of the door made him smile. Nobody called him Jack, but early on, his niece had shortened his name to that.

The door opened, and Rosie rushed past Miss Doyle, grabbing him around one leg. He brushed his hand over her dark hair and pressed her head against his thigh. "Evening, sweet pea."

She reached her hands up to him, and he picked her up, planting a kiss on her cheek. "We going home again?"

"Not today. The sun's out in full force and there's no wind, so I thought you might like to ride Horace."

"Oh boy!" Rosie clapped her hands together and looked at Miss Doyle. "We're gonna ride hossies."

Jackson wasn't certain, given the natural pale coloring of Miss

Doyle's fair skin, but he felt certain that all the blood had just rushed out of her face.

She stepped outside, closing the door behind her, and peered wide-eyed past him to the horses. "Sure now, I've never been on a horse in me whole life."

Ah, so that was the problem. Jackson flashed a reassuring smile. "It's nothing to fear. We'll just walk them."

"C'mon, Larkin. Hossies is fun."

Miss Doyle looked down at her dress. "I can't ride a horse in me dress."

Rosie giggled. "Your dress won't fit on a hossie."

A shy grin tugged at her lips. " 'Twould be a funny thing to see, for sure. What I meant to say is that I can't ride since *I'm* wearing a dress."

With a smile on her face, the young woman was quite pretty. She was always so somber and quiet around him. He'd wondered if she didn't like him for some reason.

Jackson lifted Rosie onto Horace's saddle and then offered a hand to Miss Doyle. Would she stand her ground and refuse to go? He wouldn't mind time alone with Rosie but didn't want the young woman to get in trouble with her employer. "Look, if you'd rather not go, I understand. We're not leaving town, just walking around. Rosie loves horses, and I thought she'd enjoy a short ride."

Miss Doyle darted a glance at the closed door and shook her head. "Mrs. O'Keefe says I must go, or. . ."

Jackson hated putting the young woman in such an awkward position, but since Rosie was all ready to ride, he didn't want to disappoint her. "I'll help you mount the horse, and then you can fix your skirts so they're respectable."

Green eyes stared at him as if he were a loon. "Will you be riding or leading the horses?"

"Ride with me, Uncle Jack."

He shrugged. "Guess I'm riding. But I can lead your horse if you prefer."

He could tell she didn't want to ride, but she shuffled toward the horse, stopping four feet away. His heart went out to her. Here she was being forced into another situation she didn't desire, but she wasn't complaining, and for that, he admired her.

Before she could object, Jackson scooped her up and deposited her on Maudie's back.

"Oh!" she squealed as she struggled to hide her bare calves with her skirt and cloak. That done, she glared at him. " 'Twould have been kind of you to have given me warning, Mr. Lancaster."

He grinned, enjoying her lyrical accent. She looked as ruffled as a hen being chased by a fox. "Call me Jackson—since we're seeing so much of each other."

"You can call her Larkin." Rosie smiled. "That's her name."

Jackson lifted a brow at the young woman, and she nodded. "Aye, call me by me first name."

He mounted up behind Rosie. "It's a pretty name. What does it mean?"

Glancing over his shoulder, he noticed her cheeks had reddened. " 'Tis actually a man's name. Lorcan means fierce or silent."

Well, the silent part sure fit, but not the fierce. Sweet might be a better description.

"Me da liked the name. He said it reminded him of a lark. A bird." She shrugged, as if that wasn't an acceptable reason for giving a baby girl a male name.

"It's pretty and suits you." He guided the horses toward the edge of town, wanting to kick himself for complimenting her. He didn't need her to think he was happy to have her around. She was just an intruder, an interloper, distracting him from the short time he had with his niece.

Jackson tickled Rosie. She giggled and squirmed, making him forget about his silent shadow.

Larkin concentrated on holding on to the saddle horn and not falling off the big horse while Jackson led it behind his mount. She'd made the mistake of peering down to the ground and didn't want to do that again. She rocked to the horse's gentle gait, relieved they weren't going any faster.

Up ahead, Rosie giggled as Jackson tickled her. Larkin admired his broad shoulders and the loose way he sat in the saddle. Not at all like her all-tensed-up gotta-hold-on-tight-so-I-don't-fall rigidness. Maudie's walk was gentle, making Larkin sway side to side a bit. Still, she didn't trust animals and kept a tight grip on the horn in case the horse decided to run away.

Larkin rubbed her gritty eyes and yawned. She'd lain awake late the previous night trying to make sense of things. Against her wishes, she liked Jackson Lancaster. His nearly black hair was almost the same color as Rosie's, and his blue eyes reminded her of the vast ocean she crossed after leaving Ireland. The man had a rugged, shaggy look, kind of like a lost pup that needed someone to care for it.

She knew he ran the stage line with his brother, who'd been killed. Perhaps it was too difficult to care for an ornery four-year-old and a business too.

Rosie let out a squeal, and Jackson chuckled, making his shoulders bounce.

Larkin smiled, glad to see Rosie happy again. The lass was

becoming more withdrawn at the O'Keefes', as if she were afraid she'd get in trouble for touching things, which she had.

Mrs. O'Keefe had little patience for a rambunctious child, especially one who accidentally broke an antique vase from Ireland. She had ordered Larkin to take Rosie on daily walks to help the child run off some steam. They'd been to the Lancaster Stage office several times, but to Rosie's disappointment, her uncle hadn't been there.

Why had Maura wanted the child in the first place? Did she think it lifted her up in the eyes of the community to be generous to an orphan? Did it fill a hole in her heart from losing her own child so long ago?

A rogue gust of wind flipped her cloak behind her, revealing her bare calf. Two men on the boardwalk elbowed each other and grinned at her. Cheeks scorching, she hurried to grab the corner of her cloak and secured it under her leg.

Jackson had done nothing to indicate he didn't want his niece. In fact, he acted the opposite. She was beginning to think Mrs. O'Keefe had misled her. But why?

Larkin always tried to believe the best of people. But if Mrs. O'Keefe had lied about Mr. Lancaster just to get Rosie, then she'd done the man a horrible injustice.

Jackson looked over his shoulder at her. "You doing all right?"

She smiled and nodded, warmed by his concern for her. She had tried hard to remain aloof. To not like Jackson Lancaster.

But it was too late.

Looking toward heaven, she prayed, *Father God, if Mrs. O'Keefe lied to get custody of Rosie, I pray You'll make things right. Jackson loves his niece, I can tell. They're family and should be together. Please make it so.*

Chapter 5

Mrs. O'Keefe peered over the top of her spectacles at Larkin. "When do you plan to accept Frank's offer for dinner?"

Larkin's heart skipped a beat. She'd hoped the subject wouldn't come up. "I'm not particularly interested in dining with him, mum."

Maura's pale blue eyes widened. "Why ever not? He's a fine-looking man and is vice president of the bank. It's more than a girl in your position should hope to find."

Her words cut like a surgeon's scalpel. A servant—that was the position she meant. As much as Larkin had hoped to become the daughter Maura always said she wanted, she knew she never would be. Maura had taken her in as a way to get free labor, and Larkin wasn't about to be tied the rest of her life to someone else who didn't love her. She twisted her hands together. "Mr. Barrett makes me nervous."

"That's the silliest thing I've ever heard. Why, he's a perfect gentleman." Maura's lips twisted, reminding Larkin of a snarling dog. "If he asks you again, you will accept. Is that clear?"

Larkin nodded, but inside she was screaming. Oh, how she wished she could leave this house and find a place of her own, but she had little money, and nobody would hire her if the mayor's wife told them not to. And how could she leave Rosie with Mrs. O'Keefe? The little girl's life would be miserable.

Maura enjoyed dressing her up and strutting the little lass around in front of friends and acquaintances, showing how generous she was to take in the waif. But at home, Maura couldn't be bothered with Rosie. She was relegated to the kitchen and Larkin's room and not allowed access to the rest of the house for fear she'd break another of Maura's valuable decorations. At least now Larkin had a cause to live for. She would tend the child she'd come to love and make sure that Rosie never knew the loneliness that she had.

Hurrying back to her room, she found Rosie sitting on the bed rubbing her eyes, her nap over. With her braids loosened, hair tousled, and cheeks red, she was as darling as ever. "Is Uncle Jack coming today?"

"Aye." A flutter of excitement tickled her stomach at the thought of seeing Jackson again. She was only happy for Rosie's sake. The lass was a different person on the days her uncle came. She was happy and not quiet and moody, like she'd recently become.

Larkin picked up the brush, undid Rosie's braids, and in quick order rewove them. She was thankful Rosie had quit asking for her mum and da but didn't like how she was starting to withdraw. The poor child had been through so much recently. She didn't deserve to be stuck in this house where only Larkin and Wilma loved her.

"Shall we go see if Wilma baked some sugar cookies while you napped?"

Rosie smiled and nodded. Larkin helped her into her shoes and fastened them, then took her into the kitchen, where they washed their hands. Rosie shinnied onto a chair and drank half the glass of milk Wilma had set out for her.

Larkin cringed when she wiped her milk mustache on her sleeve. "Use your napkin, lass, not your sleeve."

Rosie shrugged and picked up a cookie. As she ate, she stared off into space. Larkin wondered what she was thinking about as she helped herself to a cookie. After eating another cookie, Rosie took two more and wrapped them up in her cloth napkin.

Larkin lifted her brows. "What are you doin'? Have you not had enough cookies?"

"I'm saving them for Uncle Jack."

How sweet. Larkin glanced at the clock on the hearth. Jackson was later today than normal. She wondered if he was having a hard time running his business without his brother's assistance. Each time she saw Rosie's uncle, the bags under his eyes seemed larger and darker. Did he ever sleep? Was he eating properly?

"He'll be here soon," Wilma said as she added potatoes to the pot of boiling water.

Being separated from Rosie seemed to be more of a problem to Jackson than the fact that someone was watching her for him. He should be grateful for that, at least, as busy as he was.

Larkin shook her head. Why all the worry about Jackson Lancaster? He could have kept Rosie instead of giving her to Maura. But hadn't he mentioned something about Rosie being stolen from him?

It was all so confusing that Larkin's head was swirling like a weather vane in a windstorm. Who was right? And who was wrong?

A knock at the kitchen door pulled her from her worries. Wilma dusted her hands on her apron and opened the door. Jackson had started coming to the kitchen entrance to avoid seeing Mrs. O'Keefe. It seemed to Larkin that every time the two were together, Maura enforced some new rule that only irritated the man further. Was there bad blood between the two of them?

Jackson tipped his hat to Wilma and Larkin, but his lovely blue eyes lit up when he saw Rosie at the table.

She smiled and waved to him. "I saved you some cookies."

"Did you, now? You know I like cookies." Jackson lingered in the doorway as if afraid to come in.

A frigid breeze cooled the overly warm room, stirring up the scent of wood smoke and baking chicken. Larkin's stomach growled.

"Sure smells good in here." A shy grin tugged at Jackson's lips.

"Well, don't just stand there letting in the cold air—not that it doesn't feel wonderful to me after standing in front of this stove all day." Wilma waved her stirring spoon in the air. "Have a seat at the table and eat those cookies your niece saved for you."

He hesitated a moment and looked past them. Was he making sure Mrs. O'Keefe wasn't around? Finally, he stepped inside and shut the door, then sat at the table. Rosie shoved her napkin toward him. He unfolded it and smiled. Larkin's stomach twittered at the sight of his dimples.

"Thank you for sharing with me, sweet pea." He took a bite and closed his eyes, as if he'd never tasted anything so good.

Larkin was saddened to think of him living alone and working so hard after all he'd lost. As far as she knew, Rosie was the only family he had left. His dark hair hung down over his forehead, so different from that of the many businessmen who visited the O'Keefe house, who wore their hair slicked back with smelly tonic. His cheeks bore the tan of a man who was often outside, not the paleness of men who worked in an office all day.

He caught her staring and winked. She resisted gasping and turned to find something to do. She grabbed a glass, retrieved the milk, and poured him some. When she handed it to him, his warm smile tickled her insides as if an intruding moth were fluttering at a window, seeking escape.

"I brought you a surprise." He looked at Rosie, reached into his coat pocket, and pulled out a handkerchief. He slid the bundle across the table.

Rosie clapped her hands and rose to her knees. She opened the present, revealing four perfect wooden replicas of animals. "A hossie!"

Jackson's longing as he watched his niece confused Larkin as much as his warm smile had. He didn't seem like the kind of man to abandon a child. She never wanted to like him, but she did. A lot.

"Look, Larkin, a cow. Moooo..." Rosie walked the cow and horse across the table. "Oink, oink," she said, picking up the pig.

"I think she likes them." Larkin smiled at him.

Jackson nodded and stood.

Rosie cast a worried eye in his direction but picked up the fourth animal—a sheep.

He glanced at Wilma then turned to Larkin. "I, uh...brought you something too."

Larkin reached out and accepted the small wooden figure, her hands trembling and heart pounding. She'd never received a gift from anyone except at Christmas or on her birthday, and those had dwindled to next to nothing.

"It's a bird." He cleared his raspy throat. "It's not a lark, but I thought you might like it since you said your name reminded your dad of a bird."

Her throat went dry at the thoughtfulness of the gift and the time involved in making it. Larkin could only nod. She turned away, lest he see the tears burning her eyes, and poured a glass of water.

Wilma's upraised brow caught her eye. The cook grinned, something she rarely did.

Larkin swallowed another drink, wiped her eyes, and turned back around. "Thank you. I've never had such a thoughtful gift."

A shy smile tugged at his lips; then he broke her gaze.

She turned to Rosie. "Shall we go and put our lovely animals in our room so you can spend time with your uncle?"

Rosie stuck out her lip.

"Maybe she could bring one with her?" Jackson asked.

"Aye, that is a grand idea."

Larkin escorted Rosie back to their room, all the while examining her own gift. The bird, carved from a light-colored wood, more resembled a sparrow than a lark, but the fine craftsmanship and detail made even a plain sparrow exquisite. She probably shouldn't have accepted the gift, being as it was from a man, but she clutched it to her heart, knowing it was already one of her most treasured possessions.

Fifteen minutes later, Larkin and Jackson walked down the boardwalk with Rosie between them, holding their hands. To someone who didn't know them, they could be a family on their way to the mercantile or somewhere else. But as much as Larkin longed for a family of her own, she didn't dare hope it could be this one.

She didn't have the freedom to choose her own family. She'd always be grateful to Mrs. O'Keefe for taking her in when she was orphaned, but hadn't she paid her debt by working hard these seven years? Even indentured servants were freed after that long.

"I'm cold." Rosie blinked away the flakes of snow that had landed on her eyelashes.

Jackson lifted her up and wrapped his duster around her. "We'll be home soon. I've already got the fire going, so it will be warm."

Pulling her cloak to her chest to block the biting wind, Larkin quickened her pace to keep up with the long-legged man.

Though many people loved the snow that had started falling this morning, it only reminded her of the times in New York when her family had been cold, living in a drafty shanty with little food or fuel. She longed for the warmth of the sun and beautiful wildflowers.

"Afternoon, Miss Doyle."

Larkin stopped suddenly to keep from colliding into Frank Barrett. "Good day, sir." She attempted to go around him, but he sidestepped, blocking her way. At least the wind was less severe with his body shielding her, but the look in his eyes chilled away any warmth she'd gathered from his presence.

"When can I expect the privilege of your company for dinner? I'd hoped we could dine together before now."

She shivered, remembering Maura's warning. If she refused Mr. Barrett, Maura might put her out on the street, with no home and no job. But she wasn't a slave. She didn't have to dine with this man if she didn't want to. Perhaps she could put him off until another means of escape provided itself.

"Mrs. O'Keefe took in the Lancaster girl, as you know." She attempted to look around him to see if Jackson had heard her or noticed her gone, but Mr. Barrett blocked her view. "I've been quite busy caring for Rosie. 'Twould not be proper for me to dine with you and neglect me other duties. Perhaps after Christmas. . ."

"I'll talk with Maura and make sure that you have some free time. I've waited long enough for you."

His mouth pursed, and something flickered in his steely gaze that sent chills down Larkin's back, as if someone had dumped snow down her shirtwaist. "No. Please do not do such a thing."

"Why? Do you not wish to enjoy my company? I'm quite wealthy, you know." His mouth twisted into an arrogant snarl.

Larkin searched for an answer, but her mind froze.

"Excuse me, but Miss Doyle is with me at the moment."

Relief melted the chills at the sound of Jackson's voice behind Mr. Barrett. The shorter man spun around to face him.

"No one asked for your advice, Lancaster."

"The mayor's wife has instructed Miss Doyle to escort me and my niece. Do you want me to inform her that you kept her ward from her duties?"

Larkin hurried past Mr. Barrett to stand beside Jackson. He handed Rosie to her then faced Mr. Barrett again.

"Uh. . .no, I didn't mean to keep Miss Doyle from her duties." He glanced at her. A muscle ticked in his jaw. His cold gaze could have frozen hot water. "Another time, then." He pivoted around and marched down the boardwalk.

Somehow Larkin felt sure she'd be the one to pay for his displeasure.

Jackson double-checked the ammunition in his Winchester. He set it on the desk, then grabbed another rifle and loaded the cartridges in it. He had a payroll for Carpenter Mills that had to get through. With Shorty driving, him riding shotgun, and Cody Webster, a sharp-shooter disguised as a city slicker, riding inside the coach, Jackson hoped to deliver the payroll without incident. His customers were getting leery of traveling on the Lancaster Stage after all that had happened.

His boots echoed on the boardwalk and down the steps. The four horses fidgeted, anxious to be on their way. Jackson handed up his rifles to Shorty then passed him a canteen filled with coffee and a small satchel that held their lunch. He walked to the front of the stage, checking harnesses and talking to the horses.

"Uncle Jack!"

He pivoted at Rosie's call, his heart jumping. He'd never minded driving the stage, but going today would mean he wouldn't be back until Thursday and would miss Wednesday evening with Rosie. Mrs. O'Keefe had been stern and refused to allow him to visit his niece on another day. No amount of sweet talk or arguing could sway her. As much as he loved Rosie, he couldn't take care of her and provide for her without his business.

Rosie ran into his arms, and he tossed her in the air. Larkin followed a few yards behind, walking demurely, her cheeks brightened by the cold wind that tugged at her dark green cloak.

"We sneaked out."

Jackson raised a brow at Larkin, and she ducked her head for a moment.

"Mrs. O'Keefe had a tea to attend with the banker's wife and some of her other friends, and Mr. O'Keefe was still sleeping. Since you'll be gone tomorrow, we thought to come and see you off." Larkin shrugged one shoulder, as if it were a small thing, but to Jackson, it meant a lot.

He smacked a kiss on Rosie's cheek, making her giggle and washing away his longing of not getting to see her. She turned her head, giving him access to the other side of her face, on which he happily planted another kiss.

"I wanna go with you." Rosie clung to his neck.

"I wish you could, sweet pea, but it's too dangerous." He wanted to say, "Maybe after we catch whoever's been robbing the stage," but didn't for fear it would make her think of her parents.

"Bring me a present."

Larkin stepped forward. "Now, Rosie, 'tisn't good manners to ask for gifts."

Jackson handed his niece to her and helped a female passenger into the coach. He checked his pocket watch as Cody winked at him and stepped inside. Jackson closed the door and looked at Shorty. "Ready to go?"

His driver nodded and turned up his collar. "Yep."

Jackson knelt in front of Rosie and hugged her. "Be good for Miss Doyle, all right?"

"Her name's Larkin."

"Be good for Larkin. . .and don't correct your elders." He hugged his niece tight, never wanting to let her go. But time was ticking. The stage needed to leave, and Christmas was drawing closer.

He stood and gazed at Larkin. She was so pretty in her dark green cloak and with her cheeks rosy from the cold air. He felt a sudden urge to pull her close and hug her but shook off that crazy thought. "Thank you."

She nodded and took Rosie's hand.

Jackson cleared the huskiness from his throat, jogged around to the far side of the stage, and climbed aboard.

Rosie waved.

"We'll be praying for your safety," Larkin called out. She caught his gaze then darted hers to the ground.

Shorty let off the brake and shouted a loud, "Heeyaw!"

Rosie jumped up and down from her safe spot by the office window. "Yaw. Yaw!"

Jackson grinned and waved, his heart warmed by their brief visit. He positioned his rifle on his lap, watching as they left town to see if he noticed anything out of the ordinary.

The snow had stopped, leaving a thin blanket of white all across the open prairie. His cheeks burned from the chilly wind, and he hunkered down, keeping a watchful eye. It would be hard for anyone to sneak up on them for the next five miles, since they were on open prairie.

His mind drifted to the quickly approaching Christmas Day. It was on a Saturday this year. Would he even get to see Rosie? Would he spend the day alone, remembering last year's happy Christmas with Ben and Amanda?

And how in the world was he going to find a wife in nine days? But he had to—or lose all that mattered to him in this world.

A pheasant darted upward from a nearby bush, making Jackson jump.

Shorty chuckled. "A little edgy, huh?"

"I was just thinking, that's all." Jackson refocused on his duty.

If all else failed, he could ask the Widow Winningham to marry him. He shuddered—and he knew it wasn't from the cold. The thought of being a stepfather to her six rowdy sons made him quiver as badly as being lost in a blizzard with no coat on.

And how would little Rosie fare with all those rough boys? There had to be a better answer.

He checked the landscape for intruders—anything that looked out of the ordinary—then turned his thoughts to God. *Help me, Lord. Show me what to do. I can't lose Rosie.*

Desperate, he turned to Shorty. "I don't reckon you know any women that want to get married."

Chapter 6

Larkin sat on the edge of her bed and rocked Rosie back and forth.

The girl sniffled and huddled against Larkin's chest. "I want Uncle Jack."

Larkin stroked her hair and murmured softly. "I know, lass. He's busy with work, I'm sure of it."

As Rosie sobbed, Larkin's ire grew. How could Jackson disappoint his niece like this? Why hadn't he warned her that he'd miss two nights with her instead of just the one? She'd stirred Rosie up, thinking he was coming today, only to severely disappoint her.

Larkin rocked and prayed, hoping business had kept Jackson away rather than injury. It had been a whole week since he'd come for Rosie, but at least the child had gotten a few moments with him when they'd visited him at the stage office.

Rosie's breathing rose and fell as sleep descended. Her little body grew heavy.

Larkin tucked her in bed then softly kissed her cheek.

Caring for Rosie made her heart ache with longing. Oh, how she wanted children of her own—and, of course, a husband. But no man other than Mr. Barrett had shown an interest in her, and she had no desire to get to know him better.

She faced a dilemma similar to those of the sharecroppers in Ireland who worked the soil of the wealthy landowners. They had to give a share of their crops to these landowners and thus had barely enough to feed their families. There was no hope of a better life.

At least Maura had seen that Larkin was educated and had allowed her to attend school through the eighth grade. But she paid her no wage, only providing food, shelter, and clothing. How could she move somewhere else when she had no money? What man would want to marry a woman who was nothing more than a servant?

Jackson's blue eyes invaded her thoughts. The charming way his coffee-colored hair hung over his forehead made her want to brush it back. Would it be soft to touch, or thick and wiry?

Larkin shook her head at the foolish thought. She would never know the answer to that. Jackson Lancaster tolerated her presence only because he had to.

Dropping to her knees on the cold floor, she folded her hands and prayed, asking God to soothe Rosie, to protect Jackson—for Rosie's sake—and to provide a way for her to start a new life, outside the O'Keefes' home.

The next morning, Maura left with Rosie in tow as she went to visit the Flemings, a family with two girls a bit older than Rosie. Larkin donned her cloak and left after they were out of view. She marched down the boardwalk, her boots pounding on the weathered wood.

She'd stewed last night until she'd finally fallen into a restless sleep and then had to listen to Maura's gloating at breakfast. Maura was certain they'd seen the last visit from Jackson Lancaster. On and on she'd told Larkin and Mr. O'Keefe how much better off the child was with them.

Larkin wasn't sure if she was truly angry because Jackson had disappointed Rosie or because she had to listen to Maura's self-righteous boasting. More likely, both situations had fueled her Irish temper, one she kept in check on most days.

She knocked on the stage office door but knew by the darkness inside that nobody was there. She tried the door handle, thinking to leave Jackson a note, but found it locked.

Swirling around, she studied the town of Prairie Flats. The place lived up to its name. Located on the Illinois prairie, the town was as flat as a sheet of paper. There were few trees to block the steady winds, which was a blessing in the summer but a curse in the winter.

There was work to be done at the O'Keefes', but rarely having time to herself, Larkin wandered toward the mercantile. On occasion, Maura allowed her to purchase an item or two and charge it to the O'Keefes' account. Of course, there would be extra chores required to pay for those necessities.

Christmas was quickly approaching, and Larkin wondered what she could give the people in her life. She could make Rosie a doll, but she didn't want a new one competing with the doll the child's mother had made. Perhaps she could sew a small quilt from the scraps she'd been saving. Larkin smiled at the pleasure such a gift would surely bring the lass.

But finding something for the O'Keefes was more difficult, and the fact that it was expected took the joy out of the giving. Larkin sighed. What could she give them that they didn't already have? For just being the mayor of a small town, Mr. O'Keefe was a superb provider and often worked long hours. The O'Keefes lacked nothing.

A woman a few years older than Larkin smiled at her husband as they squeezed past in the crowded aisle. Melancholy tugged at Larkin, and she couldn't resist watching them. The husband wrapped his arm around his wife and whispered in her ear. The woman giggled and looked at him with adoration.

Larkin had never felt so lonely. Staying busy at the O'Keefes' had kept her from developing friendships, and Mr. O'Keefe, Jackson Lancaster, and Frank Barrett were the only men who actually talked to her, except an occasional guest at the big house.

The scents of spices and leather and the sweet odor of perfume that a man was testing out as a gift for his wife hung in the air. People chattered, and two children played hide-and-seek around their mother's skirt as she waited to have her purchases tallied up.

What would it be like to wake up each day next to a man you loved and to have children to tickle and hug and receive wet, sloppy kisses from?

She stopped in front of a box of colorful Christmas ornaments and picked one up. Never had she seen such elaborate decorations— or even a real Christmas tree—until she'd move in with the O'Keefes. She had vague memories of hanging holly and ivy in their small home in Ireland, and those times were the happiest she could remember. Hers was a home where a child was free to laugh and talk, not one where she had to be cautious and quiet. The faces of her parents had faded over time, but not the feeling of being loved and cherished. Would no one ever love her again?

Larkin pursed her lips. She ached for a home of her own, and at nineteen, she felt it was time to find a way to get it. Perhaps she could find a job with room and board and a small wage. It wouldn't be much more than she had now, but it would be hers and not Maura's.

Still. . .how could she leave Rosie? The child needed her.

Leaving the store and its cheery inhabitants, she plodded along the boardwalk. Her dilemma tugged at her. She crossed the street and dropped onto the empty bench in front of the stage office. Still no sign of Rosie's uncle.

In spite of her irritation with him for hurting Rosie, she couldn't help worrying about Jackson. She'd asked around and discovered he had an excellent reputation. Not at all what Maura had said. And she knew he loved Rosie.

Larkin's thoughts drifted to a vision of Jackson laughing and tossing Rosie in the air. She'd never wanted to like him—thought him an ogre for not keeping his niece. But instead of hating him, she feared the opposite was true. Her feelings had grown like the abundant wild ivy of her homeland. Did she love the man?

But what did that matter? He could never return her feelings when she worked for his enemy. Looking heavenward, she prayed, "Please, Lord, don't let me feel these things for Jackson. And please bring him home safely."

She glanced in both directions, hoping to hear the jingling of harnesses and the pounding of horses' hooves. "Jackson, where are you?"

Jackson brushed down the last of the horses and then put the tools away. Now that each horse had fresh hay and water and a measure of oats, he could go home. But where was home?

He'd tried living at the big house but hated the silence of the place. Amanda's knickknacks and utensils cried out for a woman to use them, but he was out of luck in that respect.

He'd even spent an extra two days scouring the small towns his stage stopped at to see if there was a kind woman who'd marry him. But none of the available women wanted to marry a man they didn't know so quickly, no matter that he owned his own business.

He sighed and scratched his bristly beard. He wanted to see Rosie, and it didn't matter one bit that today wasn't his day. Turning around, he headed for the O'Keefe house.

Just a hug from Rosie, and he'd know she was all right. Then maybe he could sleep.

Seeing Larkin would be a bonus. The auburn-haired sprite's name was still on his list, but he didn't dare ask her to marry him. If she said no, his visits to Rosie would be awkward and unbearable.

He'd never been friends with a woman before, except for Amanda, and she was family. Besides, though Larkin's stance toward him had softened, she'd never indicated having any affection for him. She'd been through enough in her life. She didn't need to marry a man she didn't love.

He stopped at front of the O'Keefes' kitchen door. Was he doing the right thing, coming here on a day he wasn't expected? Before he could knock, the door flew open.

Wilma stood there with a bucket of dirty water. She blinked and smiled. "Well, about time you got back. Here, save my old bones a chill and empty this on that shrub for me."

Jackson took the bucket and did as she bid, glad that she seemed happy to see him. Inside, he set the bucket by the door, taunted by the fragrant scent of baking bread and knowing there was nothing warm for him to eat at home. "I realize it isn't my day to be here, but do you think I could see Rosie?"

Wilma's lips pursed. "I wouldn't mind except that she's abed with a fever, and I don't think it's proper for you to visit her in Larkin's room."

Concern stabbed his chest. "How long has she been sick? Has the doctor seen her? Larkin's room?"

Wilma nodded and moved a pot of something to the back burner. "Rosie shares Larkin's room. Seems the madam didn't want to take a chance on her breaking something in the guest room."

Irritation battled concern. Mrs. O'Keefe had made a big deal about his place not being good enough for Rosie, but now she was living in the servants' quarters. They were probably much nicer than his room behind the office, but the thought that the mayor's wife had banned Rosie from a better room irked him. "I want to see her. Either take me to her or bring her to me."

Wilma gave him a scolding stare then softened. "I imagine it would help her to see you. Give me a minute."

Jackson removed his jacket and hung it on a chair and laid his hat on the table. He paced the kitchen, enjoying the cozy warmth but anxious to see his niece. After what seemed like hours, Larkin hurried into the room. "You're back. I was so worried."

He stopped pacing directly in front of her. "How is Rosie?"

Larkin shrugged and twisted her hands together. "She's had a fever for two days. 'Tis my fault, I fear."

"Why?" Jackson took her hands to keep them still.

Her lower lip quivered. "We built a snowman. Rosie's been wantin' to play outside, and I thought 'twould do her good to get some fresh air. I–I'm so sorry." Tears gushed from her eyes and down her cheeks.

Jackson pulled her close and patted her back, hoping to comfort her. "It's not your fault. Children catch colds and fevers."

"I shouldna have taken her outside." Larkin clung to his shirt.

She sniffled, and Jackson couldn't resist resting his head against hers, hoping she didn't mind that he was fresh off the trail.

After a moment, she seemed to gather her composure. Wilma entered the room, and Larkin stepped back. "Sorry."

"Don't be." He smiled and wiped a remnant tear from her cheek. "I know it's not a proper thing to ask, what with her being in your room, but may I please see Rosie? Just for a minute?"

"If you want to know what I think"—Wilma glanced at them over her spectacles—"you're just what that child needs to get her back on her feet. She's pined herself into a tizzy missing you. I don't know what Mrs. O'Keefe is doing keeping you two apart."

"C'mon. I'll take you to her." Larkin took his hand and tugged on it.

He enjoyed the soft feel of her small hand in his. They passed a big closet and then entered a room that was slightly bigger than his but sparsely adorned. His gaze landed on a small lump under a colorful quilt. His throat tightened.

"The doctor says she will be fine. He left some medicine for her and said not to let her outside until Christmas."

Jackson knelt beside the bed and reached out his shaking hand to brush the hair from Rosie's overly red cheeks. Clearing his throat, he forced some words out. "Sweet pea, it's Uncle Jack."

Rosie stirred, and her eyes opened. She blinked several times; then her mouth curved upward. "Hi."

Jackson glanced at Larkin. "Can I hold her?"

Her lips tilted upward, and she nodded.

Jackson lifted one corner of the quilt, but Rosie sat and climbed into his arms. Her hot cheek warmed his. *God, please touch her. Heal her.*

"I thought you'd gone to heaven. Like Mama and Poppy."

Jackson clutched her small form as tightly as he dared. "No, precious. I told you I'd take care of you, and I mean to do that."

"Good." She snuggled in his arms and was soon fast asleep.

Larkin motioned to a chair in the corner. He took Rosie and settled down. Larkin laid the quilt over them both.

"Just let me sit here and pray a few minutes; then I'll leave." Not that he knew how he'd be able to leave her.

"If you need anything, just call out." Larkin patted Rosie's head and left the room.

It held a single bed, making him wonder how both Larkin and Rosie managed to get any sleep. Besides the chair, there was a small desk and a crate that held a stack of clothes. Two pegs hung on the wall, holding a pair of dresses, both ones that he'd seen Larkin wear. There wasn't even a fireplace. The lack of amenities stunned him, considering how fancy the rest of the house was.

The bird he'd carved sat in the middle of the windowsill. There were no pictures, no decorations of any kind. He hugged Rosie closer, his irritation with Mrs. O'Keefe growing. Had Larkin lived in near poverty her whole life? Was that what Rosie was doomed to endure if he didn't get her back—to be the mistreated servant of a selfish, wealthy woman?

A racket sounded in the kitchen and moved his way. Maura O'Keefe stormed into the room, her pale eyes colder than the winter sky outside. "What is *he* doing here?"

Larkin wrung her hands together. "He learned Rosie was sick and wanted to sit with her a few minutes. Surely you can't deny him that."

"Oh yes, I can. The judge was clear in his orders. Put that child in her bed and leave my house this instant."

Rosie whimpered and cuddled closer. "Don't go, Uncle Jack."

Jackson clenched his jaw tight to keep from spewing out his anger on the woman. If Rosie hadn't been sick, he would have marched right out the door with her, but he couldn't risk her getting sicker. Against his wishes, he laid her on the bed.

Rosie tried to cling to him, but Larkin squeezed in between them. "No. . . don't go. . ." Rosie's wails followed him down the hall and into the kitchen.

Maura crossed her arms over her chest and frowned. "First thing in the morning, I'm going to the judge and tell him what you've done."

Jackson glared back at her and stepped closer.

Her ice blue eyes widened.

"And maybe I'll just tell the judge how you've relegated my niece to the servants' quarters, not even giving her a bed of her own. What do you think he'll say about that?"

Mrs. O'Keefe paled. "Get out and don't come back."

Jackson snatched up his jacket and stormed outside without even putting it on. How had things turned out so badly? The days were ticking away. He couldn't leave his niece in that woman's care. If he didn't find a wife soon, he'd leave his business and whisk Rosie away in the night. The two of them could start over somewhere else.

Even as his thoughts traveled that trail, he knew that wasn't the answer. God wouldn't have him react in anger, but where was He in all of this? So far his prayers had gone unanswered.

Jackson grabbed a fistful of snow, wadded it into a ball, and threw it against a tree.

Could he just walk away from the house his parents had built? And the business he and Ben had worked so hard to make a success?

And what about Larkin? Could he leave her to live out her days in that little room with no hope of a future?

He slammed the door to the office, rattling the window, and

strode back to his room. If he had any hopes of getting Rosie back, he had to move into the big house and put aside his hurts.

He glanced at the calendar. Only six days to Christmas.

Chapter 7

"How is your dinner, Miss Doyle?" Frank Barrett's charming smile would have won over most maidens.

" 'Tis delicious. Wilma is a fine cook." Larkin avoided his gaze and glanced at Maura, who was watching them. Why did she want to push Mr. Barrett on her? Larkin had no fortune. He had nothing to gain by a union with her.

"Christmas will soon be past; then I will expect you to accept my dinner invitation." Mr. Barrett shoved a huge bite of veal into his mouth.

Larkin's heart pounded, her appetite disintegrating. She glanced across the table.

Miss Eleanor James, eldest daughter of the town's banker, glared at her. The woman had made her interest in Mr. Barrett clear, but he seemed oblivious to her wiles. Why didn't he pursue Eleanor instead of her?

On cue, Wilma touched her shoulder just before dessert was served. "Miss Rosie is ready for you to tuck her in, Miss Doyle."

Larkin dabbed her lips with her napkin. "Thank you, Wilma. I shall see to her right away."

Frank Barrett and the other men stood as she rose from her chair, but he along with Maura scowled as she left the table.

Her heart hammered, and she almost felt guilty for prearranging her escape, but the thought of spending the evening avoiding Mr. Barrett's advances and her employer's glares had set her nerves on edge. As she passed through the kitchen and entered the servants' quarters, her heart slowed and her breathing returned to normal.

Rosie sat at the kitchen table eating a late-night snack of bread with apple butter. She smiled when she saw Larkin, then yawned. Normally she was in bed an hour earlier, but Larkin had asked Wilma to keep her up as long as she didn't get in the cook's way.

"Ready for bed?"

Rosie stuffed a final bite into her mouth and nodded. She licked her fingers, then downed the last of her milk and yawned again.

"Best get that youngun to bed before she falls off that chair." Wilma sidled a glance at them as she sliced a peach pie and placed a serving on one of Maura's favorite china plates.

Larkin carried Rosie to their room and helped her into a nightgown, then tucked her in.

"Uncle Jack comes tomorrow." Rosie's eyelids rose and closed, getting heavier by the second.

"Yes, lass, tomorrow is his day to see you." Larkin hoped his work wouldn't keep him away again. There hadn't been any robberies in the past week, but with people coming to visit family for Christmas, as well as extra orders to be shipped because of the holiday, Jackson seemed busier than ever. *Please don't disappoint Rosie again.*

Larkin brushed the hair from Rosie's face, thankful for the natural warmth of her forehead and not the burning fever that had kept the child in bed the past three days. Donning her own gown, she wondered if Jackson was poring over the stage bookwork or eating a warm meal. She wasn't certain but thought that he'd lost weight since she had first gotten to know him.

Kneeling beside her bed, she shivered and prayed, "Heavenly Father, please make a way for Rosie and Jackson to be together. Also, if You could work things out so I could leave and get my own place, I'd be forever grateful. Bless Wilma and thank You for her friendship."

She scurried into bed as she murmured, "Amen," knowing she'd be both delighted if Rosie was returned to her uncle and sad to lose the little girl she'd grown to love. She'd even miss seeing Jackson regularly.

She scooted down in the covers and snuggled up next to Rosie's warm body, hoping Maura didn't come looking for her, demanding that she return to the dinner party. And how was she going to get out of dining with Mr. Barrett? Would Maura actually punish her or perhaps even turn her out if she continued avoiding the man?

Larkin nibbled the inside of her cheek, wishing she had the nerve to tell him she wasn't interested. "Lord, make me bolder."

She closed her eyes; her body relaxed. As the fog of sleep descended, it wasn't Mr. Barrett's dreary gray eyes she saw, but Jackson's somber blue ones. He carried more than his share of concerns. She longed to rub the crease from his brow—to kiss away his pain.

Larkin's eyes darted open, and she stared into the darkness. Why hadn't she noticed before? When had it happened?

Jackson Lancaster had sneaked in and stolen her heart.

"D'you find a gal to marry yet?" Shorty peered out of the corner of his eyes at Jackson then refocused on the road in front of him, keeping the horses at a steady pace.

"Not yet." If no problems presented themselves, he'd be home by noon and have time to clean up and see Rosie this evening. Christmas was only three days away, and his hopes of finding a bride were diminishing.

"I talked with two women from neighboring towns. One was seven years older than me and had three children." It wasn't that he didn't like children, but he had Rosie to think about. Becoming an instant husband and father to one child was daunting enough.

"The other woman had an elderly mother who lives with her." Jackson's heart went out to them, but he just couldn't bring himself to ask the woman to marry him—not when a pair of moss green eyes kept invading his dreams. And that cinnamon hair. He longed to run his hand through it but tightened his grasp on his Winchester instead.

Suddenly a flame ignited, as if he'd been shot in his gut, making his whole body go limp. When had he developed feelings for Larkin? Why hadn't he noticed sooner?

Shorty chuckled. "Two women at once might be a bit to take on."

Numb with the realization that if Larkin were to accept his marriage proposal, he could have Rosie back by Christmas Eve and a wife he loved instead of some stranger, he turned to Shorty.

The driver shot several sideways glances at him and looked around. "What's wrong?"

The ricochet of rifle fire echoed across the barren landscape. The edge of the footboard in front of Jackson and Shorty shattered. Both men ducked.

"Heeyaw!" Shorty shook the reins and urged the team into a gallop as he hunkered down.

Jackson scoured the area, his heart thumping hard.

"There!" Shorty yelled and pointed with his stubbly chin.

Three riders charged out of the tree line, rifles aimed straight at the stage. Jackson fired, and one rider lurched backward out of his saddle. Below him, Cody shot from inside the stage.

How had anyone known about the payroll? He'd handled it personally. He fired again, knowing he had to live for Rosie's sake. The child couldn't lose another person she loved.

As if he'd been branded with a blazing hot iron, his left shoulder exploded with pain. Jackson didn't take time to look at his wound but raised his rifle to the other shoulder and shot another man.

The outlaw clutched his side but stayed in the saddle. He slowed and turned his horse around. With his two cohorts gone, the third thief swung around and raced back to the trees.

Even though the outlaw might have been responsible for Ben's death, Jackson couldn't shoot the man in the back, but Cody must have had no qualms about it. His weapon blasted, and the last man jerked and flew off his saddle.

Fighting intense pain, Jackson braced his feet and struggled to stay on the jarring seat as Shorty kept the team racing for Prairie Flats. Jackson yanked his kerchief out and shoved it under his shirt to stay the bleeding. Though only noontime, a foggy darkness descended, and Jackson felt himself falling.

Chapter 8

Larkin steadied Rosie's hand as she hung one of the older Christmas bulbs on the tree. Though it was still several days until Christmas, Maura had insisted the tree be up and decorated, as well as the parlor and dining rooms, before her annual December 23 dinner party. Larkin hoped the pine boughs scenting the room didn't wither before tomorrow evening.

Mistletoe hung in clumps over doorways, tied with colorful red bows. Unlit candles stood in the windows like soldiers on guard, waiting for nighttime, when they would be lit to show visitors the way. Pine boughs and red bows decorated the stairs and fireplace mantel.

Everything looked festive, but Larkin shivered at the thought of another evening with Frank Barrett. Maura had made it clear that she'd accept no excuses this time. Larkin sighed. She was expected to remain at tomorrow's dinner until all the guests left; then she was to change clothes and help Wilma clean up.

"Did you have a tree when you were little?" Rosie reached for another of the colorful glass balls.

Larkin hurried to her side. "Let me help you. And no, I never had a Christmas tree until I came to live with the O'Keefes."

"How come?" Rosie's lower lip protruded as if she thought Larkin terribly unfortunate.

"I lived in Ireland until I was eight. There are few trees to be found there, so we decorated with holly and ivy. The holly has lovely red berries on it. At Christmas, me mother would fix bread sauce made from bread crumbs, milk, and an onion with cloves stuck in it for flavoring."

Rosie turned up her nose. "I don't like yunyuns."

Larkin smiled. She turned at the sound of quickly approaching steps.

Wilma hurried into the room, her gaze jumping from Rosie to Larkin. "I need to speak with you alone."

A fist clenched Larkin's heart at Wilma's worried expression. What was wrong? Could something have happened to Jackson? That thought made her want to crumble into a huddled mass of misery. What if he died without knowing how she felt?

Larkin took Rosie's hand, forcing the horrible thoughts from her mind. She was overreacting. Wilma's distress could be the result of a simple problem, not that she was prone to hysterics. Perhaps Mrs. O'Keefe's food order for her party hadn't arrived.

"I've made some Christmas cookies." Wilma smiled at Rosie. "I don't suppose anyone would like to help me sprinkle colored sugar on them?"

Rosie bounced up and down as they walked toward the kitchen. "Me! I can do it."

"Before you can work, you need a snack." Wilma placed a plate with three cookies in front of Rosie and then set a glass of milk on the table. "Stay here and eat while I talk to Larkin."

They hurried back to the parlor and sat on the settee together. Wilma took Larkin's hands; her brows dipped down, and her lips were pursed.

"Tell me what's wrong. You're scarin' me."

"There was a stage robbery attempt, and Mr. Lancaster has been shot."

Larkin surged to her feet. "Where is he? Oh, is he. . .alive?"

Wilma nodded. "He's at Doc Grant's and will be fine. Sit down. There's more."

Larkin hurried to obey, though all within her wanted to rush out the door and over to the doctor's office.

"It seems Mr. O'Keefe and that Frank Barrett were part of the outlaw gang that's been holding up the stages. Since Barrett worked at the bank, he was privy to information about payroll deliveries. Barrett is dead, but Mr. O'Keefe is in jail. He was shot and is singing like a songbird now."

Larkin's eyes widened. She pressed her hand against her chest. "Poor Mrs. O'Keefe. Is that why I haven't seen her all day? How is she taking the news?"

Wilma's lips twisted. "Gone. On the train this morning. She was probably neck deep in all of this. That's why she kept pushing Barrett on you. Wanted to keep things all in the family."

Larkin peered around the cheerful room, such a contrast to the horrible news she'd just heard. "What will happen to all of us?"

"We're to close up the house. I don't know after that."

Larkin wrung her hands. Where would they live?

With Mrs. O'Keefe gone and Mr. O'Keefe in jail, what would happen to Rosie? Surely the judge would allow her to go back to Jackson. He would take his niece home and have no reason to visit Larkin ever again.

Could she tell him how she felt? Was it too forward of her?

She jumped up. *Please, Father, let him live.* "I must see Jackson."

"I'll watch Rosie while you go." Wilma's expression warmed, her eyes twinkling.

As the haziness of sleep fled, Jackson glanced around. He wasn't in his own bed. Where was he?

He tried to sit up, but a sudden pain in his shoulder and a pair of strong arms pushed him back.

"Hold it, young man. You've been shot."

"Doc?"

"Yep. There was a stage holdup, but you got the rascals. They won't be bothering you anymore."

Jackson lay back, his foggy mind struggling to remember what had happened. "Shorty?"

"He's fine. Just got a few scratches."

"Gotta get out of here, Doc. Need to check on Rosie." He attempted to sit up again, but the doctor held him down.

"Lie still or I'll give you something that makes you sleep. Tomorrow will be soon enough. I've already sent word about your injury and told the folks keeping your niece that you'll be fine—providing you rest."

Jackson sighed but relaxed. Had Rosie heard about his injury? Would she be worried? Would Larkin? How was a man supposed to rest when he had all these concerns muddling his brain?

A door rattled and someone entered with a swish of skirts. He hoped the doctor would pull the curtain so nobody would see him down like he was.

The swishing moved closer, and he turned his head. Larkin!

Worry wrinkled her pretty brow, and she twisted her hands together. "H—how are you? We were so concerned."

"Rosie was?"

Larkin shook her head. "Rosie's fine. She doesn't know yet. 'Twas Wilma and meself that were worried. 'Tis a relief to know you'll be fine."

He smiled and held out his hand. She stared at it, then stepped forward and clasped it. "I'll come and see Rosie when I get out of here. Probably tomorrow. Don't tell her about me. She'll just fret."

Larkin nodded. "I suppose you'll get Rosie back now."

"Why do you say that?"

Her eyes widened. "You haven't heard?"

He shook his head, wondering what she meant.

She conveyed to him what she'd heard from Wilma, who'd been at the mercantile when the outlaws were brought in to town.

Jackson stared at the ceiling. Numb. The very people who tried to take Rosie from him had most likely been responsible for his brother's death. Had it all been some big plan to steal Rosie? Or had Ben and Amanda just been in the wrong place at the wrong time? He'd probably never know.

His heart skittered. With Mrs. O'Keefe gone and her husband in jail, the judge would have to give Rosie back to him. He smiled, but when he looked at Larkin, his grin faltered. "What's wrong?"

Larkin glanced at him then stared at the floor. "I'm sure the judge will give Rosie back to you now. I'm truly happy for you."

"You don't look happy." Love for this woman warmed his whole body. He wanted to take her in his arms and kiss away her troubles. Why had it taken him so long to realize that he loved her?

"It's just that I shall dearly miss. . .Rosie."

Jackson bit back a smile. Glory be, the woman had feelings for him. They were written all over her lovely face. "Just Rosie?"

"Well. . .I. . ."

"Doc!"

Larkin jumped at Jackson's shout.

"What's all the caterwauling?" The doctor strode in, wiping his spectacles on the edge of his shirt. "Are you in pain?"

"No, but I need to sit up." Jackson sent him a pleading gaze.

"Sorry. Not today." He turned to leave.

"Wait. C'mon, Doc. A man can't ask a woman to marry him while he's flat on his back."

Larkin's head spun toward him, her beautiful green eyes wide. A slow smile tilted the lips he longed to kiss.

Doctor Grant chuckled. "Well. . .I suppose I *could* make an exception for that."

Jackson gritted his teeth, pushing away the pain as the doctor helped him up.

The man quickly left the room, a wide grin brightening his tired features.

Jackson reached for Larkin's hand and took a deep breath. She looked so vulnerable, almost afraid to hope. "Did you know the judge gave me until Christmas to find a bride or I'd lose Rosie for good?"

Larkin shook her head.

"I realized yesterday that I'd been searching in vain. The woman I love is right here. Will you marry me, Larkin? Help me raise Rosie?"

Her lower lip trembled, and tears made her eyes shine. She nodded.

He grinned.

"I love you too, Jackson. 'Twould make me very happy to marry you."

That was all he needed to hear. With his good arm, he pulled her to his side and kissed her, showing her how he felt and making promises for the future—promises he was eager to fulfill.

"Don't the candles look beautiful?" Larkin tossed the kindling she used to light the parlor candles into the fireplace. "Tradition has it that they are a symbol of welcome to help Mary and Joseph find their way as they looked for shelter the night Jesus was born."

"They'll help Uncle Jack find his way." Rosie stared at the dancing shadows the flickering flames made on the walls.

" 'Tis true. He and Doc Grant should be here soon. Let's go help Wilma."

In the kitchen, Wilma took the goose out of the oven. Its fragrant odors had been making Larkin's stomach growl for hours. "Thank you for cooking that tonight. Smells truly delicious."

Larkin lifted Rosie onto a stool. "There's one quaint custom in Ireland where the groom is invited to his bride's house right before the wedding and they cook a goose in his honor. 'Tis called 'Aitin' the Gander.' "

Rosie grinned. "You're the bride."

Larkin felt her cheeks warm. . .or perhaps 'twas just the heat of the kitchen. "Aye. Tomorrow your uncle Jack and I shall marry."

The thought of being Jackson's wife brought twitters to her stomach that had nothing to do with hunger. A knock sounded at the door, and she jumped. Her beloved was here.

Rosie slid off the seat, but Larkin beat her to the door, pulling it open. Jackson stood there, his arm in a sling and his jacket around his shoulders, blue eyes smiling.

"Uncle Jack!" Rosie wrapped her arms around Jackson's leg. He patted her head, but his gaze never left Larkin's face.

Larkin's heart flip-flopped. Oh, how she loved this man. And tomorrow he'd be her husband.

Someone behind Jackson cleared his throat. "It's cold out here. Don't suppose we could go inside where it's warm so you two could stare at each other by the fire." Doc Grant peered around Jackson's shoulder, grinning.

They hurried inside, and Larkin helped Jackson with his jacket. Rosie and Doc sat at the table. Wilma set a bowl of applesauce on the table and smiled at the doctor.

"I need to talk to you in private a moment," Jackson whispered in Larkin's ear.

She nodded and led him to the parlor. He glanced around the room at all the pretty decorations. Maura's dinner party had been canceled, but the lovely room would make the perfect spot for a Christmas wedding. Their wedding.

Jackson's gaze landed on the mistletoe over the doorway. He grinned wickedly, dimples flashing, and tugged her to the parlor entrance. "In America, we have a tradition. If two people stand under mistletoe together, they have to kiss."

Larkin's whole body went limp, and if Jackson hadn't pulled her to his chest, she was sure she'd have melted into a puddle at his feet. How was it she could come to love this man so much, so fast? His lips melded against her, and all other thoughts fled. Too soon he pulled back.

"No doubts about tomorrow?"

She shook her head. "Not a one. I've prayed hard, and God has made it clear. You and Rosie are my future."

"I feel the same way. Tomorrow can't come soon enough." He stole another quick peck on her lips and led her back to the kitchen. Jackson seated her at the table and took the place next to Larkin, holding her hand.

"I'm gonna get Christmas presents like Baby Jesus did," Rosie declared to Doc Grant.

He waggled his eyebrows at Larkin and Jackson. "I heard you're getting something really special for Christmas."

Jackson chuckled and hugged her.

"I've been looking for a cook and housekeeper." Doc Grant smiled at Wilma. "Looks like I've found one."

Larkin breathed a prayer of thanks to God, knowing her friend would have a place to work. . .and maybe more, someday.

She glanced at the table, her stomach growling. Steam rose up from the mashed potatoes. Canned green beans with bits of ham awaited them, as did Wilma's shiny rolls. Only the goose was missing.

The room quieted as Wilma carried a silver platter covered with a fragrant golden brown goose to the table. She set it in front of Jackson and stared at him. "Well. . .I guess your goose is cooked."

Doc Grant's gaze darted toward Larkin and Jackson. He burst into laughter at the same moment Jackson did. "Ain't that the truth."

Larkin failed to see the humor in the situation but laughed anyway, happy that her beloved's face held lines of joy instead of sorrow.

Tomorrow she'd become Mrs. Jackson Lancaster. She uttered a silent prayer: *Thank You, Lord.*

Bestselling author **Vickie McDonough** grew up wanting to marry a rancher, but instead, she married a computer geek who is scared of horses. She now lives out her dreams in her fictional stories. Vickie is the award-winning author of over thirty published books and novellas. Vickie is a wife of thirty-eight years, mother of four grown sons and one daughter-in-law, and grandma to a feisty eight-year-old girl. When she's not writing, Vickie enjoys reading, antiquing, watching movies, and traveling.

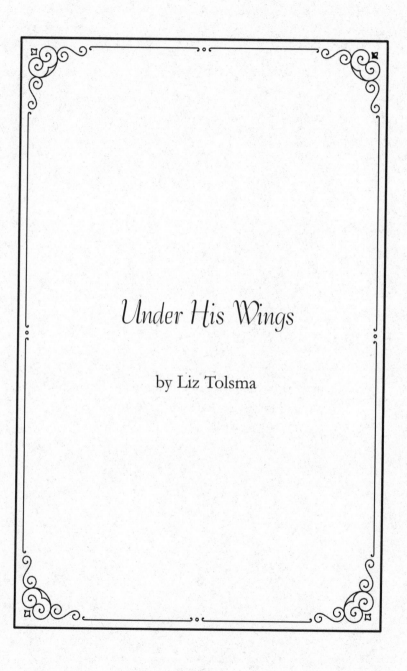

Under His Wings

by Liz Tolsma

Dedication

To Doug. Thank you for encouraging me to follow my
dream and for loving me and supporting me as
it came true. Always and forever yours.

Chapter 1

1875
Camp Twelve, Wisconsin

Adie O'Connell pictured the farm in her mind as if she'd dropped in a thousand times before. In a way she had. The little log cabin would be snug and cozy, with tight chinking and real wood floors. At one end there would be a big stone fireplace and, at the other, a loft with a ladder leading to it. She'd have a red barn, a milk cow, a chestnut mare, and lots of laying hens. In the garden she'd plant tomatoes, sweet corn, pole beans, and peas.

"Howdy, Miss Adie."

She jumped a mile, scolding herself for daydreaming again. She'd been knee-deep in her fantasy and had walked right over to Derek Owens. He leered at her as tobacco juice ran down his dirty brown beard. His perpetual habit of tobacco use had stained his teeth. The husky lumberjack spit a stream onto the floor then raked his gaze over her slender form.

"Got anything for me this morning?" Derek wiped the back of his huge hand across his mouth. A few of the men seated near him at the large U-shaped table in the mess hall tittered, though no one dared to speak. Cookie, busy in the kitchen, ruled the roost around here and tolerated no talking in his dining room.

Drawing herself to her full five-foot-three-inch height, Adie raised her chin and thumped a bowl of sausages on the wood plank table. "Here's your breakfast. Enjoy." She hoped her curt reply hid her nerves. If she let him know how much he flustered her, he would come on stronger. She'd learned that much in the years she'd worked in lumber camps.

She scurried toward the kitchen to retrieve more food for the hungry throng, not glancing back at Derek.

Cookie met her near the big woodstove, a plate of flapjacks in his hand. "Sure you don't want me to deliver these sweat pads for you? Don't want Owens giving you more trouble."

She took the dish from the slight man with only wisps of white hair left on his head. His huge gray apron hung past his knees.

"I can handle him." She smiled, loving this man who looked out for her.

Cookie wielded his spatula. "You let me know. I can give him whatnot, and he won't bother you."

"I don't doubt it." She chuckled as she pushed the swinging café doors open with her shoulder.

She paid better attention to where Derek was when she stepped into the dining room this time. She walked a wide arc around him and set the plate of pancakes on the far side of the table, not bothering to push them his way.

Derek winked at her, sending a shiver down her spine. "Hey,

Adie, I sure could use some of what you got down there."

Her hands shook, and she wiped them on her white apron, hoping to conceal their trembling. "Boys, please pass Mr. Owens some pancakes and maple syrup."

Derek sneered. "Why don't you bring it down here yourself?"

One of the jacks pounded his fist on the table. "Enough, Owens. Treat Miss O'Connell like a lady, and leave her alone."

Adie recognized the tall, lean man with eyes the color of the syrup. Everyone called him "Preacher Man" because he didn't cuss, didn't carouse, didn't womanize, and wanted to go to seminary. The moniker stuck. In fact, in the two weeks he'd been in the logging camp, she couldn't recall hearing his given name.

Derek hefted his bulk from the long bench and stood, leaning on his knuckles on the table. "What you going to do to make me?"

She feared Preacher Man's interference would make matters worse. She had enough experience following her father to the camps in the past seven years to know men like Derek Owens didn't cater to being told what to do. He might escalate his advances to spite the man.

Preacher Man rose to his feet, a head taller than Derek. "I'm asking you to be a gentleman and mind your manners. Remember what your mama taught you."

Wrong answer.

"I'll teach you what I do to a mongrel like you."

Adie knew fisticuffs would ensue, so she retreated to the safety of the kitchen, desiring not to land in the middle of the melee. If only Preacher Man had kept his mouth shut.

Noah Mitchell steeled himself for the blow to come. He'd heightened

Derek's wrath by opening his mouth to protect Adie and diffuse the situation. In the end, he'd made a mess of things.

He wouldn't fight back, but he'd turn the other cheek as the Lord commanded. He came here to earn money to go to seminary. Several winters of work might pass before he saved enough, but he would go. In the meantime, he wanted to be a Christian example to the rough, heathen men in the camp.

Around him, the lumberjacks cheered on Derek, their champion. Hoots and hollers echoed off the mess hall's log walls. Roars of approval swelled around Noah as Derek faced him. He swallowed hard, wishing the bully would get it over with. He closed his eyes. He could smell Derek's fetid breath. He locked his knees and braced himself for the pain.

Why had he made an enemy of such a man?

All at once the room fell silent. Men muttered, and he heard them shuffle to their seats.

Someone clapped him on the back in greeting. "Morning, Preacher Man."

Noah dared to open one eye.

Quinn O'Connell stood beside him, his jade-green eyes sparkling, a grin spreading across his face. Old enough to have fathered most of these men, nevertheless he was as broad as any jack and as strong.

Quinn's wild, unkempt hair made him appear a bit rough around the edges, but Noah hadn't been fooled. Quinn held a fierce love for his daughter and all that concerned her. The man had a soft heart.

Quinn commanded respect too, as evidenced by the scurrying of the men around them.

"What's going on? When I came in, Owens looked about ready to kill you." Quinn spoke softly as he and Noah took their seats next to each other on the rough benches.

"He may have if you hadn't arrived." He sat down, his knees suddenly weak.

"Did he bother my daughter again?"

Noah shrugged, not wanting to see a fight break out between Owens and Quinn. The older man wouldn't stand a chance. "I took care of it. He'll leave her be from now on."

Adie's father growled. "I'll make sure he keeps his distance."

"Please, don't."

"I won't hurt him. Not now, anyway." Quinn spun around in his seat and clomped to the other end of the long table.

Noah could do nothing more than watch the older man confront the burly lumberjack. Owens spat then nodded. He may have acquiesced for now, but Noah didn't miss the fire burning in his dark eyes.

Quinn made it halfway back to his place at the table when Adie appeared from the kitchen, a steaming coffeepot in her slender hand. Noah watched, entranced, as she sashayed to her father, stood on her tiptoes, and planted a peck on his hairy cheek.

The seasoned woodsman squeezed her and whispered in her ear. The way she gazed at him caused Noah's heart to beat faster than two jacks' sawing.

He'd better watch out. If Quinn knew how Adie affected him, Quinn would send him to the floor instead of Derek Owens. Make no mistake—the man was possessive of his daughter. He tolerated no coarse talk about her and shot dangerous looks at anyone who dared to come within ten feet of her.

Noah couldn't help but stare at the beautiful young woman. Locks of curly red hair fell about her face as she poured coffee. Her eyes, described by her father as the color of the hills of Ireland, danced in delight as Quinn teased her. Noah would give every penny of his seminary savings if she would smile at him with those full, red lips.

No, he needed a long walk in the crisp November predawn. He jumped from his spot at the table, ashamed of himself. He had no right to be thinking about Adie O'Connell in such a way.

"Thank you."

He turned and stared into her amazing green eyes.

She smiled her smile at him. "I appreciate the way you stepped in with Derek, but you didn't need to. He's not a problem for me."

"You're, uh, welcome." A smattering a red freckles crossed the bridge of her upturned nose. He couldn't bear the thought of Owens laying a hand on her. "But don't underestimate him."

Quinn stepped beside his daughter. "He won't hurt her."

Noah peered at Owens from the corner of his eye. The man scowled, and Noah didn't need to step into the Wisconsin winter to notice a chill in the air.

Noah and Quinn pulled the crosscut saw between them in an easy rhythm. Around them the music of other saws rang, punctuated by the staccato hammering of axes. The towering white pine they worked to fell had already been notched by an axe on one side. Now they labored at sawing it on the opposite side, a little above the gash. Wedges were inserted from time to time to cause the tree to fall.

"I appreciate the way you took care of Adie." Quinn wiped the back of his arm across his forehead. Temperatures may be below freezing, but the men worked up a sweat.

"My pleasure." And Noah meant it.

"I hate what this life is doing to her. I've dragged her from camp to camp in the winter and from odd job to odd job in the summer for the past seven years. It's not been easy. She's done her share of man's work without complaining, but I know she's not fond of it. She'd like to settle down, live in one spot again, but I can't. Since Claire passed, I can't stay in one place. She held our family together and helped me be a good father. Without her, I've been lost." He ran a hand through his tousled brown hair.

"Adie loves you. I can see it in the way she looks at you. She doesn't hold any of this against you."

The lines around Quinn's green eyes softened. "Adie's a good girl, especially to put up with the likes of me."

"She does more than put up with you."

Quinn shrugged. "We'd best get back to work. If I rest these old bones too long, I'll never get going again."

The men put their hands to the crosscut saw once more, working in silence. In a short amount of time they had almost completed their chore. The pine would soon fall.

Then a loud crack split the air.

A long, vertical fracture appeared, traversing the trunk and ruining the lumber. Worse, it destabilized the tree. If the jacks couldn't wedge it hastily, it would fall. And no one could predict where.

Quinn and Noah, along with other men, worked frantically, driving in wedges. The tree groaned.

"She's going, boys!" Quinn shouted.

Men scattered.

The tree leaned.

Noah watched it descend to earth.

"Quinn!"

Chapter 2

Adie plunged her hands into the hot dishwater. She hated this part of her job. Stacks of tin plates and cups surrounded her, topped by a load of greasy pans. When she completed this chore, a mound of potatoes waited to be peeled. The loggers called them murphies, which made no sense whatsoever. Over the years she had come to understand the jacks' lingo but refused to speak it.

Her hands stilled in the water as she wondered about the big, tall man who came to her defense. No doubt, he was a gentleman with perfect manners. They called him Preacher Man. Daddy told her he wanted to go to seminary someday. She didn't know his name. No one called him anything else, not even her father.

He sure was handsome—broad and strong, with brown eyes that made you think of things that caused Adie to blush. He talked like a preacher. Where did he come from?

She sighed. Her pile of dishes had not grown one inch smaller. The cup in her hand went into the rinse water.

She longed for a view of the majestic pines just beyond the log walls of the camp kitchen. Having something beautiful to look at would make her work seem to go faster. She could stand here and gaze at the snow sparkling in the sunlight.

A commotion clamored in the dining hall, jarring her back to reality.

A shout came from outside the swinging doors. "Bring him in here. Lay him on the table. Be careful. He's bad off."

Men yelled back and forth to each other.

Adie's heart rolled over.

An accident. There had been an accident.

Please, Daddy, be all right. Be safe.

She swiped her shaking hands on her apron as she hustled to see who had been injured. With every breath, she prayed she wouldn't find her father on the table.

A large crowd gathered around the wounded lumberjack. The flannel-covered backs of tall, brawny men blocked her view. Adie couldn't see who they'd brought in. She searched the sea of hats, the various sizes, shapes, and colors making it possible to distinguish the wearer. She spied Preacher Man and Derek Owens. Where was her father's dark-blue felt cap? He would be in here with the men, wouldn't he?

It doesn't mean anything that I can't find Daddy. Maybe he stayed outside with the horses. Maybe he had run to fetch the camp boss, who acted as physician. Willing her stomach to cease its jumping, she stepped into the crowd.

The noise around her ceased.

The men parted.

Her father lay, unmoving, on the table.

Everything around her became hazy. Through a narrow tunnel of light, she spied her father's pale face. Blood coursed from his temple, but his chest still rose and fell. She rushed to his side.

"Daddy."

His eyes remained closed. He lay still. So still.

Too still.

"Daddy?"

She rubbed his cold hand.

No, God, You can't do this to me again. You can't take him from me too. Do You hear me?

She turned and found herself staring into Preacher Man's warm, brown eyes. They filled with unshed tears.

"The tree split and fell. The trunk clipped him. I yelled, but he couldn't get out of the way quickly enough. I'm so sorry."

He reached out to her, but she shoved his hands aside. "He's not dead. Look, he's still breathing. Why are you standing there? Run and get Mr. Larsen. Help my father." Why was no one doing anything?

"Someone went for him, but there's not much anyone can do."

Adie stamped her foot in frustration. "Don't say that. Nothing is going to happen to him. Now do something. Anything! Boil water, or tear sheets for bandages or whatever you can think to do."

A moan sounded from beside her. She turned back. Her father's eyelids flickered.

She leaned over the man who had always been there for her and stroked his whiskered cheek. "Shh, everything's going to be all right. You'll be fine."

He parted his lips, but no sound escaped.

"Don't try to talk. Save your energy. You're going to need it when you get back to work in a few days."

Her father's mouth moved again, and this time he croaked out a word. "Noah."

Preacher Man leaned in. So his name was Noah.

"I'm here, but Adie's right. Conserve your strength. Whatever you have to tell me can wait."

Daddy moved his head from side to side, wincing. "No." He took a shallow breath. "Take care of her."

Noah's big hand covered her father's. "I will. I promise."

She didn't like the direction of the conversation. Everyone talked like her father was dying. "Why would you say that, Daddy? You're not going anywhere. We'll be together like we always have been. Come spring you'll hire on and help someone with their planting. But it will be the two of us, looking out for each other, like you said it would be, forever."

Daddy gave her hand a small squeeze. "I love you, Adie."

The lines in her father's face softened, and his hand went limp. His eyes stared blankly.

"No! Daddy, no!"

Strong arms enveloped her and kept her from falling to the floor. Noah whispered in her ear. "I'm so sorry."

She couldn't speak, couldn't think, couldn't breathe.

She was utterly alone.

Little light filtered through the cracks in the chinking of the cabin. A frigid wind blew, and ice built up on the inside of the walls.

But nothing compared to the chill in Adie's heart. When Mama had died seven years ago, she hadn't thought anything worse could happen. Well, it had. Both her parents were gone. She closed her eyes to shut out the reality of her father dying. Maybe, just maybe, when she opened them she would find this had been an awful nightmare. She would wake up, and everything would be the way it should be.

But when she did, nothing had changed. Outside, men continued to chisel her father's grave from the frozen earth. Sawing and hammering came from the blacksmith's shop next door as the jack-of-all-trades smithy constructed the coffin.

Her father's smiling eyes looked down on her from a photograph in a wood frame. Adie took the daguerreotype from the crude shelf above the stone fireplace. His hair was slicked back. She ran her finger over the glass above his image. Her mother sat beside him, prim and proper, a cameo at her delicate throat. Every chance he got, Daddy reminded Adie what a wonderful person her mother had been. He'd never stopped loving her. His grief over her death caused him to sell their farm. They became nomads, working wherever work could be had.

She couldn't blame him for wanting to escape the memories inhabiting their little log cabin. Right now she wanted to run as far from this place as her legs could carry her and never look back. Of course, it was impossible. Winter had settled into the Wisconsin Northwoods. No one would come or go for a long time.

And Adie had nowhere to go anyway. What could one woman do alone?

She sighed and replaced the picture on the shelf. Her numb mind couldn't make such decisions now. At this moment she needed to focus on getting through the next few minutes and hours. She'd worry about the future when it happened.

The cold of the room seeped into her bones, and she shivered. Without kicking off her high-button shoes, she slid under her brightly colored patchwork quilt. With frozen fingers, she traced the stitching. Her mother had sewn this quilt for her bed under the eaves in the attic. She had allowed Adie to do some of the work. Together they had chatted away the hours.

Her memories took her to the day she and her father had packed their belongings and moved from their home. They'd left so much behind, but Adie had insisted she take the quilt. Since that day it had traveled with them from place to place. Some nights it covered her in cabins such as this one, some nights in haylofts, some nights on a blanket of pine needles beneath the stars.

Always her father had been nearby. Not tonight.

Tonight she would be alone.

At last she permitted herself to grieve for all she had lost. She cried and cried until her pillow was soaked and her body exhausted.

Work stopped for only a brief time after the accident. Trees needed to be harvested, after all. The lumber company didn't want work to slack off, even because of a tragedy.

Noah sawed trees with Butch, his new partner, pulled from the swamper crew cutting limbs from trunks. Usually, the steady back-and-forth motion of the two-man crosscut saw soothed Noah. Now he couldn't keep his attention on his task. Despite the danger it posed for him, his thoughts returned time and again to Adie. His heart ached for her. Quinn had told him they had no other living kin, and Noah imagined how alone she must feel. He wanted to comfort her.

She'd felt so good, so right in his arms when he'd caught her. A wren weighed more than she did. But she was soft and warm and curved in the right places. He longed to hold her forever, to shield her from more pain.

The saw caught in the tree, and worked paused. Noah closed his eyes for a moment and erased his thoughts. He had no right dreaming about Adie like that. Her father had died a few hours ago. And he had to take care of her.

Butch yanked on the saw, and their rhythmic work started again. Noah's promise to Quinn came to mind. Even before the accident, he'd been concerned for his daughter's well-being if something should happen to him. His anxiety deepened when Derek Owens began making advances toward her.

Without her father there to watch out for her, she became a prime target for Owens and women-thirsty jacks like him. Unfortunately, there were too many unprincipled men in a logging camp. They wouldn't see another woman all winter long, so they'd try to take advantage of the one in their midst.

Noah wanted to see her protected. The thought of her falling into the clutches of someone like Owens disgusted him. She made clear her distaste for the man's suggestions.

Early on, Noah and Quinn had formed an unlikely friendship. Quinn was the only lumberjack who didn't ridicule Noah for his beliefs, the only one who listened to anything Noah had to say. So when Quinn asked Noah to make sure no harm came to Adie if anything happened to him, Noah had agreed to it without much thought. Right before he passed away, Quinn had reminded him of his promise.

He shook his head and wiped his forehead with the back of his sleeve, his plaid flannel shirt and woolen long johns damp with perspiration. His nerves were as jagged as the saw blade.

He stepped back to watch Butch hammer a wedge into the saw cut with the back of his axe. The tree creaked and moaned, then leaned. *Tiiiimberrrr.*

It plummeted to the earth with a crash.

No problems. Not like this morning.

Noah groaned. He had an obligation to the one man who didn't laugh at him or put him down. He knew he needed to keep his promise to Quinn. But how? What might be the best way of going about it? Noah felt inadequate.

Adie needed someone to watch out for her and to keep her reputation from being sullied by men like Derek Owens. A logging camp was no place for a woman alone. But what could Noah do?

Chapter 3

After work halted at nightfall, and with a hearty dinner behind him, Noah knocked on the back door of the wanigan, the company store, where Mr. Larsen slept.

"Come in."

Noah entered the boss's small and sparsely furnished lean-to. A narrow but neatly made bed occupied one wall, a colorful quilt tossed over it. Mr. Larsen sat in a straight-back chair at a long table on the opposite wall. That left little space for even as simple a task as turning around. Noah could just step inside and still have room to close the door behind him.

Mr. Larsen looked up from the books and papers spread over his desk, his glasses on the very tip of his hawk-like nose. He was probably somewhere around forty, but his importance in the camp made him seem much older. He nodded in Noah's direction. "Mitchell. Have a seat." He motioned to the bed.

Noah sat, the corn husks in the mattress rustling as he settled into position.

"I'm sorry about O'Connell. What exactly happened?"

Noah shifted, those horrible images of Quinn's accident repeating themselves in his mind. The eardrum-busting crack of the tree. The men rushing to insert wedges, racing to control the fall of the pine. The sight of the tree leaning directly over Quinn. The look of surprise, horror, fear on the man's face. The icy cold that shot through his own veins.

"It's like I told you. The tree split. Why? I don't know. We tried to wedge it to no avail. I yelled to Quinn, but it was too late." Noah closed his eyes and took a couple of quick deep breaths, trying to dissolve the lump in his throat. "He did nothing wrong. None of us did. The Lord called him home today. That's all."

"I'm sorry, Mitchell. I know you two got along real well."

"Thank you, sir." Noah cleared his throat and twisted the end of his mustache. "But I didn't come about that. Well, maybe in a way it is. I have a problem. I was wondering if I could ask your advice."

Larsen removed his spectacles and placed them on the desk. "What is it? Owens bothering you? You know, he's done nothing illegal. There's not much I can do about him. You two'll have to work it out yourselves."

The man sounded exasperated. How many others had complained about Owens?

"No, sir, it's nothing like that." He shifted, the mattress crunching beneath him. "In a way it is, though. I mean, it does involve Owens. Sort of."

Larsen tapped his fingers on his desk. He was getting impatient.

"Sir, what is going to happen to Miss O'Connell? Quinn's daughter."

"Happen to her? What do you mean?"

"She's a beautiful young woman. Some of the men have made advances toward her. Inappropriate advances." He wished he could halt the progress of the heat up his neck and into his face.

The boss leaned forward and rubbed his chin. "Go on."

"Quinn always watched out for her. Protected her. When he was around, none of the men dared to even look at Miss O'Connell. Without him here, I'm afraid of what some of them might do. She's vulnerable." A vision of Adie, her slender white hands grasping a sweating water pitcher, a red curl falling across her pink cheek, crossed his mind. "She needs someone to watch out for her."

"And you propose to do the job, Mitchell?"

"I promised Quinn several times I would take care of his daughter should something happen to him. I didn't ever think. . ."

Larsen slapped his knee. "No one ever does. And you're right. Miss O'Connell needs a protector. All the women I've ever run across in a logging camp have been married. And matronly. Never had one young and single like she is. O'Connell was a good worker and a leader. He kept the men in line, and they respected him. That's why I allowed him to bring her along. But now—well, what she needs is a husband."

Noah didn't like the way Larsen looked directly at him. His mother had that same I-have-a-chore-for-you-that-you-won't-like kind of look. One that usually meant he was about to muck out stalls.

He swallowed. "A husband?"

"If someone married her, she would come under the protection of her husband. While the men here might be wild and some would say uncouth, they wouldn't dare touch a married woman."

"Who?"

Larsen laughed. Actually laughed. The crinkles around his eyes deepened. "Seems to me, Mitchell, if you made the promise to O'Connell, it ought to be you."

Noah stood so quickly the room spun. "Me? Marry Miss O'Connell?"

"She is beautiful. Maybe a bit spirited for a quiet man like yourself, but you could do worse. Much worse."

The world tilted, and Noah reached for the rough lumber wall to steady himself. Him? Marry Adie? Couldn't he just treat her like his sister? That's what he'd had in mind when he'd promised to protect her. Not marry her. That hadn't come to mind at all when Quinn asked.

His plans did not include a wife. A spouse would change his future. With someone else to support, he would never be able to save enough money for seminary. Later, maybe, there might be room for a wife, but not now. He needed to scrimp and save every last penny to pay tuition, not have it frittered away by a woman buying lace, ribbons, and other frippery. He hadn't seen any of that on Adie, but his sisters liked those sorts of things.

He would have to give up so much to marry her.

Yet his loss couldn't compare to Adie's. He had a choice in the matter. She didn't choose to be brought to this camp, didn't choose to lose both her parents, didn't choose to be stranded, alone, and defenseless. The apostle Paul commanded Christians to care for orphans, and he supposed she fit that category. And her father told him she knew the Lord.

"Mitchell? You all right? You need a drink of water?"

Larsen's voice pierced his thoughts. For a moment the room was so silent he could hear nothing but the sputtering of the oil lamp.

Noah shook his head, clearing his mind.

He trembled at the thought of what the Lord wanted him to do. His life was about to change forever.

"I'll marry her, sir. If she'll have me."

Adie stared at the mountain of dishes that awaited her this morning.

This morning, like so many other mornings, yet so different. In one day her father had laughed with her, died, and been buried.

Everything was different.

Everything was the same.

Cookie had told her she didn't need to come to work today. If she didn't work, though, what was there to do?

She scrubbed the egg pan, telling herself her tears came from the ache in her knuckles, not from the pain in her heart.

A soft knock sounded at the swinging door. "Miss O'Connell?"

She recognized Preacher Man's—Noah's—soothing tenor voice.

She swiped away her tears with the back of her hand. "Yes."

He came through the swinging door, tall, lean, but somehow soft. Maybe it was the look of compassion in his golden-brown eyes. "I'd like to speak with you, if you have a few minutes." He shuffled his weight from one booted foot to the other.

"Just a few. I need to wash all of those." She tilted her head toward the pile of dishes.

He held the café door open for her and gestured for her to sit on one of the benches in the mess hall while he stood, then paced, rolling one end of his mustache between his fingers.

He stopped in front of her and looked straight into her eyes. "I'd like to extend my sympathies to you on the loss of your father."

She dug her ragged fingernails into the edge of the wooden

bench, willing herself not to cry. After last night, she thought she had cried all the tears in the world. But today, if she let herself give in to the grief, she knew she would weep and weep and never stop.

"Thank you, Mister. . ."

"Mitchell. Noah Mitchell. Please call me Noah."

"Thank you, Noah."

"He and I were felling the tree together yesterday. I don't know why it happened. He did nothing wrong. But he loved you very much."

She bit her lip. She couldn't speak, so she nodded. He was sweet and thoughtful, but she didn't want to talk about this.

He resumed his pacing, and she relaxed her grip on the bench. Without warning, he spun around.

"He was always concerned about you. Wanted to make sure nothing happened to you. He loved you very much and felt bad about dragging you all over the state, never giving you a place to call home."

She couldn't take any more. She rose and touched his upper arm, surprised by the firmness of the muscles. For a moment she forgot what they were speaking about. Then it rushed back.

"Mr. Mitchell—Noah—I want to thank you for your sentiments." She didn't know how many more words she'd be able to force through the narrow opening in her throat. "But truly, I need to finish the dishes and start peeling potatoes for supper. Cookie will be upset with me for wasting so much time."

She started toward the door, but he caught her by her wrist. Though his grip was firm, he didn't hurt her. She paused and turned, her face so close to his she could feel his rapid, warm breath on her cheek. "Mr. Mitchell, please."

"Miss O'Connell, I promised your father that I would be the one to take care of you if anything happened to him. For some reason he felt I could be trusted with his most treasured possession."

His eyes turned dark, and she couldn't tell what he thought.

"A lumber camp is no place for a beautiful young woman all alone. There are men who. . .who would do things."

"I assure you, Mr. Mitchell, that I can hold my own with the jacks. They don't frighten me in the least." Well, none of them but a certain Derek Owens. The man disgusted her and yes even caused her to tremble. But her father was always there to keep him in line.

Her father. Who wasn't here any longer.

Noah touched a curl that had strayed from her pins. The hairs on her arms stood up straight. This big room must be cold without the ovens going. She took a step back, and he released her wrist.

"I don't think you understand. Some men might try to take, well, advantage of you." A blush heightened the ruddy look of his face. "You need someone to take care of you, to protect you. A husband."

"A what? A husband? You have to be kidding me." Where did he get such a ludicrous suggestion? "I have no need of a husband. Besides, who would I marry? One of those ill-mannered jacks you mentioned?"

Noah turned, walked to the end of the table, gripped the edge, and then faced her. For some reason she held her breath. He put his hand over his heart and pressed his chest. "Me. You could marry me."

Chapter 4

You? You want me to marry you?" Adie's eyes widened. "What kind of crazy idea is that?"

Noah wondered the same thing. "It's not all that wild. Look, these men aren't going to see another woman until March or April. Some of them might try. . ."

Her calm voice belied the touch of fervor behind her words. "I've been in logging camps around jacks much longer than you have. Don't try to tell me what they're like. I can take care of myself."

Noah thumped himself down on the bench by the table. "I realize the idea might take some getting used to. I wasn't fond of it when Mr. Larsen mentioned it. But it's wise. If you came under my protection, as my wife, the men wouldn't dare touch you."

"This wasn't your idea? Mr. Larsen suggested it?"

"It's not that...I mean, you know, I wanted to. But I just didn't..." He was tangling himself like a dog in a leash.

She sat next to him, rubbing her hands together. "I appreciate the thought. But I'm not going to marry you. Or anyone else. I'll be fine. You'll see." She touched his arm, sending the words in his brain scrambling.

"It would be in name only. The marriage that is." Noah hated the schoolgirl blush heating his face. "If that makes a difference."

"I know you made a promise to my father, to take care of me." Her eyes sparkled with unshed tears, even as she lifted her chin. "And you're the kind of man who would never break a promise. You're noble. If it makes you feel better, I hereby release you from your vow."

Before Noah could say a word, she rose from his side and made her way to the kitchen, her skirts swishing at her ankles.

He sat there for a while running the palm of his hand over the rough wood of the bench, still warm from her body. While the idea of marrying her had sounded insane when Mr. Larsen first spoke of it, Noah knew now he had no other way of protecting her.

Cookie took one look at Adie when she returned to the kitchen and put down the potato he'd been peeling, but not his paring knife. "I seen Preacher Man out there talking to you. He giving you trouble?"

She cleared the tears from her eyes with her fingertips. "No. He, well, he proposed to me, for my own protection. If I was his wife, none of the men would bother me anymore."

"And? Are you gonna marry him?"

"No. Of course not. I have you to take care of me, don't I?" She pointed to his hand, holding the knife.

This light jesting always brought a smile to Cookie's face, but not now. "Might not be such a bad idea. I seen how Owens treats you. You can't be too careful around him. I'd think on it again if I were you."

She didn't want to think about it. Or talk about it, for that matter. "I'll finish the dishes and then help with the potatoes."

"Preacher Man wouldn't make a bad husband. He works real hard. I ain't never heard him cuss or talk coarse or nothing. Later on you might regret passing him up."

She was pretty sure she wouldn't. All she wanted was a small piece of the world to call her own, a simple log cabin, a simple life.

She stuck her hands in the cooling water and got back to her dishes. She knew her father had watched over her. The jacks respected him.

She sloshed water all over the counter, the floor, and herself, not caring about the mess. Until Derek Owens came along, she'd never had problems with any of the men. There was the time a year or two ago when a jack slapped her backside as she came around with the coffeepot, but she'd steered clear of him from then on and had no more trouble. She'd do that for the rest of the winter, and once the thaw came and the logs were downriver at the mill, she'd leave. Perhaps she'd go to Green Bay or even Milwaukee, hire on as a maid there, and save her money. If she were careful, someday she'd have enough for her own farm.

She reached for another dish to wash and with relief realized she'd reached the end of the pile. Her present state of mind had helped her get through the chore at a rapid pace.

After wiping down the counters, she headed outside to dump the dirty dishwater and to pump more. The bright sun shining off the white snow hurt her eyes but did nothing to warm the air. A chill wind blew through the clearing.

Quiet permeated the camp. Even the blacksmith's anvil remained still today. The jacks wouldn't return from the woods for hours yet, not until dark began to fall. They ate their lunch outside. Sometimes they worked at a great distance from the camp, and coming in to eat would take too much time from their jobs.

Each evening she'd waited with anticipation for her father to file into the mess hall for supper. He'd smile at her. The gesture comforted her. Someone in the world loved her.

The longing ache in her heart ripped open again. She missed Daddy. Her throat constricted. She dropped the dishwater pan on the snow and covered her face. Her breath came in gasps.

God, how could You do this to me? How could You take both Mama and Daddy from me? How could You? I'm all alone now. Do You hear me, God?

A boot crunching in the snow answered her.

A moment later, a rough hand slipped behind her neck. She ripped her hands from her eyes. Derek Owens leered at her from mere inches away. She backed up a few steps until she bumped into the log walls of the mess building. He came right after her, placed one hand on either side of her, palms against the wall, wrists against her shoulders.

He had her hemmed in.

"I've been waiting for this chance, Adie. You're a hard one to catch, but I knew I'd get you sooner or later."

Her palms began to sweat. Her heart thumped in panic. "What are you doing here in the middle of the morning?"

"I volunteered to tell Cookie we shot a deer. He needs to come skin it so we can have some good eatin' tonight. What a bonus to find you here by yourself." He touched her cheek with his rough hand.

She recoiled at his touch, trying to think of a way to escape. Maybe if she slipped under his arms and ran faster than she ever had, she could get safely back inside.

Derek spat a stream of tobacco juice into the snow, wiping his mouth on his shoulder. He leaned in, planting a hard, heavy kiss on Adie's mouth. The sickeningly sweet, pungent scent of the cheap corn liquor he loved to drink flavored his breath, to nauseating effect. Bile rose in her throat when his cracked, dry lips scraped hers.

She couldn't scream. She tried to plant her arms on his chest and push him away, but he grabbed her wrists, pinning them against the log wall. All blood flow to her hands ceased.

The blows her high-buttoned shoes landed on his shins didn't bother him. He leaned in harder. She couldn't draw a breath. The world spun. Bright colors flashed behind her eyes.

Then two hands grabbed Derek around his neck and pulled him off her. She gulped air. Noah tightened his grip on Derek, his thumbs on the shorter man's windpipe. "You'd better leave your filthy hands off this lady."

Adie wilted against the building in relief.

Noah shook him. "Stay away from her. Do you understand?"

The big man fell to his knees.

"Do you understand?"

Derek nodded. Noah released his grip and gave the jack a kick.

But then Derek stood and spun, fists balled, lunging at the slender man, who darted to the side moments before those huge fists would have connected with his stomach.

Fear jerked her legs from under her. She slumped in the snow.

The giant took another step toward Noah. Before he could strike, Mr. Larsen emerged from the wanigan. "Ah, Owens, perfect. Cookie mentioned he needed more wood chopped. Since you're free, you can take care of that. Get your axe. The woodpile's behind the kitchen."

Mr. Larsen stood with his hands on his hips. Derek searched a moment before locating his axe next to Adie. She didn't want to think about what he would have done if he'd remembered it. She'd been so afraid for Noah she hadn't noticed it beside her.

"Come on, Owens, let's go." Mr. Larsen still stood in the store doorway.

Derek surveyed Noah and Adie. Her skin felt like it crawled with ants. "This ain't over. My pa was a weak-willed man who let my ma beat up on him. I'm not like him. Not at all. I always get what I want. Watch and see if I don't."

Chapter 5

After Derek left, followed by Mr. Larsen, Noah helped Adie to her feet. Her heart trembled at his touch, along with the rest of her body. He wrapped his arms around her.

She wished she could clean the taste of Derek—with his tobacco and booze—out of her mouth.

"Can't you see you're not safe here? You need someone to protect you. You need me." He paused for a moment then tightened his embrace. "You have to marry me."

His hold warmed her. She stopped shivering, yet she couldn't bring herself to admit he was right. "You did protect me today, even though we aren't married. Derek took me by surprise and had me pinned before I could react, but Daddy taught me to fight for myself. Look, you came to my rescue at the precise moment I needed you. We don't have to be married for you to watch out for me." Relief mingled with disappointment at those words.

"I saw Owens coming through the woods as I went to join the other loggers. For a while I kept going, but God gave me this feeling that things weren't right. Part of me knew I had to go after him. If I hadn't been late today, I wouldn't have seen him. There's no telling what he would have done if I hadn't stopped him. If he surprises you again—and he will—you won't be able to protect yourself."

She tried to ignore the truth in his words but couldn't. All the labor in the camp had made her strong but hadn't made her grow or put on weight. She'd only be able to fend off Derek if she had the element of surprise on her side.

"I'll be careful. Next time I'll pay better attention."

Noah shook his head and released his hold on her.

If only Daddy were here to give her some advice. Of course, if Daddy were here she wouldn't be in this pickle. Adie didn't know what to do. How could she marry a stranger? Cookie encouraged her to do so, but what did he know about marriage and a woman's heart?

Stepping to the side and looking up, she examined Noah. A slight smile curled his lips, and something about him that she couldn't pinpoint exuded warmth and kindness.

Her father had told her Noah came to the camp this winter to earn money for seminary. He wanted to be a preacher. All the preachers Adie knew rode the circuit. They didn't settle down. Unless he wanted to be a big-city preacher. That kind lived in fancy brick houses, not in cozy log cabins. Either way, she'd be forced to give up her dream forever. She'd never have her quiet, peaceful life.

Noah reached out to her. He stopped before he touched her. "Adie?"

She turned her back to him, thinking of Derek. Her arms tingled where he'd squashed her wrists. The crush of his weight against her hadn't fully eased. What could she do to defend herself? He had well over a hundred pounds on her. If he came back for more like he promised, would it end as well as it had today? She knew the answers to her own questions.

Noah was right. She was alone. Defenseless. A lumber camp was no place for a young woman. Women worked in other camps. Much older women, married women. Or the other kind, the kind she didn't want to be, but the kind she'd end up as if Derek had his way. She'd be easy prey then for any man in the camp.

She didn't have another choice.

She turned toward Noah, staying out of arm's reach. "I'll marry you."

Noah stared at Adie as she stood by his side in her simple brown gown. He'd never seen her in anything other than her faded work clothes, covered with an apron. This must be her Sunday best.

Mr. Larsen, who served as justice of the peace among his other duties, intoned the words of the marriage ceremony. Noah didn't hear a word.

She clasped her hands in front of her so tightly her knuckles turned white.

"Do you, Noah Bradford Mitchell, take this woman. . ."

Did he? Yes, this was the right thing to do, the thing the Lord would have him do. He may never lead a congregation as their pastor, but he would serve the Lord this way.

He'd insisted the blacksmith fashion crude rings for them. Derek Owens and the others needed a visual reminder that Adie was his wife and that they had to stay away.

They said the appropriate words at the appropriate times, and so they were married.

By the time Adie returned to her little cabin after supper dishes that evening, Noah had built up the fire, and warmth enveloped the small space.

Noah. Her husband. How strange that sounded. How odd to see him in this place.

She studied him as he stirred the logs, muscles rippling under his lumber shirt. He had a strong profile with a regal-looking nose and the indefinable quality of compassion about him. And he was good-looking.

Adie heard her mother's voice in her head. "Handsome is as handsome does." So far, this applied to Noah inside and out.

She warned herself not to lose her heart to this man. God had a way of taking from her all the people she loved. Caring about another person led to heartbreak in the end. She'd have to exercise caution so she didn't come to feel for him.

He noticed her and placed the poker on the mantel, next to the daguerreotype of her parents. A picture of another couple with several children had joined it. She furrowed her brows.

"Those are my parents and sisters. While I waited for you, I brought my things from the bunkhouse. I won't get in your way, but I'd like to have my picture there too."

"I don't mind." And she didn't, until she spied his quilt on Daddy's bed. When she'd changed her clothes after the ceremony, she'd folded her father's quilt, the one from the bed he and Mama shared, and placed it in the small trunk at the foot of her bed. Noah's red star coverlet looked strange there, out of place. At least he'd kept the sheet hanging between the two rope beds.

"You are bothered. I can tell."

She shook her head, unwilling to speak the lie.

"Come on, sit down. It's been an unusual day. I made a pot of black lead." He poured them each a cup of coffee.

He sat across from her. "This is strange to both of us. We need time to get to know each other and feel comfortable together. I'll keep my promise and not, well. . .you know. But I want us to be friends. Life will be easier if we can get along."

"Thank you." She sent him a small smile to let him know she appreciated his kindness. "I'd like for us to get along." But not too well or too close. "Tell me about all those sisters of yours."

She'd picked a good topic. While she sipped her coffee, he told her about each of his sisters, their personalities, their likes and dislikes, and the families of the ones who were married. In spite of her heart's warning, she laughed when he told her how he'd teased them, pulling boyish pranks like snakes in beds and frogs in lunch pails.

"Of course, they got even with me. I remember one piece of pumpkin pie complete with a dollop of Pa's shaving cream instead of whipped cream."

She laughed, surprising herself. She shouldn't be merry so soon after her father's death, but it did warm her heart.

He leaned back in his chair and took a swig of his coffee. "Now it's your turn. What about your family? I know you don't have any siblings, but do you have cousins? Aunts and uncles?"

"I don't have any family." The ache in her chest returned full force and then some. She wanted this conversation to end. Scraping her chair back, she stood. "It's been an exhausting day. I'm going to retire. Good night."

He opened his mouth as if to question her but slammed it shut.

"Good night, Adie. Sleep well."

As she closed the sheet that served as a curtain, the one separating her from her husband, she remembered how her parents said good night. Such a tender look would pass between them. Her father would take her mother in his arms, hold her close, whisper into her hair, and kiss her for a long time.

The memories brought tears to her eyes. The knowledge that she would never have that kind of relationship sent them streaming down her face.

Noah thunked his forehead with the palm of his hand. How could he be so stupid, bringing up her family like that? They had been having a good time, getting along. She laughed in all the right places and put him at ease. Then he had to go and mention her family, right after her father passed away. What a *dummkopf*. He knew she didn't have any family; Quinn had told him more than once.

From now on he would need to choose his words with care. He knew he had to protect her from the uncouth men in the logging camp. He didn't realize he'd have to protect her from himself.

Chapter 6

Adie washed, dressed, and left the cabin the next morning before Noah woke. He marveled at the long hours she worked. At four, Cookie woke them with his call, "Daylight in the swamp," and they were at the mess hall by four-thirty. He never thought about how early Cookie and his assistant rose to have the meal ready.

Anticipation swelled in him when he thought about her. His wife. To care for and watch over. The task almost overwhelmed him. She'd be part of his life from now until he died.

On the short walk to the mess hall, he met some former bunkmates. Roger, the one with a spotty beard, clapped him on the back. "So, Preacher Man, you enjoy your wedding night?"

He tried to convince himself that the wind made his cheeks burn.

"How lucky to have a woman to keep you warm. Wish I had one."

He let them believe he and Adie had a true marriage, to keep them from bothering her.

As they entered the mess hall, he spied her bringing pancakes from the kitchen. The men broke Cookie's absolute silence rule as she came with the sweat pads. "Morning, Mrs. Mitchell," they chorused. An invisible brush painted her cheeks pale pink. My, she was beautiful. Part of him came to life when he gazed at her.

She sashayed to his side, and a red curl, escaped from its pins, bounced along. "Good morning."

He grinned like a kid with a peppermint stick.

A jack at the far end of the room shouted, "Come on. Kiss her already."

The men pounded on the table. "Kiss her! Kiss her!"

Cookie emerged from the kitchen, glaring at those who broke his no-talking rule. Noah asked Adie the question with his eyes. She nodded. He rose and wrapped his arms around her. Their first—and probably their last—kiss happened in front of a crowd. He bent and placed his lips against hers. They were warm, soft, and tasted like syrup. She leaned into him. Everything faded but the whoosh of blood in his ears.

The men cheered, and they parted after a too-short time. Cookie raised his voice. "Enough. If you want breakfast, you'd best be quiet."

As if doused with ice water, they hushed. Noah, awash in embarrassment, shoveled pancakes on his plate and drowned them in butter. Adie returned to the kitchen, a rush of cold air filling the void beside him. He missed her.

He remembered the promise he made last night. He had to round up his stampeding emotions before he hurt her.

Only the scrape of forks against tin plates made noise. But the stares of the men dug into him, like his mother's when he'd been up to something.

He hurried, wondering which dish Adie had prepared—sweat pads, cackleberries, or doorknobs. Ma would scoff at his jack lingo and tell him to speak proper English.

With his stomach satisfied, he went to find her. He had to see her. Sometimes she came with Cookie when he brought pots of steaming soup, but not always.

"Where you going, Preacher Man?" Derek, stationed in front of the kitchen door, spat the words. No one could mistake the challenge in his voice and tone. He might be sober at breakfast, but liquor was sure to make him feel bulletproof by sundown. Bulletproof enough to challenge Noah with more than words. Best to set Derek straight now, in front of everybody.

Noah leaned around his rival, placing his left hand on the table. The hand with the crude ring. "I'm going to see my *wife*."

Derek spoke through clenched teeth, his chaw bulging in his cheek. "You made a mistake. I'd wager the marriage ain't real. Hope you don't regret it, 'cause things ain't over between us."

Back in the kitchen, Adie tried to concentrate on frying bacon. Not that concentrating on anything was easy, considering Noah's kiss. She knew they had to put on a show for the jacks, but, against her will, she wished the kiss could have been real.

Noah's gentleness proved such a contrast to her vile encounter with Derek. The pleasant aroma of shaving cream clung to his face, making her want to draw closer. His lips, which she felt certain had never spat tobacco juice or touched a drop of strong drink, felt full and luxurious—yet unmistakably manly. When they broke away from each other, she'd sensed he hadn't been unaffected. Had she seen a flicker of longing, of what could be?

No. You can't think these things. This is a marriage of convenience. That's all.

The sound of the door opening completed her journey back to reality. She turned to see Noah. Instead of the soft look he'd worn after their kiss, the angles of his face were hard. He bore the stance of a rabid dog straining to be let loose. All fantasies evaporated. "What's wrong?"

"Stay away from Owens."

"Why?"

"Have Cookie bring out the platters. Or I'll serve. And don't go outside for water. Cookie can."

"He won't hurt me."

"Was I wrong about him coming after you?"

Every ounce of her hated admitting defeat. She didn't want anyone to know she was afraid. "I'll be careful. I promise."

He touched her upper arm. The heat of his hand soaked through her cotton sleeve and made her shiver. "Come with Cookie when he brings lunch. I don't want you alone."

The old man piped up from the big griddle across the room. "Don't worry none. I got my eye on her."

Adie laughed. Now two men observed her every move. Soon they'd be escorting her to the outhouse.

Noah touched her cheek then stepped back. "Don't go out alone. Cookie can walk with you wherever you need to go."

She couldn't suppress her giggle.

"What's so funny?"

"We've been married less than a day, and already we're thinking the same thoughts. Mama and Daddy finished each other's sentences." She warned her heart not to get attached. She'd had enough heartache.

Compassion filled Noah's eyes. "See you later."

"You be careful too."

She couldn't bear another loss.

Adie had two Dutch ovens from tonight's stew to wash, and then she'd be finished. She longed to return to the cabin. How would she and Noah spend their evening? She recalled Mama darned socks or mended petticoats while Daddy whittled, their cabin snug against the bitter winds. Daddy had done a great job with the chinking. Not a finger of cold had seeped through.

That was all she wanted. Not a big house with so many rooms you got lost, but a cozy cabin with a loft. She'd slept in their cabin's loft before Daddy had started wandering. In the summer, rain pattered on the roof inches from her head. In the winter, frost covered the windowpanes and hoary nails in the eaves.

Her daydreams took her so far from Camp Twelve that she jumped out of her skin like a snake when two hands grabbed her around the waist. She yelped and spun around, planting her foot in the man's belly.

She'd expected Derek. Instead she found Noah, doubled over, clutching his midsection, groaning.

She covered her mouth in horror. "I'm so sorry. Please forgive me."

Cookie rushed to Noah's side. "You gotta watch out for that gal. She's tiny, but she's got a mean punch."

Noah nodded but didn't speak. She pulled over Cookie's bean-snapping chair. "I'm sorry. I know I hurt you, but did I do permanent damage? Do you want some water?"

He waved her away. "I'm fine."

"I thought you were Derek. I was daydreaming, and you scared my heart right out of me. Forgive me? Please?"

She put on her best I-won't-do-it-again face, the one her father couldn't resist.

"Your father taught you to fight well. Next time I'll be noisier."

He hadn't forgiven her. He must be upset. But if she thought about it, he shouldn't have come from behind her. What had he been thinking?

"What are you doing here?"

"I came to see you home. I don't want you out alone, even a short distance."

She repented of the bad things she'd thought. "I'm almost done."

She hurried through the rest of the pots. Before long, she and Noah entered their cabin. A toasty room greeted her.

A book, papers, a pen, and an inkwell littered the tiny table. Curiosity overcame her, and she went for a peek. She sat in the chair, her feet grateful to rest.

The book was a Bible, its leather cover worn. Guilty about snooping, she didn't read the papers.

Noah sat opposite her. "It's a letter to my mother. I can't send it until spring. More than likely, we'll be home before it arrives. But Ma said to tell her all about camp life. I write a little every night."

"Did you write about our marriage?"

"Yes. Would you like to read it?"

She was afraid of what he might have said. "No. Will you tell her I kicked you?"

Noah guffawed, the sound as rich as pound cake. Maybe his laugh meant he wasn't as angry anymore. "Only if you want me to."

"We'd better skip that."

"Would you like to write something?"

A sudden shyness stole up on her. "I wouldn't know what to say."

"You'll love my mother. And she'll love you." He embraced her hand with his own. Unbidden tears welled in her eyes. Oh, to have a mother again.

He removed his hand, leaving her bereft. Her reaction caught her off-guard.

He opened his Bible. "I'd like to read."

She stood. "I'll leave you alone."

He motioned for her to sit. "I'd like to have devotions with you."

She perched on the edge of her chair, tentative. Daddy had read his to himself. She hadn't read the Bible in ages. Her mother's sat in the bottom of her trunk. She didn't understand how God could take Mama from the daughter who desperately needed her.

"I'm going through the Psalms. I'm up to 103. Is that all right?"

She nodded, and he began. She didn't hear most of the passage until he said, "Like as a father pitieth his children, so the Lord pitieth them that fear him."

Did the Lord pity her? Did He love her? She didn't think so. Otherwise He wouldn't have left her without parents and married to a man she didn't know.

He finished reading and she stood suddenly, knocking over her chair, hurrying from the room.

Chapter 7

As it often did, the rhythm of the crosscut saw grinding through the sweet pine carried Noah's thoughts far away. In the past weeks, they'd wandered to Adie.

Butch, his partner, broke the tempo, wiping his sweaty forehead and stretching his muscles. "What's eating at you, Preacher Man? Your eyebrows are scrunched."

Noah made an effort to smooth them. "Nothing."

"There can't be trouble with your wife already. You've been married less than a month."

If Quinn were here—and if he weren't Adie's father—he'd let the words flow like water. But Butch wouldn't understand. On the surface, things with Adie sailed smoothly. Noah anticipated the evenings, when they sat and chatted.

But when talk turned personal, things changed. She withdrew. Most of the time she fled before prayer.

Why couldn't he break through her defenses? They'd be together forever. He wanted to know her. Why couldn't he get close? What caused her to shut herself away?

Butch wouldn't understand.

"No trouble. I couldn't ask for a better wife."

"You sure couldn't. You landed a beauty, with her curves and the way she swings her hips."

Noah's breakfast hardened in his stomach. "That's no way to talk about a woman, especially not my wife. Let's get back to work."

Butch picked up his end of the saw and shrugged. "Sure wish I had a woman like that."

The lump in Noah's gut grew. Were others speaking the same things about his wife?

Adie inhaled, enjoying the soft, cool air after the heat of the stoves. Her boots crunched on the snow as she and Noah walked home one evening. The stars in the inky-black sky danced for them. Not a breath of wind blew. Temperatures were almost balmy.

"Do you mind if we take a walk?" She had a question to ask him, but her nerves acted up. Perhaps it would be easier if she couldn't see him.

Noah, wearing his lumberjack coat with a bright-red scarf, strode beside her. "Let's stay around the clearing. We don't need problems with Owens." He sounded troubled.

They strolled in silence, their feet breaking the sheen of ice before sinking into soft snow. All the while, she contemplated how to phrase the question. Her future loomed in front of her. She knew it wouldn't be what she wanted, but she desired to know what it would be.

Without warning, she stumbled into a hole in the snow left by another's foot. Noah reached to steady her and then offered his arm. She wrapped her fingers around his elbow. Now her heart tripped.

When the tip of her nose stung from the cold, she decided she had to ask. No better way, she supposed, than to come out with it.

"Where is your seminary? Will we go there right away in the spring?"

The footfalls beside her paused, and she stopped too. She could almost hear him holding his breath.

Very softly, so quiet she almost missed his answer, he said, "I won't be going. I'm not going to be a pastor."

Did he speak those words? "Why not?"

"Things have changed." He didn't elaborate, and she chose not to press him.

Her hopes for the upcoming years brightened. His father farmed, and perhaps Noah would too. "We could homestead somewhere. Minnesota or Iowa."

"No, I'm not going to farm."

"Cattle ranching? One of the farmers Daddy and I worked for last summer headed west." The desert and mountains were dry, but there had to be trees along the rivers for their cabin.

"Maybe I'll try my hand at banking. Bankers lead a settled life. We'll go to my parents' home while I look for a job. I think Madison or even Milwaukee."

A banker? In the city? His voice fell flat, devoid of enthusiasm, not like when he spoke about pastoring. Banking wasn't his dream. What had changed that he couldn't or didn't want to go to seminary?

Her. That's what.

They had married. Now the lumber company fed and housed

them. When spring came, that would disappear. He'd be financially responsible for her. The money he'd saved for seminary would be used to provide food and shelter for her.

All her energy drained away. She withdrew her hand from his elbow. "I'm tired. Let's go home."

What could she do? Her best course of action might be to have the marriage annulled as soon as the thaw came. Then he'd be free.

It could be her Christmas gift to him.

The moon rose and cast its pale light across Noah's face. Lines radiated from his eyes and etched paths around his pinched mouth. He'd given up everything to marry and protect her. She hadn't realized that. Her husband was the most unselfish man she'd ever met. Her heart swelled even as it broke into thousands of tiny pieces.

Noah walked beside his wife, gulping lungfuls of mid-December air. Adie's question started him thinking. He hated contemplating the future.

Since he was little, he'd loathed farming. The smells from the cows and pigs had caused him to upchuck more than once. He'd been ashamed of being so weak, but he was powerless against it. As the only boy, he'd had no choice but to help his Pa. He'd had to do his share of the chores.

When he was fifteen or sixteen, a guest pastor spoke at church. He'd never forget the passage the reverend preached on. "Lift up your eyes, and look on the fields; for they are white already to harvest." God had stirred his soul, and Noah had known he'd found his calling.

Or he thought he had. Now he needed a new profession. One that didn't require an education he had no means to finance. Banking sounded dreary and dull. He hated the idea of being surrounded by money all day. But he had to find work because he had a wife.

Adie finished the dishes early a few nights later. She swept the floors and insisted Cookie retire. Noah hadn't arrived, but she decided not to wait for him. What could happen between here and the cabin? She wouldn't be out of screaming range of her husband.

She slipped on her long, blue wool coat and snuffed out the lights. In the depths of winter, the nights were dark and long.

Jack Frost worked hard. A frigid blast met her as she stepped outside, the weather far different from a few nights ago. Fat snowflakes whirled around her, a storm in the making. Lowering her head, she pushed forward.

She hadn't progressed more than a few feet when she ran into a hard, solid object. A man. "Noah, I'm sorry I didn't wait. We finished early, and I started home. But I'm glad you're here."

"I'm glad you're here too." Derek sneered.

Chilled to the bone, Adie attempted to sidestep the tree-trunk frame of the man in her path. He shifted behind her, grabbed her wrists, and held them both in his huge hand. With his other hand, he covered her mouth. Pressing forward, he pinned her against the mess hall wall, his hand still over her mouth. His rancid breath passed across her neck.

She struggled against his weight.

He crushed her.

She gasped.

He spit tobacco into the snow then wiped his beard across her back. Her stomach heaved, but she refused to vomit.

"You listen up good. I aim to have you. You tell your old man that he needs to be on watch. One day, I'm gonna come for him."

Chapter 8

T he snow drifted through the air.

Adie no longer thought it pretty as Derek crushed her against the rough logs.

His lips stung her neck.

She detested him.

He backed away.

She crumpled to the ground. The crunching of his boots faded.

Then she heaved.

She sat and trembled for a while before Noah arrived.

"Adie? Adie!" He rushed to her side, wrapping her in his arms. He felt so wonderful, so secure, that once her stomach was empty she cried.

He lifted her as if she were a child and carried her to the cabin.

He tucked her in bed, folding the quilt around her. All the time, she sobbed, unable to stop her tears.

With the coverlet over her, he removed her high-button shoes. His respect for her modesty touched her. She wept harder. He sat beside her, holding her hand, stroking her hair.

A while passed before she'd exhausted her store of tears.

He touched her forehead. "You don't have a fever. Do you still feel ill?"

She shook her head. Though her stomach had quit heaving, it rolled whenever Derek's words echoed in her mind.

"Did you eat something that didn't agree with you?"

She didn't want to alarm him or make him worry, but she had to tell him. He needed to know.

"Derek threatened us."

Owens. Hot anger and cold fear blasted through Noah as he stood over Adie. "What did he do to you?" He became aware of a bruise darkening her forehead. *Dear God, don't let him have touched her.*

She sat and steadied herself. Regret coursed through him. He shouldn't have been so harsh. He knelt beside her. "I'm sorry. It's just that if he. . .I couldn't stand it."

"No. No. He didn't hurt me." The black-and-blue mark on her face belied that. "Cookie and I got the dishes done ahead of time, and I wanted to get home, so I left without you. I walked smack into Derek."

She closed her eyes and took a deep breath. "He told me you needed to watch out for him, that he was coming for you. When he was finished with you, then he could have me all to himself. I think he was threatening to kill you."

She might be right. He wasn't afraid for himself, however. His concern lay with her. Their marriage had done nothing to halt Derek's advances. Instead, it emboldened him.

Quinn had entrusted Noah with his beautiful, beloved daughter. She'd had two run-ins with the louse. He'd failed to protect her. What if Owens didn't back off next time?

The picture of Owens with his hands on her blinded him with rage. She'd become important to him. A sense of comfort and a feeling of home had filled him as he'd watched her mend his shirts and darn his socks, shadows from the flickering firelight dancing across her freckle-spotted face. The gesture was personal and intimate.

She stared at him, her pupils wide in her emerald eyes.

He held her hand, rubbing small circles over the back of it. "Don't worry about me."

"But Derek can't get to me unless he gets rid of you. Our marriage was a mistake. Now you're in more danger than me."

He remembered the emotions streaming through him when he'd discovered her in the snow, sick and sobbing. Her tears felled him. He was as helpless to stop his feelings as he was to stop a toppling pine.

He studied her. Her sunset-colored hair, her sparkling eyes, her proud chin, her soft cheeks, her gentle hands—all mesmerized him.

Far more than that, her lively, charming disposition and caring spirit captured him. She adored Cookie and worked hard to make the older man's burden lighter.

What were these strange, tingling feelings coursing through his soul?

She cupped her hand over his whiskered cheek. "Please be careful, Noah. I couldn't stand it if I lost you too."

In that instant he identified his feelings.

He loved her.

Noah ambled with Adie through the freshly fallen snow on the way back to their cabin the following night, her arm looped through his. They were joined, connected, and it felt right. He hadn't expected love to happen, but it had. You can't put water back in the pump.

He'd walked her to the mess hall this morning, not leaving until Cookie had arrived. Before breakfast, he'd reported last night's incident to Mr. Larsen. His boss had claimed he could do nothing.

Nothing.

No one had witnessed last night's exchange. Derek would deny it. Mr. Larsen warned him to be extra vigilant the next few days.

He kept his eye on Owens during work, barely caging his rage. He stayed in the dining hall after supper, helping her, and now walking her home.

His newly discovered love grew. He wanted to learn everything about her. Maybe she would trust him enough someday to open up. He wanted to woo her.

When he'd hung up her coat last night after she'd slept, he'd tucked her mittens into her pockets. A crinkling had come from one, and he'd felt a piece of paper. Had Owens slipped her a threatening note? He'd retrieved it. Before him, sketched in pencil, had been a little log cabin. She must have drawn it herself. He'd held his breath as he stared at the beautiful likeness. The proportions had been perfect, the details amazing. She'd included knots in the trunks and traced each chimney rock.

He twirled his mustache as they walked along, wanting to ask her about it, but she yawned. "I'm so tired. You must be exhausted, doing my chores after logging all day."

He stifled a yawn and chuckled. "Guess I am. Maybe we should have devotions and head for bed." The drawing could wait.

Once at the chilly cabin, they settled in for Bible reading. He chose Psalm 91. He wanted to reassure Adie—and himself—that the Lord watched over them.

"'He that dwelleth in the secret place of the most High shall abide under the shadow of the Almighty. I will say of the Lord, He is my refuge and my fortress: my God; in him will I trust. Surely he shall deliver thee from the snare of the fowler, and from the noisome pestilence. He shall cover thee with his feathers, and under his wings shalt thou trust: his truth shall be thy shield and buckler.'"

He peered at her. Tears ran in rivulets down her pale cheeks. He bolted from his chair, flying to her side, grasping her hands. "What's the matter? Did Derek threaten you again?"

Adie shook her head, unable to turn off her tears for the second night in a row.

She'd never been one to cry, but the words Noah read tonight probed all her pain. Ever since Mama had died, and then Daddy, she'd had difficulty reconciling the idea of a loving God with the things happening in her life. Why did He leave her alone in the world? Why did He allow Derek to threaten her and force her to marry a man she'd spoken less than a dozen words to? In this passage, God spoke to her. After all these years, He had a message for her.

"Read it again."

He returned to his chair and traced his finger over the page. "'And under his wings shalt thou trust.'" She stopped him.

"Under his wings." The concept drew her back to sunny childhood days. Daddy had bought Mama laying hens as a birthday surprise. At first they hadn't collected many eggs. They'd allowed some to hatch to increase their flock. She'd loved to watch the fluffy chicks scurry about the coop. When she'd bend to scoop some into her apron, they'd scatter and dart under the hens' wings. Their mothers protected them from Adie's chubby, too-tight grasp.

Was God like that? Did He protect her like the hens protected their chicks? Another memory bombarded her—their log cabin, alone in the Big Woods. No matter how fierce the winter winds had howled, her family had remained snug and secure.

"Is that what God is like? Like the walls of a log cabin keeping out the snow and the predators?"

His eyes shone in the lamplight like melted chocolate. "Yes, I suppose He's as dependable as these four walls. That's a beautiful idea. So perfect. We need to trust with a childlike trust that God will protect us."

She wanted to believe him more than she had wanted to believe in fairy princesses and handsome knights when she was young. "If only I could."

Noah lay in bed and stared into the darkness. Adie had yet to open up to him, but after tonight he held out hope that perhaps he'd thawed the tiniest bit of her barrier. To get her to confide in him might take a long, long time. Noah would wait. Love demanded patience. One wrong word might send her skittering away forever.

His plan to win her heart would commence, though. And he knew the perfect Christmas gift for his wife.

Chapter 9

Adie turned the bread dough, dug in the heels of her hands, stretched away, gave it a quarter turn, and dug in again. She loved to knead. The rocking lulled her, pulling her into her dreams. She imagined firelit shadows on a log wall and a family, happy, laughing, loving. Turning the dough, the dream changed, new shapes appearing.

Two heads, bent over a book, one lean body much taller.

The dreams faded, and her musings wandered to Noah. Gentleness tinged his touch when he'd tended to her after the run-in with Derek. His arm around her ill body had lent her peace and comfort. It had been right that he was there. She'd seen Daddy embrace Mama much the same way when she'd felt sick or had been upset.

When he'd scooped her up and carried her home, his beating heart had knocked against her ribs. They connected. They shared the same fear and pain and formed a marriage union. That circumstance linked them forever.

Adie rounded the dough and patted it. Smooth as a baby's bottom. She divided it into four pieces, shaped them into loaves, set them in pans, covered them with towels, and pushed them to the back of the counter to rise.

She wiped her flour-coated hands on her big apron.

After Noah had laid her in bed the other night, he'd clucked over her like a mother hen.

There appeared that hen image again. This time Noah was the hen, removing her shoes, tucking her into bed, watching over her, protecting her. If she had both God and Noah shielding her, then why did Derek continue to bother her? If God took care of her like He said He did in that psalm, why did she find herself in this situation?

She turned toward the pantry to get flour for pies. Distracted by her contemplations, she rammed into a body. She jumped.

Derek!

Gnarled fingers clasped her forearms. "Whoa, there!"

It was Cookie. She told her heart it could start beating again.

"You're 'bout as skittish as that colt I bought for my Jane one year. He'd eye her, watching, wary, and when she'd get close to him, he'd back up in his stall so far I was afraid he'd kick himself a hole in the wall and take off for the pasture."

"I'm sorry. Did I hurt you?"

The wizened man released his grip and examined himself. "Looks like I'm pretty much in one piece. When you're my age, that's a mighty good thing to say."

She giggled. Cookie had a way of turning on the sunshine. He watched out for her too. Between him and Noah and God, Derek shouldn't be a problem.

But he was.

"Now you've gone and gotten sad looking. What's troubling you?"

Would he understand everything happening inside her soul? "I have so many things whipping around my brain, I wouldn't know where to start." Her life felt like river rapids, running over rocks, redirecting course at a moment's notice.

"Things been changing for you an awful lot. That's enough to upset anyone. But you want to know a secret?"

She brightened and leaned near so he could whisper in her ear. She loved secrets. As a schoolgirl, her classmates had confided their deepest and darkest desires because they knew she'd never tell. "Go ahead."

"Noah loves you."

She hopped back. Did Cookie murmur those three words? "Noah loves me?"

"Hush now, gal—it's supposed to be a secret."

"How do you know this? Did he tell you?"

"Nope. He didn't have to. I just looked at him looking at you. He can't help himself. He's got it worse'n a cat's got fleas."

"That's such a lovely, romantic picture, Cookie."

He tipped his head and shrugged. "My Jane seemed to think I was pretty romantic. Anyways, only a man crazy in love would do dishes without being hounded. And I seen the way he puts his hand on your back when you two leave. Yup. He sure does love you."

Cookie must have been touched in the head, perhaps even a mite senile. Noah didn't love her. Theirs was a marriage of convenience. At his suggestion.

He couldn't love her.

Cookie continued toward the stove and his simmering soup while she continued to the pantry. As she loaded the apples in her apron, she considered the old man's words. She had married the kindest, most thoughtful man. He took his promises and obligations seriously. The look in his cinnamon-brown eyes caused a giggle to slide up her throat. Maybe a bit of truth hid in Cookie's words.

And Noah gave up his one dream for her. He didn't speak of it much, but when he did she caught the pain that flashed in his face. He wanted to be a preacher. And he'd be a good one. He answered her few questions with care and listened to her thoughts as though they were profound.

Put all together, did that mean he loved her? She dumped the apples on the big scarred farmer's table in the middle of the room. She'd forgotten the flour. Before she could retrace her steps, Cookie interrupted with a wave of his wooden spoon. "I got you a Christmas present."

Her heart skidded. She didn't have anything for him. "What is it?"

"Now, if I up and told you, it'd ruin the secret."

She could keep secrets, but she detested not being told one. Cookie knew that. "That's not fair. Please tell me."

"Nope. You gotta guess."

The worst punishment. "I hate guessing."

"Then I won't tell you." He turned his attention to the beef soup.

She gave an exaggerated sigh. "A palace of gold?"

"Be reasonable, gal."

"Okay, a new apron."

"Better guess. But not right."

The man downright relished teasing her. "A china doll with eyes that open and shut."

"Now where'd I get that? The wanigan don't have none."

"I guessed three times. Now you have to tell me."

"Who made up that rule? I'm not telling you."

Men were the most infuriating creatures God made. She took two steps toward the pantry.

"I'm giving you Christmas Eve supper off so you and Noah can spend it together, without them other men there. Maybe he'll even tell you he loves you himself."

Christmas Eve. Tomorrow night. The night she planned to give Noah her gift. "I can't leave you to do the cooking and dishes yourself. That's too much."

"It'll be soup and cold sandwiches. The men'll have their Christmas goose the next day." He took the empty water pail and exited through the back door, ending the conversation.

Daddy had always made Christmas a nice celebration for them. Before they came to the camp in the late fall, he'd hide away a few sticks of peppermint candy and some small item—hair combs, fabric for a new dress, the photograph of him and Mama that sat on the mantel.

This year she dreaded it. Knowing Noah loved her would make it a hundred times more difficult to set him free.

Noah and Adie hung their coats on the peg driven into the log near the door before rubbing their hands together in front of the fire. Even though the walk between the mess hall and their tiny home took three minutes at the most, with the temperature plummeting below zero tonight, their fingers froze in that short time.

Noah cast a glance at his wife. She turned away and studied her red hands as if they fascinated her. Several times this evening, while they'd done dishes and swept the floor, she'd also glanced his way. She peeked at him again, a quizzical look slanting her auburn brow.

"What is it? Do I have crumbs in my mustache?" He twirled the end.

Ribbons of pink streaked her cheeks.

She shook her head. "I was thinking."

"About what?"

She paused. "Nothing." With a swish of her skirts, she twirled toward the table and sat down. "What is this? Where did you find it?"

Adie held the log cabin drawing in her hand. He'd neglected to put it away before he went to fetch her. The few minutes each day he had here without his wife he spent whittling and fashioning her gift. He'd finished it tonight, imagining the look in her green eyes when he presented it to her.

"I wasn't snooping. The night of your encounter with Derek, I stuck your mittens in your coat pocket. The paper crackled, and I was afraid I'd wrinkled it, so I took it out to see. It's beautiful. It's so realistic it could almost be a photograph. Did you draw it?"

She nodded. "My parents and I lived there. I never wanted to leave. Every night I dream of returning. I drew this picture a summer or two ago, so I would never forget."

He couldn't wait to give her the replica he'd made. If he hoped before she'd be pleased, now he knew without a doubt that she'd love it. He almost reached under his bed to give it to her now, but then decided against it. Tomorrow, Christmas Eve, he'd hand it to her. Perhaps in her eyes he'd spy the same love he felt.

Chapter 10

Adie's ham, baked in apple cider in the kitchen's oven, sat on the tiny table in the cabin. The mashed sweet potatoes, smothered in butter, were whipped up fluffy. At the center of the table, on top of her mother's special violet-dotted tablecloth, stood a three-layer spice cake, slathered in buttercream frosting.

She sat in her chair, its curved arms smooth from years of use. Tonight she didn't mend or knit but twisted her fingers as she thought about giving Noah his Christmas gift, the gift of freedom. If he did love her, he wouldn't be happy. She'd have to convince him it was for the best.

And it was.

An inexplicable sadness settled over her. She'd miss him. She'd come to care for him. He'd been so good to her—how couldn't she?

When she left in the spring, she'd be alone, nowhere to go, no one to go there with, only God and His promise to keep her under His wings. That would have to be enough.

Tonight she'd taken her time to look her finest, sweeping up her curls and putting on her best dress, her wedding gown. She smoothed the brown poplin against her lap.

The door swung open, and Noah arrived in a blizzard of snow and sleet. "That storm is something." He stomped the snow from his boots and unwound his muffler.

She ran to assist him. "Warm yourself by the fire, and I'll pour the coffee."

He looked at the table. "Is this your surprise?"

She tugged at her sleeves. "Do you like it?"

He stopped in front of the fireplace and rubbed his hands together. "You made all of it?"

She nodded.

"I say we hurry and pray so we can eat."

He liked it. Now if only he'd eat slowly, prolonging the time before she told him the rest.

An hour later, he wiped the ends of his mustache with his napkin and leaned back. "That was the best meal I've had in a long time. Almost as good as Ma's."

Though better than his mother's would have been nice, she accepted the compliment. She wanted to enjoy the evening, but anxiety was about to burn a hole through her stomach. Maybe it was best to just say it.

She wished she didn't have to hurt him. She felt his pain as her own.

"Adie, what's wrong? You look distressed."

She couldn't hide it any longer. "I have to tell you something."

He sat forward. "What? I'm not going to like it, am I?"

"It's my Christmas gift."

"Why are you upset? I'm sure I'll love it."

"I appreciate how you stepped forward to take care of me. That cost you your dream. I don't want to steal that. I'm giving you your freedom. Come spring, I'm leaving. Alone. We'll have our marriage annulled."

Mama would've told him to shut his mouth 'cause he'd catch nothing but flies. "What are you saying?"

"In the end, you'll be happy. It's for the best."

He stood, towering over her, his words firm. "No, it's not." He lowered his voice. "*I* made the decision to marry you—voluntarily. I knew the cost."

She peered back, not intimidated. "I won't stand in the way of what you want."

"What if I want you?"

He didn't know what he said. Adie shook her head. "My mind is made up."

He stomped to the door and grabbed his jacket from the hook.

"Where are you going? It's storming, and the temperature's dropping. You'll freeze to death."

"And that wouldn't bother you much, would it?"

Tears blurred her last glimpse of him.

Noah walked into the storm, not knowing where he was going and not caring. How could she do that? Just say she would leave him in the spring. He loved her. He thought she at least liked him.

He'd been mistaken.

Her rejection smarted worse than the snow pellets stinging his face. Tears filled the corners of his eyes.

He walked a few more minutes, blinded by his hurt, wondering what he'd done wrong. Had he said something that had driven her away? He had to think of a way to convince her she was his dream. He wanted her to stay.

Lost in his thoughts, he never heard anyone approach. Rough hands grabbed him from behind and dragged him into the snow. Rock-hard fists slammed into his face and belly. "I always get what I want." A blow with each word.

Owens.

Noah fought back. He landed several punches to the side of Owens' head. He connected hard, injuring his hand. The heavier man wasn't fazed. The strikes kept coming. He tasted blood.

Then Owens knocked him on the temple. Hard. His ears rang. Dots danced in his vision.

His last thoughts were of Adie.

Adie must have paced a mile or more between the door and the table. She had done it all wrong, springing the news on Noah like that. On the most blessed of days too.

Now, because of her, he'd been gone a long time. Frigid air seeped under the door. She feared for him. If anything happened to him, she'd be to blame.

Lord, cover Noah with Your feathers. Keep him warm and safe under Your wings.

She needed to find him.

A few minutes later, wrapped in as many layers as she could manage, she grasped the knob to open the door. She pulled, and someone pushed and then stumbled into the room.

"Mr. Larsen." At least she thought that's who was under the floppy hat.

"Where are you going on a night like this, Adie?"

"Noah and I had a disagreement. He walked out and has been gone too long. I'm worried."

He handed her a bulging envelope. "I came to deliver this. You stay here." He raised his lantern. "I'll look for him."

"But..."

"Stay put. It's too cold for you. He couldn't have gone far. I'll find him."

Before she mounted another protest, he left. She unwrapped herself and tried to settle in front of the fire. She had no heart to clear the table.

"What ifs" assailed her. What if he didn't come back because he was so angry? What if the storm worsened and he couldn't find the cabin? What if he never came back?

She didn't want to lose him. She crumpled with the thought. Without him, life would be empty. By her own actions, she'd lost another person she loved.

Loved.

She sat up with a start. She loved him. Why hadn't she realized it before?

Her mind had closed itself to the possibility of love, but her heart hadn't. Without even knowing, she'd fallen in love with her husband.

And sent him away.

She needed to make things right. Again she pleaded with the Lord to bring him home.

As she finished her prayer, something—or someone—crashed into the door. "Open up."

She let in Mr. Larsen, who dragged Noah with him. "Found him in the snow. He's taken a pretty good beating, and he's cold. Get some coffee while I settle him in bed."

Mr. Larsen peeled off Noah's shirt. She turned to coax the fire to life but glanced over her shoulder from time to time. She'd never seen her husband like this. Her pulse throbbed wildly in her neck, and her legs trembled. His arms, though thin, bulged with muscles. Dark, curly hair covered his chest, and his flat stomach caved inward.

Heat suffused her.

She brought the coffee, and Mr. Larsen rose. "He's bruised, and I suspect his ribs are cracked, but he should be fine."

"Thank you for saving his life."

Mr. Larsen nodded. "Now I need to take care of Owens."

A rush of alarm swept over her. In all her concern about her husband, she'd shut Derek from her mind. He might be out there. He might come after them.

"Do you think he'll. . . ?"

Mr. Larsen patted her back. "I found him in the snow about fifty yards from Noah. Don't know what happened to him, whether your husband landed a good blow to his head or he drank himself to his grave. Either way, he'll never bother you again."

She wilted in relief. Here in this cabin they were safe, snug, secure.

Chicks under God's wings.

After Mr. Larsen left, she checked Noah, brushing a sandy lock from his brow.

"Did you hear that? I'm safe. But I didn't think it would be this hard to let you go."

He stirred and opened his eyes. "Adie?"

"Right here." She ceased breathing for a moment as she realized she was right where she wanted to be.

"I love you."

Her heart asked if this could all be a dream. No, Cookie had been right. He did love her. "I know."

"Please don't leave me."

She didn't want to. But no reason remained for the marriage. "Derek's dead. I'll be safe. I won't let you give up your dream."

"You're my dream."

She couldn't reply.

"Your present is in the top of my chest. Get it."

"You don't have to give me anything." Especially after the disaster her gift had turned out to be.

"I want to."

She'd upset him enough for one night and didn't want to distress him further. Going to his chest, she discovered a package clumsily wrapped in brown paper.

"Open it."

She wondered what could be inside the strange, lumpy parcel. Her hands shook as she tugged away the paper. She pulled out a miniature cabin and gasped. Turning it, she inspected it from every angle, not able to believe what she saw.

"It's perfect. Just like my drawing, like the log cabin from my childhood."

"Do you like it?"

"I love it." She sat facing him on the edge of the bed. "Thank you." Her supple lips brushed his.

Her touch ignited him. He embraced her and, ignoring the pain it caused, drew her close, claiming her kisses. She reciprocated. When they parted some minutes later, they were both breathless.

Something changed in Adie. She shone. The words burst from him. "I love you."

She began to cry. "Don't say that."

He saw the truth in her face, in the soft curve of her pink lips. "I know you love me."

"Nothing's changed. No matter how we feel about each other, I won't allow you to trade what you've always wanted for me."

He moaned in pain as he struggled to sit. "You're the most stubborn woman God ever put on this earth."

She giggled through the tears. "Daddy told me that all the time." She went to sit at the table. Her eyebrows creased as she picked up a large envelope.

The parcel caught Noah's curiosity too. "What's that?"

"I don't know. Mr. Larsen brought it. That's when he offered to look for you."

She unfolded the flap. Her eyes grew as large as tree trunks, and her hands shook as she withdrew a sheet of paper and read it. Then she laughed.

"What's inside?"

She came and handed him the envelope. "This is for you."

He gasped when he saw the number of bills inside. Why would she give him all this money? Where had it come from?

"The note says Daddy saved it to buy me a farm, like I'd always wanted. Use it for seminary. Don't give that up."

He couldn't take Quinn's final gift from her. Not deserving, he held out the envelope. "I won't take it. You can't give up that for me."

She picked up the miniature log cottage. "I won't be giving up anything. I'll always have this, wherever we go. Whether we live in a palace or a hovel, or even a little log cabin, it will be home. Because you'll be there."

Would she give it all up for him? Them? "Are you sure?"

"I love you. God protected you for a reason and gave us both our dreams."

His heart pattered in disbelief. God had blessed him beyond measure and graced both him and Adie with everything they'd ever wanted. His throat clogged, but he squeezed out the words. "I love you too. Marry me."

She swept her fingertips across his temple, and he pressed her hand to his cheek. "We're already married."

"I want to be married the way two people should be."

A soft pink touched her cheeks. "I do."

He drew her close. "Merry Christmas, Adie."

"Merry Christmas, my love."

Liz Tolsma is the author of several WWII novels, romantic suspense novels, prairie romance novellas, and an Amish romance. She is a popular speaker and an editor and resides next to a Wisconsin farm field with her husband and their youngest daughter. Her son is a US Marine, and her oldest daughter is a college student. Liz enjoys reading, walking, working in her large perennial garden, kayaking, and camping. Please visit her blog, *The Story behind the Story*, at www.liz tolsma.com and follow her on Facebook, Twitter (@LizTolsma), and Pinterest. She is also a regular contributor to the Midwest Almanac blog.

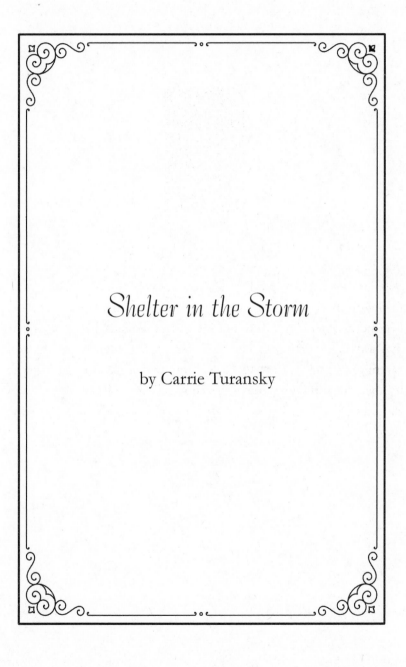

Shelter in the Storm

by Carrie Turansky

Dedication

To my husband, Scott, who encouraged me to follow my
dreams and has helped me live them out for more than
forty years. Happy anniversary and all my love!

*"Then the Lord will create. . .a shelter
and shade from the heat of the day,
and a refuge and hiding place from the storm."*
ISAIAH 4:5–6 NIV

Chapter 1

A gust of wind rattled the shutters over the parlor windows. The lantern flame flickered, sending shadows dancing across the walls. Rachel Thornton's hand stilled, and she looked up from her sewing.

Her younger sister, Susan, stopped reading aloud mid-sentence and glanced at her, questions shimmering in her blue eyes.

A shiver raced up Rachel's back, but she forced a smile for her sister's sake. "It's just the wind, dear. Go on."

Susan nodded, though uneasy lines creased the area between her slender brows. She tilted the Bible toward the lantern light. "Thou, O Lord, art a God full of compassion, and gracious, long-suffering, and plenteous in mercy—"

A shot exploded outside. Rachel gasped and pricked her finger. A shout and second shot followed.

Susan dropped the Bible and spun toward the windows. "Do you think that's Father?"

"I don't know. Stay here." Rachel strode into the wide entrance hall.

Her sister ignored her words and hurried after her. "Maybe it's Colonel Hadley and his men on patrol."

Rachel's mind raced with possibilities. It could be the colonel. Union troops occupied the Nashville area and often called on their family, but they rarely came to Springside this late at night unless they needed medical help from her father.

"Do you think they're chasing a deserter or a Confederate spy?" Excitement overshadowed any fear in fifteen-year-old Susan's voice.

A more alarming question rose in Rachel's mind. Had Father been attacked on his way home by one of the bushwhackers who lurked along the roadside, robbing travelers and stealing their horses?

She hurried to her father's library, jerked opened the desk drawer, and pulled out his revolver.

Susan gasped. "What are you doing?"

Rachel opened the chamber, checking to be sure that all six bullets were in place. Her father had taught her how to fire it, though she'd never shot anything but a homemade target in the pasture beyond the stable.

She swallowed and tried to steady her voice. "I'm going to make sure everything's all right." If she hadn't been so frightened, she would have laughed at those words. Nothing had been *all right* for more than three years, ever since this terrible war had broken out.

Gripping the revolver, she returned to the entrance hall and approached the front door. She would not stand by and let someone hurt her family or destroy their home. Not after all they had endured.

Susan ran after her. "You can't go outside."

"I have to. What if Father's been shot and needs our help?"

Panic filled her sister's eyes, and her chin trembled.

Rachel laid her hand on Susan's arm. "Don't cry. I'm sure it's just—"

A solid thump and low moan sounded beyond the front door.

The sisters froze, their eyes locked on each other. Rachel swallowed and grasped the revolver with both hands.

A loud pounding rattled the door. "Miz Rachel? Open up. It's Amos."

Relief melted through her. She lowered the gun, though she had no idea why Amos didn't go around back and let himself in with his key. She laid the revolver on the side table and hurried to the door. Susan stayed behind her as she turned the heavy lock.

Dim light from a lantern on the table shone past them to the tall figure on the portico. Amos stepped forward carrying a lifeless man in his arms.

"Who is it, Amos?"

"I don't know, Miz Rachel. I ran out front when I heard the shots. I found him layin' in the road by the gatepost."

Susan leaned around Rachel. "Is he dead?"

"Not yet, but he's gonna be if we don't do something to stop the bleedin' in his arm."

Rachel surveyed the man's pale face and bloodstained jacket. Weary lines etched his forehead and the area around his closed eyes. A scraggly blond beard and mustache covered the lower half of his face, making it difficult to tell his age, though he looked young rather than old. His tattered clothes gave no clue to his identity. Was he a rebel on the run or a Union man?

Saint or sinner, she couldn't banish him to the stable. "Bring him inside."

"But what if he's a bushwhacker or a thief?" Susan asked.

"We'll worry about that later. Right now he needs our help."

"But what will Father—"

"I'm sure he would agree. Now, go get some towels and a basin. And find Esther. I'll need her help."

Susan stood her ground. Rachel met her sister's gaze with a firm, steady look. Finally, Susan huffed and flounced off toward the kitchen.

Rachel turned to Amos. "Take him up to the front bedroom."

Amos hesitated, his dark eyes regarding her cautiously. "You sure about that, Miz Rachel?"

"Yes." She motioned to the large, curving staircase at the back of the entry hall. "Put him in Nathan's room."

"I don't know what your daddy gonna say about you bringing this man inside when he's gone." Amos grunted as he shifted the man's weight. Then he headed toward the stairs.

Rachel bit her lip, debating her decision. Father might not return from town for several hours. She would have to treat the man herself. Her palms grew moist at that thought. All she knew she'd learned at her father's side as they attended wounded soldiers in makeshift hospitals in and around Nashville. Rebel or Union soldier, each man received the best care her father could give. She could do no less.

But did she have the skills she needed to save this man's life? That question weighed heavy upon her as she lifted the lantern and followed Amos up the stairs.

Rachel pressed her lips together and leaned closer to examine the man's wound. The bullet had passed straight through his upper left arm. With a gentle hand, she washed away the blood. "Bring the lantern closer."

Esther grimaced and turned her face away. "I don' know how you do that, Miz Rachel. Makes my head swim just takin' a peek."

Rachel held back a smile. Esther never had liked the sight of blood. "You don't have to watch. Just hold the lantern steady."

"All right. Long as you do the doctorin', I'll be fine."

Rachel certainly wasn't a doctor, though she had assisted her father for many years. This was the first time she'd treated such a serious injury on her own.

The man moaned and rolled his head toward Rachel.

Her stomach clenched, and she lifted her hand away. Of course she wanted him to wake up, but she'd hoped to clean and bandage his wound first. She had nothing to give him for the pain. What if he became delirious?

The man slowly opened his eyes and looked up at Rachel with a dazed expression. His Adam's apple bobbed as he swallowed. He licked his lips and mumbled something she couldn't understand.

Rachel bent over him, bringing her face into the circle of light. "You've been injured, but we're taking good care of you."

Confusion filled his pain-glazed eyes. "Hettie?" He slowly lifted his hand and reached toward her face.

Rachel froze as his cool fingers skimmed her cheek. Then his hand fell to his side, and his blue eyes drifted closed again.

Esther clicked her tongue. "Oh, my. He thinks you're his sweetheart."

"Or his wife," Susan added with a delighted grin.

Rachel sent her sister a sharp look. But she couldn't silence the questions circling through her mind. Who was this man? And who was Hettie?

Footsteps sounded in the hallway. She looked up as her father opened the door. "Oh, Father, I'm so glad you're home." She wiped her hands and greeted him with a hug, thankful for the comfort of his strong arms around her.

He stepped back and looked at her with concern in his eyes. "Amos tells me you've taken in a patient."

She nodded. "He was attacked on the road by our gate."

"We heard two shots and men shouting." Susan came around the bed to greet Father. Though his focus was already on their patient, he leaned down and kissed Susan's forehead.

"He was bleeding badly when Amos found him. I had to bring him in."

He studied the man then gave her a quick nod. "Good decision. Let's take a look and see what we can do for him."

Rachel released a breath. Everything would be all right now. She would assist Father, and together they would do all they could to be sure the man survived.

Father hung his jacket over the back of a nearby chair. Then he washed and dried his hands on a clean towel. He had always taught her that cleanliness was an important part of good medical practice. Others suggested his meticulous ways wasted time, but she believed he was right.

The man never stirred as Father checked the wounds then listened to his heart and lungs with a stethoscope. He asked for more light, then lifted the man's eyelids and leaned in for a closer look. Finally, he clasped the man's wrist and felt his pulse, his calm expression revealing nothing.

Rachel's stomach twisted like a butter churn. "How is he, Father?"

"Will he be all right?" Susan's serious tone suggested she'd finally realized the man's life hung in the balance, and this wasn't some silly adventure.

"His heartbeat is regular, and his lungs are clear." A shadow of uncertainty crossed Father's face. "But his pulse is weak, and it looks like it's been a long while since he's had a good meal." Father placed his hand on the man's forehead. "No fever. But his being unconscious this long concerns me. He may have hit his head when he fell or have internal injuries."

Rachel's throat tightened, and she pressed her lips together. She'd seen too many fine young men lose the battle against their injuries and pass from this life to the next, clutching tintypes of their sweethearts or letters from loved ones back home.

Please have mercy on him, Lord. We don't even know the poor man's name. Don't let him die.

"Let's bandage him up."

Rachel nodded and passed Father several strips of clean cloth.

Lines furrowed his forehead as he wrapped the man's arm and then tied the bandages in a knot. "We'll have to watch him closely. The next few hours are very important."

"I'll sit with him." The words spilled from Rachel's mouth before she had time to think them through. "I mean. . .you must be tired, Father. Why don't you rest for a few hours and let me keep watch?"

Father straightened and met her gaze. "I suppose that's a good plan. But come and get me right away if he wakes up, or if you see any change in his condition."

Rachel nodded, pulled the blanket up to the man's shoulders, and smoothed it over his chest. Her father and sister bid her goodnight and left the room.

"You want me to stay?" Esther asked. "I don't mind. That old Amos snores like a bear. I'd probably get more rest in here with you."

Rachel smiled. "No, I'll be fine. You go on to bed."

"Well, you keep that fire burnin' and bundle up. I don't want you catchin' your death o' cold. Then you be the one needin' nursin', and

I don't even want to think about that." Esther's mutters faded as she disappeared out the door.

Rachel leaned over the man and studied his pale face. Blue-gray half-circles shaded the area under his eyes. A smudge of dirt streaked one side of his forehead. An old scar under his left eye caught her attention. Had he been wounded while leading a line of troops into battle or from losing a barroom brawl? She hoped it was the first scenario; but if he was a courageous officer, then where was his uniform? What if he was one of those dreadful bushwhackers who had plagued the countryside and made traveling so dangerous?

She looked at him again and shook her head. There might be more behind his trouble than a gunshot wound, but she didn't believe he was an outlaw or a deserter. At least she hoped he wasn't.

Closing her eyes, she whispered a prayer, "Lord, please spare this man's life."

Chapter 2

Burning pain throbbed in James's arm, pulling him awake. He blinked and waited for his eyes to adjust. A lantern with a low flame sat on the bedside table. Beyond that, heavy drapes hung over a tall window, but no light seeped in around the edges. Next to the window, a tall dresser and wardrobe sat in the shadows against the wall.

He slowly lifted his hand and ran his fingers over the bandages wrapped around his left shoulder and arm. Heat radiated from his wound.

Fuzzy memories of the attack replayed through his mind. He had been riding down the road in the moonlight when an explosion sounded and a sharp pain shot through his arm. Two men jumped from the trees. One knocked him off his horse, while the other grabbed the reins. Stunned by the surprise attack, he lay on the ground, trying to defend himself while the first man kicked him and hit him with a heavy club.

What happened after that? He had no memory of coming to this room. The men must have stolen his horse. What about his clothes and saddlebags?

He turned his head to look for them, and another wave of pain pulsed through him. Clamping his jaw, he closed his eyes. *Relax. Let it pass.* He shifted his thoughts and focused on the feeling of the soft pillow under his head then blew out a deep breath.

How long had it been since he had slept in a comfortable bed like this with smooth, clean-smelling sheets and warm blankets? Eight months? Nine?

A soft sigh and the rustle of fabric broke the silence.

His eyes flew open, and he turned toward the sounds. In a shadowed corner, near the fireplace, a young woman slept in a large chair.

Surprise rippled through him. Who was she?

Light from the fire flickered across her pleasant oval face and dark hair. She looked to be in her early twenties, though it was difficult to say for sure. She wasn't strikingly beautiful, but there was a certain sweetness in her expression that made him wish for his drawing pad and the opportunity to capture her with his pencils.

He lay back and tried to ignore the incessant pounding in his head and make sense of the situation. This young woman must have found him and taken him in. She must also be the one who had bandaged his arm and put him to bed in this comfortable room. Though that would be difficult for her to do alone. Perhaps there were others who had helped. Whoever they were, he was grateful for their kindness.

But what would they do with him in the morning? Had he made it to the Union lines, or was he still in Confederate territory? And more importantly, which side did these people support? Would they offer him a safe haven or turn him over to the rebels as soon as the sun rose?

He didn't intend to wait around and find out. Going back to that filthy Confederate prison was not an option. He'd rather die on the road than return to that hopeless pit of despair.

Gathering his strength, he lifted the blanket and rolled to his side. Pain shot through his ribs, sucking the air from his lungs.

He must have injured more than his arm in the attack. That made sense as he recalled the brutal beating those thugs had given him. Shuddering, he rose to a sitting position. The bed squeaked. His head swam, and his empty stomach surged in protest.

Had she heard him? He glanced over his shoulder. Her slow, steady breathing and peaceful expression didn't change.

Gritting his teeth, he used his good arm to push himself to his feet. The room tilted and spun, and he gripped the head of the bed like a drowning man clutching a lifeline.

Taking one shaky step, then another, he dragged his feet across the carpet. His legs trembled, and he felt as weak as a newborn calf. A strange buzzing in his head grew louder. The light around him rippled and faded. He felt himself falling, and he hit the floor. Pain crashed over him, and darkness swallowed him whole.

A loud crash startled Rachel from her sleep. She sat up, scolding herself for dozing off. Her gaze swung to the empty bed. She gasped, jumped from the chair, and ran across the room. On the other side of the bed, the man lay on the floor in a crumpled heap.

"Oh no!" She dropped to her knees and grabbed his hand. "Sir? Oh, please, sir, wake up."

Tangled blankets hung from the side of the bed. He had either rolled off or come to and tried to get up. Either way, she had to get him back in bed. But she had no idea how to do that alone. Going to get Father seemed like the most sensible plan, but she hated to leave the poor man lying on the floor.

She raised his head and tucked the pillow underneath. At least she could try to make him comfortable.

He stirred and slowly opened his eyes.

"Oh, thank goodness." She leaned closer, searching his face.

He squinted up at her, looking as though it was a challenge for him to focus.

"You've fallen, and we've got to get you back in bed." She glanced at the door. "Just lay still now, and I'll go get my father."

His eyes flashed, and he reached for her arm. "No. Please."

"It's all right. My father's a doctor. You have nothing to be afraid of."

He loosened his hold, but lines still creased his forehead. "There's no need to wake him." He pressed his lips together and slowly sat up. But he swayed, and his face drained of color.

"Let me help you." She placed her arm around his back. Working together, they got him up on the bed. He sat on the side, his bandaged arm cradled against his chest.

She returned his pillow to the bed. "Just lay back now, and I'll help you get situated." He lowered his head to the pillow, and she lifted his legs. Then she pulled the covers over him. "There, are you comfortable?"

He nodded but looked deathly pale. "Thank you," he whispered. "You're very kind." His English accent became clearer each time he spoke, stirring more questions in her mind.

She folded down the sheet and smoothed it over the top edge

of the blanket. "I'm glad to help. Now, why don't you rest, and I'll let Father know you're awake."

He reached for her arm. "Please, wait. . .who are you?" His eyes seemed to plead another unspoken question, and she had the feeling he wanted to keep her there or keep her father away.

"My name is Rachel Thornton."

"This is your home?"

"Yes. This is Springside."

"How far from Nashville?"

"About eight miles."

His eyes flickered, and he nodded.

"And you are?" She smiled, hoping to put him at ease.

He glanced away, then turned back and met her gaze. "James Galloway."

"And where are you from, Mr. Galloway?"

He hesitated. "Bristol, England."

She waited, hoping he would explain why an Englishman happened to be traveling at night on a country road in Tennessee. But he stared at the fireplace, looking lost in his thoughts.

"Well, I'm sure my father will be happy to hear you're awake." She turned to go, half expecting him to reach out and stop her again.

But this time he simply closed his eyes and released a heavy sigh.

Chapter 3

Father took over care of their patient a little after midnight. She offered to stay longer, but he insisted he would be fine and sent her off to bed.

The next morning she slept in later than usual. She hurried to wash and dress, then checked her reflection in the mirror and ran her hand over her dark brown hair, smoothing it back from her face. The center part drew attention to her large dark brown eyes, straight nose, and high cheekbones. It was more fashionable to have blue eyes, an upturned nose, and a round, full face like her sister Susan, but she had not been blessed with those features.

Remembering her mother's words, *"A cheerful countenance improves everyone's appearance,"* she put on a smile. It helped some, but it couldn't disguise the fact that she was willowy and almost as tall as her father.

Her thoughts shifted to her sister again. Susan had developed a lovely figure that was full in all the right places—places where Rachel had only slight suggestions of her womanhood.

She turned away from the mirror, scolding herself for stirring up jealous feelings. She dearly loved her sister, and she'd watched over her since their mother died five years earlier when Rachel was fifteen and Susan was eleven.

The memory of her father's compliments brought her a bit of comfort. *"You have character, warmth, and intelligence, my dear, and those qualities are more valuable than a full figure and a round face."*

She hoped he was right, but she doubted they would improve her marriage prospects. Most of the eligible young men in the area had been called away to fight in the war, and her family's Union loyalties separated her from all but a few who remained.

Perhaps she would stay at Springside forever and take care of Father. Most days, that seemed preferable, especially when she thought of the officers who visited their home and showed an interest in her.

Not one could compare to Andrew Tillman. She reached in her top drawer and pulled out a small tintype. Dressed in his Confederate uniform and wearing a solemn expression, he looked older than his twenty years. Her heart ached as she gazed into his eyes and recalled the dreams she had envisioned for their future.

But all that had changed two years ago when he'd been killed in his first battle. Hope for a life with Andrew died that day, leaving only bittersweet memories in its place.

Her pain had lessened over time, but she made up her mind she would never give her heart to another soldier.

She tucked his picture away next to a sachet of rose petals and a handkerchief embroidered by her mother, then turned away and left her room.

Voices carried into the hall from her brother's bedroom. The door stood slightly ajar. She slowed to listen.

"So, Mr. Galloway, tell us more about yourself." Her father's voice sounded warm and relaxed.

"Please, sir, call me James."

"Where are you from, James?"

A second passed before he answered. "I'm originally from Bristol, England."

"Ah, yes, I can hear the accent."

James chuckled. "It's helped me out of a scrape a time or two. Seems both North and South respect the English."

Susan giggled. "I just love your English accent. It's so charming."

Rachel cringed. Her sister never had been one to hold back her thoughts or opinions. She knocked and stepped into the room.

"Ah, Rachel, good morning." Father smiled at her then turned to their patient, who still rested in bed. "I'm sure you remember my oldest daughter, Rachel."

A faint smile lifted James's lips. "Yes." His gaze connected with hers. "Your father tells me I owe my life to your quick actions last night. I'm very grateful. Thank you."

Her face flushed. "You're welcome. How are you feeling today?"

"Like I've been trampled by a herd of wild horses, but I expect to improve soon." He did look a bit less intimidating with a clean face and combed hair.

"I believe you're on your way to recovery," her father added. "So, tell us what brings you to the Nashville area."

James frowned slightly and glanced at the window. "It's a rather long tale."

"We have plenty of time." Father sat down and told Rachel to pull up another chair next to Susan.

"Tell us your story, Mr. Galloway." Susan leaned forward with an eager expression.

He shifted his gaze from Susan to her father and then to Rachel. "First, I'd like to ask if your loyalties lie with the Confederacy or the Union."

A shadow of concern crossed Father's face. "We're loyal to the Union. Have been since the beginning. I was one of the first to sign the loyalty oath when the Union took control of Nashville in sixty-two."

The tension in James's face eased. "That's good to hear. I'm for the Union as well, but I know many in Tennessee support the Confederacy."

"That's true, but Governor Johnson has had a very strong influence here in the Nashville area. Most of those who are opposed to the Union have left or been sent away. You can't do any business in Nashville unless you sign the loyalty oath."

James nodded. "When I woke up last night, I wasn't sure who you were or what you would do with me this morning. That's why I tried to leave." His gaze returned to Rachel. "I didn't want to take a chance you'd turn me over to the rebels."

Father shook his head. "You're safe here and welcome to stay with us as long as you need to recover."

"That's very generous, sir, especially since I'm a stranger to you."

"Well, stranger or neighbor, you would've been treated with the same care and respect."

"Thank you. I appreciate it very much."

"So, are you with the Union Army?" Father asked.

"Not in the usual sense. But I've traveled with them as a special artist since the beginning of the war. I sketch battle scenes and camp life and send those drawings back to New York where they're made into lithographs for the *Harper's Weekly* newspaper."

"Ah, so you're a newspaper correspondent." Father beamed a smile at Rachel. She released a deep breath, glad to hear he had an honorable occupation and reason for traveling through the area.

"Yes. I do the drawings and my associate, Thomas Beckley, writes the articles. We usually travel together, but we've been separated since I was captured during the battle at Cold Harbor in early June."

Susan's eyes widened. "Captured? By the rebels?"

"Yes, I was a prisoner until my escape about a month ago."

"But you're not a soldier," Rachel said. "Why would they take you?"

"The Confederates don't appreciate *Harper's* views on the war, and since I was carrying a weapon when I was captured, they shipped me off to prison with the rest of the men."

"Why that's terrible!" Indignation filled Susan's voice. "I can't believe they imprisoned a civilian—and a journalist at that."

"Where did they send you?" Father asked.

"To Richmond first. I spent two months in Libby Prison, and then I was sent south to a prison in Salisbury, North Carolina. That was an intolerable hole. The worst conditions you can imagine. I spent a month there. Finally, in mid-September I escaped with three other men. We split up after the first day, and I made my way west searching for the Union lines."

Father frowned. "You traveled all the way over the mountains of Carolina and halfway across Tennessee? Why, that's several hundred miles."

"Yes, sir. I found a horse, saddled and wandering in a field the third day after my escape. There were even saddlebags filled with items I needed for the trip." He hesitated and shook his head as though it still surprised him. "I traveled at night and kept off the roads, heading toward Nashville, hoping it was still in Union hands."

Father shook his head. "I hope you know it's a miracle you made it this far. God was watching over you."

James nodded. "Yes, sir. I believe you're right. And I'm deeply grateful to Him, especially for bringing me here."

Rachel's eyes misted. What amazing strength and courage it must have taken to make such a long journey. A hundred questions rose in her mind, but this wasn't the time to ask them.

"Oh, Mr. Galloway, I've never heard such an exciting story!" Susan clasped her hands. "You have to tell us how you managed to escape—"

Rachel gave the slightest shake of her head, but Susan ignored her.

Father rose from his chair. "I'm afraid that will have to wait for later. Mr. Galloway needs to rest and regain his strength."

Susan's lower lip jutted out. "But, Father, I'm sure it wouldn't tire him to tell us—"

"Susan, I'd like you to go downstairs and help Esther in the kitchen." He sent her a warning look she couldn't ignore.

She rose from her chair. "I hope you will tell us more about your adventures later, after you've had time to rest." She smiled at James then turned and left the room.

"Rachel, I'm going to get some clean bandages. I'd like to check and redress James's wound before we leave him to rest. Will you get some fresh water?"

"Yes, Father." She rose from her chair.

Father nodded to them and walked out the door.

"I'm sorry I caused you so much trouble last night when I tried to leave."

"It's all right. I'm just glad we convinced you to stay." As soon as the words left her mouth, her face flushed. She hadn't meant to sound so forward. "Excuse me."

She turned and fled the room with the memory of his twinkling eyes quickening her steps.

Chapter 4

Rachel entered the warm kitchen and found Esther bent over the hearth, stirring a bubbling pot. A cheerful fire crackled in the large stone fireplace.

Esther glanced over her shoulder. "Morning, Miz Rachel. How's that young man doin'?"

"He seems much better today. Father's with him now."

"Good. Where's he from?"

Rachel relayed highlights of James Galloway's story, including his capture at Cold Harbor and escape from a Confederate prison.

"I would've never guessed he was a newspaperman. He looks mighty rough. More like a travelin' man of some sort."

"I'm sure that's because of his prison experience." How would James Galloway look with a clean-shaven face and new clothes? The question sent a shiver through her. She reached up and took a clean pitcher from the cabinet.

"Poor man. Spendin' all that time in a prison and then escapin' over the mountains. We're gonna have to take good care of him and fatten him up." Esther lifted a large wooden spoon to her lips and took a sip. "Mm-mmm. This is just what he needs."

Rachel smiled. "What is it?"

"Chicken soup." Esther took another taste. "Nothing better for healing than my soup."

Susan entered the kitchen humming a tune. She spun around and waltzed up to Esther. "Did you hear James is an artist for *Harper's Weekly* newspaper?" A dreamy look filled her eyes. "And he's from England."

Esther clicked her tongue and pointed the spoon at Susan. "Now, don't you go gettin' all worked up over that man. He's probably married or has a sweetheart back home. He was calling for her last night. Isn't that right, Miz Rachel?"

Rachel pumped water into the pitcher. "Mr. Galloway hasn't told us if he's married or not, but it doesn't matter. Susan is too young to be thinking about men in a romantic way."

"I am not too young!" Susan scowled. "I'll be sixteen in eight months, and that's certainly old enough to start thinking about men, especially handsome men like James."

"You're to call him Mr. Galloway." Rachel set the pitcher on the counter and snatched a dish towel to wipe her hands. "And you must stop gushing over him. It's not ladylike."

Susan lifted her eyebrows. "I am *not* gushing."

Rachel batted her eyelashes, imitating her sister. "'Oh, I just love your English accent. It's *so-ooo* charming.'" She dropped her false smile. "That's gushing. And it gives a bad impression."

Susan's eyes flashed. "You're just jealous because I know how to carry on a conversation and keep a man interested."

An angry response rose in Rachel's throat, and she struggled to hold it in. It was true her sister could converse with anyone and was a favorite of the Union officers who visited their home. But they thought of her as a younger sister, didn't they?

Rachel smoothed her hand over her skirt. "You may not like what I said, but I'm trying to help you see how you appear to others and keep you from embarrassing Father."

Susan's mouth dropped open. "How can you say that? I am not—"

Esther raised her hand. "Whoa now. There's plenty of battles goin' on in the countryside. I don't need no more in my kitchen." She pointed at Susan. "Now you best listen to your sister and mind your manners around Mr. Galloway." Esther's expression softened, and she patted Susan's cheek. "Besides, a pretty young lady like you don't want to lose her heart to some newspaperman who's gonna run off and leave as soon as he's able."

Susan warmed to Esther's sweet talk. "I suppose you're right, but he is a very charming man."

"Well, whatever kinda man he is, we best get busy. We've got dinner to fix, and your father's not gonna be too happy if it's late."

Rachel pulled in a sharp breath. Father was waiting for her to bring the water. She grabbed the pitcher and hurried out of the kitchen.

James examined the painting of a horse on the wall above the fireplace. She was a beautiful black mare with a white blaze on her forehead. He stared at it so long, he felt certain he could re-create it in his drawing book—if it hadn't been stolen. Discouragement washed over him as he recalled all the sketches and thoughts he had recorded during his months in prison and then after his escape. They were all gone now, probably tossed in some muddy hedgerow where the wind and rain would destroy them.

Anger burned in his stomach. If he ever found the men who attacked him, he'd make sure they never did that again.

He huffed out a breath and rolled to his side to gain another view. A knock sounded at the door.

His spirits rose. He would welcome a visitor. Any visitor. "Come in."

The younger sister, Susan, entered carrying a tray with a covered dish. She smiled, her pretty blue eyes sparkling. "I hope you like chicken soup and corn bread."

"That sounds wonderful." He shifted, preparing to raise himself.

"Oh, don't worry about sitting up to eat. I can help you." She placed the tray on the table next to his bed and scooted a chair closer.

The idea of being spoon-fed, even by this attractive young woman, didn't agree with him. "I'm sure if you brought another pillow or blanket to put behind my back, I could sit up and handle a spoon."

Her smile faded slightly. "All right." She opened a wooden chest at the foot of the bed and took out a quilt. He leaned forward, and she placed it behind him. "How's that?"

The effort to sit up left him feeling lightheaded and short of breath. "That's fine. Thank you."

"The soup has a lot of carrots and potatoes with nice chunks of chicken." She set the tray in his lap and removed the cover from the bowl.

Flavorful steam rose and warmed his face. His stomach growled, and his mouth watered. "This looks heavenly. Excuse me." He bowed his head and sent off a brief prayer of thanks. When he lifted his gaze,

Rachel walked through the doorway carrying a second tray.

She stopped halfway across the room and stared at her sister. "I didn't realize you prepared a tray for Mr. Galloway."

A triumphant gleam lit Susan's eyes, and she nodded.

What was this, some sort of rivalry between the sisters?

Rachel moved toward the bed and looked down at the tray in his lap. A slight smile lifted her lips. "Perhaps Mr. Galloway would like a napkin and a knife to spread the butter." She took those items from her tray and handed them to him.

Susan's cheeks turned pink, and she tossed her blond curls over her shoulder. "Maybe he doesn't like butter."

James chuckled. "Oh, I love butter, especially since I haven't had any for several months." He tucked the napkin over his chest and dipped his spoon in the soup. "Mmm, this is delicious. My compliments to the cook." He glanced back and forth between them, wondering which one had prepared the meal for him.

Rachel smiled. "I'll be sure to tell Esther you like it."

"Ah—and who is Esther?" He directed the question to Rachel, but Susan answered.

"Oh, she's our cook and housekeeper. She and her husband, Amos, used to be slaves. But when Grandfather Morton died seven years ago, Father set all our slaves free. Most moved on, but Amos and Esther stayed to work for Father. And old Samuel stayed to care for the horses, even though his son Caleb—"

"Susan, I don't think Mr. Galloway wants to hear about every person who has ever worked for Father."

James grinned. "Well, I am interested in hearing what motivated him to free his slaves."

Susan sat in the chair next to the bed. "Oh, Father never believed in slavery. He was born in Philadelphia, and his father was a Quaker.

But then he met and married Mother and moved here to Tennessee with her family." Her blue eyes widened and she leaned closer. "He and Grandfather used to have terrible arguments about slavery. That was the only time I ever heard Father—"

"Susan!" Rachel held out the tray toward her sister. "Please take this back to the kitchen and relay Mr. Galloway's thanks to Esther."

"But I don't—"

"I know. But it's time."

Susan stood and shot a heated glance at her sister. With a swish of her dress, she turned and left the room.

Rachel exhaled and lowered herself into the chair. "I'm sorry, Mr. Galloway. Susan tends to be outspoken at times."

"She's young and spirited. No harm done." He took another spoonful of soup, savoring the delicious broth. "It sounds like you have quite an interesting family. Susan mentioned your mother. . ." His voice faded as he noted the sudden sadness in Rachel's eyes.

"She passed away about five years ago."

He hesitated a moment. "I'm sorry for your loss."

"Thank you."

"Your father seems very devoted to you."

Rachel's face brightened. "Yes, he is. And we love him dearly. What about your family?" She glanced down at her lap. "Are you. . . married?"

He held back a smile. "No, I'm not. My parents are in England and my brother as well. But I haven't seen them since before the war."

She looked up, compassion in her eyes. "That's such a long time. You must miss them terribly."

"Yes. . .I do." His eyes burned, and he turned away. All those months in prison, he had focused on survival and escape. He hadn't allowed himself to feel how much he missed his family. "Even before I was captured, it was difficult to get letters back and forth to England. I doubt they knew I was a prisoner, which was probably for the best. I hate to worry them."

"They must be concerned since they haven't heard from you in so long. I'm sure Father or Amos could take a letter into town and mail it for you. With the Union in control of Nashville, we do get some letters through."

His spirits lifted. "That's an excellent idea. And I must contact my editor at *Harper's* as well."

"Perhaps, after you finish eating, I could help you with that."

"I'd be most grateful." He set his spoon aside and picked up the knife, intending to butter his bread. "I'm not sure if I can do this one-handed."

"Oh, let me help you." She rose from her chair, bent over him, and sliced open the square of cornbread.

The scent of roses floated around her. He pulled in a deep breath.

She spread a thick layer of creamy butter over the bread. A soft flush filled her cheeks, and the corners of her mouth tucked in and formed a smile. "There you go."

"Thank you." He watched her settle in the chair again. "Do you have any other sisters or brothers?"

"I have an older brother, Nathan. He's twenty-four. This is his room." She glanced around.

"I hope I haven't put him out of his bed."

Rachel smiled. "No. He isn't living here now. He was attending medical school in Philadelphia when the war started. He joined the Union Army and works in a field hospital near Washington."

"That must be a difficult job." He had seen enough injured soldiers to know that was an understatement.

"Yes, he writes to us about it." A shadow crossed her face. "We haven't had a letter in over a month." Her voice faltered, and her eyes glistened.

He reached over and touched her hand. "He's probably just busy taking care of his patients. I'm sure you'll hear from him soon."

She released a deep breath. "I hope so. That would certainly lift some of Father's burden." Rachel slid her hand out from under his and smoothed it over her skirt. "These last few years have been difficult for him. He loved my mother deeply. Her death was a terrible loss. And now, with his only son off in the war. . ."

"I imagine you and your sister are a great comfort to him."

"We try to be, but sometimes I'm afraid we just *try* his patience." Dimples creased her cheeks, and her warm brown eyes glowed.

He laughed. "I'm sure he would say you are his delightful daughters who brighten his days and give him more than enough reason to keep pressing on."

She laughed now. "Oh, Mr. Galloway."

"Please, call me James."

"Then, you must call me Rachel."

He grinned and nodded, his heart feeling much lighter than it had in months. "All right. Rachel it is."

Chapter 5

Rachel tucked the needle in her sewing box and shook out the shirt she had altered for James. It was an old one that belonged to her brother, but there was still plenty of wear in the material.

She held it up, checking her work, and then gave a satisfied nod. The thought of James wearing a shirt she had altered warmed her heart.

For the past six days, she had delivered his meals, tended to his needs, and was pleased to see him regain some strength. Susan also visited him each day. He was polite to her, but he seemed to prefer talking with Rachel.

Her plan to maintain a proper distance had faded away by the second day. James's warm personality put her at ease. They had discussed everything from his childhood in England to his first job in

New York, painting scenery for a theater company. When she asked him about his work as an artist for *Harper's*, he shared a few stories, but he usually shifted the focus to her. With a little prompting, she told him about her fondness for English poetry and her love for their three remaining thoroughbred horses.

She smiled at the memory of those long talks. Though she'd only known him for a week, she felt a special attachment forming.

Did he feel the same? Or was he simply lonely?

Hope rose in her heart. Maybe she had finally found someone who would care for her as Andrew had. But doubts nibbled away at her dreams. Why would a handsome man who had traveled so extensively be attracted to a simple Tennessee girl like her? And what about his sweetheart, Hettie? He hadn't said anything more about her since that first night when he had called her name, but Rachel didn't want to risk opening her heart to a man who belonged to someone else.

She sighed and pushed those confusing thoughts away.

Picking up the shirt, she draped it over her arm and headed to James's room. Father said he was well enough to dress and come down to dinner with the family today. She imagined James sitting across from her at the dining room table, and then scolded herself. She had to stop thinking about him all the time. He was their patient, not her beau.

As she approached his room, she saw James sitting at the dressing table with his back to her. Father stood behind him. He looked over his shoulder. "Ah, Rachel. Did you finish the shirt?"

"Here it is." She stepped forward and glanced in the mirror.

James's reflection smiled back at her with a clean-shaven face and a neat new haircut.

Rachel swallowed. *Oh my.* He was good-looking with the beard, but he was ruggedly handsome without it. "I hardly recognize you."

He laughed. "That's precisely what I said when your father finished helping me shave." He ran his hand down the smooth side of his face and along his strong, square jaw. "Feels quite different."

She broke her gaze and held up the shirt. "Will this do?"

He nodded and sent her a warm smile. "I appreciate you altering it for me. Seems I'm now indebted to you for the clothes as well as your excellent care."

Her father lifted his hand. "Please, there is no debt. We've come to think of you as our friend." Father glanced at Rachel in the mirror. "Almost like family."

Rachel looked away, praying Father wouldn't say anything else. Did he sense her growing attraction to James? Was it that obvious? If Father saw it, did James? Mortified by that thought, she turned away and laid the shirt on a nearby chair.

Amos entered the room carrying a pair of leather saddlebags over his shoulder. He pulled a folded envelope from his pocket. "I have a telegram for Mr. Galloway. And on my way back from town, I found these saddlebags in the bushes down the road from the gate."

James turned to him. "Why, those are mine."

Amos handed him the saddlebags. "I was thinkin' they might be, sir."

"Thank you." With his arm still in a sling, James struggled to undo the buckle. "I can't believe it. I'd given up all hope of ever finding them."

Rachel helped him open the buckle and lift the flap.

James pulled out a thick drawing book. Next came a metal dish, a fork and spoon, a folding knife, a case of drawing pencils, a pocket-sized New Testament, and a small revolver. He grinned as he examined each item.

"Is everything there?" Father asked.

"All except a little money." James's eyes glistened as he pulled out the final item, a tintype of a beautiful young woman with blond hair and a sweet, pale face. He gazed at it for a moment and then laid it carefully on the dressing table.

Rachel bit her lip. Was that Hettie?

"This means the world to me. Thank you, Amos."

"Glad I spotted it. Here's that telegram, sir."

James thanked him again, then took the envelope and opened it.

"Is it from...your family?" Rachel asked. James had sent only two letters, one to his parents in England and one to his editor at *Harper's*. Why hadn't he written to Hettie?

"No, it's from my editor, George Curtis."

Rachel's heart began to pound. Would he recall James to New York or send him back into battle? "What does he say?"

Father lifted his brows at her, and heat flooded her cheeks.

James didn't seem to mind her asking. "He says he's glad to hear I've escaped. He wants an article and drawings about my experiences. He'd also like me to rejoin my associate, Thomas Beckley, in Virginia as soon as possible."

Father frowned. "I don't believe you're ready to return to the battlefield. You not only have the wound and beating to recover from, you've been deprived of nourishing food for several months."

A perplexed expression settled over James's face.

"You need at least another three or four weeks to rest and build up your strength before you travel a great distance like that."

"Father's right. You mustn't go back too soon, or you might become ill."

James lifted his gaze to meet Rachel's. "I appreciate your concern." He glanced at the message again. "But I must go as soon as I'm able."

Rachel's fingers curled in and grabbed her skirt. "Surely there are other artists who can cover the battles."

"There are a few, but I made a commitment to my employer, and I owe it to the men. My drawings bring their story home. I raise morale and persuade people's opinion. It's a great responsibility." He straightened his shoulders. "I'll be rejoining them as soon as I'm well enough to travel."

"But you've already given your best for more than three years, and you were imprisoned for it. Couldn't you work from New York? Do you have to put yourself in danger to help the war effort?"

Father cleared his throat. "Rachel, it's not our place to question James concerning his duty and commitments. I'm sure he'll pray and take his health into consideration when he makes his decision."

Fire burned in Rachel's heart. "Excuse me." She gave a curt nod to her father and James and fled the room.

She had lost one man she loved in this war, and she could not tolerate the thought of losing another.

A shock wave rippled through her, and her steps stalled. Did she truly love James? She had only known him for a week. Was that even possible?

It didn't matter. He didn't return her feelings. She felt certain of that. If he did, he would never consider leaving her and going back into battle.

A cozy fire burned in the fireplace, warming the parlor against a chill in the air. James glanced out the window, marveling at the contrast between the brilliant blue sky and the fiery orange maple leaves.

He had been with the Thorntons for more than two weeks. The pain in his arm had eased, and he didn't need to wear his sling all day.

He shifted his focus to Rachel, and gratefulness warmed him from the inside out. Her constant care and companionship had been the key to his recovery. She sat across the room from him now with a basket of mending at her feet, her attention focused on her sewing. She had stayed behind today to keep him company while Dr. Thornton and Susan went to visit a sick neighbor.

A smile lifted one side of his mouth as he thought of the discoveries he had made about her over the past few days. Though he would've never guessed it by looking at her now, she was quite a rough-and-tumble girl when she was young—riding horses and tramping through the woods—all to the exasperation of her mother and the delight of her father.

But her life had changed dramatically when her mother died. She became the caretaker for her younger sister, the overseer of the household, and the assistant to her father in his medical practice. Quite remarkable roles for such a young woman.

Every day he felt more drawn to her, eager to hear her thoughts on the topics they would discuss. She was not overly flirtatious like her sister, but he did sense she enjoyed his company. And being with her stirred desires in his heart he had set aside for the past three years.

What was he going to do about it? Covering the war for *Harper's* had to be his priority right now. That was his duty, and soon it would take him away from Springside—and away from Rachel.

He closed the door on those thoughts for now. His editor was waiting for his story and drawings from his prison experiences and escape. Recounting the conditions in the prisons and the hardships he and the other captives had endured was a grim prospect, but that story needed to be told. Perhaps it would push the decision makers in Washington to press for peace and the release of all prisoners, both North and South.

Opening his sketchbook, he ran his hand over the dove-gray page. Memories washed over him as he thumbed through his earlier drawings. Starry nights around the campfire with the men. The bugler standing tall, sounding reveille as the sun rose. Men charging into battle, their shouts echoing across the fields. Smoke rising from the battlefield as cannon fire thundered in the distance. A lone soldier at the edge of camp, weeping over a lost friend.

He pulled in a sharp breath and closed the book, fighting a choking sensation in his throat.

"James?" Concern filled Rachel's eyes. "Are you all right?"

He blinked and nodded. "Yes. I'm fine."

She regarded him more closely. "Perhaps you should lie down for a bit. Let me get you a blanket." She set aside her sewing.

"No. I just need. . ." He shook his head slightly. How could he shift his thoughts away from the battlefield, the prisons, and the friends he had left behind?

He lifted his gaze to Rachel's face. Her gentle brown eyes seemed to probe his thoughts. She was certainly a lovely distraction. Perhaps that was his answer. He opened the book once more and turned to a new page. "I'd like to draw your portrait."

A rosy glow filled her face. "Why would you want to do that?"

His gaze traveled over the soft curves of her cheeks and the dark lashes surrounding her beautiful eyes. "So no matter where I go, I can always remember you."

His throat tightened, and he looked down, trying to regain control. What was wrong with him? Ever since he'd come to the Thorntons', emotions he'd hardened for so long seemed to be softening, like a wax candle before a fire.

He cleared his throat. "I must've left my pencils upstairs."

"I'll get them for you."

"No. The walk will do me good." He rose from his chair. "Save that smile. I'll be right back."

Her blush deepened, and she nodded.

He strode from the room, doing his best to hide the discomfort each step caused. He had to push himself and build up his strength. He wouldn't get stronger by resting all day. Soon he would have to return to the battlefield. The Union had to be preserved. Slavery must be stopped. Countless men had given their lives for those ideals. He couldn't forget their sacrifices.

One day soon, he would have to say goodbye to Rachel. No matter how much he cared for her. A cold, hollow feeling grew in his stomach. Gritting his teeth, he forced himself to climb the stairs to his room.

Chapter 6

Rachel pressed her lips together as she watched James walk through the parlor doorway. She could tell his ribs were still hurting. But at least he was up and walking.

Lord, thank You that he has come this far. Please complete his healing.

Her prayer faltered as she thought of what would happen then. James would leave, and she would be left behind again to wait and worry about him. Perhaps he wouldn't even write to let her know how he fared. Andrew had only penned one letter, and it had arrived after the devastating news of his death.

A wave of panic rose and made her heart pound. Would the same thing happen to James? How could she live with the fear of not knowing if he was dead or alive? She blinked away hot tears and stared at the worn sock stretched over her darning gourd. The gaping hole in the toe seemed to mock her, daring her to try and close it.

The sound of horses approaching drew her attention. She set aside her darning and rose to look out the window. Two men on horseback rode up the long drive toward the house. They wore blue officers' jackets, but the rest of their clothes looked dirty and worn. She didn't recognize them.

A shiver raced up her back. Amos was mending broken fences in the hillside pasture. Esther had gone to lie down after dinner, complaining of a headache. She and James were virtually alone in the house.

The men dismounted and climbed the steps to the front portico.

Rachel's heartbeat pounded in her ears. Who were they? Did they bring news about her brother?

A loud knock sounded on the door. She looked over her shoulder, wishing Amos or Esther would appear.

"Help me, Lord," she whispered, then crossed the foyer and opened the door.

The taller man looked her over with a sleazy grin. "Afternoon, ma'am. Is this Doc Thornton's place?"

Rachel's stomach quaked, but she forced her gaze to remain steady. "Yes, it is."

"We'd like to talk to the doctor." The tall man exchanged a brief glance with his shorter companion.

The hair on Rachel's arms prickled. She didn't feel comfortable telling them her father wasn't home, but she didn't want to lie, either. An idea flashed into her mind. "I'm sorry. He's with a patient. He can't see you right now."

The short man grinned and rubbed his dirty hand on his pants leg. "Well then, we'll just have to come in and wait till he's free." He pushed past her into the entrance hall.

Rachel gasped and clutched the door. "You can't just barge in here. You'll have to wait outside."

The other man chuckled, then grabbed her arm and pulled her away from the door.

"Let go of me!" Rachel tried to pull free, but he only held on tighter.

The tall man kicked the door closed, and the short heavyset man stepped up next to her. "Now, maybe you'd like to tell us the truth. Is your daddy home?" He reeked of wood smoke, sweat, and tobacco.

Revulsion rose in her throat, and she clamped her mouth closed.

"Now listen here, missy," the tall man said as he gave her a little shake, "you better open that pretty little mouth of yours and start talking, or we'll have to find a way to loosen your tongue. Who else is in the house?"

Her face flamed, but she maintained her silent glare.

The short man glanced around the room. "Whooee, look at this place. Your family must be mighty rich. How'd you hold on to all these fine things? Your daddy in cahoots with Governor Johnson and the rest of those filthy Union men?"

Alarm raced through her like an electric shock. These men weren't Union officers. "Those uniforms you're wearing obviously mean nothing to you."

The short man grinned and slapped his hand against the front lapel of his jacket. "Oh, these? We helped ourselves to these fine jackets from some dead officers down Murfreesboro Way. And I ain't gonna tell you how them officers died." He cocked his head, grinning like a drunken fool.

Her eyes widened, and she felt like she might be sick to her stomach.

"Shut up, Horton." The tall man tightened his grip on her arm. "Now, I asked you real nice if anyone else is home, and I'm still waiting for an answer."

Where could he have put that tin of drawing pencils? Just yesterday he'd seen them on the small table next to the bed. James knelt and looked under the bed. He spotted the tin and carefully maneuvered himself into position to pull it out.

The sound of a door closing downstairs and male voices made him stop and listen. Rachel hadn't said she was expecting anyone, but people often came calling unannounced. He rose and made his way to the top of the stairs.

"I told you, my father is seeing a patient, and we have a few servants working around the place." Rachel's voice sounded unusually high.

"Go get your father and bring him out here."

James frowned, then knelt and looked through the baluster of the curving stairway without revealing his presence.

Two men stood with Rachel. One gripped her arm while the other looked her over with a leering grin.

"I can't disturb my father," Rachel insisted. "You'll have to leave and come back another time."

The men laughed. "Oh, no, missy. We aren't going anywhere."

James's anger seethed. He had no idea who these men were, but they were up to no good, and it was up to him to defend Rachel.

He dashed back to his room as quietly as possible, dumped the contents of his saddlebags on the bed, and grabbed his pistol. Checking to be sure it was loaded, he hurried back to the top of the stairs.

"You must have some money or valuables hidden around the place." The bigger man pulled Rachel closer. "Come on. Give us what we want."

James focused on the men, searching for weapons. He didn't see any, but they could be hidden in their clothes. If he stepped out now and challenged them, would he be able to protect Rachel? The element of surprise seemed to be his best advantage. He stood, took aim, and fired.

A vase on the side table exploded. Shards of glass flew in every direction. Rachel screamed. The tall man cursed and jumped back, dropping his hold on her. The short man yelped and crouched, covering his head.

"I have five more bullets where that one came from," James announced.

The tall man looked up and spotted him. "Why, you—" he snarled and took a step toward the stairs.

"Stay where you are." James descended two more steps. "I'm a crack shot, trained in England."

The man reached for Rachel, but she stepped back.

"Leave her alone." James shifted his gaze to her for a split second. "Move away from them."

Though her face was pale, she nodded and backed up toward the stairs.

"Now, very slowly, I'd like you men to leave." James motioned toward the door, praying they would go without a fight.

"What if we don't want to?" the tall man said in a surly voice.

"That mistake could cost you your life." *Help me, Lord.* James's gaze remained steady, but he could feel the beads of sweat forming on his forehead. Would they see the tremor in his arm or suspect he'd only recently regained the strength to stand?

The short man tugged at the other man's jacket. "Come on, Porter. Let's go."

Porter cursed then turned and walked toward the door. James kept his pistol trained on them. The short man passed through the doorway and stepped outside. As he did, Porter reached into his coat and spun around.

James fired as the gun flashed in Porter's hand.

Porter yelled, grabbed his side, and fired at James.

The bullet whizzed past his ear. He returned fire as Porter ran out the door.

James rushed down the stairs and across the entrance hall. Glass crunched under his boots. Once outside, the men jumped on their horses and galloped down the drive, heading for the main road. He shut the door and locked it, then turned to Rachel.

She stared at him, her face still pale.

He laid aside the gun and wrapped her in a comforting hug. She trembled in his arms. "It's all right," he said softly.

"But if you hadn't been here. . ."

He tightened his hold and tried to chase away that dark thought. "But I am here, and I won't let anything happen to you." He held her close for a few more moments as silent prayers rose from his heart.

Finally, she stepped back and looked up at him. "Shooting that vase. . .scared me to death. . .but it worked."

"I'm sure the Lord gave me that idea. I hardly had time to think."

Rachel sent him a wobbly smile. "He rescued us both today."

James nodded. It was true, the Lord had taken care of them; but he couldn't push Rachel's comment from his mind. What if he hadn't been here? What would those men have done to her? How could he leave, knowing the danger the war could bring to her door?

Chapter 7

O h, Mr. Galloway, you don't have to bring those dishes in here. We'll get them." But Esther's glowing eyes told how much she appreciated his help.

Rachel smiled as she set the empty platter on the kitchen table. James had won Esther's heart with his continual compliments of her cooking and his habit of clearing the dishes from the table.

"Esther, this was such a fine meal, I'm honored to give you whatever assistance I can provide." James stacked the dishes on the sideboard and gave her a small bow.

"Mercy, listen to you goin' on like that." Esther shook her head and laughed. "You're gonna spoil us all, then what are we gonna do when you're gone?"

Rachel's smile melted away, and her hands suddenly felt cold.

There had been no more discussion about when James would leave, but each day he was getting stronger. Somehow, she would have to find the strength to say goodbye when the time came. Right now, she didn't want to think about it.

James moved past her through the swinging door then held it open for her. She smiled her thanks, and they returned to the dining room. Susan met them there, slowly making her way around the table, collecting the soiled silverware, looking none too happy with the task.

Father grinned at them from the head of the table. "Thank you for cleaning up. Quite different than the old days, eh, Rachel?" He lifted his brows.

She smiled and nodded as the memories flooded back. Before the war, and even further back, when their mother was alive, they had several maids and an assistant cook to help Esther prepare and serve meals. Rachel and Susan rarely helped with any common duties. But all that had changed in the last few years.

Most of their servants left to travel north and make new lives for themselves. Rachel was sorry to see them go, not so much because it meant more work for her, but because she thought of them as family, and she missed each one.

But it was probably for the best. Father could never afford to pay that many servants now. Though he worked harder than ever, few people could pay him his normal fees. He often returned from a house call with a chicken or a bunch of vegetables as payment. At least they didn't go hungry.

Amos strode into the dining room with a broad smile on his face. "I picked up three letters while I was in town."

Esther followed him in, clutching a dishtowel.

"One is for you, Mr. Galloway." Amos handed a thick envelope to James. "And the other two are for you, sir." He passed the letters to Father and then stood by, holding his hat in his hand while Father examined the first envelope.

"Thanks be to heaven," Father whispered in a choked voice. "It's from Nathan."

Rachel hurried to his side. "Open it, Father."

"Oh, praise the Lord." Esther grabbed Amos's arm. He nodded and patted his wife on the back. Susan joined Rachel and gave her a quick hug, while Father tore open the letter.

He adjusted his spectacles and read aloud. "'My Dearest Family, I am well and now working at the Armory Square Hospital in the center of Washington. We have a thousand beds here, and they are almost always full of sick and wounded men. I know my training is not all that it should be, but I am glad I can help these brave men and ease their pain. We are able to save many lives, but sadly, not all.'"

Tears misted Rachel's eyes. She swallowed and tried to blink them away. James walked over and laid his hand on her shoulder. How thoughtful he was to notice her response. She looked up and sent him a grateful smile.

Father continued, "'Your wonderful letters have been a great comfort and encouragement. I am sorry I have been slow to reply. Many times I sat down to write, but the weight of the day seemed so heavy on my soul that it was hard to put the pen to paper. I know you understand.

"'I hope to be home to celebrate Christmas with you all this year. I will write again to tell you when I'm coming, but know that my heart is already there, and each night I fall asleep with visions of Springside and my dear family on my mind. Please write again soon. Your loving son, Nathan.'"

Rachel sighed and gazed toward the fireplace. Nathan carried a heavy burden, treating so many injured soldiers day after day; but he was well, and they would all be together again at Christmas. That would make their celebration so special.

Father folded the letter and patted her hand. "Can you believe it? Our Nathan will be home in just a few weeks."

"Who sent the other letter?" Susan leaned over Father's shoulder.

He opened it and scanned the page. "It's from my brother Edward." He read the first section to himself, then nodded and smiled. "He and your aunt Julia plan to come for a visit later this month. They'll arrive next week and hope to stay through the end of November to celebrate Thanksgiving with us."

Rachel squeezed Father's arm. "Oh, it'll be wonderful to see them again." She laughed and looked at James. "So much good news in one day. I hardly know how to take it all in."

He returned her smile and nodded, still holding his unopened letter in his hand.

"Edward says they'll also bring his wife's cousin Daniel Kincaid, a young lawyer who has just opened his practice in Bowling Green." Father looked at Rachel. "I've never met him, but of course he's welcome." He put his arm around Rachel's shoulder and gave her a quick squeeze. "That will make it a fine Thanksgiving with so many gathered around our table."

"What about your letter, Mr. Galloway? Is it from your family?" Susan sat at the table, and Rachel joined her.

Sadness flickered in James's eyes then faded. "No, it's from my editor. That's why I'm in no hurry to open it. I imagine he's not too pleased that I haven't sent the story and sketches he asked for."

"But you're still recovering. He ought to understand that." Susan pushed her hair over her shoulder. "Perhaps Father should write him a letter on your behalf and explain your condition."

James smiled. "That's a thoughtful suggestion, but I doubt my editor would appreciate it." He tore open the letter, and several bills of currency fell to the floor.

Susan gasped. "Oh my, look at all that money."

Rachel tugged her sister's sleeve as James stooped and picked it up.

"It looks like your editor must not be too upset with you," Father added with a chuckle.

James laughed along with him. "Apparently not." He stood, tucked the money in his vest pocket, and glanced at the letter. His face brightened as he read.

"Is it good news?" Susan asked.

Rachel tugged at her sister's sleeve again.

Susan turned and glared at her "What? I just asked a simple question."

James grinned at them. "My associate, Thomas Beckley, will be coming to Nashville. My editor wants me to wait here to meet him rather than traveling to Virginia." As he continued reading, his expression darkened.

Fear knotted Rachel's stomach. "What is it, James?"

"He says the election is stirring up deep feelings all over the North and the South. Even with the colder weather, both sides appear to be sending troops to Tennessee. He expects a major battle will be fought here soon."

An icy shiver raced along her arms. She glanced at Father and then at James. "In the Nashville area?"

"It's possible. I'm sure the Confederacy would like to retake Nashville if they can. But no one knows their plans for sure."

Father turned to Amos. "Did you hear any news of troops moving toward Nashville when you were in town?"

Amos shook his head. "I just picked up the mail and ordered that new part for the wagon like you asked." He rubbed his chin. "I'm sorry, sir. If I knew you was wanting war news, I could've gone down to the newspaper office or asked around at the livery."

"It's all right. I have to go into town tomorrow to see a few patients. I'll see what I can learn then."

Rachel's stomach tensed. The Union's control of Nashville had allowed them to live in relative peace and safety for the past two years. If the South regained control, everything would change. Their loyalty to the Union would put them in a dangerous position.

A sense of foreboding rose in her heart, and she gripped the edge of the table. Looking across the room at James, she saw his eyes reflecting the same troubling emotions. The war was coming to Nashville, and there was nothing they could do to stop it.

Chapter 8

Rachel stared at her book and read the same lines for the third time, but their meaning still didn't sink in. She glanced at James.

He frowned slightly and motioned for her to look down again. "You have to maintain the same pose."

She felt heat stealing into her cheeks as she lowered her gaze again. Did he like what he saw? Or did he think her face was too thin and her nose too long? What about her prominent cheekbones and high forehead? She stifled a groan. Why had she agreed to let him draw her portrait again?

Of course she knew the answer to that question—he had insisted his last drawing didn't do her justice and had asked permission to draw another. How could she say no to him?

His kindness and generosity toward her family had made a deep impression on her. He'd insisted on giving Father most of the money he'd received from his editor, saying he owed his life to them. It would take care of their needs for the next few months and provide wonderful feasts for Thanksgiving and Christmas.

She heard the sound of horses' hooves and carriage wheels on the front drive and looked up. Father laid aside the newspaper and rose from his chair.

Susan rushed to the window and pushed the curtain aside. "Oh, they're here!" She sent them a jubilant smile then hurried to open the front door. Father followed her.

Rachel rose and brushed her hand down her skirt. It had been more than a year since she'd seen Uncle Edward and Aunt Julia. Though it was only sixty miles to Bowling Green, the war made travel too dangerous for frequent trips.

James set his drawing book on the table and walked with her to the front portico. She glanced at his handsome profile as he watched the carriage approach. She treasured these days with him. His associate from *Harper's* was due to arrive in Nashville any time. Every day brought his departure closer.

He hadn't said anything about his feelings for her, and he'd made no promise to write or return for a visit. She pushed those painful thoughts aside, but she couldn't keep them from dampening her spirits.

The carriage rolled to a stop, and the side door flew open. Uncle Edward stepped down then turned to help his wife. Finally, a tall young man with dark wavy hair and a full mustache stepped from the carriage.

Father greeted his brother with a warm handshake. "Edward, it's so good to see you."

Father took Julia's hand and kissed her cheek. "Welcome, Julia."

"Thank you, Josiah." Julia turned to the young man beside her. "This is my cousin, Daniel Kincaid. Daniel, this is Dr. Josiah Thornton and his family."

"I'm happy to meet you, sir." Daniel shook Father's hand. He looked past Father's shoulder and smiled at Rachel.

Father turned to her. "This is my oldest daughter, Rachel."

Rachel held out her hand to Daniel. "It's a pleasure to meet you."

His dark eyes lit up. "The pleasure is all mine." He bowed, lifted her hand to his lips, and kissed it.

Rachel swallowed. Few men had greeted her that way.

Daniel looked up, still holding her hand. "Cousin Julia told me so much about you. I've been looking forward to our meeting."

James frowned and clasped his hands behind his back as he watched them.

Father introduced Susan. She smiled and held out her hand. Daniel repeated the kissing gesture, but he didn't linger over her hand as he had with Rachel.

"And this is our friend, James Galloway," Father continued. "He is an artist covering the war for *Harper's* newspaper."

James's gaze held a challenge as he shook Daniel's hand.

"Interesting line of work. Perhaps you'll share some stories from the battlefront."

James gave him a brief nod then turned and shook hands with Edward and Julia.

"How long have you been with *Harper's*?" Daniel asked as he crossed the portico, walking between her and James.

"Four years."

Daniel studied him. "Where are you from?"

"England." James's tone was clipped and formal.

"I thought so. I'm from Kentucky myself," Daniel added with a proud nod. "Born and raised in Louisville. I studied law at the university there. I've recently moved to Bowling Green to begin my law practice."

"So you never enlisted in the Union army?" James raised one brow.

"Oh, no." Daniel chuckled. "Kentucky is neutral. I wouldn't think of taking sides in this dreadful war."

James glanced at Rachel, his disapproval of Daniel obvious.

Daniel turned to Rachel. "Cousin Julia tells me you're a fine horsewoman. Perhaps we can go for a ride together soon. Nothing like a jaunt in the crisp fall air to enliven the senses."

James grimaced and looked away.

"Why, yes, riding would be lovely." She forced a smile, hoping Daniel wouldn't notice James's response.

"I love to ride too," Susan said. "We had more than a dozen horses before the war. But Father gave all but three of them to the Union Army."

Rachel sent Susan a warning glance. Would she ever learn to think before she spoke? There was no need to announce their reduced circumstances the minute their guests walked in the door.

Father ushered them into the parlor. "I'm so glad you've arrived safely. I was concerned with all the rumors of troop movements that you'd cancel your trip or run into trouble."

Edward chuckled. "We didn't have any trouble at all. Union soldiers stopped us as we came through Nashville and asked where we were going. After I told them, they waved us through."

Father turned to Rachel. "Would you tell Esther our guests have arrived and that we'd like some refreshments?"

"Of course, excuse me." Rachel headed to the kitchen, but she didn't find Esther there. Looking out back, she spotted her hanging laundry on the line. As she pushed open the back door, their eleven-year-old neighbor, Aaron Tillman, ran across the pasture toward the house. He ducked under the fence rail and dashed up to her.

"The rebels are at our place, looking for horses." He pointed over his shoulder, panting for breath. "My father sent me to warn you. He says they're coming this way."

Rachel grasped his shoulder. "You're sure?"

"Yes, ma'am. They took our horse Clover, even though she's old and swaybacked."

Rachel scanned the road leading to the Tillmans'. She didn't see any rebel soldiers yet, but no doubt they were on their way. "Thank you, Aaron. You hurry home and be careful."

"Yes, ma'am." Aaron held on to his hat as he ran back across the pasture.

Esther hustled over, toting the empty laundry basket. "What's got into that young'un?"

A plan formed in Rachel's mind as she repeated Aaron's message.

Esther gasped. "Lord, help us. The rebels are coming!"

"Go inside and tell Father I've taken the horses to the Chestnut grove by the lower spring."

Esther grabbed her arm. "This ain't no game of hide an' go seek. Those rebels will do somethin' awful to you if they find out you hidin' horses from them."

"Then I won't let them find me." She pulled away. "They can't have our last three horses." Determination pulsed through her as she ran to the stable and pushed open the door. The smell of sweet hay and warm horseflesh greeted her. She grabbed the lead rope from the first stall and attached it to Ranger's halter. He whinnied and nuzzled her shoulder.

"It's all right. We're just going for a little walk. Everything will be fine." She wasn't sure if her whispered words were more for her sake or the horse's.

Hoofbeats sounded in the distance. She crept to the stable door. Peeking out the crack, she spotted four Confederate soldiers riding toward the house with two horses tied behind. One was old swayback, Clover.

Rachel shivered and hurried to the second stall. With trembling hands, she grabbed Lady's lead and tried to clip it to the halter. "Lord, help me get this on."

What about her uncle's two horses and his carriage? Their driver must have taken them out on an errand in town because they weren't in the stable. She didn't have time to worry about them now.

The stable door squeaked open. Rachel froze. Her heart pounded so hard she thought it would jump out of her chest. Footsteps crossed the stable toward her. She closed her eyes and prayed to be invisible.

"What do you think you're doing?" Frustration edged James's voice.

She whirled around. "You nearly scared me to death!"

"You can't take three horses out of here by yourself."

"Then perhaps you should help me." She pushed past him and moved into Moonbeam's stall.

"There's no time. The rebels are already here."

"These horses are the only way my father can get around to see his patients, and they're our only hope of rebuilding our stock when the war is over."

He studied her for a moment. "All right, but I hope you know they'll cook us and the horses for dinner if they catch us."

A strangled laugh rose in her throat. "I can't believe you're making a joke at a time like this."

"I've found humor is helpful in desperate moments." He grinned and held out his hand for Moonbeam's lead rope. "I suggest we go out the back way."

"Good idea." She grabbed Lady's lead in one hand and Ranger's in the other then followed James out the door. Gratefulness rose in her heart. If she was going to outrun the rebels there was no one else she would rather run with than James Galloway.

James held a low-hanging branch aside while Rachel led Lady under the cover of the large tree. A few seconds later, she returned for Ranger. James followed her in, leading Moonbeam. He paused and looked up at the leafy canopy. Crimson and gold leaves hung around them in a near perfect circle almost touching the ground.

"This is a great spot." He tied Moonbeam to a low branch.

"We used to play here when we were children." Though they were at least a quarter of a mile from the house, she kept her voice low.

James smiled, thinking of Rachel as a young girl playing make-believe in this magical place.

Rachel looped Lady's lead rope over a branch. "Do you think we're safe here?" The vulnerability in her eyes made his stomach clench. She'd been so strong up to this point. Now he could clearly see the fear she'd kept hidden.

"No one will find us here." He prayed that was the truth.

A gust of wind ruffled the leaves overhead. A crow called in the distance. She shivered and rubbed her hands down her sleeves.

He wished he could take her in his arms and calm her fears, but that didn't seem right when he would be leaving soon. What did the future hold? Would he ever see Rachel again after he left Springside? The weight of those questions made him feel like a heavy stone pressed into his chest.

He moved to a sturdy, low-hanging branch. "Come sit with me."

She joined him and eased herself onto the branch. "What shall we do now?"

He forced a smile. "I suppose we could have a cup of tea and a nice chat while we wait."

She laughed softly and shook her head. "Sometimes I don't know what to think of you."

He feigned surprise. "What do you mean?"

"One minute you're seriously discussing important issues, and the next, you're making me laugh and forget all my troubles."

"And this is a problem?"

"No. . .I just don't know which is the real James Galloway."

"They both are." He cocked his head and grinned. "Life would be very boring if you could only have one mood, wouldn't you agree?"

She pushed back with her feet and made the branch swing a little. "I suppose that's true. The Bible does say a cheerful heart is good medicine." Her smile faded. "But it's difficult to always have a cheerful heart, especially with everything that's happening with the war."

His expression softened. "That's when we need it the most."

"I try, but. . ." She bit her lip and looked away.

"What is it?"

She lifted her gaze to his. "I'm afraid, James. I don't want you to go."

Her honest words snatched his breath away, and he struggled to form a response.

She rose and turned away. "I'm sorry. I shouldn't have said that. I know you have a job to do and no reason to stay here."

Her words tore at his heart. He longed to tell her there was nothing he wanted more than to stay here with her. But how could he make a declaration like that without a plan for the future? And what about his commitment to *Harper's* and his duty to his friends?

"This is hard for me, James. I've already lost someone I cared about deeply."

"You have?"

"Yes. His name was Andrew Tillman. We grew up together. His parents are our closest neighbors." The tenderness in her voice made it clear that she and Andrew were more than neighbors.

"What happened?"

"He joined the Confederate Army as soon as Tennessee seceded. He died fighting in his first battle just a few months later."

"I'm sorry. Were you engaged?"

"No, but we had promised our hearts to each other before he left."

He leaned closer until his arm touched hers. "I can understand a little of what you've gone through. I lost someone dear to me not too long ago."

She tilted her head and looked up at him. "Who?"

"My sister died last December. I didn't realize how ill she was until it was too late for me to return to England. We never had time to say goodbye."

"Oh, James." Tears shimmered in her eyes.

"I wanted to go home as soon as my parents wrote and told me she was ill, but Hettie sent another letter and insisted she'd be fine."

Rachel lifted a startled gaze to his face. "Your sister's name was Hettie?"

"Yes. Well, her real name was Henrietta, but we called her Hettie."

"Is she the woman in the tintype you carried in your saddlebag?"

He nodded. "Why do you look so surprised?"

"You called for Hettie the first night you were here." She lowered her gaze. "I thought she was your sweetheart."

"No. A dear sister, but not my sweetheart."

"Oh, I'm glad." She looked up, and her eyes widened. "I mean. . . it sounds like you were very close. I'm sorry for your loss."

"Thank you." He paused for a moment. "I think Hettie would've been very fond of you."

She ducked her head and smiled. "What makes you say that?"

"She loved horses as you do, and somehow she found a way to tolerate me."

Rachel laughed then covered her mouth to stifle the sound.

"You'd better be careful, my dear, or you'll give us away."

She nodded, her eyes glowing with affection. She slowly lowered her hand, revealing her tender smile.

His heart soared. She obviously had feelings for him. Surely he could tell her he cared for her even though he had no idea what was to come or how they could be together.

Taking her hand, he pulled in a deep breath. "Rachel, though I've only known you a few weeks, I want you to know that I—"

"There you are!" Susan pushed through the branches into their shady hideaway, followed by Daniel Kincaid.

James stifled an irritated sigh and dropped Rachel's hand.

"The rebels are gone. Father says it's safe to come back." Questions flickered in Susan's eyes as she glanced at Rachel and James.

"We thought you might need help with the horses." Kincaid moved toward Rachel.

James clenched his jaw. If Kincaid tried to kiss her hand again, he'd knock that hat right off his head.

"That was quite a daring plan to hide your horses," Kincaid said. "But it could have ended in disaster if you'd been discovered."

"Well, no one found us, and for that I'm grateful." She turned and sent James a private smile.

His heartbeat quickened. He returned her smile, hoping she understood he had more he wanted to say.

Chapter 9

The next morning a bright blue sky hung overhead as Rachel and Daniel walked back to the house following their ride. She would've rather spent the morning with James, but there had been no gracious way to decline Daniel's request. Susan had begged to go along, and Rachel was more than willing, but Father insisted she stay in because she seemed to be coming down with a cold. Rachel released a soft sigh. Now the day was half spent.

"Springside is certainly beautiful this time of year." Daniel gazed across the pasture.

"It's beautiful all year round." She tried to keep the hint of impatience out of her voice, but she wasn't successful.

He chuckled. "I'm sure it is, I was simply pointing out how impressed I am with your property."

"Thank you." She got the words out, though it pained her.

"On our way to Nashville, we saw many homes that had been damaged or deserted, but the war hasn't seemed to touch you here. You're very lucky."

"I believe in Providence rather than luck."

He tipped his head. "Of course. I believe in Providence as well."

"We're grateful for God's protection, and we pray daily for a Union victory." She lifted her skirt and hurried up the back steps.

"Rachel, wait." He removed his hat and joined her on the back porch. "This morning hasn't gone as I'd hoped. Have I done something to offend you?"

She glanced away. "No. You've been a perfect gentleman. I'm sorry I've been. . .distracted."

He took her hand and kissed it. "Of course. All is forgiven."

She wanted to pull her hand away, but she waited until he released it then turned and went inside.

Susan met them in the entry hall. "I need to speak to you." She took Rachel's arm and steered her away from Daniel.

"Excuse me," Rachel called over her shoulder then leaned closer to Susan. "What is it?"

"James just received a message," Susan whispered. "Thomas Beckley has arrived in Nashville."

Rachel clutched Susan's arm. "Where's James?"

"Upstairs packing. I knew you'd want time to say goodbye."

"Thank you." She squeezed Susan's hand. They might clash over silly things, but in a crisis, their loyalty ran deep.

Rachel hurried to James's room. Through the open doorway, she saw him by the bed placing his drawing book in the saddlebag.

He looked up. His gaze locked with Rachel's. Then he clamped his jaw and continued packing.

"May I come in?"

"Yes, of course." He spoke without looking at her.

"You're leaving?"

"Yes, I'm meeting Thomas in town."

"What will you do then?" She crossed the room to stand beside him.

"We're headed to Franklin. The Confederates are gathering south of there. We believe they hope to take Franklin then push north toward Nashville."

Goosebumps raced up her arms. "Franklin is only fourteen miles from here."

He looked up, apprehension flickering in his eyes. "I didn't realize it was so close." Frowning, he paced to the window and looked out. "Does your father have a plan to move you to safety if the battle comes this way?"

Rachel shook her head. "Father won't leave Springside unless troops march across the pasture. Even then he'd probably stay to care for the wounded rather than flee."

"Perhaps you and your sister should go to Bowling Green with your aunt and uncle. . .and Daniel."

Questions swirled through Rachel's mind as she lifted her hand to her forehead. Was the war finally coming to their doorstep? Were they truly in danger? Would they have to leave Springside?

James moved to her side and took her hand. "I'll speak to your father about taking you north, at least until things settle down. You should be safe there."

All the hair-raising stories James had told them about rushing to the front lines to capture the action for his drawings flooded her mind and sent a terrifying shiver through her. "How will you stay safe?"

"I'll be fine. Nothing's going to happen to me."

She pulled her hand away. "Is that what you said before you were captured at Cold Harbor?"

"Rachel, please, let's not quarrel."

"How can we avoid it when you have so little regard for your safety?"

"That's not true. I take every possible precaution."

"But you admitted the risks you took led to your capture. You could have remained in a safer position, but you stayed to finish that final sketch, and that's when you were taken."

"Yes, but that was before I spent three months in a Confederate prison." His expression softened. "And before I met you." He took her hand again and looked in her eyes. "Rachel, I promise I'll be careful. But I have to go. Please try to understand."

She waited, hoping he would promise to speak to her father about his feelings for her. But he only searched her face once more then released her hand.

"How will you get to Nashville?" she asked, her voice thick with emotion.

He placed a shirt in the saddlebag. "Perhaps your uncle will allow his driver to take me in his carriage."

"I want you to take Lady."

He frowned and nodded. "I suppose that would work. Amos could ride Ranger and bring Lady back after I get to the hotel."

"No, I want you to keep her."

His expression softened. "Oh, Rachel, I know how much Lady means to you. I can't take her."

"Just keep her until you buy another horse. Then you can return her to me." Hopefully, Lady would carry James out of danger and bring him safely back to her.

James nodded, his eyes shining. "Thank you. I'll take good care of her."

"I know you will." She sent him a tremulous smile. "Please, take care of yourself."

"I will." Then he leaned down and placed a feather-light kiss on her cheek. "I'll write. I promise"

Rachel's spirit lifted like a floating cloud. Surely that kiss and promise to correspond meant James cared for her. He would return, not just to bring Lady home but to see her again.

Chapter 10

James's back ached as he hovered over the desk in his hotel room in Nashville, finishing the drawing depicting the Battle of Franklin. He yawned and rubbed his eyes, trying to wipe away the gritty feeling.

For the past seven days, he and Thomas had traveled with the Union troops as they took their stand at Franklin and held back the surging Confederates. But there had been devastating losses on both sides. General Hood and his Confederate soldiers weren't giving up. Troop movements seemed to indicate they were regrouping, and this time, Nashville could be the target.

James dipped his brush in the China white paint and stroked highlights on the clouds over the sketch of the battlefield scene. He needed to finish his drawings tonight. First thing tomorrow, they would be sent to New York by special courier along with Thomas's article. Hopefully they would convey the bravery of the troops and stir up prayer and support for the dire situation in Tennessee.

But what would happen in the week or two before the story and drawings were published? Would Nashville be able to defend itself against the Confederates, or would it become another casualty of the war?

And what about Rachel and her family? His stomach twisted as he tried to suppress his anxiety. Before he left Springside, he urged Dr. Thornton to take Rachel and Susan and travel north until the danger passed. The doctor assured him their safety was his highest priority, but he didn't believe that would be necessary.

James shook his head. Surely, after all the injuries the doctor had treated, he realized a cannonball was no respecter of persons. If the battle came to Springside, they would all be in great danger. Perhaps the doctor would change his mind and send them away.

Thomas entered the room, his expression grim. "I spoke to Colonel Clarence Miller. He says they're pulling out in the morning. I believe we should go with them."

James nodded and wearily rinsed his paintbrush.

"Are you about done?"

"I have a few more details to add to General Schofield's horse."

Thomas sat on the bed and tugged off his boots. "It'll be good to sleep in a warm bed for a change rather than out in the open."

James nodded and focused on his drawing. The sooner he finished, the sooner he could get some well-deserved rest . . .but would he be able to fall asleep with so many disturbing thoughts on his mind?

Had Rachel left for Kentucky? Would Kincaid be able to protect her if the need arose? Would she fall for the lawyer's charms? The thought of her riding off with Daniel Kincaid made his hand shake.

A black mood descended over him. He tossed his paintbrush aside and rose from the chair.

What did it matter? He had no idea how long this blasted war would last. It could be years before he'd be free to settle down and give Rachel the kind of life she deserved. Maybe she should marry Kincaid. With his family connections and new law practice, he could provide a safe and stable life for her.

But a knife pierced his heart as he thought of Rachel in Daniel Kincaid's arms. He had to get back to Springside, but how could he do that with troops from both sides encircling Nashville?

Rachel lifted the evergreen garland and handed it to Esther. "Drape it a bit more before you reach the next nail."

Esther stepped up the ladder. "All right, but it don't seem right puttin' up decorations when we just come through a terrible battle and there's wounded men in the house."

"That's precisely why we need to decorate. Our victory at Nashville is worthy of celebrating, and Christmas is an even more important reason."

"Well, celebratin' is the last thing on your father's mind. He hasn't had a good night's sleep in three weeks, ever since those rebels attacked Franklin."

"I'm sure it will cheer him to see our decorations." Rachel stifled a yawn. She'd been up late several nights in a row helping Father care for the five wounded men he'd brought home after the battle of Nashville.

With all the turmoil in the area, her uncle, aunt, and Daniel had decided to stay through Christmas and do what they could to help.

There had been no word from James. Her hands felt clammy as

anxious thoughts taunted her again. Had he been captured or injured at the Battle of Franklin? Much of the fighting had happened at night, and there were frightening stories of hundreds of casualties on both sides.

Then, early in December, the Battle of Nashville had been fought south of the city. Springside lay several miles to the east; so thankfully, they'd only heard the cannon fire and seen the smoke of the battle from a distance.

Now Christmas was only three days away. She prayed James was safe and well, but each day, when no letter arrived, she fought her own battle against fear and despair. How could she go on if she lost him as she had Andrew? Oh, why didn't he write and set her mind at ease? At least she would know he was alive and not locked in some terrible Confederate prison or dying in some dreadful field hospital.

She pulled in a calming breath and lifted her face to the sunlight streaming through the ruby colored glass above the front door. *Lord, please take care of James, and help me to trust You.* She could not let fear win. Her victory would come as she turned each anxious thought into a prayer and held on to hope. James would write soon, just as he promised.

Susan came in the front door toting a basket of holly with Daniel at her side. "Oh, now it looks like Christmas!"

"Yes, you've done a wonderful job." Daniel sent Rachel a lingering smile.

"Thank you." She couldn't deny she enjoyed his attention and compliments. He obviously hoped to win her affection, but thankfully, he hadn't spoken to her about his feelings. She wasn't sure what she would say if he did.

"Where do you want me to put this holly?" Susan removed her cloak.

Rachel nodded toward the parlor. "Why don't you arrange it with the evergreens on the mantel?"

Susan nodded. "Come help me, Daniel." She took his arm and guided him away.

He glanced at Rachel with an imploring look as he passed.

She glanced up at Esther and pretended not to notice.

As soon as they entered the parlor, Esther clicked her tongue. "That man has feelings for you."

Rachel tugged on the hem of Esther's skirt. "*Shhh!*"

Esther chuckled. "It's true."

"Well, you don't have to announce it to the world."

"I'm not. I'm just sayin'—"

The front door flew open, and a Union officer burst in.

Esther yelped and grabbed the ladder. Rachel's hand flew to her mouth.

The bearded officer spun toward her with a broad smile and held out his arms. "Merry Christmas!"

She gasped and dropped the garland. "Nathan! Oh, Nathan!" She leaped toward her brother and hugged him tight. He felt more solid than before, and his jacket carried the delicious aroma of wood smoke and pine needles.

"Thank You, Jesus!" Esther hurried down the ladder

Susan ran into the entrance hall and squealed. Nathan laughed and swung her around. Daniel joined them, smiling at the happy reunion.

"What's all the commotion?" Father called, coming down the stairs.

They all turned and grinned up at him.

His eyes widened, and his mouth dropped open. "Nathan?"

"Hello, Father." Nathan's voice cracked.

Father opened his arms, and they embraced. "Oh, son, it's so good to see you."

Rachel blinked back happy tears and placed her arm around her sister's shoulder. Seeing her brother safely home was such a wonderful gift. Now, if only she would hear from James, then her heart could be at peace.

Chapter 11

With the last rays of sunlight fading in the west, James walked across the front drive at Springside. He'd risked his friendship with Thomas and his editor's wrath to make it back to Nashville by Christmas Eve.

Candles flickered in the parlor windows as shadows of dancing couples floated past. The melodious strains of a waltz reached his ears as he mounted the front steps. His heartbeat quickened. Soon he would take Rachel in his arms and dance with her around the room. Then he would tell her everything in his heart, and she would answer with a promise to be his.

Before he could knock, the door opened, and Susan appeared on the arm of a young Union officer.

"James! What a wonderful surprise." She invited him in and

introduced him to her companion, but James barely heard what she said.

He removed his hat and set it on the side table, then strode to the parlor doorway. The furniture had been pushed to the sides of the front and rear parlors, opening a large center area. Several couples danced to a tune played by a fiddler and pianist, while at least a dozen others, including three men with bandaged injuries, sat around the edge watching. The scent of pine and cinnamon hung in the air.

James spotted Rachel on the far side of the room, and his heart beat faster. She wore a wine-colored dress with rows of ruffles and a tempting view of her neck as she danced with a tall, bearded Union officer. He guided her into a turn, and she gazed up at him with a look of pure delight in her eyes.

James's spirit sank like a heavy rock thrown in a pond. Maybe he was too late. Perhaps he shouldn't have come at all. He stepped back and bumped into someone.

"Whoa there." Dr. Thornton steadied him.

He turned and faced his friend. "Hello, sir."

"James, welcome! We didn't know you were back in the area. Glad you've come to join us." A merry smile lit the doctor's face as he leaned closer. "There's a certain young lady who will be very happy to know you're here."

James cast a solemn glance over his shoulder. "I don't know. She seems quite taken with her current partner."

Dr. Thornton chuckled. "She always has been fond of her brother, but I'm sure she'll save you a dance."

"Her brother?"

"Yes, Nathan is home with us until the New Year." Dr. Thornton clapped him on the shoulder. "Why don't you go in and let Rachel know you're here?"

"Yes, sir. Thank you. I will." He spun around and headed through the parlor door. Searching the room, he found Rachel again, but she had changed partners. Now she danced with Daniel Kincaid. Her bright eyes and beaming smile made it clear how she felt toward him.

Setting his jaw, he marched across the parlor and tapped Daniel's shoulder. "Excuse me."

A soft gasp escaped Rachel's lips. Daniel turned. His dark brows dipped, but he released his hold on Rachel. All around them, couples slowed and exchanged concerned looks.

"Shall we?" Before she could answer, James took her in his arms and waltzed her across the floor in perfect time to the music.

She sent him a flustered look. "I didn't know you were coming."

"I wouldn't miss my chance to dance with the most beautiful woman in the room." He tightened his hold, bringing her closer.

Her cheeks blazed. "It's not polite to break into the middle of a dance like that."

"I'm sorry, but I've missed you terribly, and I couldn't stand seeing you in the arms of that. . .Kincaid."

Doubt filled her eyes. "If you missed me so much, why didn't you write?"

He missed a step but quickly recovered. "We were in the field at Franklin for several days, and then behind the lines in Nashville—"

She stiffened. "You've been in Nashville, and you didn't send a message?"

Suddenly the room felt too warm, and he wished they would open a window. "I was working night and day, then we were called away to follow General Schofield. I just returned to Nashville today, and I didn't have time—"

Her eyes blazed. "James Galloway, I was worried half to death about you for an entire month, and you couldn't find time to write me one letter?"

People slowed and turned to look their way.

Heat flooded his face, and his collar felt entirely too tight. He swallowed and looked around at the festive room and dancing couples. "I'm sure you've had a miserable time with Daniel here to keep you company through the holidays." He didn't usually resort to sarcasm, but her irritation was uncalled for.

"If that's what you believe, then you don't know me at all." Her eyes glistened with angry tears as she pulled away.

The song ended, and the other couples clapped. She glided away to the refreshment table. Daniel approached and offered her a glass of punch. She accepted it with a smile. He leaned closer and whispered something in her ear. She nodded and took Daniel's arm. They walked past James, across the entry hall, and into her father's library.

James's anger roiled like a bubbling cauldron. He grabbed his hat and strode out the front door without a backward glance.

Rachel buried her head in her pillow to stifle her sobs. James was gone, and she'd probably never see him again. Oh, what a terrible mess she'd made of everything!

A soft knock sounded at her door. "Rachel? It's Susan."

She wasn't sure she wanted to talk to anyone, but she sat up and wiped her cheeks. "Come in."

Susan tiptoed in and shut the door. "I heard you crying." She sat beside Rachel on the bed. "What's wrong?"

"Oh I feel awful about the way I treated James tonight."

"What happened?"

"I scolded him for not writing, and then I tried to make him jealous by flirting with Daniel."

Susan's eyes widened. "No wonder he left in a huff."

"I never should've let my temper get the best of me, but I was so upset he hadn't written. Then he marched in, so cocksure of himself. He broke right into the middle of my dance with Daniel and whisked me away." Remembering how he'd pulled her into his arms and danced with her across the floor made her heart pound.

"Oh, that sounds wonderful."

"But everyone was watching us, and I had no idea what to do. He tried to flatter me by saying I was the most beautiful woman in the room, but he wasn't the least bit sorry he hadn't written. He's been in Nashville almost the entire time, but he never bothered to send me one message, even after he kissed me and promised he would write."

"He kissed you!"

"Yes. . .well, it was just on the cheek."

"He did come to see you on Christmas Eve. That counts for something."

Rachel sniffed. "Yes, that's true."

"And Amos said he kept his promise to return Lady."

Rachel nodded, feeling more miserable than ever.

"He couldn't wait to dance with you. . .and he thinks you're beautiful," Susan added with a dreamy smile. "I know he should have written, but I'm sure he cares for you. He wouldn't have come if he didn't."

Rachel's tears spilled over. "Oh, Susan, I've been so foolish. I love James, but now he'll never come back because he thinks I care for Daniel."

"Oh, dear, that is a problem." Susan grabbed a pillow and hugged it to her chest. "But there's got to be some way to straighten this out."

Rachel stood and paced to the window. "Maybe I could write to him and apologize." Her shoulders sagged. "But I don't know where he's staying. He might have already left the area."

"I doubt it. The weather's so cold he's probably staying in Nashville at one of the hotels."

Rachel glanced out the window into the dark, moonless night. Tiny pinpoints of starlight twinkled down at her, reminding her of that first Christmas so long ago. The world waited in darkness for the light to come, and God saw the need and sent His Son.

Hope rose in Rachel's heart. She might not know how to find James, but she knew Someone who would help her, Someone who delighted in overcoming impossible problems and providing hope when there seemed to be none.

She clasped Susan's hands. "Maybe we could pray and ask the Lord to help me get a message to him."

"All right, but I think you might also want to confess your part of the problem."

Rachel blew out a deep breath and bowed her head. Susan was right. She needed to look at her own heart before she asked God for anything else. "O Father, please forgive me for being prideful and foolish and for letting my emotions lead me into so much trouble. I'm sorry I've been fearful and anxious and unwilling to trust You or James. Please help me find a way to make things right."

Chapter 12

Christmas morning dawned clear and bright with a touch of silvery frost dusting the grass. James's breath puffed out in a cloud as he dismounted his new horse, Samson, by the back door at Springside. Glancing left, he noticed the open stable door. Perhaps Amos was already up, caring for the animals. A warm stable was a much kinder option for his horse, so he headed that direction.

When he stepped inside, he saw Rachel throwing a saddle blanket over Lady's back. She wore her royal blue riding outfit with a jaunty matching hat.

"What are you doing?" he asked.

She spun around, her eyes wide. "James." The tender way she said his name sent a thrill through him. "I was going to Nashville to find you," she added with a tremulous smile.

His eyebrows rose. "You were?"

She crossed the stable toward him. "Yes, I wanted to tell you how sorry I am for the way I behaved last night. I didn't want you to think—"

"Please, I'm the one who should ask your forgiveness." He shook his head. "I should have written."

"I understand. You were busy and—"

"No. . .I mean yes, I was busy, but I could have sent a letter." He took her hand. "Last night I was so upset I couldn't sleep. I wrestled this through with the Lord, and He showed me I may be brave on the battlefield, but I've been a coward in matters of the heart."

"What do you mean?"

"I love you, Rachel. I have for a long time, but I haven't had the courage to tell you."

Her eyes widened. "You love me?"

"Yes, and when I saw you with Daniel last night, I felt insanely jealous and acted like an idiot. I hope you'll forgive me."

"Of course." She placed her other hand over his. "The Lord spoke to me as well. He helped me see how my fear of losing you, the way I lost Andrew, made me anxious and unable to trust. But He's so kind and forgiving. He not only showed me what I was doing wrong, He helped me see the right path."

"And what's that?"

"I need to be honest with you, let go of my fears, and trust God to take care of us both. We don't know what the future holds, but I believe God can see us through whatever comes."

"Those are very wise words." He ran his finger down the side of her face.

She responded with a smile. "I asked Him to help me find you, and here you are."

He took her in his arms. "And this is where I want to stay."

"But what about your job with *Harper's*?"

"I'd like to finish my commitment through June, but I'll be free after that. How does a June wedding sound to you?"

Her eyes danced. "A June wedding sounds wonderful. . .but perhaps you should speak to my father."

"Of course. That was my intention, to speak to you first, and then ask him for your hand."

"Oh, James, nothing would make me happier." She folded into his embrace and rested her head over his heart. "I love you so much."

"My heart is yours as well." He gently lifted her chin and kissed her. She responded with a warmth and passion that delighted him.

Father tapped his glass with a spoon. "Attention, everyone. I have an announcement to make." He smiled across the table at Rachel with misty eyes. "Today, James Galloway has asked for Rachel's hand in marriage, and I have given them my hearty consent."

Rachel's heart felt like it would burst. James took her hand under the table and gave it a little squeeze.

Susan rushed to her side. "Oh, I am so happy for you both." She kissed Rachel's cheek then turned to James. "We'll be family."

He grinned. "Yes, indeed, you'll have another brother to tease you."

Nathan shook James's hand. "Congratulations. Rachel talked my ear off, retelling all your exploits. That's a grand job you're doing, keeping the country informed and supporting our troops."

"You're the one deserving praise," James said. "Caring for the wounded takes a special kind of bravery."

Nathan nodded. "Thank you."

Her aunt and uncle added their best wishes. Then Daniel shook

James's hand and wished them both well. His smile seemed sincere, though Rachel noted a hint of sadness in his eyes.

Amos opened the door for Esther as she carried in a tray of ginger cakes. "What's all this fuss and noise?" she asked.

"Rachel and James are getting married!" Susan danced toward Esther. "Isn't that wonderful?"

Esther placed the tray on the table and hugged Amos. "Thank You, Lord! My prayers have been answered."

"Mine too," Rachel whispered and smiled at James.

After Christmas dinner, James led Rachel to a quiet corner in the library. They sat on the window seat, and he took her hand.

"What gave you the courage to come back when I treated you so terribly last night?" she asked.

He kissed her hand and looked into her eyes. "About midnight, I was praying, and God reminded me of that first Christmas. He didn't just sit in heaven and think about how much He loved us. He acted on that love and sent His Son to earth. Suddenly, I knew I shouldn't just sit in my hotel room thinking how much I loved you. I needed to get on my horse and come tell you, and see if there was any way you might return my feelings."

Her heart swelled from the sweetness of his words. "Oh, James, I'm so glad you did."

He leaned closer. "So am I. Merry Christmas, darling."

"Merry Christmas." She lifted her lips to his, hoping her kiss would show him she intended to act on all the love in her heart as well.

Carrie Turansky is an award-winning author of more than twenty inspirational novels and novellas set in Edwardian England and the US. Her latest, *No Ocean Too Wide*, follows an unlikely pair's adventurous quest to rescue countless British Home Children from an unjust emigration scheme and reunite a family torn apart. She loves weaving heartwarming tales about family, faith, and lasting love. Her novels have been translated into several foreign languages and enjoyed by readers around the world. She and her husband, Scott, have been married for more than forty years and have five grown children and six grandchildren. When Carrie is not writing, you'll find her walking around the lake near her home in New Jersey, working in her flower gardens, or enjoying a cup of tea with friends. Carrie loves connecting with reading friends on social media and through her website and blog: http://carrieturansky.com

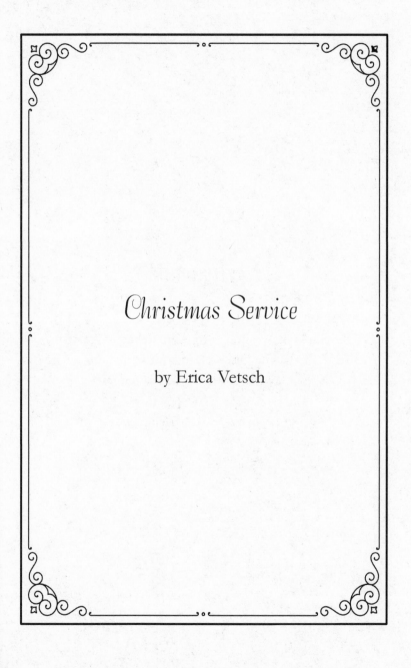

Christmas Service

by Erica Vetsch

Dedication

To the Sorensen family, Kevin, Ann, Rebecca, Jonathan, and Elizabeth, who know a thing or two about serving in church and chaotic Christmas programs.

Whether therefore ye eat, or drink,
or whatsoever ye do, do all to the glory of God.
1 CORINTHIANS 10:31

Chapter 1

December, 1875
Minnesota North Woods near Grand Rapids

Y ou'll just have to tell him no. I'm not interested." Beth Sorensen wet her finger and tested the bottom of the sad iron. No pop and sizzle. Still not ready. She mentally ran down her list of Saturday chores.

"I don't understand you, Beth." Her grandpa laid aside his glasses and pinched the bridge of his nose. "Todd Rambek is a fine man. Why won't you let him call on you? Or for that matter, the three others who have tried to court you. You're going to wind up a spinster if you're not careful."

She laughed and crossed the puncheon floor, bending to kiss his bald head. "I'm barely twenty-one, Grandpa. Hardly on the shelf yet. You've always taught me to listen for God's leading. None of the men who have asked permission to court have been the man God wants for me. Especially not Todd Rambek. He's a blacksmith, of all things."

"What's wrong with being a blacksmith? It's an honorable profession. He makes a good living, and more importantly, he's of good character—a deacon in our church. I had such high hopes that you might look favorably on him." He tapped together his sermon notes and tucked them into his Bible. "I do wish your parents were here to give you counsel. I'm hopeless with this sort of thing."

Returning to the stove, she threw another log into the firebox and tested the iron once more. Perfect. The smell of hot cotton pricked her nose as she went to work on the wrinkles in Grandpa's best shirt. She wished Mama was there too. She'd understand. After all, it was Mama who had most often said what a wonderful preacher's wife Beth would make someday.

She shook her head. A blacksmith? No, she couldn't abandon the calling she had been born to, not even for a man as handsome as Todd Rambek—deacon or not. Grandpa was a preacher, her father had been a preacher, and if she had been born a boy, she would've gone into the pastorate as well—the next generation of Sorensens to serve in a little log church somewhere in the American wilderness. It was a family tradition, a calling. She didn't know when God would bring a single preacher into her life, but He moved in mysterious ways, and she was confident He could accomplish the task.

"Did you shovel a path over to the church?" Last night's storm had decorated the Minnesota woods with a fresh half foot of snow. "I should get over there to freshen things up before church tomorrow."

Grandpa opened a newspaper and adjusted his glasses. "I didn't have to shovel. Todd took care of it first thing this morning. He's thoughtful that way." He eyed her over the top of the *Grand Rapids Gazette*.

"Nice of him." She kept her voice neutral. "Did you decide on the opening hymn?"

He flipped open the cover of his worn Bible and consulted his notes. " 'O, Sacred Head Now Wounded.' If you could, play 'When I Survey the Wondrous Cross' for the offertory, and we'll finish with 'O Come, All Ye Faithful.' That should get folks into the holiday spirit."

"So should practice for the Christmas Eve service. I'm excited about how we've switched things around. I think the adults will enjoy putting on a pageant for the children for once. We certainly had a lot of volunteers when you announced the idea last week."

"I think you've taken on too much. You'd best consider delegating some of the responsibilities. You can hardly direct the choir, the play, and the gift giving, and see to all the food by yourself."

Beth shook out the shirt and held it up to the morning light streaming through the small window set in the heavy log wall, examining the sleeves and collar for any stray wrinkles. "Perfect. I've already brushed and sponged your suit. Will you need me to polish your shoes?"

Grandpa shifted and crossed his legs. "I'm capable of polishing my shoes all by myself. You fuss too much. I don't think the church roof will fall in if I have a scuff or two on my boots or a wrinkled cuff or collar every once in a while."

She wagged her finger at him. "Nonsense. You must look the part. You're very handsome when I get you all spiffed up, and you must command the respect due your office of pastor. We can't have you looking less than your ministerial best when it's time to preach God's Word." With quick, efficient motions, she folded the ironing blanket and placed it in the cupboard under the washtub.

Cutlery and plates clinked as she set the table for lunch. "I've got stew simmering, and as soon as I get back from the church, I'll make some biscuits. How does that sound?"

"Like you work too hard. I can make the biscuits, or we can do without. I wish you'd slow down. You don't have to tackle everything in a day. Between your household responsibilities and all the things you take care of at the church, you've no time to relax and enjoy life. You've no time for gentlemen like Todd Rambek."

She lifted her coat and bonnet from their peg by the door. Clamping the edge of her red bonnet between her teeth, she shrugged into the sleeves of her dark-green coat. Once she had the wooden buttons done up, she settled her bonnet on her head. Checking her reflection in the looking glass, she smoothed dark-brown hair off her temples and tied the bow under her chin. Neat and tidy. She gave her reflection a cheeky wink. "That's right. I don't have time for men like Todd Rambek. Now, I'm off to the church. I'll be back before lunch. Don't worry about me. I'm quite content to 'Do with my might what my hands find to do' and wait for the *right* man to come along. He's out there, and I'll know him when I see him."

Just before she closed the door, Grandpa muttered, "Be careful you don't miss what's under your nose because you're too busy staring at the horizon."

Todd Rambek pumped the bellows and shoved the tongs into the white-hot coals of the forge. A bead of sweat trickled down his nose, and he swiped at it with his shirtsleeve. A little more hammering and shaping, and this peavey would be done. He had been blessed to pick up extra work from the nearest logging camp, repairing and making peaveys and cant hooks.

The camp blacksmith had gotten kicked by a horse and broken his leg, but he should be back on the job just after Christmas. Until then, Todd had all he could handle keeping their horses shod and tools in good repair as well as meeting the needs of the settlement.

The money wasn't bad either, especially since he was hoping to have need of a bigger cabin in the near future.

His hired man, Billy Mather, brought in another bucket of water. "Do you want me to haul these tools out to the camp tonight, or will they come and get them?" He tugged off his cap, leaving his hair a spiky mess.

"The Push said they'd send someone, but first thing on Monday, he wants me out there to work on the water wagon and to fit a pair of ice shoes to their best team. Can you hold down the fort here if I have to stay overnight?"

"Easy. Who is the Push this year? It isn't McGowan, is it?"

"No, a new man. Caffrey, I think? To hear the loggers complain, he must be the hardest-driving foreman they've ever worked under, but I hear they're looking to fell more than a million board feet before the spring log drive. Their blacksmith going down hampered them some. They offered me good money to move out there until he was healed up, but. . ." He shrugged and pumped the bellows again.

A grin spread across Billy's open, likeable face. "But. . .lemme guess. You didn't want to leave our little settlement without a blacksmith?"

"I have a lot of work to do here, and not just in the shop. I have other responsibilities too. They just made me a deacon at the church. Wouldn't look right to abandon my post so quickly, would it?"

"Could it be you didn't want to leave a special someone?"

Wielding the long-handled tongs, Todd yanked the peavey spike from the flames. He hefted his favorite hammer, so familiar it was almost an extension of his arm. Laying the spike on the horn of the anvil, he pounded the glowing metal and sent a shower of sparks toward the floor. Billy didn't miss much that happened in this hamlet. A few more whacks, and Todd stuck the hook back into the coals.

"So, am I right?" Billy swept his hat across a stump and examined it before taking a seat—a wise move, for any surface in the shop might have a hot coal or piece of cooling metal on it. Todd kept a sign over the forge that read SPIT BEFORE YOU SIT to warn customers.

"Right about what?" Todd wiped his hand down his leather apron.

"Don't play games. I'm talking about Beth Sorensen. You like her. I think you more than like her."

He did, and he had for a long time, but he wasn't ready to spill his longings to anyone, much less Billy Mather, good friend though he might be. Todd had finally reached a financial position to consider marriage. He'd gone to the preacher to ask if he might call on his granddaughter, and waiting for the reply had driven him to distraction for most of the day. Even as cold as it was, he'd kept the door propped open so he could see the path to the preacher's log cabin. He pumped the bellows again. "Don't you have some chores to do?"

"Sure, but what happened when you called on Pastor Sorensen? You asked him if you could court Beth, right?"

Todd whipped around. "You know about that?" His tongs clattered off the front edge of the forge, and he sprang backward to avoid getting burned.

"I do now. You just confirmed my suspicions." Billy grinned. "I saw you talking to him up by the church this morning when you were shoveling snow, and I figured you might be asking permission to call. So, what's the verdict? Is she willing?"

A groan started somewhere around Todd's toes and worked its way up. He throttled it before it squeezed through his teeth. "He said he'd ask her and get back to me, but he didn't say when that would be."

"Did he sound like he thought it was a good idea?"

Todd shrugged. "He said he'd ask but not to get my hopes up."

Which was ridiculous, since if his hopes weren't up, he wouldn't have asked in the first place.

"That doesn't sound positive. What if she says no? Will you try to get her to change her mind?"

"You're worse than an old woman wanting to gab when there's work to do. Suppose you take those buckets of ashes out and spread them on the pathways to and from the church? Melt some of that snow and ice and make it safe for the old ladies." Todd didn't worry that Billy would be offended. Nothing seemed to offend him.

Billy craned his neck to peer through the open doorway. "Wouldn't you rather do it yourself? Beth's coming over to the church from the parsonage right now." He shoved his hands into his pockets and leaned back against the log wall by the workbench. "It'd give you a chance to say hello and maybe test those courting waters." The grin spread across his face irked Todd for a moment.

Sweat slicked his palms, sweat that had nothing to do with the forge or hard work. His heart popped in his ears like gunpowder under a hammer. "Maybe I will. Anything to get me out of here and your old-woman nagging." He flung off his leather apron, snatched up the buckets of ashes from beside the door, and strode out into the cold, not bothering to put on his coat.

Beth spied the giant of a man approaching and wanted to sink into a snowdrift until he passed by. He dangled two buckets from his hands, and in spite of the cold, he wore no coat, only a plaid shirt with the sleeves rolled up.

Todd Rambek. Why did she have to run into him before Grandpa had a chance to talk to him? She cast about for some place to. . .not exactly hide, but rather to avoid him. Knee-high piles of snow blocked her escape. Like it or not, she was going to have to speak to him.

He drew nearer, his stride eating up the ground. At almost six and a half feet tall, he dwarfed Beth by more than a foot. Hours bending over a forge, molding metal to his will, and wrestling recalcitrant horses into submission for shoeing had given him a physique not too far off the tales of Paul Bunyan.

She shook her head at that fantasy, clasped her hands at her waist, and composed her countenance. "Good day, Mr. Rambek." Better to speak to him first.

"Miss Sorensen." His rich, deep voice sent a tickly sensation through her middle. She looked up—way up—into his equally rich dark-brown eyes. "On your way to the church?"

Knowing this man wanted to court her caused her to see things, to see him, differently. Hoping her appraisal didn't show, she collected his features—the broad shoulders, well-muscled neck, square jaw, lashes thick and straight, and a smile that made her heart bump. She'd known he was handsome, but standing this closely, knowing he would like to call upon her, that he had sized her up and found her to his liking, that heady combination took her breath away.

"Yes," she managed to get out, gathering her scattered wits and reminding herself not to be silly. He might want to call upon her, but she had turned the offer down. Not that he knew of that yet, but he would. And her reasoning was sound. Her life had been mapped out long ago. Marry a minister, and serve God in the church. No blacksmith, not even a deacon blacksmith, had any part of her future.

"Would you like me to go with you? I could light the fire in the stove if you're going to be there awhile. The church will be too cold for you to play the piano."

"Thank you, but I don't want to take you from your errand." She motioned toward the buckets.

"No trouble. I was heading to the church anyway. Thought I might spread these ashes on the path to melt some of the snow. I'd hate to see anyone slip on the stairs." He turned on the narrow path and headed back the way he'd come, his buckets clanking.

Beth followed in his wake. It was thoughtful of him to think of the safety of others. Very thoughtful. Too bad he wasn't a preacher.

Chapter 2

At the end of the Sunday service, Beth closed her hymnal and lowered the keyboard cover on the piano. She turned down the kerosene lamp next to the music stand before rising from the bench. Congregants stood in little knots in the aisles and amongst the pews, chatting, greeting one another, everything harmonious.

Grandpa gathered his Bible and papers and strolled toward her.

She offered her cheek for his kiss. "Wonderful sermon, Grandpa."

"Thank you, dear. You played beautifully." He took her arm and steered her to the back of the log church. They took up their accustomed places, side by side, shaking hands and giving each parishioner a personal greeting.

Beth loved this part of her duties, a substitute for her grandmother, who had passed away in the same epidemic that had taken her parents, leaving her an orphan and her grandpa a widower.

Mrs. Sophie Amboy tottered up, leaning hard on her cane. "Pastor, thank you for opening the Word for us today. We surely appreciate having a fine pastor like you to lead us." She offered her gnarled hand in its fingerless lace glove. The scent of lavender drifted off her rusty-black dress. "And Beth, the music lifted my spirits. So festive. Well, I won't keep you, but I will see you this afternoon. Looking forward to taking part in this program you're planning. I haven't been in a Christmas program since I was a girl."

"I'm glad you're looking forward to it. I'll see you back here at 2 p.m. sharp." She held out little hope that Sophie would be on time. She, like many of the members of the congregation, had a rather fluid take on timetables and was apt to show up late more often than not.

"Miss Sorensen."

She jerked. Mr. Rambek stood before her. A rock lodged in her throat, and heat rushed into her cheeks. A quick glance at Grandpa told her he had yet to speak to Mr. Rambek about her refusal of his suit. Grandpa became engrossed in the story the grocer's wife told.

"Mr. Rambek." Beth held out her hand, and his came up, clasping it and dwarfing it between his palms. His work-roughened skin rasped against hers, warm and tingly. Beth smiled politely and withdrew her fingers.

"I'll see you for lunch." His brown eyes so mesmerized her she failed to take in his words. "Thank you for the invitation."

Finally what he was saying penetrated her fascination. "What?" Her voice shot high, and her mouth fell open.

Brows bunching, he tilted his head. "Your grandfather invited me to share the noon meal with you."

"Oh, he did?" She tore her gaze away and sought out Grandpa's face.

Shrugging, a sheepish grin on his lined face, Grandpa stepped closer. "Didn't I tell you? I meant to, but I guess I forgot. Must've had my mind focused on my sermon. No matter. Beth always makes plenty. A great little cook, she is." Grandpa put his arm around Beth's shoulders and hugged her.

She painted a pleasant expression on her face. Grandpa would hear about this, but not in front of the blacksmith. "Of course, Mr. Rambek. You're most welcome. If you don't mind, I believe I'll head home now to make preparations. You can come with Grandpa as soon as he's done here."

"No, child," Grandpa cut in. "Todd here can escort you to the cabin, and I'll be along shortly. He can help you lift that roast from the oven. I won't be long."

Neatly hemmed in unless she wanted to cause a scene, Beth acquiesced. Perhaps it was better this way. Grandpa clearly hadn't spoken with Mr. Rambek about his desire to call upon her, so it was up to her to disabuse the blacksmith's mind that there could ever be any feelings between them.

He helped her with her coat and held her Bible for her while she tied her bonnet strings. When she went to take back her Bible, he shook his head. "I'll carry it for you." He held the door and took her elbow to help her down the stairs. Her boots crunched on the cinders he'd spread yesterday, and with the thin winter sun filtering through the pines, they made their way along the path to the parsonage.

With every step, she knew she should tell him. But how did one get started? Just blurt it out? *Mr. Rambek, you're welcome to lunch with us, but after that, I don't want you to call ever again.*

Wouldn't that sound lovely? A fist of tension pressed under her ribs, and she wished she had her Bible to hang on to, something to do with her hands. It might not sound lovely, but the man had a right to know. *Stop dillydallying, and just say it.*

"Mr. Rambek—"

"Miss Sorensen—"

They spoke at the same time, and she stopped on the trail.

"Please, go ahead, and I'd be obliged if you'd call me Todd." He ducked under a low-hanging branch—a branch that she'd walked under with no trouble—and waited.

Her mouth went dry, and she tugged her lower lip, letting the scratch of her woolen glove distract her for a moment. Finally, she mustered her courage. "Mr. Rambek—Todd—my grandfather informed me that you asked his permission to call upon me…socially." Warmth surged through her cheeks, further intensified by the light that leaped into his eyes. "While I am flattered, I must decline the offer." There, it was out.

"You don't care for me?" He tilted his head, the gleam dying from his eyes, leaving puzzlement and hurt behind.

"I don't really know you."

He shifted his weight from one great boot to the other and switched the Bibles to his other arm. "Then why turn down the request? You could get to know me better before deciding. That's what courting is for, to spend enough time together to see if we would suit one another." Thankfully, he kept his voice low so none of the people walking home around them would hear.

And while what he said sounded reasonable—and would be if she weren't so sure of God's calling on her life—she knew she had to stand firm. "I'm sorry, Mr.—Todd, I have my reasons."

"Does someone else have your affection?" He crossed his arms over her Bible and his against his chest.

She blinked. "No. Not yet."

"Then I see no valid reason why you shouldn't allow me to call upon you. We're both believers, of good health, near enough the same age."

His logic made her feel rebelliously illogical. "Really, this is silly. You've asked to call, and I've declined. I would prefer not to go into why. I was trying to be polite, to break it to you as gently as possible, but I can see I must be blunt. I do not wish you to call upon me socially. I could never have tender feelings for you. You're obviously well qualified to make someone a wonderful husband, but you will not be mine." She turned and marched up to the parsonage door, flung it open, and closed it in his face before she remembered he was supposed to dine with them.

Pastor Sorensen was right in one respect. Beth Sorensen was a fine cook. Roasted beef and vegetables with thick, brown gravy, hearty wheat bread, and dried-apple pie with a crust so flaky it shattered when he cut it. Todd forked a portion into his mouth.

Beth held herself so stiffly he thought she might shatter like the pie crust. She picked at her food and avoided looking at him.

Pastor Sorensen alternated between amused tolerance and exasperation, smiling and frowning by turns. He kept the conversation going but had to ask Beth questions point-blank to get any response.

Todd pressed the tines of his fork into the bits of syrupy apple filling and crusty crumbs on his plate and savored the last bite. Pushing his plate back, he rubbed his stomach. "An excellent meal. Thank you for your hospitality. As a bachelor, I don't often enjoy such fine cooking."

Beth rose and began clearing the plates. She lifted an apron from a peg beside the washtub and tied the strings into a perky bow at the back of her tiny waist. Moving efficiently, completely at home in her kitchen, she poked the fire, poured water from the kettle over a cake of soap in the washtub, and began washing dishes.

Everything about her spoke of what a great wife and homemaker she would be. Why had she spurned him? Was she being coy? That didn't line up with what he thought he knew of her.

Pastor Sorensen cleared his throat, jarring Todd, making him realize he'd been staring. Winking, the pastor inclined his head.

Todd grinned, a spark of hope lighting his chest for the first time since Beth had slammed the door in his face. Though her response had set him back for a while, he knew himself well enough to know he wasn't finished yet. He loved a challenge. If Beth could just get to know him a little better, she'd see what he'd known for a long time. That they were meant for each other. If she thought she could just brush him off and he'd fade away, she had another think coming. "I'll dry." He scooted his chair back and plucked a towel off the counter.

Pastor Sorensen chuckled and opened his newspaper.

When Todd reached for the first wet plate, his fingers brushed hers, sending forge-hot sparks up his hand.

Beth flicked a glance up at him from under her long lashes, giving him a glimpse of the blue-green depths of her eyes. "Thank you."

"My pleasure. Not long now until practice." The clock on the mantel nudged past one thirty. "Seems like everyone I spoke with this morning was looking forward to the service. Are you?"

She whisked dishes through the hot water so fast he was hard-pressed to keep up. "Of course. It will provide something different for the children. I'm sure, come Christmas Eve, you'll be surprised at what we've come up with." This time her eyes looked right into his.

So, she didn't intend for him to be part of the cast? A grin tugged at his lips. "Oh, but I won't have to wait until Christmas Eve. I plan to be there for every practice."

Before she could protest, Pastor Sorensen broke in. "That's terrific, Todd. I'm sure you can help Beth in so many ways, like building the set and hanging the decorations. She's told me some of what she's planned, and I have to say, it's an ambitious undertaking. I've told her she might be flying too high for the time and people she's got to work with, but with you helping her out, it's sure to be a success." He beamed on them over his half glasses.

Todd didn't miss the twinkle in Pastor's eyes, nor the exasperated sigh from Beth.

"Really, there's no need." Beth added more hot water to the dishpan. "I can handle the decorations, and I thought perhaps Billy Mather would build the stable for me. I'm sure you're much too busy with the shop to volunteer for the Christmas service."

"I'm never too busy to serve in the church. I've been looking forward to it. Billy can give me a hand if I need it, but it won't be any trouble at all for me to volunteer wherever there's a need."

She plunged her hands into the dishwater, and a fluff of soap floated up and clung to her eyebrow. Blinking, she tried to rub it with the back of her wrist, but Todd grasped her arm.

"Hold still. You'll get soap in your eye. Let me." He stepped close, inhaling the scents of cinnamon and apple that clung to her. The top of her head came to about his collarbone, and the bones of her forearm were light and small. He swallowed. "You'll have to look at me, so I can wipe that soap off."

She turned her face upward so slowly he thought his heart would stop completely. No woman had ever affected him like Beth did. Her blue-green eyes held a challenge, but the way her breath hitched told him she wasn't immune to his nearness. Carefully, he dabbed her brow with a dry corner of his dishcloth.

Pastor Sorensen cleared his throat, and they sprang apart. Beth handed Todd a fistful of cutlery and edged around him to put away the dry dishes. Pastor yawned and stretched. "Todd, you'll walk Beth over to the church, won't you? I think I'm going to take a nap."

"Yes, sir. And I'll see her safely home too." He wanted to laugh at the look on Beth's face, as if she'd somehow been betrayed.

Her mouth was set in a straight line, and her movements were more jerky than smooth as she snagged his coat from the hook and shoved his hat into his hands. "We might as well go then. It wouldn't do for me to be late." She took her own coat from the peg and stepped away from him before he could offer to hold it for her.

Here's your hat. What's your hurry? Yep, courting Beth Sorensen was going to be a challenge.

Chapter 3

I want to thank you all for coming." Beth turned up one of the lamps hung between the windows on the log wall. Though it was midafternoon, the log church sat in a grove of pines that—while protecting the structure from howling blizzard winds—blocked out a great deal of sunlight. "If you'll find a place in the front pews, we can get started." She took her place behind the lectern and consulted her notes, flipping through the pages while men and women jostled and settled, some still chatting while others stared expectantly.

A bubble of anxiety lodged in her stomach. Was she up to the challenge of shepherding a dozen adults through a program? Most of whom were nearly twice her age? Todd took a seat at the end of a row, crossed his arms over his broad chest, and watched her. She turned her shoulders a bit to put him on the edge of her vision and mustered her best "in-charge" voice. "I thought it might be easiest to break the service down into the different areas. We have the choir, the living nativity, the Christmas tree, and the food. First, the choir."

A hand shot up. "Who's going to direct the choir?" Mr. Hampton inclined his head.

"I had thought to direct." Beth toyed with her pencil and leaned on the lectern her grandfather used when he taught Sunday school.

"How can you direct when you'll be playing the piano? I don't mind directing." He tucked his thumbs under his braces and leaned back.

Mr. Hampton direct the choir? She consulted her list, buying time, searching for a way to say no that wouldn't wound him. "Mr. Hampton, that's very generous of you, but if you're directing, the choir wouldn't have your fine tenor voice. I had planned to have the choir stand behind the piano, so I can play and direct at the same time."

Mary Kate Bormann raised her hand. "What kind of food were you thinking of having? We always have *krumkake* on Christmas Eve."

"I don't want any of that foreign food. Plain old shortbread cookies should be enough for anyone." Clive Jenkins rubbed his round middle and stuck his red whiskers out. "Maybe some cider."

"Cake would be nice. Maybe fruitcake?" Sophie Amboy piped up. "I've got a new fruitcake recipe that I would love to try. I just know it will be the right one this year."

Beth's stomach knotted. Sophie had been trying—and not quite succeeding—at making Christmas fruitcake for the past several years. One year they would be hard as bricks, the next squishy and oozy.

Suggestions and counter-suggestions flew through the group, and a dozen conversations blossomed. "Please, if we could all be quiet and handle this in an orderly manner. . ." She might as well be talking to the white-pine log walls for all the attention her words garnered.

"Excuse me." Todd's deep voice rolled over the conversations. Talking ceased. "Maybe we should move on to something else. The menu for the treats doesn't have to be decided this minute." Heads nodded, and Todd waved for Beth to continue.

She took a deep breath and consulted her lists again. "I'd like to move on to the living nativity. I need a Mary, a Joseph, a couple of shepherds, and some wise men. Of necessity, we'll have to have some of the choir members do double-duty in the play. There will be time to shed the costumes before the last choral piece."

Immediately the chatter started again. Everyone seemed to know who should be doing what, and there were several volunteers for each part in the play.

"I think Mary Kate should be Mary. She's got such pretty yellow hair."

"Everybody knows Jesus' mother didn't have yellow hair. She was Jewish. It's only in the paintings and such where she's got yellow hair. Maybe Mary Kate should be an angel. Everybody knows angels have yellow hair."

"Are we having angels in the play?"

"I thought angels were boys in the Bible."

"Christmas tree angels are girls."

"Please, if we could quiet down, I have a few ideas—" It was like trying to herd butterflies. Beth rapped her pencil on the lectern, but no one paid any heed. Except Todd, who remained silent, never taking his eyes off her face. Chatter continued.

"That doesn't mean Mary Kate wouldn't make a good Mary. She's already got the name."

"I don't know if I could play that part. I mean, all those people looking at me. Mary is the center of the whole play."

"I thought Jesus was supposed to be the center of the whole play." This dry remark from Mr. Hampton caused both frowns and a ripple of laughter.

"Perhaps we should focus on—" Beth tried again, but the discussion didn't stop. How could she prove what a good pastor's wife she would make, how excellent her organizational skills were, if people refused to stop talking and listen?

Mary Kate's face flushed, and she smacked Mr. Hampton on the arm. "You know I didn't mean that Jesus wasn't important, but are we going to have a real baby to play Jesus? Last year they tried that when the kids put on the Christmas service, and little Arnold Harrison screamed the rafters down the entire time. I thought he was going to break all the new glass windows and we'd have to go back to those drafty wooden shutters again. Maybe we should just use a doll or wrap a towel in a baby blanket."

"Please, everyone, if we could just quiet down." Beth raised her voice and slapped the podium. The sound ricocheted off the log walls, and heads swiveled. Heat swirled in her cheeks and ears, but at least everyone had stopped talking.

She cleared her throat, trying to ignore the smile teasing Todd's lips. How dare he laugh at her? She narrowed her eyes in his direction and pulled back her shoulders. "I'm going to ask you to all remain quiet. I've given each aspect of the service considerable thought, and I believe, if you'll just listen, you'll agree it is a plan we can all work with."

Without waiting for any comments, she barged ahead. "For the choir, we'll be singing three songs. 'Silent Night,' 'Hark, the Herald Angels Sing,' and my favorite, 'Joy to the World.'"

"I like 'O Little Town of Bethlehem.' That would be the best one to sing, since we're doing the nativity play." Clive scratched the hair over his right ear.

Todd cleared his throat and rose. His head almost brushed a crossbeam. "Folks, we all seem to be laboring under the idea that this service is still in the planning stages. Miss Sorensen says she's got it all mapped out. Why don't we listen to the director all the way through before we throw around any more opinions?"

Beth's lips trembled, but she grasped the edges of the podium and gathered herself while Todd resumed his seat. "Thank you. Now, I'd like to explain how the gift tree will work, then the food we'll serve, and finally, I'll assign parts for the play."

She plowed ahead, and for the most part, folks stayed quiet. Until she started casting the play. Nobody was happy. If she put people in, they declared themselves unfit. If people weren't cast, they took umbrage. Her head spun, and through the entire process, she could feel Todd judging her, weighing up her lack of skill in corralling this renegade congregation.

She glanced out the window at the fading sunlight and realized they'd been thrashing things out for over two hours. And they hadn't even managed to practice one song yet. Nothing had gone the way she'd planned.

Shuffling her papers, she blew out a breath. "Folks, it's getting late. The last thing on my list is the schedule of practices. We've got two weeks until Christmas Eve. In that time, we'll have four evening practices and one afternoon dress rehearsal the day of the service. We'll also meet on the twenty-third to decorate the church and build the stable for the play."

Once more everyone jumped into the conversation, objecting to or agreeing with the schedule. The room swayed. Beth closed her eyes as a wave of tiredness washed over her. She hardly dared look at Todd to see what he thought of this turn of events. The noise tapered off.

She opened her eyes and found herself staring right at Todd, who had stood once more. His eyebrows rose, and a smile quirked his lips. "I think the schedule sounds just fine. I'm sure we'll all do our best to fit in with what you've got planned."

Billy Mather's hand went up. "You're gonna need help getting all the pine and holly and the Christmas tree and such. And the lumber to build the stable. Maybe you need an assistant director. I'm thinking Todd is your man."

At his phraseology, heat charged up Beth's neck and pooled in her cheeks.

"Todd's a fair hand with a hammer," Billy went on, "and he'll be driving through the woods nearly every day between the logging camp and here. Lots of time to scout out a Christmas tree and the decorations you might need."

The only thing the entire group agreed on that night was that Todd would make an excellent assistant for Beth.

"Are you all right?" Billy got up from the table and flopped into the chair before the fireplace in Todd's cabin. "You haven't said a word since the practice ended. Are you mad because I volunteered you to help Beth? I figured with you two starting to court, you'd be happy to have an excuse to spend more time with her."

Todd scooped leftover ham and beans into a crock and covered them for his lunch tomorrow. He was no great shakes as a cook. Their supper had tasted nothing like the flavorful roast he'd eaten this noon at the Sorensen table. What would it be like to eat that well every day? And how much better would the food taste if he could look across the table and see Beth there? "I'm not mad."

"You're sure not happy. What's wrong?"

Stowing the crock in the cupboard, he returned to straddle his chair backward. The wood creaked, but he'd built it strong, and it fit his long frame so he could cross his arms across the back and rest his chin to stare into the fire. "She said no. She doesn't want me to come calling."

"What?" Billy struggled upright. "Why not?"

He shrugged, feeling the tug of his suspenders. "She didn't say. Just a 'no thank you.'"

"I'm sure sorry. I thought, from the way you were watching each other and how she blushed every time her eyes lit on you, that she'd said yes."

She had blushed every time she'd caught his eye, but it wasn't from pleasure and anticipation or the beginnings of tender feelings. It was embarrassment, pure and simple.

His chin dug into his forearm. The optimism and challenge he'd felt before had faded with each of her attempts to pretend he wasn't at the rehearsal. What had started as a drizzle of doubt that he could win her heart had developed to a downpour in his chest the more he thought about things. "She had her hands full today."

Billy laughed and plonked his elbows on his knees. "She sure did. Seemed like we'd just get headed down one road and somebody would make a break for it down another. If all the practices are this chaotic, I don't imagine we'll be ready for the service in just two weeks."

Two weeks until Christmas. "We might need more than just a few practices between now and then."

"You'll get to spend a lot of time with her, especially if you're helping with the decorating and set building. Maybe you can get her to change her mind... see what a terrific fellow you are. A real catch."

"A man can't do his courting with all those people around." Todd grimaced. "With Clive and Sophie sniping at each other, and Mary

Kate arguing with every word that comes out of Hampton's mouth? Not exactly the most romantic of settings."

"Pshaw! You're not trying. I bet if you put your mind to it, you can find ways to show her you care, and there won't always be so many people around. Don't give up so easy."

Was he giving up too easily? How did a man go about courting a woman who wouldn't be courted?

"What you need is a little outside help." Billy studied his fingernails. "I bet if you asked them, every last person in the Christmas service would be happy to nudge things along."

A spark of hope lit in Todd's chest, but he shook his head. "Would that be fair?"

" 'All's fair in love and war.' Beth wouldn't stand a chance if the whole group was working to get you two together. You do love her, don't you?"

He did. And he had for a long time. Since the first time he'd laid eyes on the preacher's granddaughter. He'd scoffed, telling himself he didn't really know her and that being pretty wasn't enough of a recommendation to be a wife. But the more he watched her, the more he learned of her character, the more his love grew. As did his certainty that she was the one God wanted him to marry. Was all fair in love and war? "Let me think about it. I thought she was perfect for me, but maybe God has another plan."

His friend rose, stretched, and yawned. "I'd best head home. The boss will be after me tomorrow if I'm late and droopy from staying up." He grinned and got into his coat. "Thanks for supper. Don't give up on Beth. She might not know what she wants until you show her. Think of some ways to romance her, show her how much you care. No woman can resist a man who is truly in love with her."

The door closed, leaving Todd alone in his single-room log cabin.

He stirred up the coals and added more wood. Firelight pushed the shadows to the corners of the room.

How did one go about romancing a woman? The dead of winter was a rotten time for flowers.

He could give her a Christmas gift. But what? He could purchase something from the store, but if he made something, that would be more personal, right? What could he make? She was hardly in need of a new cant hook or wagon wheel rim. Ice skate blades? A bridle bit? A string of harness bells?

He thought up ideas and cast them aside until a flash of inspiration sparked. Bounding up, he went to the bed, knelt, and fished underneath. He dragged out a flat-topped wooden trunk. His father's toolbox. He carried it to the table, lit his kerosene lamp, and opened the lid. Ranks of picks, screwdrivers, tiny calipers, delicate chains, and ingots of silver and gold. His father had worked with metal too. But where Todd used hammer, anvil, and forge to bend steel and iron into implements and horseshoes, his father had been a silversmith, a jeweler.

Lifting the tools from their places one at a time, he examined them. He couldn't make her jewelry. That wouldn't be proper. No girl would accept jewelry from a man she wasn't engaged to marry. But he could make her a gift. A Christmas ornament for her tree.

As he laid out the tools and sketched ideas on a scrap of paper, he prayed. "Lord, You know my heart. You know how much I love Beth. I'm asking You, if she's the one for me, that You'll make it plain to her and to me. And if she's not. . ." He sucked in a breath and made a few more pencil strokes, gathering his courage to say what needed to be said. "Lord, if she's not the one for me, I'm praying that You'll make that plain to me too. If she's not Your best plan for me, then I'm asking You to take these desires from my heart."

Even as he said the words, he knew how hard it would be if God chose for him not to have Beth. And yet, he had to trust that following God's will, even if it meant a future without Beth, would be better than going his own way.

In the meantime, he would concentrate on making something beautiful that showed what was in his heart. Surely if she knew how much he cared, she'd consider his suit. Patience usually wasn't too hard for him, but where Beth Sorensen was concerned, he couldn't seem to lay hold of any.

Chapter 4

Todd strode toward the log church. Light streamed from every window, and through the panes, figures moved. He shouldered open the heavy church door, his arms wrapped around a bundle of pine boughs, stomping in the entryway to rid his boots of snow before entering the big room.

Feminine laughter and the pounding of hammers greeted him. Church folks clustered at the far end, busy transforming the stage into Bethlehem and a piney bower rolled into one.

Tomorrow was Christmas Eve, and he'd made little headway with Beth. Perhaps tonight would be different.

"Hey, you finally made it." Billy reached for the branches. "I thought you'd never get here. What happened?"

"Sorry. I got held up out at the camp. Half the logging chains decided to break today." He shrugged out of his heavy coat and hat and ran his fingers through his hair to straighten it. "Did I miss much?"

His eyes sought out Beth, bright as a cardinal in a red dress. Lamplight shone on the smooth wings of her hair pulled into a fancy knot high on the back of her head. Color danced in her cheeks as she laughed at something one of the ladies said.

"Hello? Are you listening?" Billy tipped his head to the side and nudged Todd's elbow.

He jerked his attention away and focused on his friend. "Huh?"

Billy rolled his eyes. "I said we were waiting to do the rafters until you got here, but it doesn't look like you've shown up, even though you're standing right there." He grappled with the branches and wound up dumping half of them on the floor.

Beth and several others looked over at the noise.

"I'll get 'em." Todd bent and scooped up the fragrant limbs.

"Follow me." Billy made a beeline for the women. "Think they'll work for the rafters?"

The ladies pounced on the decorations Billy carried and began weaving them into wreaths and tying them into long strings.

Todd stood there with his arms full, feeling like a bull moose in a herd of graceful deer. His heart thudded against his shirtfront and stopped altogether when Beth turned away from draping the piano with a crimson cloth and looked right into his eyes.

God, if this is You taking away the desire to be with Beth, I don't think I've quite got the hang of it yet.

Skirting a group of men hammering together a set of risers for the choir, she came to stand before him. "Here, let me take those. We thought maybe you weren't coming." She sounded like a teacher scolding a tardy student.

So she'd noticed he was late. That was good news, wasn't it? She gathered the boughs he held, and when her hand brushed his, his heart leaped into a gallop.

"Sorry I'm late. Where would you like me to help?" A board clattered to the floor, drawing his attention to the stage.

Beth sighed, her mouth twisting. "Help Mr. Hampton. He insisted he knew how to construct the stable, but he's been at it all evening, and he won't take any direction from me. 'A little lady like you couldn't possibly know one end of a hammer from the other.'" Her voice, though low enough that only he could hear, wavered in a perfect imitation of Hampton's nasally twang.

"Sure thing. Glad to help. And I'm sorry I was late." But she'd already turned away to direct the hanging of the wreaths in the windows.

Hampton heaved and shoved, his face turning purple as he struggled to lift a plank over his shoulders and brace it on a crosspiece.

"Let me help you." Todd grasped the rough wood and hoisted it onto his shoulder. "Go ahead and nail it to the supports. I've got this."

Hampton growled and hefted a hammer. Instead of whacking in the nails, he tapped and tinkered and took his time. Though Todd could hold the heavy plank easily all evening, he had no desire to, and after a few minutes of Hampton messing around, Todd lifted the hammer from his inept hands. With two mighty blows, made awkward by still holding the plank on his shoulder, Todd sent the nails home, anchoring the roof of the stable to the wall of rough-barked pine logs that he'd helped raise into place when they'd first constructed the church three years ago. The pine still gave off a resin scent and leaked pitch when the weather got hot. "There. That should do it."

The shopkeeper's mouth puckered like he'd just kissed a sourball.

"Thank you." He snatched the hammer out of Todd's hand and marched away.

Todd shrugged and stood back to survey the construction. The plank he'd nailed formed the roof of the "stable" and was supported by another upright board that formed the side wall of the temporary structure. Todd stood a foot taller than the peak of the stable roof. Since he was supposed to play Joseph in the nativity scene, he'd have to kneel or sit. Standing would make him look like a lone pine in a pasture.

Beth seemed to be everywhere, overseeing everything, and though she kept her distance from him, he supposed he was the only one who noticed. She remained tactful and calm, juggling opinions and quirks. And she'd planned a very nice program. The only problem he could see was that she tried to control everything and wasn't much for delegating, not even to her assistant director.

After the stable was completed, Beth kept Todd and everyone else hopping with projects. Hanging more lanterns, moving the piano, and finally winding yards and yards of pine and fir garland around the exposed rafters crossing the sanctuary.

Since the peeled-pine logs that formed the rafters were only a few inches above his head, Todd had no need of a ladder. Billy fed him ropes of boughs. When they'd finished the next-to-last beam, Todd lowered his arms and flexed his shoulders. The quietness of the room caused him to turn around.

Nearly empty. Only Beth and Billy remained. A mischievous glint lit Billy's eye. He stretched and let go a fake-sounding yawn. "I sure am tuckered. I think I'd best get home. You can finish up here, can't you?" Before Todd could comment, Billy sprinted for the door, snatching up his hat and coat and slamming the door in his wake.

Todd grimaced at the obvious ploy. He turned to where Beth

swept up loose pine needles and bits of ribbon, his collar growing tight. Would she think he had conspired with Billy to be left alone with her?

But her expression was clear of accusation when she looked up. She stacked her hands atop the broom handle and rested her chin on them. Candlelight reflected in her blue-green eyes. "It's starting to look like I imagined it would. It's beautiful."

He swallowed hard and took a steadying breath. Better get busy before he did something stupid. Like giving in to the urge to kiss her. "I'll just finish this last rafter."

Without his having to ask, she took Billy's place, handing up the garland and lengths of string. They worked in such harmony Todd had a hard time believing she had refused his suit. Again he petitioned God to make it work or make these feelings stop.

When the last bit of greenery was in place, he stepped back to survey their work. A wreath hung in every window. Red ribbons decorated the greenery. Fat, white candles stood on a tray atop the piano. "What about this corner?" He pointed to the only empty space in the room.

"That's for the Christmas tree." She laced her fingers under her chin and breathed deeply. "You'll bring that tomorrow to the dress rehearsal?"

Mention of the tree reminded him of her gift. Her present was complete, a delicate silver ornament, a tiny nativity scene inside a heart frame. He'd labored over it for hours, calling upon every skill he possessed and drawing upon every lesson his father had taught him. It was the finest, most detailed metalwork he'd ever done.

Would she like it? Would she think him too forward? Would she even receive it? Maybe he shouldn't give it to her at all. Maybe it had been a dumb idea from the first.

She stirred. "I had no idea the decorating would take such a long time. I'm sorry to have kept you so late. You don't need to stay. I can finish up here. You've probably got a lot of work to do tomorrow." Picking up the broom once more, she dabbed at the floor.

"I wouldn't dream of letting you walk home alone. Let's just blow out the lamps and go. The sweeping can wait until morning." He lifted the glass on a wall lamp and snuffed the flame.

Walking with Beth under the stars. Like a courting couple. He grinned to himself. Not much she could do to stop him.

Beth reminded herself as she accepted his help with her coat that they were not courting and that the thundering of her heart was ridiculous. He was seeing her home, a gentlemanly gesture, nothing else. Even Mr. Hampton would do the same. Todd had been helpful and steady at every practice and had done nothing to indicate he hadn't taken her refusal in his stride, which she had to admit both relieved and perturbed her.

He doused the final light and took her elbow. "It's bright tonight. We shouldn't need a lantern." He guided her out the door and jiggled the handle to make sure it was closed.

She puffed out her breath in a white plume, testing the air. Ice crystals formed instantly and hung like a cloud before drifting away. The starlight made bluish shadows on the snow under the trees. Everything lay under an expectant hush. Anticipation lodged in her chest, and she couldn't dispel it. But, she assured herself, the feeling had everything to do with Christmas approaching and nothing to do with the fact that she was alone with Todd Rambek.

"Thank you for walking me to the parsonage. It isn't far, though. If you want to head home, I can make it by myself." The instant the words were out of her mouth, her shoes hit an icy patch and shot out from under her. If it wasn't for his quick action and his firm grasp on her arm, she would've gone down hard.

He grasped her like she weighed nothing, saving her from a tumble but hugging her against his chest. "Whoops. Be careful." His arms remained about her, solid as tree trunks. "Are you all right?"

Except for the fact that he was squeezing the breath out of her lungs. Then she realized her breathlessness wasn't because he was holding her too tight. His arms were gentle. It was her lungs that refused to work properly.

Moonlight shone on his face, outlining his features. He bent, and for a moment she thought he was going to kiss her, but he smiled and released her. "I guess I'll have to spread more ashes on the path tomorrow."

When his arms dropped away and he clasped her elbow again, disappointment coursed through her. And if that wasn't plain ridiculous, she didn't know what was. She sought to get things onto a more normal footing. "You'll be on time for the dress rehearsal tomorrow?" Great, now she sounded as if she were scolding him about being late tonight.

"I'll be there. And I have a little surprise for you. Something I think will really lend authenticity to the play." His boots crunched on the snow.

"Really? What?"

"No, it's a surprise. You'll find out tomorrow. And if you don't think it is too late, there's something else I wanted to show you."

She stopped on the path, trying to formulate a refusal. It *was* late, and she didn't want to give him the wrong impression. If she agreed, he might think she really did want him to court her and was just being coy saying no the first time.

As if conscious of her hesitation, he said, "It's related to the Christmas service, I promise. And it won't take long."

Relief poured over her. If it had to do with the service, she had a legitimate reason to prolong their time together. That thought brought her up short. She did *not* want to linger in the snow with Todd Rambek, did she? "If it's church business and it won't take too long, then that's fine."

"This way then." He plunged off the path and headed toward the river. "Step in my footprints. I'll break the trail."

The snow was shin deep to him but clear to her knees. "Wait." She floundered a few steps. "Your strides are longer than mine." She giggled and clapped her hand over her mouth at the sound of such girlish silliness coming from her.

He turned back, a grin tugging at his lips. "Sorry about that. I forget." He took her hand and shortened his steps. "You're so tiny—I must seem like a clumsy giant."

Giant yes, clumsy no. The way he'd made short work of assembling the stable tonight and the deft way he'd handled the garland proved he wasn't clumsy. But how did she answer without revealing that she'd been watching him? "Where are we going?"

"To see something I came across when I was heading back from the logging camp this evening. I thought it would be just right for the service."

"Is it far?"

"Not too far." He led her around a stand of white-trunked birch trees. There, in the center of a little clearing, the moonlight reflected off the prettiest little pine tree she'd ever seen. Pillows of snow clung to its branches.

She stopped walking and drank in the sight. "Perfect."

"I thought so too, the minute I saw it." His voice rumbled in his chest, and when she looked up, he was staring at her instead of the tree.

Her heart beat fast, and an empty, quivering feeling started in her middle. Her lips parted to say something, but she couldn't think what.

Todd stepped closer and lifted her hands in his. Even through their gloves she imagined she could feel the engulfing warmth of his fingers. "Beth, I. . ."

She should stop him. She should hold firm to her resolution. She had a calling she couldn't ignore.

Then he gathered her close, and despite everything her head was telling her, she went into his arms willingly. His lips came down on hers, so soft and warm, drawing a response from her that sapped her strength and infused her with feelings so strong she thought she might cry. Her arms entwined about his neck, and she allowed him to crush her to his chest.

So, this was love. . . .

Reality hit her like the whiplash of a snowy branch to the face.

She struggled, and he immediately loosened his hold. His chest heaved as if he'd run a long distance.

"Todd, I'm so sorry." She put her gloved fingertips to her lips where she could still feel of his kiss. "I should never have let that happen. Please, forgive me."

"Beth, you've nothing to apologize for. You felt it, didn't you? You have to know I love you, and you feel something for me. I know you do. You can quit all this nonsense about us not courting." He grinned. "I knew we were meant for each other the moment I laid eyes on you."

Aghast at what she'd done, what she'd allowed to happen, she stepped back, floundering in the snow. "No, Todd. Please. We're not meant for each other. I can't let myself be in love with you. I'm sorry!"

She flung the last words over her shoulder as she turned to get away from him, to outrun her conscience and her mother's words.

"You'll make a perfect pastor's wife, someday, Beth. You were born to it."

Tears blinded her vision, but she didn't stop until she reached her cabin.

Chapter 5

How could she have been so foolish as to let her guard down and fall in love with someone she *knew* wasn't right for her? Beth asked herself that question a hundred times throughout a sleepless night. Scratchy-eyed and with nerves bare and twanging, she managed to fix breakfast for Grandpa.

"How are the preparations? Will you be all set for the service tonight?"

She dished up his eggs and ham and set his plate before him. "We'll be ready. Just the dress rehearsal to manage."

"You were awfully late getting in last night. I'm sorry I dozed off. I should've walked up to the church for you. You didn't walk home alone, did you?"

Not alone. Not really. Not all the way. "I was fine, Grandpa.

One of the men walked me most of the way home." She dug in the cupboard for the flour and molasses. "I've got ten dozen cookies to bake before tonight. Gingerbread with icing. I best get cracking." If she could fill her mind with all the details of the program, maybe she could stop thinking about what a fool she'd been.

"Ten dozen? Who else is bringing treats?"

Beth sorted through her spices until she found the ginger. "No one. I've got it under control. Mary Kate is bringing the cider, but it was easier to do the cookies myself. Sophie offered to bring her fruitcake." Her lips twitched. Grandpa had been the recipient of more than one of those chewy bricks when on visitation.

He grunted and finished his ham. "Cookies will be good, but don't you think you should've spread it around a little? You're doing so much. There are lots of good folks in the church who are willing and able to help you out. Though I'm glad we're not having fruitcake tonight."

"Sometimes it's just easier to do it myself."

"Maybe, though I don't see how taking on so much yourself is easier. Easier doesn't always mean better."

She dropped a kiss on his head as she passed behind him to take down her mixing bowls. "You do talk nonsense sometimes. Easier is always better."

After spending the morning baking and the early afternoon spreading icing on dozens of cookies, trying all the while not to think about Todd and what she would say to him when they met again, rehearsal time loomed. Beth mustered every ounce of courage she possessed to force herself to walk into the church.

Happy faces greeted her, along with the aroma of pine needles. "Here she is." Mr. Hampton came forward, took the box she carried, and breathed deeply. "Gingerbread? My favorite."

She scanned the small crowd, but Todd wasn't there. Strangely, her heart didn't calm. Here she'd hoped to get the first awkwardness behind them, and he wasn't even there. Guilt clawed up her chest and smothered her racing heart. Her foolishness had sent him all the wrong signals, and now he couldn't face her. Not only would she not have a chance to apologize, but if he stayed away, who would play Joseph in the pageant, and who would anchor the bass section of the choir? Had she ruined the service by failing to control her feelings?

"Honey, are you all right?" Sophie patted Beth's arm. "You look a little. . . distracted. I'm sure you must've worked too hard making all those cookies."

"I'm fine, really. Everything's under control." She shrugged out of her coat and bonnet and smoothed her hair. "All right, folks. How about we all get into our places, and we'll run straight through the service without any stops. Let's see if we can make it mistake free."

The door behind her opened, sending a gust of cool air swirling through the room. Beth whirled to see who had arrived, hopeful and fearful that it would be Todd.

Those hopes and fears were confirmed. Todd stood in the doorway, the trunk of a pine tree over his shoulder and a rope in his other hand. "Sorry I'm late. Can someone give me a hand?"

Beth froze. She'd thought she was prepared to see him again, prepared to be an adult, to apologize as soon as the situation afforded an opportunity, and move on. But she'd been wrong. She wasn't prepared at all.

Her knees went a bit wobbly, and she grabbed the back of the closest pew while several men hurried by to help with the Christmas tree. They dragged the pine up the aisle and set it up in the corner, chattering and laughing.

Todd remained by the open door, talking to someone outside. Beth did a quick head count. No one was missing. Who could he be talking with? If whoever it was would go away, perhaps she could talk to Todd in private before the rehearsal got started. She'd just peek and find out who it was.

A strange sound stopped her midstride. Todd flicked a glance over his shoulder and pulled on the rope in his hand. The sound occurred again, preceding a black face and a pair of marble-like eyes. Four hooves and a mass of wool.

Her jaw dropped. "Wha—" She gulped. "What is that?"

Todd's eyebrows rose. "It's a sheep. Goldenrod, to be specific. I told you last night I had another surprise for you." He patted the animal's shaggy head. "Don't you think she'll add authenticity to the stable scene? I borrowed her from Anders Granderson's kids. They keep her as a pet, and she's as gentle as"—he shrugged, a grin teasing his lips—"a lamb." He led the ewe a few more steps into the church and shut the door on the cold afternoon air.

Beth tugged at her lower lip and studied the sheep. The ladies in the cast and choir huddled together, whispering and frowning. "I don't know, Todd. A live sheep?" His name slipped out easily. At least the animal had managed to break the ice between them—though Todd didn't seem to be out of sorts at all.

"Don't you think the kids will like it?" His eyes held a challenge as if to ask if she was going to let personal feelings interfere with the reason for the service.

Her chin went up, and she folded her arms at her waist. "Be my guest. Just remember, you're the one who will need to clean up after the animal." If he wanted to pretend nothing had happened, that was fine by her.

Todd led Goldenrod up to the stage. The animal let out a single bleat and folded her legs to subside in a gentle heap on the straw under the stable overhang. She looked bored with the proceedings. Perhaps all would be well after all. Certainly a sheep would entertain the children.

"All right, folks. Let's start from the top. Straight through just as if this was the final performance. Don't stop, even if something goes wrong." Beth sat at the piano and began the soft opening strains of "Silent Night." Perfectly on cue, the choir came in. She smiled and nodded. Sweet harmony filled the church, and she could almost see the happy faces of the children beaming in the candlelight. The choir continued into "Hark, the Herald Angels Sing" without a pause.

Billy Mather stepped to the pulpit and opened his Bible while the nativity players donned their rudimentary costumes and took their places. A quick peek at Goldenrod—eyes closed, slowly grinding her cud. Any minute now, the ewe might begin to snore. At Beth's nod, Billy began reading from Luke chapter two. Todd knelt beside Mary Kate and the manger, and Sophia and two of her friends in white robes held their arms up when Billy got to the part about the angels appearing to the shepherds. Mr. Hampton and Clive, dressed as shepherds complete with crooked staffs, moved from near the piano to crowd into the stable area to see the Baby Jesus. Everything was subdued with Billy's voice the only sound in the room.

Beth, from her position on the piano bench, couldn't have been more pleased. Not one single stoppage of the program, no arguments, no suggestions, no helpful advice. The dress rehearsal was unfolding nothing like the previous practices, where she couldn't seem to get any continuity for the interruptions. Everything was coming together. Billy read slowly, as if savoring the story, just the way she'd asked him to, giving the players time to move without seeming rushed, which would allow the audience time to soak in the sights and sounds.

Billy closed his Bible after the last verse, and solemnly, the cast stepped onto the risers beside the piano. Time for the finale. She poised her hands over the keys, meeting the eyes of her singers, asking them to give this closing song their very best. Determination glinted in each expression. She raised her wrists and crashed down on the opening chord as the choir launched into "Joy to the World." The sound was loud and joyful, nearly deafening her with their enthusiasm.

A very *un*-joyful noise erupted from the stable area, drowning out the choir, who stumbled to a halt. Beth's hands faltered on the keys, adding several sour notes to the cacophony. The plank ceiling of the stable rocked, creaked, and disappeared downward with a crash. Necks twisted and craned, and a look of horror shot over the faces of the back row of the choir. Beth was halfway up off the bench when a wool-covered tornado plowed into the singers, sending shepherds' crooks, angels' halos, and sopranos' songbooks skyward.

Mary Kate screamed and threw herself into Mr. Hampton's arms. Together they toppled into the bare Christmas tree. Sophia fainted. Fortunately Clive was able to grab her and ease her to the floor. Billy lunged for the rope dangling behind Goldenrod, swinging wildly but coming up empty. Todd leaped after the wooly beast, but she bounded away from him straight toward Beth.

Beth scrambled backward to avoid the onrushing sheep and stumbled. Her foot caught on the edge of the piano drape and dragged it half off the instrument and right onto Goldenrod's head.

Beth tumbled to the ground, smacking her backside on the puncheon floor and toppling backward against the log wall.

The candles and holly wreath went flying, and Goldenrod—seemingly enraged by the red cloth now enveloping her—went entirely berserk. Bleating and crying, she dashed here and there, plowing into people, pews, and party decorations. In seconds the church was in shambles, and Beth could only sit and watch as her carefully erected plans exploded.

Mary Kate continued to emit scream after scream. Choir members huddled and scattered according to their personalities, and through it all Todd and Billy ran and dodged, shouted and pointed, trying to corner the demented sheep long enough to at least drag the piano drape off her head.

The final coup de grâce occurred when Goldenrod managed to shake loose from the cloth and, looking for a target for her rage, barreled into the refreshment table. Jugs of cider, a punch bowl, ranks of punch cups, and ten dozen iced gingerbread cookies defied gravity and hovered in midair before plummeting to the floor in a cinnamon-spicy, glass-shard-inducing crash.

The sheep skidded to a halt, wheeled, and lowered her head to charge in another direction. Before she could move, Todd pounced on her and brought her to the floor near the door, where Billy caught up to them and added his weight to the kicking ewe. He wrapped his arms around her legs while Todd leaned on her neck.

Thus subdued, Goldenrod gave one last bleat and stopped squirming. This turn of events did nothing to stop Mary Kate's screams, though the rest of the choir seemed to relax a fraction and stop contemplating climbing to the rafters for safety.

Beth blinked, ran her hand over her eyes, and stared at the disaster. "What happened?" she shouted to Todd over Mary Kate's screams.

"I think we scared her." His reply seemed a bit strangled.

"Of course she's scared. A sheep just launched herself into the middle of the choir." Beth rounded the piano and patted Mary Kate on the arm. What she'd really like to do is clap her hand over that mouth and muffle the shrieks. The danger had subsided. It was time for Mary Kate to quit peeling bark off the walls with her ear-piercing wails. Beth pushed herself up and headed toward the pile of men and wool on the floor near the door.

Billy choked and snorted and then gave up the fight, collapsing into laughter. Todd grimaced and appeared to be trying to hold it in, but he too lost the battle. His loud guffaws echoed off the log walls and nearly lifted the rafters. "I meant"—he managed between bouts of laughter—"that we scared the sheep."

A river of sticky-sweet cider raced toward them, carrying soggy gingerbread cookies like life rafts on a current. Snatching up the piano drape, Beth stemmed the flow. The fabric darkened as it soaked up the beverage.

From her position by the door, Beth assessed the damage while trying to hold on to her temper. Christmas carnage greeted her eyes everywhere she looked. Praying for patience, she tried to hold back the wave of despair building in her chest.

"Enough!" Beth spat the word at Mary Kate, who had just sucked in another enormous breath, ready to let loose another screech. Mary Kate swallowed her scream with a hiccup. "The animal is subdued. There is no reason to go on with your hysterics. Pull yourself together." She rounded on Todd and Billy, who still laughed uncontrollably, pinning Goldenrod to the floor. "You too. Stop laughing. It's not funny. Todd Rambek, this is all your fault. You brought that beast in here deliberately to ruin my Christmas service. After all my hard work."

The sob she had tried to quell forced its way up her throat and past her clenched teeth. Horrified at losing control, she stumbled outside, slamming the door on the debacle.

Chapter 6

Todd levered himself off the floor and made sure he had a firm hold of Goldenrod's rope. Billy rolled off her legs and sat up, still chuckling, though he had a guilty tilt to his shoulders. He grasped Todd's offered hand and allowed himself to be pulled upright.

Goldenrod lumbered to her feet, bent her head to sniff the puddle of cider, and lapped a few tonguefulls. She lifted her head, shook herself, and looked around the room with a quizzical expression as if to say, "What happened in here?"

Todd shrugged and rubbed his palm up the back of his head. "What a mess." At that moment, one of the carefully constructed wreaths hanging in a window gave up the fight and dropped to the floor, taking a string of garland with it.

"What are you going to do?" Billy shoved his hands in his pockets and grimaced.

Guilt, Todd's constant companion since he had lost his head and kissed Beth last night, stomped through his chest and set up a racket near his conscience. Why did it seem that everything he did with the intention of pleasing her ended with her running away from him? He gritted his teeth and called himself all kinds of a fool.

"We're going to get this cleaned up." He handed the rope to Billy. "Stay here, and don't let go of that sheep." Marching to the front of the church, he began issuing orders. "All right. This little disaster is my fault, and we don't have much time to get it cleaned up before the program is supposed to start. Beth is really upset, and I know she must be thinking there's no way we can have a program now, but that's not true. We can, but not without her. First, we all need to pitch in and get everything put to rights. Clive, you and Hampton rebuild that stable. Mary Kate, are you all right?"

She sniffed and swallowed. "I think I've hurt my wrist." Still trembling, she held up her arm, bracing it with the other hand.

"I'm so sorry, Mary Kate." He motioned to one of the ladies. "See if you can help Mary Kate out. The rest of you, get cracking on the cleanup. Salvage what you can; throw out the rest. Be careful with that broken glass." Todd turned to Sophie. "I don't suppose you have any of that fruitcake available, do you?"

Sophie gave him a gamine grin and patted his arm. She motioned for him to bend down so she could whisper in his ear. He had to bend a very long way to hear her. "I made up a big batch this morning, just in case. I was planning to give them out as Christmas gifts, but this need is more pressing."

He engulfed her little hand in his. "That's great. Why don't you head home and get the cakes? Take someone along to help if you need to. And round up some cider if you can. If not, we'll serve water."

As soon as everyone set to work, Todd returned to Billy. "See what you can do about hanging up that garland and stuff. Set that tree up. You can start putting the presents on it when everything else is done. That was the last thing we needed to do after the practice anyway."

"What are you going to do? And what should I do with her?" Billy lifted Goldenrod's rope.

Todd took the rope. "I'm going to tie her up outside, and then I'm going after Beth."

Billy pulled a face. "She was pretty upset. Don't you think you should give her a little time to cool off?"

"We can't afford to. There will hardly be time for us to finish here, get home for a quick supper, and get back before the service is supposed to start. We can't let Beth down. She's worked so hard." He lifted his coat from one of the back pews and shouldered his way into it. Giving the rope a tug, he scowled at the sheep. "C'mon, you. Let's get out of here before you start another riot."

Stepping out into the frosty air, he noted that the sun had gone down. Faint stars winked through the treetops, and as the darkness intensified, the stars glowed brighter. He made Goldenrod's rope fast to a hitching post out front and studied the snow around the church. Hundreds of footprints pocked the path, but one fresh set caught his eye, a set that veered toward the track he and Beth had taken last night to see the Christmas tree.

His heart beat thick. She hadn't headed home. And she had no coat. He hurried inside and tossed through the stack of coats on a back table until he found the green plaid he'd know anywhere.

Tramping through the woods, he tried to formulate what he would say to her, but everything after "I'm sorry" got stuck. He walked faster as the cold settled in and flowed over his face like icy water.

He found her standing in the snow, arms wrapped around her

waist, chin on her chest, beside the empty place where the Christmas tree had stood until he'd removed it to bring into the church. Her look of utter defeat ran him through like a peavey spike. His lungs sent plumes of frosty breath into the air.

When he stood only a few feet from her, he called her name, not wanting to frighten her. There'd been enough frightening going on today. "Beth?"

She flinched but didn't look up.

"I brought your coat." He stepped closer and held up the garment. When she didn't move her arms to slip it on, he draped it around her shoulders. "Beth, I'm so sorry. I had no idea Goldenrod would go mad like that." At the mental image of the maniacal sheep wearing the piano drape, a chuckle bubbled into his chest, but he stifled it. "If you think about it, it *is* a little bit funny." He tilted his head and invited her to laugh with him.

Nothing. Not a trace of humor. In fact, her lower lip trembled in a way that made his insides turn to water. Surely she wasn't going to cry? And what on earth would he do if she did?

"Beth, please. I truly am sorry. Don't cry. Everyone's pitching in to clean things up. We can still have the service tonight. Nothing's really ruined." He scratched his head. "Well, the cider and cookies are, but we're taking care of that."

She gave a strange hiccupping sound and clutched the edges of her coat. "You don't understand."

He spread his hands. "Then tell me. I want to understand. I want to make everything all right—with the church service and with us." Moving to stand before her, he put his finger under her chin and raised her face to look into her eyes. Starlight softened her features, and tears hung like diamonds on her dark lashes. "Beth, I stood right here last night and held you in my arms, and I *know* you felt something for me. You have to know that I love you. If we could just talk this out, you'll see that everything is going to be fine."

She rocked back, jarring his finger from her chin. "You don't get it, do you? I can accept your apology for the sheep disaster, but I can't accept your love." She took a couple steps back, putting distance between them. Her coat slid from one shoulder and trailed in the snow. "I can't allow myself to love you, because I've been called to serve God."

He blinked. Somewhere his chain of thought had broken a link. Or hers had. He squinted and shook his head. "How would loving me mean that you couldn't serve God?" Though thoroughly puzzled, a spark of hope fanned to life in his chest. She hadn't said, "I can't love you," but rather, "I can't let myself love you."

"I'm not supposed to fall in love with a blacksmith." She grappled with the coat and hunched it back over her shoulder. "I have to marry a preacher and serve God in the church."

His jaw went slack as he struggled to make sense of her words. "Who told you that? Your grandpa?" That didn't mesh with what he thought he knew of Pastor Sorensen.

"It's been my destiny since I was a little girl. My mother always told me so, and I come from a long line of preachers. If I had been born a boy, I would've joined the pastorate. That's just how it is. It's a calling, a responsibility. The Sorensens serve God in the church."

Disappointment trickled through him as he began to understand. He folded his arms and braced his legs. "So do the Rambeks." He spoke slowly, so she wouldn't miss a word. "We always have, though there's not a preacher among us." Shaking his head, he took a deep breath. "So a humble blacksmith isn't good enough for you because he isn't a preacher? You think preaching is the only kind of service that counts in the church?" He swung his arm wide in the direction of the log church. "What do you think the people who have volunteered for this Christmas Eve program have been doing if not serving in the church? What do you think they're doing right now?" A scornful growl rose in his chest. "For someone who comes from a long line of preachers, you sure don't know your scripture too well."

She gasped as if he'd slapped her, and though it hurt to be so blunt with her, she needed to hear the truth.

"Doesn't the Apostle Paul tell us that the church is like a body, made up of all kinds of members that have all kinds of jobs? If one of those members doesn't do his job of serving in the church, the whole body is less effective. We're warned against elevating one role in the church body over another. You've done that to such an extent that nobody else in the church matters." He pursed his lips. "Just how do you think you'd even put on a Christmas Eve service without those volunteers? Without Clive and Billy and Hampton and Sophie and Mary Kate and all the rest? Without this blacksmith?" He thumped his chest with his thumb. "You've been so busy organizing and dictating and being in control, you've lost sight of not only who was doing all the work, but also who the work was being done for."

Knowing he'd said more than enough, and with his heart like a wound in his chest, he turned away from her to go back to the church. He might not have been able to mend his relationship with Beth—most likely, his words, though truthful, had slammed the door forever on her loving him—but he could help mend the damage caused by the renegade Goldenrod.

Beth clutched the edges of her coat around her as Todd disappeared into the woods. The tears on her lashes lost their hold and tumbled down her cheeks in warm streaks that turned icy almost at once.

His words hit like darts, piercing her. The disgust on his face when she told him her reason for refusing to let him court her—she squirmed at the memory. How she wished she could curl up in the snow, sink down, and make herself as small as she felt. Because he had been right. And the truth, spoken through the scripture, straight from his own lips, shamed her.

Beth sought to maintain her hold on her firm belief that her destiny lay in being a preacher's wife, but the threads of that argument had already frayed and broken under the weight of Todd's words. She bowed her head and her heart to whisper a prayer in the frosty night.

"God, I'm so sorry. Everything he said was right. I—" She choked on a sob and sniffed. Whispering didn't seem appropriate, as if she still sought to hide her confession. Bracing her shoulders, she slipped her arms into her coat sleeves and dug in the pocket for her gloves. "God"—she tilted her head back to address the heavens—"I've been so wrong. I've been prideful. What I should've been using for Your glory, I've used for my own. This Christmas service, it wasn't about sharing the joy of the Christmas season with the people in our church." It hurt to admit, but she had to say the words. "I was using it to prove to myself and to others what a good preacher's wife I would make someday. I discounted the service of others and elevated myself." The tears flowed freely now as she opened her heart. Her feet moved, carrying her in the direction of the church, but slowly, for she wanted to thrash everything out with God before she faced anyone.

"God, I wounded Todd too. I made myself out—at least in my own mind—as being too good for him. And the opposite is true. He's too good for me." At this admission, her heart burst wide open, and her legs gave out. She dropped to the snow, hugged her knees to her chest, and begged for God's forgiveness. Peace flooded her insides, a weight lifted from her, and after a while, she became aware of the cold seeping through her coat. Wiping her cheeks, she stood and brushed at the snow clinging to her clothes.

She frowned, her stomach muscles tightening. How long had she been out here? Surely it had to be nearly time for the service to start. Did she have time to run home and change? What about the mess at the church? Had they gotten everything squared away?

Brushing through the trees, getting dumped on with gouts of snow each time she encountered a low-hanging branch, she hurried toward the church. Along the way, she reminded herself of Todd's words. The good people she'd yelled at were cleaning things up. They were serving, and they were just as capable, and in a lot of cases more capable, of taking care of things as she was.

When she reached the church, everything was dark. She ducked inside and lit a candle, checking the clock on the wall first. Forty minutes until the service. She hurried up the aisle. The stable, a new piano cover, the Christmas tree. Everything that could be put to rights had been. One would never know that disaster had struck only a short while ago.

She turned to the refreshment table. Six new jugs of cider sat at one end, flanked by a row of shiny tin cups. The floor beneath the table shone dark and damp from a recent mopping. She lifted the corner of a tea towel gaily embroidered with poinsettias and holly. Eight dark loaves of spicy fruitcake stood all in a row. Beth poked one of the loaves. It gave way like a sponge and sprang back. Not dry and crumbly, but moist and redolent. It appeared Sophie had finally hit on the right recipe for Christmas fruitcake after all.

The clock showed the half hour. In the candlelight she glanced down at her wet coat and the soaked hem of her dress just brushing the floor. If she hurried, she'd have time to change and be back for the service.

Her breath hitched. If she thought it took a lot of courage to face Todd after he kissed her, how much more would she have to muster after their latest confrontation?

Chapter 7

Her fingers shook with a trembling that had nothing to do with the plummeting temperature or the falling snow. Light shone from every church window, and dark figures made their way from the cabins of the settlement toward the pine structure. Lines of chinking stood out white between the solid logs, and overhead, pointing to the sky, a cross stood atop a small cupola. The church bell sent out round, reverberating rings, calling everyone to worship.

Grandpa put his hand under her elbow to help her along the path. "I sure am looking forward to tonight. It isn't often I get to sit with the congregation. I'm going to enjoy being ministered to by the members of the church."

Her heart pinched. How had she missed understanding the truth of the whole body ministering and working together? Grandpa clearly believed it and had probably mentioned it many times, both in their home and from the pulpit. And yet, she'd been blinded by her own pride. But no more.

She entered the church, her nerves playing a fugue in her stomach, and laid aside her coat and bonnet. Brushing her hands down the polonaise of her new, burgundy dress, she took a few steadying breaths.

A low hum of excited conversation buzzed in the room, enhanced by the many lanterns and lamps brightening every corner and the heady scent of pine boughs and cinnamon. Billy and Clive ushered the children to the front rows, and several of the choir members and cast stood off to the side awaiting direction.

Though aware of his presence from the moment she stepped into the building, Beth had avoided until the last possible minute looking directly at Todd. When she did, her heart did an unpleasant flip and jumped up into her throat. He stood talking with a group of men, a full head taller than they and heart-stoppingly handsome in a black suit.

"You'd best get up there." Grandpa nudged her arm. "It's time to start."

As she walked up the center aisle, conversations ceased and the choir assembled. Taking her place at the piano, she didn't know if she was glad or sad that she hadn't any time to speak to Todd before the service. Her mouth was as dry as pillow ticking, and her fingers froze on the keys. Every choir member looked at her expectantly. She sent up a quick prayer.

Of their own accord, her fingers played the introduction to the first song. The singers harmonized beautifully, coming in when they should, even remembering to repeat the last line and hold the last note. How many times had they stumbled over that in practice?

Billy's rich voice reading the Christmas story while the cast members acted out the nativity play sent gooseflesh marching across her skin. The faces of the children in the front rows all attentive and illuminated with candlelight made her heart glow. These were the ones they had come to serve. Mary Kate with a maternal expression, Clive with his Adam's apple lurching with each swallow, Mr. Hampton, face shiny with pleasure, Sophie, hunch-shouldered with age but singing with gusto. And Todd. Broad-chested, tall, strong in body and in spirit, big in stature, and big of heart. Every last one of them had come to serve the body of Christ.

Todd, as Joseph, stared right at her. She blinked, caught off-guard, and looked away. A cold fist wrapped its fingers around her chest and squeezed. What if he was so thoroughly disgusted with her that she'd lost any hope of his love? She swallowed as Billy finished the scripture passage and closed his Bible. What would she do if Todd didn't want her anymore?

She concentrated on the hymnal in front of her. The notes swam and danced and made no sense. They were supposed to sing about joy, but at that moment, she could muster none at all.

The actors shed their costumes and took their places for the final song, shuffling along the risers and opening their songbooks. In spite of her efforts to the contrary, her eyes found Todd's once more. Chocolate brown, warm, and caring. The corner of his mouth lifted in a hint of a smile, and he nodded ever so slightly. A promise that they would talk later.

The fist around her heart eased, and her fingers found the right notes. When the choir crashed in on the first words of "Joy to the World," she wanted to laugh at the memory of poor Goldenrod frightened to the point of panic and rampaging through the church. She didn't dare meet the eyes of any of the choir members. How she wanted to call down blessings on that poor demented animal. If it wasn't for that crazed ewe, she might never have told Todd her foolish thoughts, and he might never have had the chance to show her the error of her ways.

When the last strains of music faded away, a rustle went through the crowd, centered mostly in the front rows. It was time for the giving of Christmas gifts from the tree. Beth rose, covered the piano keys, and moved to the side of the room to watch. Her grandpa and several helpers surrounded the tree, reading off names and passing out bags of candy and small gifts that had been delivered to the church all week. Eager hands received toys, books, games, puzzles. Cheesecloth bags of hard candy—donated by Mr. Hampton—spread happiness amongst the small-fry.

Todd didn't come near her, instead helping with the distribution of gifts. He lifted a small child onto his arm so the little girl could see the tree better. A hard lump formed in Beth's throat, and she willed the time to pass quickly until she could speak to him.

Billy Mather sidled up to Beth, a grin revealing a great many of his teeth. "This one has your name on it."

She blinked and took the small packet of tissue paper. Turning it over, she read her name in bold, black letters. Who could this be from? She and Grandpa had agreed to exchange their gifts tomorrow. Beth untied the ribbon and edged back the paper.

Lamplight gleamed on a beautiful silvery ornament. Delicate whorls and flares of metal formed a heart, and in the center, a silhouette of Mary, Joseph, and a manger. The ornament hung from a red velvet ribbon. The workmanship was so fine it took her breath away.

She looked up to ask Billy who had given her such a fine gift, only to find Todd before her. Everything she wanted to say to him flew right out of her head. Her tongue became a wooden thing, and the sound of her heart and breath collided in her ears.

"Do you like it?"

She nodded.

"I made it for you after the first practice."

Before he knew what an idiot she was. Was he sorry now that he'd given it to her in light of the words they'd exchanged earlier?

Heat prickled her skin. She opened her mouth to offer the gift back to him and to apologize, but before she could, he took her hands in his, engulfing her fingers and the ornament.

"I'm sorry, Beth. I feel terrible chastising you like that. I should've found a more gentle way to say what I was thinking and feeling."

His apology loosened her tongue. "Todd, you have nothing to apologize for. I'm the one who is sorry. Everything you said was true." She moved her hands inside his. "I'll understand if you want the gift back, since you made it before you knew. . ." Her gaze dropped along with her voice, too embarrassed to go on, but she gave herself a mental shake. *No shirking*. Lifting her chin, she swallowed and forced the words out. "Todd, I apologize for the way I treated you. You are a good and kind man, and you are right. You do serve God in this church, much better than I have. I'm only sorry I realized it too late." Tears stung her eyes, but she forced them back.

A ridge formed between his eyebrows, and his hands tightened on hers. "Too late? Too late for what?"

He was going to make her say it. Well, it was no more than she deserved. "Too late to do anything about the fact that I've fallen in love with you."

His lips spread in a grin, and his hands crushed hers. "I don't think it's too late for anything."

She put all her love for him into her eyes. He leaned down to whisper in her ear, and the low rumble of his voice and the warmth of his breath on her temple made her shiver. "If we weren't standing in church surrounded by all these people, I'd be kissing you right now."

"Maybe, if you're free, you could walk me home after the service, and we'll see who kisses whom." She gave him a saucy grin.

"I'm going to hold you to that." He tucked her hand into his elbow and escorted her to the refreshment table, where Sophie served up slabs of fruitcake and Mr. Hampton poured cider. Beth tasted the rich, dark cake, and her eyes widened as the flavor burst on her tongue.

"It's my new recipe. I never could quite get it right until this year." Sophie winked at Beth. "I was hoping to have a chance to share it, and thanks to that ridiculous sheep. . ." She shrugged and winked again.

An hour later, Beth and Todd walked arm-in-arm through the woods. Grandpa had given his hearty blessing on Todd seeing her home, slapping Todd on the back and kissing Beth's cheek. "I'm glad for you, Beth." He flipped his hat onto his head and left them to close up the church.

When she and Todd reached her cabin door, Todd took her face between his palms and kissed first her eyelids then her nose. His arms came around her, and his lips descended on hers. She sighed as he deepened the kiss.

When he finally released her, he smiled down into her eyes. "Merry Christmas, Beth. May it be the first of many for us."